THE COMPELLING SEQUEL TO PRAYER WARRIORS

CELESTE PERRINO WALKER

Pacific Press Publishing Association
Nampa, Idaho
Oshawa, Ontario, Canada

Edited by Jerry D. Thomas
Designed by Dennis Ferree
Cover illustration by Brian Fox

Copyright © 1997 by
Pacific Press Publishing Association
Printed in the United States of America
All Rights Reserved

ISBN 0-8163-1407-1

97 98 99 00 01 • 5 4 3 2 1

To Ethel Young,
who uses the sword of light to
fight in prayer and
point the way in love.

Note From the Author

I would like to take this opportunity to thank all the people who contacted me about *Prayer Warriors* and how it afffected their lives. It is exceedingly humbling to know how profoundly it has changed them. I don't take credit for that. There were days in the writing of these books when I would sit down and write twenty-five pages with no more effort than it would take to write a letter. I am as surprised as anyone at the end and can hardly recall the content although I planned it out myself. I would be horribly remiss and ungrateful if I did not point to my Saviour as the Inspiration for every word I write.

Still, writing books has not been as easy task. Some have wondered if I have been privy to the conversations between angels and demons, as though I have some sort of spiritual easedropping device. Unfortunately, there is another way, which is much less exciting, to obtain knowledge of good and evil for "the heart is deceitful above all things and beyond cure."

In his preface to *The Screwtape Letters*, C. S. Lewis explains the absence of angels by saying, "Ideally, Screwtape's advice to Wormwood should have been balanced by archangelical advice to the patient's guardian angel. Without this the picture of human life is lopsided. But who could supply the deficiency? Even if a man—and he would have to be a far better man than I—could scale the spiritual heights required, what 'answerable style' could he use? For the style would really be part of the content. Mere advice would be no good; every sentence would have to smell of Heaven. And nowadays even if you could write a prose like Traherne's, you wouldn't be allowed to, for the canon of 'functionalism' has disabled literature for half its functions."

I do not claim any superiority to Lewis in attempting to portray the angelic host. My purpose in writing these books was to condense *The Great Controversy* into one practical idea, answering this question: What is the great controversy? The answer—that it is the battle for our wills—became the plot for *Prayer Warriors* and *Guardians* in order that we might draw aside the curtain for a time and become aware of this battle and to explore ways to become warriors in it rather than victims of it.

People are also curious about the storylines. As in everything that is written, much of it is based on real people, but rather than being an exact rendering of their lives, it becomes more a composite of many individuals in order to serve the story. The elements of the story that would probably be the most suspect to my invention are likely to be those based most closely on fact, which proves out the old adage that fact is stranger than fiction.

I would also like to thank all those at Pacific Press who have worked tirelessly to put this book together. I would especially like to thank everyone who purchased *Prayer Warriors* and trusted me with their valuable time in reading it. I hope if it, or *Guardians*, has touched your life in some way you'll take a moment to share your story with me. I can't answer all the letters I receive, but I would consider it a great privilege to read each one.

God bless each of you, always, and real good.

1 Thessalonians 5:17

Celeste perrino Walker
RR 3, Box 4913
Rutland, Vermont 05701
cpwalker@together.net

CAST OF CHARACTERS

Billie Jo Raynard:
 Billie Jo's husband, Jimmy, was injured in a logging accident that left him in a coma. Since his miraculous recovery, things have been hard for the family. Life is made worse by Jimmy's mother, Helen, who continues to devise ways to control their family. Billie Jo and Jimmy have two children, Cassidy (8) and Dallas (5).

Jimmy Raynard:
 Billie Jo's husband. His accident left him unable to log any longer. He works mostly at fix-it jobs he can find.

Helen Raynard:
 Billie Jo's mother-in-law. A very controlling person. She dislikes Billie Jo. A buried secret from her past surfaces and prompts her to a desperate act.

Leah Moreau:
 Billie Jo's friend. Part of the mothers' prayer group.

Angel: Jewel

Demon: Nog

Ethel Bennington:
 The prayer warrior. These past four years have seen Ethel's

health increasingly deteriorate. She continues to pray feverishly because she senses that her time on earth is nearly over. She is mostly concerned at how Cindi will take her death and that she never found out what happened to her daughter Carol.

Cindi Trahan:

Ethel Bennington's visiting nurse. Cindi is overwhelmed by the care of her adopted daughter, Esther, and has been letting her relationship with God edge out of her life. She doesn't see the changes in Ethel's condition because she is with her every day and she is too preoccupied.

Marc Trahan:

Cindi's husband.

Pastor Hendricks:

Pastor of the church they all attend.

Angels:

Supervising angel: Reissa

Angel: Shania

Recording angel: Michel

Angel: Calum

Angel: Gaye

Demons:

Sparn

Rafe

Don Germaine:

He has spent the last four years working through the bitterness he developed during the war in Rwanda. He is poised on the brink of a new relationship, and things are going very well at the clinic he runs just outside of Niamey.

Shay Beauregard Okeke:

Young Cajun girl from Louisiana. She has been working at the mission clinic for five years. She is married to Nwibe and is pregnant with their first child.

Nwibe Okeke:

Native African man who is married to Shay Beauregard. Having lost his sight to river blindness, he is led around by a stick held by his son, Marcus. His first wife died several years before he met Shay. He works at the clinic.

Marcus Okeke:
Nwibe's son.

Madina Okeke:
Nwibe and Shay's adopted daughter.

Wahabi Okeke:
Bartender in Niamey. Brother of Nwibe.

Toby O'Connell:
Nurse who was stranded at the clinic and then decided to stay. She was divorced by her husband after a plane crash in which he lost his memory; she is considering the possibility of getting married again.

Davy O'Connell:
Toby's ex-husband. As he begins to regain some of his memory, he realizes that he is lonely and missing something in his life. Nightmares about the plane crash haunt him.

Julia and Ray Vargas:
Married now and registered nurses, Julia and Ray have decided to enter the mission field and request placement at Don's mission.

Angels:
Julian (Don)
Gaius (Shay)
Lileah (Toby)
Jes (Davy)

Demons:
Merck (Don)
Jezeel (Shay)
Lucien (Toby)
Belial (Davy)

Lyle Ryan:

Is preparing to marry Calla Kendall. He has become the youth pastor at his church and will soon graduate and become a fully ordained minister. He's excited about his work but is increasingly uneasy about his relationship with Calla.

Calla Kendall:

Tempted with a new relationship, Calla begins to get cold feet about the wedding. She has her own problems to work through and begins to see that there are some real issues in her relationship with Lyle that were never addressed.

Berniece Kendall:

Calla's aunt. Calla lives with her. It was Berniece's husband who caused the accident that claimed Lyle's legs.

Jesse Redcloud:

Down on his luck, Jesse plans to rob the church Calla and Lyle attend. He is accepted and welcomed by the church members, who think he is a nice, clean-cut young man.

Angel:

Shelan (Lyle)
Atli (Calla)
Saiph (Jesse)

Demon:

Warg (Lyle
Balor (Jesse)

Also:
Archangel: Noble

PROLOGUE

The bright sunshine streaming in through the open window illuminated Ethel Bennington's silver hair, sending shafts of light through it. If you looked just right, with your eyes a little squinty, it seemed as if she had a halo floating gently above her head. At least, that's how it appeared to Esther Trahan as she crept into the old woman's room and peered over the bed at her.

Ethel had been sitting there, in that exact position, for a very long time. Even longer than when Mommy made her take a nap, even though Esther insisted that she was a big girl now and didn't need to take naps like a baby anymore. At first, Esther thought her old friend had fallen asleep. Then she saw her lips moving.

"There you are!" A voice hissed behind her. "I told you not to bother Grammy while she's praying." Strong hands reached around her middle and picked her up, swinging her onto her mommy's hip.

"I wasn't bothering," she said defensively. "I was just watching."

Ethel's eyes fluttered open, and she smiled softly. The myriad of wrinkles that lined her face had deepened over the previous four years, and her skin was so pale you could easily see the blood pulse through the veins on her hands. Her eyes, still alert and observant, appeared tired, and the lids drooped heavily as if she was preparing to drift off into a deep and irreversible sleep.

"The child is right," she agreed. "She wasn't bothering at all. In fact, I've rather enjoyed her company."

"You didn't know I was here," Esther said in an accusing tone. "You couldn't see me. Your eyes were closed!"

Ethel chuckled. "I can't see the angels, either, love, but I know they're here too."

Esther's eyes widened, and she looked around quickly, expecting to see the angelic host suddenly materialize. "There are angels here?" she asked in a whisper.

Mommy laughed out loud, and Ethel's smile broadened. "Don't you ever doubt it, young lady," Ethel admonished, shaking a crooked finger at Esther. "There are angels surrounding us every minute of every day, strengthening us, guiding us, and comforting us. They are Jesus' messengers, and they work very hard for Him."

Esther's brow wrinkled as she thought about this. "Do I have an angel?" she asked finally. "I mean, my very own angel?"

Ethel nodded. "You certainly do. You have a guardian angel who watches over you and protects you."

"Does everyone have an angel?" Esther remembered the program Mommy and Daddy had been watching the night before. It was called the "News," and whatever the "News" was, it was always bad. Last night there were pictures of some children in Africa who had lost their mommies and daddies. Esther had asked Mommy what happened, but she looked like she was going to cry, and she'd turned off the TV. Esther knew that Uncle Donny lived in Africa, and she hoped that maybe he could help the children, but she didn't dare say anything about that to Mommy in case it made her sadder.

"Of course everyone has an angel of their very own," Mommy chided as she tickled her under the chin.

Esther evaded her fingers with a squeal and an agility born of experience. "Then how come some people's angels don't keep them safe?" she asked. Instantly, both Mommy and Grammy looked sad.

"You see, sweetheart," Ethel began, but Mommy interrupted her.

"No," she said gently. "Let me." Sitting down on the bed, she lowered Esther onto her lap and held the child tightly. Esther squirmed against the pressure. Mommy's lips were white as she pressed them together before she spoke, and Esther began to wish she hadn't asked the question.

"You see, honey, God has promised to protect His people. He tells us in the Psalms that because we love Him, He will rescue us and protect us. And He will. He will keep us safe from Satan. We never have to be afraid of Satan, ever. If we love God, we can always be sure that we will someday be with Him in heaven." Esther closed her eyes as Mommy smoothed the hair back from her forehead. "And lots of times, God will send His angels to protect us from physical harm, but not always. Satan will rule on earth until Jesus comes back, and he may win many physical battles, but Jesus has won our souls for eternity."

Esther smiled up at Mommy. She didn't understand everything that Mommy had said, but she understood enough. Jesus didn't want people to get hurt, Satan did. And Jesus would always protect their souls, even if Satan hurt their bodies. And there were angels all over the place. That was especially interesting.

Esther hopped off her mother's lap and headed out Ethel's bedroom door at full speed. "Essie, where are you going?" Mommy laughed after her.

"To find a book about angels," Esther called back over her shoulder.

Reissa smiled gently from her position beside Ethel's wheelchair. She placed a comforting hand on the old woman's shoul-

der as she coughed, her shoulders shuddering with the strain. Her strength was nearly spent, but she was so desperately needed. Concern tugged at the corners of Reissa's lips as she studied her charge.

Hands clasped, she had again begun to pray. Cindi, seeing this, moved quietly about the room, straightening things up. Every now and then she glanced at Ethel, but Reissa could see that she saw with eyes of love and missed the reality. She had witnessed the changes wrought in the previous four years by such slow degrees that she barely noticed a difference. It was Cindi that Reissa was most concerned about.

Angels streamed from Ethel's side toward heaven and returned just as quickly to gather more requests from the old lady's fervently moving lips. She pushed herself more these days. It was as if she could sense that the race was almost through and she had been given her second wind. But, the strain was beginning to tell.

Around the perimeter of the room a gathering of demons had begun to boil. They had started showing up lately, as if they could smell death, like vultures drawn to carrion. A half dozen skulked at the opposite side of the room. They had made no moves, betrayed no plans . . . yet. They simply waited.

This also concerned Reissa. Although they could make no headway with Ethel, their presence bothered Cindi. Distracted by Esther, Cindi's frame of mind was more open to their suggestions than Ethel's was. They didn't attack Cindi with the ferocity or the tenacity Reissa knew them to be capable of, but they caused her to stumble occasionally all the same. Each time, she had picked herself up a little sheepishly, berated her lack of watchfulness, and gone on. But they were wearing her down.

Calum moved and drifted toward Reissa, and she glanced at him. His face was particularly striking, with eyes so blue they defied description. He smiled pleasantly.

"She is hard at it today," he observed. "Never have I seen a *warrior so dedicated."*

Reissa nodded. "Yes, she really should be napping, conserving her strength. She has a hard fight ahead of her yet."

"Yes," he agreed and jerked his head in the direction of the demons. "They will do everything in their power to make it difficult for her."

Reissa laid one strong hand on Calum's shoulder. "I must return to the Master for a short time. I leave you in charge of this precious one and the others under my care."

Calum bowed his head in humble acceptance. "You can count on me to do my best for the Master," he assured her.

"I will be back soon," Reissa promised. In a blinding flash of light, she traversed the space between earth and heaven. `One day soon,' she thought, `mankind will make the same journey.'"

CHAPTER

Objects began to emerge from the dark as the sun struggled to crest the skyscrapers. Pink rays shot into the gray sky like paint hitting wet watercolor paper. The moment the color touched the sky it exploded, and suddenly there was color everywhere. Orange bled into the pink until the whole sky seemed to be on fire.

But, it was not the fireworks display in the heavens that woke Davy O'Connell that morning. It was the sound of the city waking up. A refuse truck just down the street pulled to a jerky halt, brakes screeching. A few doors away, the owner of a bakery chased away a derelict from the doorway where he had spent the night. Curses hounded the man down the street as he stumbled a few paces before crumpling to a heap, retching violently.

"Worthless drunk!" the bakery owner screamed, throwing an empty wine bottle after him. It hit the sidewalk, the glass spraying the oblivious drunk. He heaved a few more times before staggering to his feet and moving off down the street. The bakery owner went to get a broom to clean up the mess he'd left behind.

Davy shifted uncomfortably. The door frame dug into his back.

GUARDIANS

As he rubbed his hands over his face, the scratchy stubble of his beard reminded him of why he was not in his own warm bed at his apartment.

She'd kicked him out. Again. He remembered that. She told him that he didn't appreciate her — she always said that — and that she'd found someone who did, so not to bother coming back. He hadn't planned to either. Until he had a few drinks in his belly.

Who did she think she was, kicking him out of his own place? He'd been there first. So, he'd gone back. She wasn't there, and the apartment was locked up tighter than Fort Knox. His belongings were outside the building. It looked like they'd been there a while because passers-by had been pawing through them.

He'd gathered up what was left and hidden it in an alley until he could figure out what to do. Then he'd gone back to the bar. He had a vague memory of being kicked out of a taxi for throwing up, but that's where he blanked out.

He stood up shakily, stretching some of the stiffness from his limbs. The fresh aroma of brewing coffee drifted down the increasingly busy street. It awakened a gnawing ache in his stomach. Somehow, he had to get some money today.

Davy headed to the alley where he'd left his stuff. He squeezed into the crawl space between two garbage dumpsters and groped around in the darkness, fumbling for the slick plastic of the garbage bags his belongings were in. Just as his fingers brushed the surface of the bags, a crash in the alley made him freeze. He was in an awkward position, his lower body exposed in the alley while his torso was wedged into the crevice.

One hand went automatically to the gun in his pocket. Its weight was reassuring in his hand, and he palmed it gently, almost lovingly. Davy had never shot the pistol. He backed out of the crawl space, heart triple-beating in his chest. He squatted back onto his haunches with a growl, his eyes scanning the alley, the gun in his hands weaving uncertainly.

It was Crazy Carol.

She was looking at him the way a bird might, head cocked to one side, as if he were an oddity, not a threat. Matted black hair, liberally streaked with gray, poked out from beneath a woolen ski hat that belied the seventy degree temperature. Her face reflected the effects of her harsh living conditions.

She carried all her clothes on her back, the layers padding her thin frame with their tattered insulation. Black eyes blinked rapidly at him, and she grinned a wide, toothless smile. A curious purplish birthmark shaped like a half-moon beneath one eye made it look as though she'd been involved in a street brawl and walked away the loser.

Beside her was the dog she rescued from a garbage bin while looking for lunch one day. At least that was the rumor. He stood taller than her waist and was thinner than any dog had a right to be. Huge feet splayed out from his long legs. He was covered with wiry hair, a gift from some Irish wolfhound ancestor. His tail wagged gently as he watched Davy. His eyes were intense, almost human.

"Whatcha doin'? Whatcha doin'? Whatcha doin' there?" Carol sang. "Move along. No loitering. No gun. Bad man." She shook her finger at him, and he looked down at the pistol in his hand, suddenly embarrassed. He waved it at her.

"Aw, go on, Carol. Take your dog with you."

"Come on, Come Here," she told the dog, tugging on the frayed string that was tied around his neck. Come Here turned around obediently and followed her on down the alley as she talked to invisible people. "Get along, Bob, ain't got no leftovers today. Tell ya what, come back tomorrow, Janet. Gonna rain, it is. Shore is. Shore is."

Davy pulled out the garbage bags and began to paw through them trying to locate the few items he wanted to take with him. A change of clothes would be nice, if he could find something that 'she' had managed to wash. He was so preoccupied that he didn't notice the change in weather until a few premature raindrops splattered on the hot pavement and evaporated instantly. The sky swirled moodily, mixing charcoal clouds in angry circles before opening up, the deluge obscuring sight. Davy cursed his luck and hunkered into the crawl space to wait for the storm to pass.

That was when it dawned on him that Carol had been right. And for just one second he was sure he heard her odd cackle float down the alley as an undertone to the pounding of the storm.

Although Davy couldn't see them, two angels loitered in the alley nearby. Both were radiant in their brightness, a sharp contrast to the dingy weather. Rain fell in black sheets around them, but they acted as though it didn't exist. Their concentration was completely absorbed by the exchange they had just witnessed between the recently homeless Davy and the permanently homeless Carol.

"He doesn't see his condition in its true light," Jes mourned. "He is so blind that he thinks he is fine, that things will work out. He is so self-centered, so self-absorbed, that it doesn't even occur to him that 'she' may not take him back. And she won't. She's had enough. Of course, he doesn't know that, and so he plans and schemes to make things the way they were. To make them 'normal.'"

Saiph nodded sagely. "Normal may be comfortable, but it's certainly not a catalyst for growth."

"Can't he see what a shallow, meaningless life he leads?" Jes asked. "It is so far removed from what Christ the Master intended, and yet he is happy with it! How can that be?"

Balor, a shriveled old demon, sat hunched up along the opposite wall of the alley. He picked his teeth nonchalantly with one long, dirty fingernail. "He is happy with it because he's doing what pleases him," he informed the angel with a patronizing smile. "And he will continue to do what pleases him because he hasn't got a sacrificial bone in his body." He scuttled aside to get a better view of Davy while he waited out the storm.

Jes turned her back on the demon, wrapping her wings protectively around her body like a shimmering cloak of light. She leaned toward Saiph and lowered her voice. "I have been talking to him. The other day the taxi driver almost beat him up because he didn't have any money to pay for his fare. I impressed him that there was money in his pocket. When he saw it, he was so relieved that he thanked God for saving him."

Balor snorted. "You think that did any good? He didn't mean it, I assure you. God is a curse word to Mr. O'Connell. He's an atheist through and through."

"There is no such thing as a true atheist," Jes replied softly, not making direct eye contact with Balor. "When their lives are on the line, they will call on God whether they claim to believe in Him or not. An atheist is someone who does not choose God, not someone who does not believe in Him."

"Semantics," the demon scoffed disdainfully. "And it doesn't matter what optimistic definition you give it. Davy O'Connell does not believe in God now, and He never will."

"Humans are free to choose life or death," Jes countered evenly. "He is free to listen to you or me."

Balor studied his fingernails as if they held some sort of secret. "And it is my job to see that he listens to me." Deep-set black eyes looked up without warning, and an evil grin split his homely, deteriorated face. "It's nothing personal, you understand. But we're right, and you're wrong. Simple."

"Yes, yes, it is personal," Jes corrected. "Because you chose the path of destruction, because you were wrong, you hope to drag down as many innocent people as you can."

Balor shrugged. "Misery loves company," he joked. "I wouldn't let it get to you," he added sarcastically. "It won't be much longer until it's all over anyway. The end is near, isn't it?"

"It ended two thousand years ago," Jes said grimly. "You know that. It is that fact that makes you so desperate."

"That's not desperation, my enemy, that's confidence," Balor replied smugly.

Saiph turned slightly and peered down the alley through the rainfall. Carol was trudging back up the alley. Come Here padded softly at her side, head low, eyes almost closed against the pelting rain. Saiph flew to her, wrapping a wing around the homeless woman. "Carol, follow me. I know a safe place where you can wait out the storm."

Carol's head snapped up and she smiled. "Follow me. Follow me," she said. And while humming Jesus Loves Me, she allowed herself to be led by the angel.

"It's mine!"

"Is not!"

"Is too! Daddy gave it to me last week!"

Billie Jo stepped into the middle of her shrieking offspring and lifted the toy in question out of their grasp. She closed her eyes and counted to ten before she attempted to speak. Even though she kept her voice soft, the awful headache pounding in her skull made it sound loud even to her own ears.

"OK, looks like it's time for some time-out." Groans greeted this statement, and Cassidy slunk off with a glare and a pout. Dallas hugged one of her legs and refused to let go.

"Mommeeeee," he whined. "Daddy did too give that to me. I want it back. Why can't I have it? Why? Mommeeeeee . . ."

Billie Jo put both hands to her ears to block out his voice. One more syllable and she just knew her head would explode. "Dallas, this toy is in time-out for awhile. Please be a good boy and go find something else to play with."

She tried to take a step, but he clung to her, refusing to let go.

There was a stubborn glint in his eyes that Billie Jo recognized. It was the same one his father got from time to time. "Dallas, let go," she warned. "Let go, now. One, two . . ." She never made it to three.

Suddenly the front door burst open, and Helen was in the room as large as life. Billie Jo was tempted to think that it was a headache induced nightmare until Dallas relinquished her leg with a squeal and flew toward his grandmother. Even Cassidy, who was a little reserved around Helen, came running at the sound of Helen's voice.

Nog clung to Helen like a second skin. His eyes were red-rimmed and glazed over. He'd been working overtime on her, and it showed. Digging, digging, always digging. It had been easy to reopen old wounds, rekindle old insecurities. With him around, Helen would never run out of ways to try to keep her claws tightly locked onto the life of her son.

And Nog was determined to keep it that way.

He sized up Billie Jo like a boxer entering the ring. She was easy prey today. Even without the benefit of her weakened mental state resulting from her headache, she would react to the least provocation, and there was hardly an angel in sight to help her. A few well-placed jabs and kerpow! Out of the ring she'd tumble.

"Push her," he urged Helen. "But be nice about it. Don't give up an inch. Take what's yours."

Lately Helen's moods had been swinging back and forth from downright chilly to nauseatingly happy. Today, Billie Jo realized with a sinking feeling in the pit of her stomach, was a happy day. Although Helen gave her nothing besides a cool 'hello,' she instantly pulled a bag from behind her back and presented it to the children.

Cassidy dropped the last of her reserve and accepted a new doll before hugging Helen around the waist. Dallas was no less appreciative of a remote controlled monster truck, which he proceeded to try out immediately.

"And I brought you some candy," Helen crooned, giving them each a thick chocolate bar.

"No candy before . . ." Billie Jo began, but Helen cut her off.

"I hope you don't mind," she simpered apologetically, her eyebrows lifting along with one slim shoulder. "Please don't take it away from them. It's just a little treat. It won't hurt a thing."

Billie Jo swallowed the retort on her lips. She knew she was being manipulated, but she couldn't bring herself to ruin the look of joy on the kids' faces. It was always this way. Helen would do something nice, and Billie Joe would come out looking like the ogre when she took it away or spoiled their fun. Today, she just didn't have the strength to fight it.

"Take a moment," Jewel pleaded. "Ask for the Master's strength. You must see that you have none of your own. Only in His strength can you stand firm in love. All you have to do is ask." The angel stood poised to infuse Billie Jo with unlimited power from above at her request, but it wasn't forthcoming. He watched with an overwhelming feeling of helplessness as Billie Jo plowed on in her own strength, relying on her own judgment and her own ability to control her temper.

"It's just that it's so close to suppertime," she said, hoping that an explanation would do what it had always failed to do in the past. "We don't usually let the kids eat between meals. It ruins their appetites."

Helen rolled her eyes. "Well, a little treat now and then isn't going to kill them," she replied, some of the old bite back in her voice.

"No, of course not," Billie Jo muttered as she walked into the kitchen to get a glass of water so she could swallow the aspirin tablets that were melting in her hand.

"What was that?" Helen barked.

Billie Jo ducked her head to avoid Helen's glare. "Nothing," she mumbled. "Nothing at all."

But Helen was on her like a hound dog scenting its quarry. "No, you said something. What was it? I want to know."

"Don't do it, Billie Jo," Jewel pleaded. He watched as a gang of demons surrounded Billie Jo, taunting her.

"You gonna let her talk to you like that?" one hollered, buzzing circles around her head, making little jabs at her.

"Mean old witch, who does she think she is barging in here and bossing you around?" another asked haughtily. "I'd give her what for. After all, she deserves it. Give it to her. Go ahead."

"Billie Jo, nothing good will come of an argument. Reason with her. It may take more time, and it won't be as immediately gratifying as appeasing your anger, but in the end it will be so much more satisfying to follow the Master." Jewel wrapped Billie Jo in his strong arms, but she wrestled away from him to confront Helen.

Billie Jo tried counting again, but before she reached ten, she spun around and faced her mother-in-law nearly nose to nose. She felt as if her head had come clean off her shoulders. *"And we have liftoff!" she heard a little voice in her head say as if it were narrating the sequence of events.* "I said 'of course not,'" she ground out, jaw clenched, hands balled up at her sides.

"And just what is that supposed to mean?" Helen asked, lifting her nose a few degrees into the air.

"It means," Billie Jo said slowly, enunciating each word, "that it wouldn't do them any harm to wait either. In fact, that's what is best for them. But you don't care about that, do you? You just want them to like you. You know we don't give them candy, let alone between meals. Why do you have to bring it in the first place? Give it a rest already. Don't you know when you're not wanted? GO HOME AND QUIT BOTHERING US!"

It was as if she could feel their eyes burning holes through her. Everything moved like a dream-state. She swung her head around. Cassidy and Dallas were staring at her, dumbfounded, frightened.

Guardians

Gael and Boreas, the children's guardian angels, struggled to protect them from the angry emotion Billie Jo was carelessly spraying, but it was as futile as trying to block the spray of a skunk. It saturated the air and made it impossible to breathe. They retreated as the demons moved in, chortling at their victory. One infused the children with fear, and another battered them with anger.

Jewel took in the whole scene with tears streaming down his golden cheeks. The whole of the army of heaven waited—just waited—for the command to protect Billie Jo and the children. A few words would have placed a barrier around them that Satan and his demons could not have penetrated. But those words, that prayer for help, never came.

Instead of fighting back and vindicating her whole tirade, Helen averted her eyes and dashed toward the door gulping back tears.

"You hate me," she wailed. "You've always hated me. No matter what I do, it's never right. I don't know why you hate me so much!"

Billie Jo stared after her and then turned to face the accusing looks on the faces of her children. Before she could even offer an explanation, Jimmy came through the door, his face dark with anger. "What in blazes has got into you, woman?" he roared. "My mother's out there just a'bawlin' her eyes out saying you hate her and she always knew you did. Whatever did you say to her?"

Nog moved forward like a bullfighter parrying the final thrust. "You worthless piece of nothing," he said with smug satisfaction. "How could you do that? She was only trying to help you and look at what you did. She's crying! Crying! Don't you feel bad now? You did this. You crushed her. I hope you're happy with yourself."

"I . . . I . . ." Billie Jo struggled to say something, anything, in her own defense. *'What have I done?'* her mind wailed. *'Oh, God, please forgive me. I lost my temper again. When will I ever learn?'*

The bridge of her nose stung the way it always did just before she had a real good crying jag, and there was a horrible sick feeling in the pit of her stomach, as if she'd swallowed a boulder and it was thinking of making a return trip. She looked up, trying to meet Jimmy's eyes and felt it coming on like gangbusters. Her shoulders shook, and she dissolved into tears as he watched in bewilderment. Then Dallas started crying, and Cassidy joined him. Jimmy took one panicked look at them and fled.

The instant the prayer left Billie Jo's lips, Jewel was at her side. He wrapped his arms around her and assured her of God's love. He was barely aware of Nog's hollow victory laugh as he left to follow Helen. The rest of the demons scattered but stuck around in case Billie Jo should regret her hasty petition.

"Too late now," one of them scoffed. "The damage has been done. Why don't you just curse God and get it over with. After all, it isn't like He helped you when you were down, now is it?"

But his words fell on deaf ears. Billie Jo sank to her knees and gathered her children in her arms. She murmured apologies mixed up with prayers, and they clutched each other for comfort. Over and over she tried to erase the look of fear she had caused in their eyes, but it wouldn't go away. She mourned that *even more than the outburst itself.*

By the time Jimmy came back home, she had managed to get her emotions under control. She had apologized to her children for the scene, apologized to her God for her sin, and was ready to make peace with her mother-in-law. Her headache had subsided enough to allow rational thought. The kids were playing quietly in their room when Jimmy opened the front door and found her in the living room straightening up.

He didn't say a word, just walked over to her and wrapped his big, strong arms around her, enveloping her in forgiveness. Billie Jo sank into him and gripped him tightly around the waist.

"I'm sorry," she whispered.

"I know," he said, his breath warm against her neck. "Me too.

I just don't understand how come you and my mother can't get along together. It don't seem that hard to me."

Instantly Billie Jo's anger returned, and she pulled away from him. "No, it isn't, as long as I let her have her way. She bullies me around, and you know it. And you always stick up for her."

Jimmy scowled at her. "That's not true. Just so happens this time she's right. Wasn't no big deal her giving the kids a present."

"No, maybe not this time," Billie Jo agreed. "But what about last time and the time before that? It's like she's trying to buy their love. And what about me? It's my job to be the police, to monitor her. I shouldn't have to do that. And it makes me look like some kind of ogre. She's a grown woman. Why can't she respect us?"

"She respects us," Jimmy replied defensively. "In her own way."

Billie Jo snorted. "You got that straight. In her own way—the land of no way. We've asked her before not to bring the kids candy, but does she ever listen to us?"

"Aw, I used to eat candy before supper," Jimmy said, "and nothing bad ever come of it. Didn't stunt my growth or nothing, did it?"

Billie Jo stifled a smile. Jimmy was built like a sequoia. "That's not the point," she forced herself to reply with an even voice. "The point is that we've asked her not to do it."

"And we'll just have to ask her again," Jimmy said. "It'll get through that thick head of hers sooner or later."

"I just wish you wouldn't stick up for her," Billie Jo whispered. Her stomach was convulsed into a thick knot, and tears slipped softly down her cheeks. "It makes me feel second best."

Jimmy shook her shoulders sternly. "That ain't true, and you know it. Now buck up, hear?"

Billie Jo nodded. *What choice do I have?* she thought to herself. *She's won again.*

"Yeah," she said aloud. "I'm bucking."

CHAPTER

Noble faced the other angels gathered at the meeting. Their usually serene faces wore sober expressions. It was plain they wondered why they had been summoned together. Each angel present was assigned to the mission compound just outside of Niamey in Niger, Africa. Gaius, Julian, Lileah and a handful of others studied him expectantly.

Noble found no pleasure in what he must tell them, but he knew that the events about to take place would afford all of their charges a growing experience. The humans at the mission were poised to enter a new phase of the battle. Their commander had wearied of the fight and her end was near. Comrades were about to be wounded on all sides. The entire future of the mission was at stake and each angel present would soon be caught up in the gritty fierceness of battle. They had to understand exactly what was involved and how things would soon change.

Don Germaine placed his worn canvas bag full of medical supplies in the back of the ultralight, right under the seat. Squinting up at the sun, he wiped one sleeve over his already perspiring forehead. It was going to be a scorcher, he thought.

Guardians

Toby O'Connell, who was making some minor adjustments to the engine of the little plane, jostled him with an elbow and nodded at a dust-covered Land Rover that had pulled up in front of the clinic. Several young men dressed in khaki shorts, crumpled and stained white shirts, and heavy boots hopped out of the vehicle.

They all staggered slightly, but one nearly crumpled the instant his feet hit the ground. His companion shoved one shoulder beneath him to hoist him back into a standing position. His head rolled wildly, his long, straight blonde hair falling in damp wisps across his face, obscuring it. The driver hopped out and walked briskly towards Don and Toby.

"'Ello chaps," he said with a wide infectious smile. He stuck out his hand and shook Don's with a firm grip. His thick brown hair looked freshly cut and a little too short. A bushy, almost handlebar, mustache punctuated his smile and the laugh lines around his frank blue eyes crinkled as he spoke.

"The name's Thomas, John Thomas. One of the boys picked up some kind of bug in our travels. 'Ave you got a shot of penicillin about? Good, then." He waved his buddies into the back of the line of people waiting for shots in front of the clinic.

He turned back to face them, an apologetic grin on his face. Then he slapped one hand to his forehead and began rummaging around in his shirt pocket.

"Say, would either of you know where I could find Shay Okeke? I've a letter 'ere for 'er." He held out a rather dirty letter with Shay's name printed in ominous, legal, businesslike letters on the front of it.

Don reached for the letter. "I'll deliver it to her for you. She's probably not up yet." He ran his fingers over the crinkled edge of the letter and stared moodily at the return address: Thornton, Edgerton, and Battles; Attorneys At Law. Didn't look promising. He felt a wave of dread pass over him.

"Where did you get this letter?"

"Chap from Niamey, some sort of bar where me and the boys stopped for some, er, liquid refreshment, asked me to pass it along as we were coming in this general direction."

Toby laughed out loud. "Wahabi. Had to be. Real aristocratic type? Looked down his nose at you, did he?"

Thomas shook his head. "No, pretty friendly." He ducked his head sheepishly. "Of course we were rather loose with our money. He also thought my friend there," Thomas glanced towards his companions who were advancing in line, "might be able to get a shot of antibiotic here."

"I'll take a look at him if you like," Don volunteered. "I'm the doctor here."

"No need," Thomas replied. "I'm a doctor myself. Careless, I'm sure, but I left my medical bag behind. No, I'm certain it's nothing. Just a bug, as I said."

One of the children at the mission ventured too close to the Land Rover and the air was suddenly split with the shrieks and howls of monkeys. This drew a child-sized crowd. Don peered around Thomas's shoulder at the Land Rover. His eyebrows crept up and he ran one hand through his black curls. "What's with the monkeys?"

Thomas laughed. "Lunch," he replied with a wink at Toby who shuddered. "There are my boys. Right, we're off. Thanks ever so much."

The Land Rover kicked up a wave of dust as Thomas punched the gas. Wheels churning, rear-end weaving, it continued on in the direction of Agadez. Don stared after it for a few minutes.

"I said, I'm going to the compound, do you want me to bring that to Shay?" Toby repeated. Don snapped his head around to find her grinning at him.

"Where'd you go?" she asked playfully, giving him a little shove. "Zoning on me?"

Don felt his heart stop for a second, the way it did every time he saw her smile. She seemed nothing like the angry woman who had wandered into his mission a few short years before. But then, he was nothing like the angry man she had met.

They had worked hard, the two of them. They'd had to. They had a lot of baggage to discard before they could concentrate on each other. Now they were at the same place, standing on the brink of a whole new relationship, a whole new life together. And it felt right. It felt exactly right.

Don handed Toby the envelope. She stood on her tiptoes and gave him a quick peck on the cheek, as if she could read his thoughts, then she turned and ran towards the mission compound. He watched until she disappeared and then turned with a sigh to finish getting ready.

"I wouldn't be getting too comfy in that relationship if I were you," Merck said smugly.

"Merck! Merck! Where are you, worthless, no-good, conniving . . . there you are. What are you just standing around for? There's work to be done." Lucien fairly bristled with importance these days. Merck purposely dragged his feet as he approached Lucien. Passive aggression was what the humans called it. Whatever it was, it got under Lucien's skin.

"Can't you move any faster than that?" he howled irritably. "Do I have to do everything myself? It's no thanks to you and the rest of these worthless, lazy do-nothings that this mission will be brought to its knees. No, I'll do it single-handedly."

"Go ahead," Merck replied flatly. "Sparn will get all the credit. He's still in charge of this post. Remember?"

"Sparn?" Lucien shrieked, as if he'd forgotten all about the demon. "Sparn?! He's done nothing. He DOES nothing but sit all day in that chair and brood. He will not receive credit for my work. I won't have it. Now, move!!!

"I've gone to great lengths to institute my plan and with no help from any of you. Now I have work for you. Take one contingent of demons to follow the vehicle that just left. I want you to make sure they reach Agadez. When they do, make sure they

run into lots of people." Lucien rubbed his hands together glee-
fully. "Yes, every person in the town, if possible."

Merck shrugged. "Sure, no problem."

"It might well be a problem if you don't get a move on!" Lucien
screamed. His eyes bulged from their sockets and Merck couldn't
help thinking that there was something just a little desperate
about his tone. Before he could think of anything to say, Lucien
had wandered off muttering to himself. He flew at a small group
of demons blocking his path, scattering them like pigeons.

Whatever his great "plan" was, Merck didn't want to be the
cause of its failure and Lucien's subsequent wrath. He sum-
moned a group of his friends and they set out to find the Land
Rover. He thought idly that it might be the first time in history a
group of demons was sent out to protect someone.

Shay Okeke, formerly Beauregard, tried to roll over but a sharp
pain in her side prevented a completion of the movement. Giving up, she rolled back and flung an arm into the middle of the
bed expecting to find her husband beside her. But her fingers
touched only the cool sheet. She grimaced. Nwibe was up already.

Groaning, she struggled into a sitting position, wondering exactly how long they had let her oversleep today. It seemed like
lately all she did was sleep. At least it was better than the vomiting. That had just begun to subside and she was still too grateful
to mind the exhaustion or her expanding girth.

She probed her abdomen with curious fingers, but it was still
too early to feel much. Sighing, she ran her fingers through the
tangle of long black hair that fell well past her shoulders. Somehow today, she had to find enough energy to bathe. There just

never seemed to be enough time in the day.

The door opened a crack and Nwibe stuck his head in, smiling. His white eyes gazed sightlessly into the room. "Ah, Madame, you're awake."

Shay chuckled. "You amaze me, you know that? How did you know I was awake?" She shook her head. "No, don't answer that. I like the mystery of it. Besides, sometimes I think it can't be explained."

"Akueke has been keeping your breakfast warm. Do you think you'll be able to eat anything this morning, sweetheart?" The affectionate American term still sounded foreign on his lips and Shay ducked her head to hide the smile he couldn't see but would surely sense.

"I think I would like something this morning," she replied, struggling to keep her voice even.

"You don't fool me, Madame," he said, titling his nose skyward with a haughty sniff. "You find my use of your Americanisms amusing. If you would prefer, I won't use them any more."

Shay struggled to her feet and rushed to him, throwing her arms around his waist. "I find them amusing, yes, and adorable. Just like you." She buried her face against his chest and nestled against the vibrations of his laugh before turning her face up for a kiss.

"Come now, you make Akueke wait and you know how impatient she gets. Besides, you need to get some nourishment before you waste away."

"Like that's possible," Shay mumbled sarcastically with a sheepish glance towards her middle. She looked fat. She felt fat. And she didn't like it. "Where is Madina?"

The little girl they had adopted three years ago had been feeling the effects of Shay's condition. Until her pregnancy, Shay had spent a lot of time with her. Now she felt as though she hadn't even seen Madina in days. Whenever they did get a chance to play, Shay tired easily or just did not feel up to it.

"She has gone to play at the house of a friend," Nwibe replied.

Shay groaned. Madina had been at Felia's house too much lately. It made Shay feel guilty. Still, she should feel fortunate that Felia's mother took compassion on Madina, Shay told herself.

She allowed Nwibe to lead her to the dining room which had long since been vacated by the rest of the mission staff. Akueke fussed over her as if she were an invalid and Shay half suspected that she had kept the best of the meal aside from the others just to tempt her into eating.

"Really, I'm fine," she kept repeating, but Akueke paid no attention to her.

"You must eat," she insisted. "You get too thin. Not good for that baby."

Shay nearly choked. "Thin? I'm a whale!"

"Nonsense," Akueke retorted. "Why, I think you've actually lost weight. You know," she admonished, punctuating her words with stabs of a wooden spoon, "my mother when she carried her babies was big, very fat. She had a baby almost every year."

"Wow, every year?" Shay contemplated the implications of this, doing the arithmetic while Akueke went on.

"She had so much milk she could have fed an entire village of babies. Once, she nursed the daughter of a neighbor who became sick and couldn't feed her own baby—at the same time she nursed my brother."

"Where is your mother now?" Shay asked.

"Dead," was the laconic reply. "Too many babies too soon." She shrugged. "It is this way with many of my people. That is why it makes my heart glad when I see those like the Doctor Germaine and Miss Toby and you teaching the people about birth spacing and such. The babies who come now will have a better future and so will their parents."

Shay nodded. "That's what we hope too."

"Hey, kiddo, how you doing this morning?" Toby asked as she

burst into the kitchen. Seeing Shay's full plate, she helped herself. "I don't remember seeing this on the table for breakfast," she said, casting an accusing glance towards Akueke who made threatening motions with the wooden spoon.

"That is for Madame Shay and her baby," Akueke sniffed.

Toby licked her fingers. "I need my nourishment too," she argued. "I've got to fly that cantankerous doctor around to the outposts today." Her grin suggested that the chore wasn't nearly as distasteful as she made it out to be.

Shay pushed her plate of food aside. "I'm sorry. Have I been keeping you?"

Toby put a hand on Shay's shoulder and propelled her back to her chair. "Take your time. Flory's getting stuff ready for the shots today. Her first solo. She's quite excited about it. I don't know what the big deal is. It's not like she's never given a shot before. She says the nuns let her give shots all the time at Our Lady of Whatever.

"Anyway, there's not much else that needs doing at the moment. Don's fiddling with the ultralight. I half regret teaching him how to take care of it," she mused. Then added, "I've still got to get some things from my room. You've got plenty of time."

Shay sank back into her chair. "Did you say Flory's giving shots today?"

Toby nodded. "Yup, and she's got a line of customers already. Why?"

"Oh, nothing really. Nwibe needs to have a Hepatitis B vaccine. I'll make sure he gets it today. He's been putting it off." She scrunched up her nose. "He doesn't like shots."

"Me either," Toby admitted. "But, it's better than getting Hepatitis B, that's for sure."

"I know. I'll send him over just as soon as I find him."

"Almost forgot," Toby mumbled around a mouthful of food. "Some Brit with a Rover full of monkeys dropped this off. Said Wahabi gave it to him." Toby handed Shay the letter and then snagged a toast off her plate narrowly missing having her fingers rapped by Akueke's spoon before ducking down the corridor towards her room.

Akueke muttered under her breath and began to prepare another toast while Shay turned the letter over and over in her hands. "Looks serious," she said more to herself than Akueke. She tried hard to ignore the uneasy feeling in the pit of her stomach. The letter had to be from her father's attorney, William Battles. But, why?

If it was bad news, she wanted to read it on a full stomach. She laid the letter aside and did her best to eat what was on her plate. For the first time in days, she was actually hungry. Nwibe came in before she was finished.

"Honey, you need to go over and let Flory give you your vaccine," she said, fully expecting him to put up a fuss about it.

"You will be happy to know, Madame, that I have already taken care of that little matter," he replied with a slight grin.

Shay studied him, her brows knit thoughtfully together. "Nwibe, you wouldn't start lying to me after all this time, would you?"

"Certainly not," he replied. "But, if you do not believe me, you may ask Madame Florentine."

"No," Shay replied lightly. "I believe you. I just didn't think it would be so easy to convince you that you needed the vaccine, that's all." She pushed herself away from the table, forgetting about the letter. "Thank you for breakfast, Akueke. It was wonderful."

"But, you hardly ate a morsel," the old woman clucked disapprovingly. "You will waste away. Mark my words."

"I'm stuffed, really," Shay insisted. "Now, I'd better get to work before they fire me."

Shay waddled—at least she thought of it as waddling—towards the clinic. Toby had been right. There were at least thirty people waiting in line for shots of penicillin and vaccines. Mothers waited patiently with their babies on their hips, uncomplaining in the hot sun. Some of the children had red hair, a sign of malnutrition, and Shay made a mental note to remind their mothers to stop at the clinic so they could be treated.

Florentine Pelligrino was a young nurse from Our Lady of Mercy Mission Hospital who was training with Doctor Germaine. The sisters at Our Lady had hoped that Florentine could be trained to do simple operations with simple equipment and Doctor Germaine had agreed to teach Flory in exchange for her help around the mission.

Ever since he and Toby had started the outpost clinics, help had been a little scarce. Fortunately, they were expecting some nurses' from the States to arrive any day. Flory was picking up the slack until they arrived.

Shay liked the quiet Italian girl. Sometimes in the evenings, she could hear her clear, sweet voice singing *Solo Mio* or snatches from an opera. Her hands were always busy, always helping. She had picked up what Don taught her with amazing speed and proved herself to be a competent student.

Her long black hair was drawn up into a neat chignon that Shay could never have managed. It framed a small, thin face with large, soulful black eyes. Although she stood taller than Shay, nearly as tall as Don, she was thin almost to the point of being skinny.

"Hello, Flory, how are you this morning?" Shay put her hands at the base of her spine and stretched backwards, trying to relieve some of the pressure put on her back by her ever-increasing girth.

"I am fine, Mrs. Okeke. And how are you and that precious little bambino?" Florentine asked, as she loaded a syringe for her next patient.

"Please," Shay begged, "call me Shay. Somebody's got to. My own husband refuses to call me anything but Madame or Madame Shay and we've been married for three years now. And when Doctor Germaine calls me by name, it's like when your mother yells and you know you've done something wrong." Shay lowered her voice to mimic Don. "Shay Judalon Okeke what did you do with my new scalpel?" The young nurse laughed with her.

A patient coughed and Shay let her eyes roam down the line of people waiting for shots. Judging from appearances, she could see a few penicillin's, a couple tetanus, and one that looked suspiciously like malaria. Flory gave the man in front of her an injection of penicillin, washed the needle in a basin of water beside her and prepared her next shot.

Shay's lips and hands blanched. They felt tingly, as if they had gone to sleep. Her hand shot out and clamped on Flory's forearm. "What are you doing?" she asked hoarsely.

Flory looked at her, eyes wide. "What do you mean? I'm giving the shots today. Doctor Germaine said that I should since he and Miss O'Connell were going to be away. Don't look at me like that! Are you all right? Should I call for Doctor Germaine?"

Shay swayed, her grip on Flory's arm tightening. "Have you used that same needle on all of the patients you've given shots to?" Flory nodded dumbly.

"And how many shots have you given today?"

"I don't know. Maybe twenty so far. Maybe thirty. I don't know. I wasn't counting. What is it? What is wrong?" she begged.

"Come with me," Shay pulled the girl after her into the clinic behind them. Inside the whitewashed concrete walls, it was cooler. She led Flory to a shelf full of hypodermic needles. Grabbing a handful she shoved them at Flory. "From now on, use one needle per patient. Do you understand?"

Flory nodded, a puzzled look on her face. "Yes, but, isn't that a waste? At Our Lady of Mercy, we use only five needles per day. That is all we can afford. So, we wash the blood off between shots . . . at least when we have time."

Shay felt the floor tip beneath her. "That's not how we do it here," she said. Somewhere in the back of her head little bells were ringing and someone was banging a loud drum. "Go ahead and finish up, but remember to use a new needle for each patient."

Flory nodded obediently and headed back out to her duties while Shay sank against one of the walls, her breathing heavy and jagged. What Flory had done was almost unthinkable. Who knew what viruses she could have been passing along using that infected needle. And Nwibe . . . Nwibe had gotten his vaccine with that same needle.

Shay lifted herself off the floor and made her way outside to find Don. She had to tell him. She found him outside towing the ultralight to the makeshift runway.

His face paled as she talked. "It's my fault. I never told her how. Just showed her the equipment and let her take over. She seemed to know what she was doing. I sure hope . . ." The rest of his sentence went unspoken, but they both knew what he hoped.

"Mama!" Marcus' voice made them both spin guiltily. "Daddy said to bring this to you. You forgot it."

Shay reached out trembling fingers to take the letter from her father's lawyer. "Thank you, Marcus."

Hooking one nail under the flap, she opened it. Marcus and Don looked on while she scanned the letter. As the words registered, she could feel all the color drain out of her face. The world spun crazily and when she looked up there was a haze over everything.

"My father is dead," she said slowly just before her knees gave way and she slid with relief beneath a blanket of darkness.

CHAPTER 3

The roar in his head obscured every other sensation. And the speed was incredible. The tops of the trees approached the cockpit of the plane as if they were being hurled out of a canon. Davy O'Connell's hands gripped the controls of the plane long after it ceased being necessary. He felt his body bounce from one end of the cockpit to the other just before gentle hands lifted him up and set him down next to the base of a tree. He sat there, dazed, as the remnants of his plane burned all around him.

"Remember, Davy?" Jes coaxed persistently. She'd been through this same scenario with him before. Davy continued to choose the leading of the enemy and was deeply under his influence, so Jes's pleas fell on deaf ears. Somehow, she had to get through to him. "Davy, think about the hands. The hands that lifted you out of the plane? Do you remember them? They were my hands, Davy."

As if watching a movie in slow motion, Jes could see him play back the scenes of the crash in his mind. Even as he stood behind the bank counter, his pupils dilated and his breathing quickened. He flinched perceptibly on impact, and then he was out of the plane.

"Remember?" Jes whispered fervently. "Remember?"

"I don't know what you're trying so hard for," Belial commented. "He wasn't saved before the crash, and he won't choose to be saved now. What difference does it make if he remembers the crash? He could care less about your Jesus."

"Jesus saved him from death . . . twice now," Jes replied. "He will care about that if he only would realize it."

"Well, he won't," Belial assured her. "He listens to me now. Not you. Get lost."

"I won't," Jes replied stubbornly. "There are those who remember him in prayer, and they give me strength and purpose."

Belial spat a string of black sputum from between the gap in his front teeth. "They must not be giving you too much strength if he still doesn't remember anything. Why don't you give up?"

"Every human being has been given a conscience. Jesus won't force Davy to choose Him," Jes replied sadly. "And I can't either. But I can offer the hope of salvation to him, and you can't stop me."

"Oh, can't I?" growled the demon menacingly. He turned to a bank customer and gave her a rough shove forward in line. "Hey, lady," he said, his voice oily and urgent. "You're late, you know. Hurry! Hurry! What are you waiting for? He's not paying any attention to you, is he? Doesn't that just make your blood boil? That is so irritating! Remember the last time you came in here and that customer service representative was on the phone with her boyfriend and made you wait ten minutes before she even acknowledged your presence? And now it's happening again. It just never ends.

"You're going to be late. Really late. And then Mr. Crampton is going to fire you because you'll lose the account and then who's going to feed your kids? Certainly not your good-for-nothing husband who can't even send his child support check more than once in a blue moon. Butt in already!"

Belial crowded in behind the woman, his hot breath bathing

the back of her neck, causing her to squirm anxiously. She glanced uneasily toward the door as a muscle in her face jerked spastically. "Do something!" Belial shouted, jumping up and down, waving his arms like a maniac.

"Excuse me! I'd like to make a deposit. Sir? EXCUSE ME!" Davy blinked at the customer in front of him and her annoyed expression. She drummed her fingers rapidly on the countertop and chewed nervously on her lip. Definitely the signs of someone who needed a vacation.

"I'm sorry," Davy apologized, shaking his head to get the daydream to go away. Sometimes it felt too real to be a daydream. "You said a deposit?"

"Yes, and make it snappy. I'm double parked, and I'm late for a meeting." She glared at him as a muscle near her eye twitched. "I ought to report you, you know," she said coldly.

"Careful, Davy," Jes cautioned. "You don't know why she's reacting this way. She's obviously in a hurry, and she has no idea why you were ignoring her. Show compassion."

"Aw, let her have it!" Belial shouted gleefully. "What right does she have to berate you? She doesn't know what you've been through. Give her what for!"

Jes knew that she wasn't getting through to Davy, but she could tell that what she was saying was at least beginning to make an impression when he took a few minutes to compose himself before replying.

"Yes, Ma'am, you ought to," Davy said smoothly, biting back a caustic reply. "But if you bear with me, I'll have you out of here in a jiffy. There you go. Thank you for banking with People's Trust and have a nice day." He managed to get a smile from her before she turned and hurried out of the bank.

Jes breathed a sigh of relief, and Belial shrugged his shoulders. "I'll get him the next time. Or the next. You'll see." Jes ignored him and turned back to Davy.

"Will you quit flirting with the customers, Davy?" Laurie teased as she set five bundles of twenties by his cash drawer. "How many times have you been asked out this week already?"

"Oh, only a couple hundred this week," Davy replied smoothly. "But last week I almost topped a thousand."

Laurie stuck her lip out in a pout. "Not fair," she said. "How come nobody ever asks me out?"

"'Cause you're not as cute as me," Davy joked. He quickly threw up his hands. "Kidding, just kidding. Hey, careful with that letter opener. In some states it's considered a deadly weapon."

Laurie poked him gently in the ribs. "If you take me to dinner, nobody will get hurt."

Before Davy could answer, a smooth female voice answered for him. "I'm sorry, but he has other plans tonight. Isn't that right, Davy?"

Deniece Daignault leaned across the teller counter as Davy turned, a flush on his face. What would she think? He felt like a kid caught red-handed in the cookie jar. He snapped his fingers. "That's right, we're going out. Aren't we?"

"You said it; I didn't," Deniece retorted. She stood back from the counter and tugged at the hem of her red linen blazer to straighten out the line. Her hair flipped out at the bottom and swung when she turned her head. It was distracting, Davy decided, but not as distracting as her perfume. "You can't back out on me now. It's not every day the Bengals come to New Orleans, and I intend to see every moment of that game. And you said something about an expensive restaurant."

Davy's brow furrowed as Laurie turned back toward her own teller window, a sour expression on her face. "I don't remember anything about an expensive restaurant," he said.

"It was worth a try," Deniece joked. "With your memory, who knows?"

Davy sobered instantly. The look on his face brought Deniece up short.

"Oh, Davy, I didn't mean it. Truly. Forgive me?

Davy nodded and took a deep breath.

"What is it? Did you have another one of those visions?" Deniece snapped her sunglasses up so that he could see her eyes.

"They're not visions," Davy corrected her. "They're more like daydreams. But it's no use. I can't remember anything past the crash."

Deniece reached over and patted his arm. "Not right now, maybe. But, in time you'll remember. If that's what you want."

"Maybe," Davy admitted. Sometimes he wasn't even sure why he wanted to remember. After all, Toby was gone. The only thing he remembered about her was her name. And he had one vague fleeting memory of the stricken look on her face the last time he'd seen her.

He'd been with Linda then. Linda Turlington who owned a yacht. He'd stayed with Linda on the yacht for six months, and then they'd had a spat, and she'd kicked him off. He'd tried to make a go of it in Boston for a while, but he kept running into people who knew him, and he didn't remember them. Finally, he decided to move. It was the only thing to do.

It had been like drawing a defining line between his two lives. The Davy O'Connell before the accident and the Davy O'Connell after the accident. So he had packed up everything and moved to Ooltewah, Tennessee, just outside of Chattanooga. Except for the heat, he liked everything about it.

He started out in an apartment but made the mistake of letting his girlfriend, Meg, move in with him. Inside of three months, she'd kicked him out the first time. By the time the year was ended, he'd been kicked out for good. He'd heard since that she had gotten married, and he wondered if it was happily ever after.

There had been a few rough months when he'd been homeless or mooching off "friends." Then he'd gotten a lead, from one of his friends who had recently lived in New Orleans, on a modest duplex in Laplace, Louisiana. With nothing tying him to Tennessee, he'd moved out the next day and rented the duplex. In the entire time he'd been there, about two years now, no one had ever moved into the other side. There was never even a sign out to rent it.

He asked the landlord about it one time and was told that it was being saved for his daughter when she moved back to the States. That suited Davy just fine. He wasn't crazy about neighbors anyway, and it left him the entire backyard to keep a garden.

Why he liked gardening he wasn't sure, but then, he was used to that. It was the same with banking. For some reason, he felt drawn to it. When he saw an ad in the paper for a teller position, he'd applied right away. He'd proven immediately that he was more than qualified.

Then one day during a mortgage closing, he'd been delivering some paperwork to the branch manager, and the lawyer handed him a check to pass to the manager. Without thinking, Davy had signed the check. It had gotten him in a lot of trouble at work, but it also made him think that maybe he'd worked in a bank before in some other position. At times, he regretted not finding out more about his life before the accident, especially now that he wanted to know more. Occasionally, he thought about tracking down someone who could fill him in, but he had never gone through with it.

The relationships he'd had with women had taught him something else. Until he figured out who Davy O'Connell was, he was in no position to begin a serious relationship. And so he dated. A lot, according to Laurie, who seemed extraordinarily interested in his love life. But nothing ever came of his dates, and quite often he realized that he was lonely.

Not the kind of lonely that passed. More the kind of lonely that ached deep inside him. It was a feeling that had been getting stronger. And it made him think of Toby. He wondered where she was and what she was doing. He even worried about what she thought of him. And he tried to remember her. But he couldn't.

"Look, I'll meet you outside the Superdome, OK?" Deniece was saying.

Davy nodded. "Sure. Outside the Superdome."

Laurie grunted. And Deniece ignored her. And Davy smiled. Outside the Superdome.

When he saw her, she looked more like his kid sister than his date. She was dressed in black leggings and a ridiculously large Cincinnati Bengals T-shirt. The shirt earned her dirty looks from nearly everyone around her. Her baseball cap was on backward, her hair drawn up into a ponytail. She smiled broadly when she saw him.

"Whatever possessed you to wear a Bengals T-shirt here?" Davy asked as he grabbed her hand. "You of all people ought to know how rabid this city is for the Saints."

"I know," Deniece replied, snapping her gum. "I like to be different."

"Tell me again why you like the Bengals?" Davy asked.

"They had a cute quarterback a few years ago," Deniece replied. "Besides, I like the tiger."

"Yeah, that's the criteria I use to pick a football team, too," Davy agreed with a snicker.

"Hey, I was young. My friend Shay and I got into football a little because our fathers were big fans. She picked the Colts before I could . We liked horses at the time. But there was something about the Bengals . . ." Deniece mused.

"Yeah," Davy joked. "The quarterback."

"Actually, this was before that quarterback, but he didn't hurt anything." Deniece lapsed into silence, and Davy glanced at her and saw that her eyes were a little misty. He felt a quick pang of sympathy.

"Something wrong?" he asked gently.

"I miss her," Deniece whispered.

"The quarterback was a woman?" Davy shook his head. He took her arm as they were jostled by the crowd and moved ahead a few paces in line. "Impossible."

Deniece laughed. She played idly with the hem of her T-shirt, balling it up and then stretching it out. "No, not the quarterback. My friend Shay. She's in Africa being a missionary. And she's about to have a baby. I'm going to be an aunt. Well, not technically, but we've always been sisters at heart."

"So are you going to go? To Africa, I mean? To see the baby? Or are you going to wait for her to come visit?"

Deniece shrugged her shoulders. "I'm not sure. She may be coming back for a little while. Her dad passed away a few weeks ago. We've already had the funeral, of course, but she might want to have a memorial service for him. I just don't know. I sent her a letter, but I haven't heard anything from her yet."

Davy squeezed her hand. "You will. Don't worry."

Deniece looked up at him. "You're a good friend, Davy," she said.

But inside he didn't feel like a good friend. He felt like a fake. After all, who was he anyway? Even he didn't know for sure. But, he determined, it was something he very much wanted to find out.

Reissa surveyed the room with a look of peaceful resignation. By her side, Ethel Bennington's head nodded, her eyes fluttering until they drooped shut. Although her respirations were regular, they were shallow, and the effort of them lifted her shoulders sharply with each intake of breath.

It wouldn't be much longer, she knew, before the faithful

warrior's fight would be over and she would be at rest waiting for the return of the One she had loved so much and so well. And all of heaven was concerned about who would take her place. The torch had been passed to Cindi Trahan, but more and more, as the days went by, Reissa doubted Cindi's ability to continue carrying it at Ethel's passing.

The gift of the child, for whom she had waited so long, consumed her every waking moment. Of late she had even been neglecting her devotions. The Master came repeatedly to meet with her, only to return saddened by her indifference. His disappointment tugged on Reissa's heart, and she wished with all her might that Cindi might once again seek His presence.

The ever-present clutch of demons continued to grow like a malignant tumor. Their jubilation was hard to mistake. Beady eyes watched shrewdly for life signs as they hovered expectantly, anticipating the feast of misery and glorious victory when Ethel drew her last breath.

Reissa was suddenly conscious of the presence of another angel at her elbow. She looked up to see Noble standing there. His face held no shadow of darkness, although he knew what the future held as surely as she did. Instead, there was a confidence and strength about it that made the demons across the room squirm uncomfortably.

"She does not have much longer to wait," he observed, reaching out one strong, golden hand to stroke the forehead of the old woman. Ethel stirred contentedly in her sleep but didn't waken. Her lips twitched into a brief smile.

Reissa took one of the gnarled hands into her own strong, smooth ones and held it gently. "No. She sleeps so much of the time now. I have tried to open Cindi's eyes to the fact that she is slipping away, but she is too preoccupied to notice it."

Noble's head dipped in acknowledgment. "She has seen the changes too gradually to notice them. Soon one will come who can comfort her, but I fear he will arrive too late to help her *prepare her heart for what is to come."*

"Will he help?" Reissa asked curiously, wondering who the archangel was referring to.

"It is too soon to tell. He has been hurt many times himself. His faith will be tested yet again. You must watch out for him carefully when he arrives. He may need your help as well." His gaze traveled to Ethel. "This faithful prayer warrior will soon be resting and have no more need of you. It will be time for a new assignment."

Reissa's eyes misted over. A new assignment. How many new assignments had she had since the world was first created? Someday soon, she knew, there would be no more "new assignments." The long wait would be over, and she would meet all the charges who had been in her care over the ages. But the first person she wanted to meet on that day was Ethel Bennington. She would miss the faithful old woman.

Noble's hand gripped her forearm. "Have courage. The time is almost at hand." In the next instant he was gone, and Reissa was left to contemplate his words and to carefully keep guard against the plotting demons who edged ever closer in Noble's absence. It was important, very important, that they not shorten the little time she had left.

Cindi Trahan burst into the room with a tray holding a snack and a cup of herbal tea. Cheerful words of greeting died on her lips when she realized with a start that Ethel had fallen asleep. She set the tray down quietly on the night stand and lowered herself into a formal Victorian-style chair that didn't so much as invite respite as it grudgingly put up with it.

Esther had gone down for her nap in the guest room that Ethel insisted belonged to her and with Ethel asleep, Cindi was at a loss for something to do. It was so rare that she had any free time that she wasn't quite sure what to do with herself.

Idly she picked up the Bible that lay near the tray on the night stand. It was Ethel's favorite one. Her husband, Bert, had given it to her on their wedding day. Cindi was amazed that it had held up so well. The leather had softened until it was as buttery as velvet in her hands. She opened it up and thumbed through the thin onion-skin pages, seeing where Ethel had marked her favorite passages, sometimes writing in the margin in her spidery handwriting.

Reading the words of God awakened a yearning in Cindi that almost overwhelmed her. With longing, she remembered the days before she and Marc had adopted Esther. She had spent hours reading her Bible and praying. Her relationship with God had been so primary, so focused.

But then Esther had come into their lives, and Cindi was fortunate to grab a few hurried moments in the morning to read through a devotion before the day started as if it had been shot from a sling. Gone were the long, leisurely hours spent in prayer and meditation. Worse, she was so busy all the time that she barely had time to even miss them.

Her eyes skimmed the pages hungrily, and she had a vague sense of connectedness with God, but her spirit felt rumpled inside her. It was as if something internally had been set to fast-forward and she couldn't settle down enough to really absorb and contemplate the words she was reading. When she reached the bottom of the page, she realized with dismay that she had no idea what she'd just read.

She set the Bible down in frustration. Her head sank down into her hands, and she tried desperately to clear her thoughts to pray. Maybe that was it. She'd forgotten to invite God's Holy Spirit to be with her and open her eyes as she read. Maybe that was why she couldn't settle down mentally.

"Dear Lord," she began. And then she blanked out. Her thoughts were so jumbled she couldn't figure out how to phrase her request. She shook her head. "Lord," she started over, "please send Your Spirit to open my eyes to Your words. Help me to see how they apply to my life."

She heaved a big, convulsive sigh. "You know how my life has been lately, Lord. It seems like it never ends. Not that I'm complaining, mind You. We love Esther so much. So very much that sometimes I ache when I watch her playing. I can't imagine life without her now.

"But You know, Lord, she's a very energetic child." Visions of Esther racing all over the house while Marc chased her while both of them laughed filled Cindi's head, and she smiled. "She's sure an in-your-face kind of kid. It's impossible to ignore her even if you were trying. And bright? It's almost frightening. Why, just the other day . . . But, You don't have time for that, Lord. Well, maybe You do, but I don't. I've already forgotten what I was praying about." Cindi looked upward as if searching for a clue that might be written on the ceiling.

Shania watched the one-sided exchange with interest. "Cindi, the Master wants to hear everything you have to tell Him. He's waited such a long time for you to meet with Him. He misses you, Cindi. And I know you miss Him too."

"She does not," Rafe contradicted her. "If she missed Him she'd make time for Him. What kind of person could miss someone who was available twenty-four hours a day? After all, He's supposed to be just a prayer away, isn't that right?

"But maybe prayer isn't all it's cracked up to be. Is it, Cindi? You sure seem to be having a hard time with it. Why don't you give up for now?" he suggested. "There are so many other things you need to be doing. You can pray later."

"Clear your mind, Cindi," Shania urged. "Invite the Master to come into your heart. He wants to hear every little detail about your life. He wants to hear your concerns about Esther and your financial problems. He wants to hear that funny story you told Marc the other night. Most of all, He wants to spend time with you. Won't you try?"

"Don't bother," Rafe sneered. A few other demons, interested in the conversation, moved in closer to discourage Cindi.

"Don't listen to her," one said, his voice raspy and low. "If your Master wanted so much to spend time with you, He'd come back. What's He waiting for anyway? He's just sitting up there in royal splendor while you twiddle your thumbs down here suffering."

"Yeah, I'd say He's real anxious to bring you all home with Him all right," another piped up, jeering. "He's got the host of heaven waiting on Him hand and foot. He's in no hurry."

"Cindi, the Spirit is right here. Won't you talk to your Lord?" Shania begged.

Cindi wearily lifted herself off the chair. It was no use. She couldn't focus her thoughts enough to pray. Every time she started, they just rambled off in one direction or another. Maybe later, when it was quiet and Esther was in bed for the night. She tried to push out the thought that by that time she'd be so exhausted she wouldn't be able to string together a coherent sentence.

She wasn't accomplishing anything by sitting here letting her thoughts ramble. Maybe later . . .

She backed out of the room and shut the door quietly behind her, oblivious to the rejoicing of the group of demons. And yet a vague sense of disappointment and guilt followed her as she left. No matter how hard she tried throughout the rest of the day, she couldn't shake it. When at last she put her head down on her pillow that evening, she thought again fleetingly about praying.

"Dear Lord," she murmured as a wave of fatigue washed over her, sapping every good intention. Within moments she was asleep.

CHAPTER

The scream of agony echoed inside Billie Jo's head all the way to the hospital. As Jimmy sat slumped and sobbing against the passenger side door and Cassidy and Dallas sat wide-eyed and scared in the back, she replayed the last few minutes of her life over and over again.

She'd been making dinner when the phone rang. "Jimmy, would you get that?" she'd hollered.

"I got it, I got it," she'd heard him reply. She'd been vaguely aware of the first low tones of the conversation. "Hello, Dad," she'd heard him say. And then, "What happened?" The strain in his voice made her heart stop and then pound furiously. In that instant she'd known something terrible had happened.

The wail that came out of Jimmy's mouth reawakened the recently healed wounds of her own suffering. He'd never even said goodbye to his father. He'd just hung up the phone, blindly stumbled to the closet, grabbed his coat, and headed for the car.

Billie Jo had turned off everything on the stove, collected her terrified children, and run out after him. He was sitting behind the wheel, but he was shaking so hard he couldn't even turn the key in the ignition. Billie Jo buckled the kids into their car seats and gently pulled him out of the driver's seat and propelled him around the car to the passenger side. He had crunched his big frame inside and mechanically buckled his belt.

He hadn't spoken a word as she backed out of the driveway and headed out to the road.

"Where are we going, Jimmy?" she'd asked gently.

"Hospital," he'd managed between sobs.

Now he was moaning and rocking back and forth. The straps of his seatbelt tightened and released with the motion. Billie Jo cast a furtive glance at him. He looked awful. His face was ashen and his eyes bloodshot.

"Jimmy?" she said quietly. "Honey? Can you tell me what's wrong? Why am I headed for the hospital?"

He looked over at her, anguish tugging at his rugged features and making him look suddenly like an old man. "My mom," he sobbed. "She . . . she tried to kill herself."

Billie Jo gasped and shot a quick look at the kids in the rearview mirror. Cassidy burst into tears, and Dallas strained against the restraints of his car seat.

"What happened to Grandma?" he demanded. "What's wrong with Grandma? She can't kill herself. Then she'd be dead, and she wouldn't come to visit me no more and bring me candy."

"Sweetie, Grandma Raynard ain't dead," Billie Jo said firmly. "She ain't dead, and she ain't gonna die." She glanced at Jimmy to confirm this fact. "How . . . how is she?"

Jimmy shook his head, sobbing helplessly. "She . . . she shot herself. In the head," he choked out.

Cassidy began crying even louder, and Dallas's lip began to quiver. Billie Jo fought the bile that rose in her throat. She had a feeling that at any moment she was going to be sick.

She gripped the steering wheel and began to pray as hard as she could, out loud, although she didn't realize it. "Oh, Lord, we got us a problem this time. Please be with us. Help Jimmy through this. Protect his ma, and don't let nothing bad happen to her.

Keep her safe and let the doctors know what's to be done for her." Billie Jo snuck one hand over and grabbed Jimmy's big, meaty palm, clutching it tightly. "We know You'll be with us, Lord, 'cause You promised. Help us to accept Your will, whatever that may be. Help this situation to bring us closer to You. Please send Your angels to watch over Grandma Raynard. Amen."

Jimmy's hoarse and whispered "Amen" almost startled her. So did the two little sniffling "amens" from the back seat. She felt a wave of peace wash over them, almost as if the car were being bathed in love. She sucked a deep breath into her lungs and concentrated once more on the road. They were almost there.

The first thing Jewel did was to dispatch a legion of angels to the hospital to gather around the bedside of Helen Raynard. Her condition was critical, more critical than any of the humans involved realized. With their limited vision, they looked only on the outside. And right now, that was bad enough. But they failed to see what was inside.

Helen's husband, James, sat beside her bed, head bowed, with tears running down his face. Every now and then, he would raise his head and direct a solitary question toward the ceiling. "Why, God? Why?"

Over and over, the angels attempted to explain to him the Master's love and to show him how the tragedy had happened. His heart burdened with grief and guilt, he ignored them and continued to grieve, stubbornly refusing to listen.

Helen herself was not conscious. She lay with her head swathed in bandages, needles and tubes attaching her to monitors. Earlier that day, to escape the pain of severe depression, she'd taken her husband's .22 Remington pistol, put the end of the barrel in her mouth, and pulled the trigger. That should have been the end, but the bullet ricocheted inside her skull and came out her cheek. She passed out from the shock.

Hearing the shot, James rushed upstairs and immediately

dialed 911. EMT's had worked on Helen for twenty minutes, stabilizing her condition before transporting her to the emergency room. There she underwent reconstructive surgery on her jaw and brain surgery to remove a bullet fragment. Amazingly, she had missed injuring anything vital, but her condition was listed as critical, and she had not yet regained consciousness.

Nog stood close by, gloating in his victory. "I knew I could make her do it," he chortled. His cohort, Fenris, bobbed his head up and down in agreement until Nog's hand shot out and grabbed the luckless demon by the throat. "I said," he snarled, "I knew I could make her do it."

"Yes," Fenris gurgled, trying to pry Nog's fingers from their stranglehold. "You were wonderful. Magnificent. Masterful. No one could have done it better."

"Yes," Nog agreed amiably. "I was wonderful, wasn't I?" A faint smile flickered across his homely features, barely lifting the saggy skin that covered his face. His black eyes were thoughtful. "Still, it's a shame she didn't have better aim. Maybe I should have lobbied for the pills. Although it does seem like any idiot should be able to blow their brains out."

He brightened up and walked with a light step around the bed. "But there's still hope. After all, even the doctors aren't sure what kind of damage she did. It's extremely possible that she won't make it. If fact, I'd bet on it."

Fenris let out a wild laugh that ended like the bray of a donkey. "That's funny! Bet on it! Ha-ha!"

Nog's eyes narrowed, and he glared at Fenris. "I wasn't trying to be funny."

Fenris sobered instantly. "Oh. Of course not. I knew that."

Nog's attention was drawn by a long, ragged sigh from James. He sidled up to the man and put his face so close that his leathery cheek almost touched James's wrinkled one. "You knew she'd do it, didn't you, James? You knew it all along. Too bad *you don't love her enough to have protected her from it."*

Fresh tears sprang into James's eyes, and his shoulders shook with soundless sobs. "All these years, but still you knew it would happen one day. Remember how you used to dread coming home at night because you wondered if she'd hurt the boy or herself while you were gone? Remember? And after the boy left home and she got so depressed, you were sure it would happen then."

The tortured look on James's visage twisted and shifted. He threw one arm across his face as if to block out painful memories. The red checkered sleeve of his flannel shirt was damp with tears. "You saw the signs this week, but you didn't care enough to keep a closer eye on her, did you? No, all you cared about was that stinking newspaper so you could keep track of your stocks and your television. Helen was right. You're just a lazy couch potato, without a spark of fire in you. I don't know why she married you in the first place. Just look where it got her."

Nog pointed one gnarled finger triumphantly toward Helen's inert figure, and James buried his face in his hands and began sobbing in earnest. "I'm sorry, Helen," he wept. "I should have known. I should have seen it coming. I should have protected you. Why, God? Why?"

Jewel fluttered to James's side, and Nog wilted away from him with a threatening hiss. "James, listen to me," he pleaded gently. "It's not your fault. You couldn't have protected Helen from herself. You did your best. God is watching over Helen, and He is watching over you. Won't you seek His face? He will help you through this time. Rely on His strength; He wants to lift you up."

James shrank away from Jewel, and Jewel watched helplessly as he sobbed, refusing any comfort. Nog threw him a haughty look of superiority before resuming his place beside the man. He draped one long crooked arm heavily on James's shoulders. Fenris crowded in close to him and with a snotty look toward the angel began to heckle James as well.

Billie Jo crowded into the room right behind Jimmy but hung back as he embraced his father. Like two old college buddies, they clapped each other on the back and tried not to let the other see they'd been crying. Even this tragedy, it seemed, would not serve to draw them closer together.

Billie Jo wrapped her long gray wool coat tighter around her and shot a concerned look out to the nurses' station where one of the intensive care nursing students was amusing the children. Jimmy hadn't thought it would be a good idea for them to see Helen. Sneaking a peek beyond Jimmy and James to where Helen rested on the bed, Billie Jo swallowed past a lump in her throat and silently agreed with her husband.

The sight of Helen, helpless and injured, stirred compassion and sympathy in Billie Jo's breast. In that instant, she forgot how irritating and annoying Helen could be. She forgot how hard she'd fought against Helen since the first moment they met. She forgot how tenaciously Helen still clung to Jimmy and how diffi-cult that made life. For that one second, she realized how very much God loved Helen, even if she didn't.

And then it passed. In its place there was simply sympathy. She wondered what had driven Helen to this. What could possi-bly have made her want to take her own life? Slowly she became aware of James and Jimmy talking in low tones.

"You couldn't have stopped her, Dad," Jimmy was saying, his voice hoarse from crying. "It's not your fault."

"But I knew it would happen someday," James replied, shak-ing his head morosely. "Ever since her mother . . ." James never finished what he was saying. He glanced up and caught Billie Jo listening to their conversation and closed his mouth with a snap.

"Billie Jo," he said, nodding politely toward her. They had never had what Billie Jo would have called a "close" relationship. Mostly James ignored her. Sometimes she got the idea that he felt sorry for her and that he understood what she was going through; but if he did, he never said a word to her about it. "It was good of you to come."

James offered her his hand, and when she took it in her own, she found it was limp and clammy. She gave it a sympathetic squeeze and placed her arm around his shoulder in a half-hug.

"I'm so sorry, James," she said. Somehow "Dad" had never applied to him, and Billie Jo had settled on calling him by his given name early on in her marriage. James didn't seem to mind. "How is Helen?"

James shrugged, and his lips tightened up perceptibly. "She's hanging in there," he said. "The doctors aren't sure if there will be any brain damage. They are pretty hopeful. I guess the . . . bullet," James staggered over the word and stopped to take a steadying breath. "The bullet didn't hit anything major. Still, they can't say for sure yet if anything was affected. There hasn't been much swelling though."

Jimmy patted his father on the back. "She'll pull through, Dad. You know Mom. She's a fighter."

James dissolved into tears. "I just wish she could have held on a little longer. Given me time to see how desperate she was. Maybe I could have . . ." The rest of his sentence went unfinished as he began to weep. He put his hands over his face, refusing to let his son witness his grief.

Jimmy sobbed with him. "Dad, there was nothing you could have done," he assured him over and over through his own tears.

Billie Jo felt her eyes mist, and her throat squeezed tight. "I don't understand. What was Helen so desperate about? What had happened?"

James wiped his face as if he could wipe the emotions away. Suddenly, he was James again. Unflappable, unemotional, imperturbable James. He was the stoic, if emotionally absent, man she was well acquainted with.

"It was that fight the two of you had the other day," he

replied, refusing to look in Billie Jo's eyes. "It got her down. 'Course the two of you was never real close, but that about put her over the edge. She's been mighty dicey the last few years but nothing compared to these last few months. I should've been watching more carefully, but what with the stock market the way it's been, I just haven't been able to pay attention like I ought to have."

"Are you saying it was my fault?" Billie Jo squeaked as panic clutched her stomach, and she nearly doubled over.

James shook his head hurriedly. "No, no, 'course not. It's not your fault. It's not anybody's fault." He appeared to ponder this statement as if he wasn't sure if he really believed it himself yet. "It would've happened anyway. It was bound to. What with her history and all. I just should've paid more attention. Maybe I could have prevented it."

"I don't understand." Billie Jo's hand snaked up and clutched Jimmy's arm. "What do you mean it was bound to happen? What history are you talking about?"

Instantly, she regretted asking. James gave her a tortured look and clamped his lips together. "Nothin'," he muttered. "Never mind."

Billie Jo looked up at her husband, but Jimmy wasn't paying any attention to her or his father. His eyes were glued on his mother, and he was crying silently. He pulled away from Billie Jo's grasp and made his way to Helen's bedside. Careful of the tubes and needles, he took one of her hands in his own and held it gently.

"Momma?" he said quietly. "It's me, Jimmy. You gotta come back to us, Momma. We need you. I need you. And the kids. They need you too. Come on back, Momma."

Billie Jo watched him and chewed on her lip. She knew she ought to be thinking the same thing. Feeling the same way. But she couldn't help but realize how her life would change if Helen simply slipped away. She could almost feel the burden of dealing with Helen slide off her shoulders. And a heavy load of guilt settled in its place. She sighed deeply. This was a lose/lose situation.

Lyle Ryan could see a small square of the night sky from where he lay restless on his bed. A sprinkling of stars appeared to be dripping from the bright heelprint of the moon. Cool air drifted through his open window in delicate gusts, bringing the fragrance of honeysuckle. Tomorrow the air would be heavy with humidity, but tonight it was refreshing. Lyle rolled over and tucked one hand under his head so he could better see out the window.

A row of trees on the opposite side of the road hunched over like squatting giants in the dim moonlight. Dogwoods—blooming, he knew—but tonight their shapes were menacing, playing tricks on his imagination. He thought he heard a creak somewhere in the house and for a half-second assumed his mom was wandering around. Then with a rush of pain, he remembered that she had passed away.

"I know You're out there, God," Lyle said out loud. The sound of his own voice startled him. "I know You're out there, and I know You're watching over me. I just wish You were here. Right here, in this room with me. And that You had skin on. I could use some company." His muscles clenched unconsciously as a floorboard squeaked. *I really hate old houses.*

Restlessly, he pushed himself up in bed and maneuvered into his chair. A baseball bat stood propped up beside his bed, and he grabbed it, cradling it on his lap as his eyes strained to see in the darkness. But there was nothing. No sound. Even the breeze had stopped riffling the curtains.

Lyle breathed a sigh of relief. It was just his imagination. Living alone was starting to get to him. He relaxed a little, his hand dropping down to the wheel of his chair to move himself into position beside the window. Then something cold and wet touched his hand.

"Arghhh!" he screamed, scrambling for the bat. A soft whine stopped him. "Hershey, you scared me to death!" he yelled at the dog whose tail thumped on the hardwood floor, blissfully unaware of how close he'd come to being beaned.

Calla had left the dog with him the night before, certain the pet would be great company. Until now, Lyle hadn't even seen him. Hershey had immediately found a comfy spot and had been sleeping there ever since. Apparently, the dog had awakened feeling lonely. Lyle reached down and rubbed the broad head as the tail-thumping increased.

"Some company you are," he muttered to the dog. "Here you had me thinking you were an intruder. You'd better stay in here with me, Hershey. You'll be better off. And maybe if there is a real intruder, you can protect me." Lyle chuckled at the thought of Hershey protecting him. The only way that would happen was if he was able to lick the intruder to death.

Without realizing it, Lyle drifted off to sleep. The bat slipped from his hands and fell to the floor. Lyle slept on, and Hershey turned around several times before dropping to the floor and curling up in a tight ball at the foot of Lyle's chair.

When he woke, his neck was stiff, and the dog was gone. A sharp bark let him know what had wakened him, and he wheeled himself to the kitchen door to let Hershey out. The dog wandered around the yard, did his business, and then trotted off confidently toward Calla's house down the street. Lyle called until he was hoarse, but Hershey never even looked back. He sighed and peered outside at the early morning sunshine. As far as summer days went, Lyle mused, you couldn't get one much nicer. He decided to suggest going for a walk.

He'd missed enough of life already. Opportunities like this one were meant to be grabbed and held firmly with both hands. He grinned boyishly as he thought about trying to convince Calla to go for a walk instead of taking her customary afternoon nap. He could already hear her protests, but he also knew she'd cave in.

Lyle spun his wheelchair around and rolled toward the mirror hung at just the right level on the wall of his room. Four years had wrought serious changes in the face that stared confidently back at him. The blue eyes were the same, only now they sparkled with purpose and joy. The face had a few more lines, perhaps the result of time spent outdoors in the sunshine rather than hiding beneath a tree in the shade.

There were fine wrinkles punctuating his eyes from studying. Already a youth minister, he would soon graduate from college and be fully ordained. His stomach fluttered slightly at the thought. Leaning forward on large, rock-hard arms with biceps the size of cantaloupes, Lyle studied his reflection in the mirror. Yes, a lot had changed in the last four years.

He whistled *Joyful, Joyful We Adore Thee* while he set about getting ready for church. Putting the finishing touches on his tie, his eyes wandered around the room, taking in the shabbiness of it. Not that it mattered much. Calla had more plans for the house than he even knew about. Sometimes he wondered if she didn't think more about redecorating their house than the actual wedding. Since his mother had passed away six months before, though, she'd been pretty subdued about mentioning it. Lyle got the idea that she thought it bothered him.

In a way, he guessed it did. Sometimes he thought he'd hate to change one stick of furniture. Other days, he wanted to redecorate the whole house until it was unrecognizable. Maybe then he wouldn't miss his mom or his dad when he saw certain things. After his mother died, he'd asked Calla to place Mom's things in her room and close the door. He hadn't had the nerve to open it since.

The familiar crunch of Calla's tires on the gravel of the driveway shook him out of his reverie. He grasped the wheels of his chair firmly and made his way down the ramp by the kitchen door to the driveway. Calla flashed him a smile as she hopped out of the car to help him in. Her aunt Berniece sat in the back.

"Hello, Lyle, how are you this morning?" she asked. Except for a few more gray hairs, Aunt Berniece hadn't changed at all. She was still the same sweet lady who had helped Lyle by her ceaseless prayers and her quiet compassion.

"I'm good, Aunt Bernie," Lyle replied with a grunt as he maneuvered into the front seat. "How are you doing?"

"Never better," Berniece chirped.

Calla folded Lyle's chair and stowed it in the trunk before sliding back into the driver's seat and backing the car out of the driveway. Lyle reached over and grasped her hand. It felt natural after all this time. He didn't even mind that Aunt Berniece was watching from the backseat, although that used to bother him.

Calla squeezed his hand and winked at him. Lyle felt a rush of warmth course through his body. He could hardly believe that in four months they would be married. If anyone had told him how his life would turn out after the accident, he would have laughed in his or her face. He still had to pinch himself occasionally just to be sure he wasn't dreaming.

"You're going to wish it was a dream," Warg sneered. "I have plans for you." He glanced over at the ever-present Shelan. "You should never have taken him out of my hands. You'll regret it, and so will he." He rubbed his hands together as his eyes narrowed in contemplation. Shelan shuddered at the evil light shining in them. "I swear you will," he promised.

"Lyle follows the Master now," Shelan warned. "You cannot harm him."

"See if I can't," Warg growled. He began coughing loudly, spitting up a wad of vile-looking phlegm. "He only listens to you because everything is going his way. His future looks so

bright. We'll see how much he listens when I take it all away."

"He will follow the Master still," Shelan replied confidently.

Warg watched Lyle stroke Calla's hand absently with one finger. His eyes narrowed, and he leaned forward to whisper in his ear. "Ever think she might just be settling for the consolation prize?" he asked.

Lyle shook his head as if a bumble bee had flown into it by accident. A flush brightened his face, and he squirmed uncomfortably. Warg laid a shriveled hand on his shoulder, pinning him to the seat. "Do you ever wonder if she wishes she had stayed with Brick Brody?"

Lyle's movements became increasingly agitated. Calla glanced at him, a worried expression on her face.

"What's the matter, honey?" she asked. "Are you in pain? What is it? Are you OK?"

Lyle wiped a bead of sweat off his brow. "Nah, nah, I'm fine. Just had a nasty thought, that's all." His eyes shifted uneasily to the back seat where Aunt Berniece was politely pretending to be absorbed in the scenery.

"Do you want to talk about it?" Calla asked anxiously.

Lyle shook his head. "No. Not right now."

Calla looked for a minute as if she was going to say something; then she shut her lips tight, causing a white line to appear around her mouth. "OK, whatever you say."

Warg chuckled. "No guts. You got no guts, kid. Ask her straight out. She won't be able to deny it. Not a chance. You'll see it in her eyes, even if she does."

"Calla is not so shallow that she loves you for superficial things," Shelan told Lyle. "She loves you for the person you are inside."

"Ha!" Warg shouted. "See? Even the angel admits it. You're nothing to look at. You're just a crippled loser. If you really loved her, you'd let her marry someone who is worthy of her. Someone normal."

"Do not listen to him, Lyle," Shelan urged. "Your worth is

determined by the value Christ the Master places upon you, not by human standards.

"Yeah, sure," Warg said sarcastically. "But you aren't living in heaven, now are you? You're living on earth and being judged by human standards. And according to those standards, you're a loser."

Lyle bolted forward. His seatbelt tightened and caused him to fall backward, panting in the seat. "Too easy," Warg observed, and in the next instant he was gone. Shelan saw Calla watch Lyle nervously out of the corner of her eye, but she said nothing.

"He is insecure," Shelan explained to her, certain that the girl would understand. She had an empathetic heart, and she 'felt' Lyle's pain. She felt it so much that it was a concern of Shelan's. At times, she was unsure exactly why Calla wanted to marry Lyle and how much she just wanted to continue patching him up. Calla's gaze grew sympathetic, and she squeezed Lyle's hand reassuringly.

Lyle spent the rest of the trip hunched over miserably in his seat. Bad feelings weighed him down as if they were bags of sand tied to his body. Time and time again, he'd had to shake them. He sighed quietly. At least, now he knew how. He bowed his head. "Lord," he breathed silently, "please take these bad feelings away from me. I know they are not from You but from Satan. Make me strong so that I can serve You. In Jesus' name, Amen."

By the time they arrived at the church, Lyle felt a little better. Calla helped him out of the car and into his chair. Soon she was pulled away by one of her friends, and Lyle's duties kept him from seeing her again until after the service.

"Hey, Lyle, man, it's time to say goodbye," a voice said as he scanned the departing church members for Calla's face. Lyle swiveled around to see Ray and Julia Vargas, friends of his who had recently gotten married.

"Goodbye? Already?" Lyle scrambled to take his mind off Calla. Ray and Julia were leaving to be missionaries in Africa. They had become good friends, and he would miss them. "I can't believe you're really going!" he exclaimed.

Ray and Julia exchanged excited looks. "We can hardly believe it either," Ray replied. "Julia says I'm going to have to knock her out to get her on the plane. I'm not so sure they won't have to knock both of us out. I'm not crazy about flying either."

Julia took one of Lyle's hands in her own and gave it a squeeze. "Best of luck to you, Lyle," she said softly. "I wish we could be here for the wedding. Where is Calla? I wanted to say goodbye to her too."

"I don't . . ." Lyle began, but Ray cut him off.

"There she is," he said, pointing to where Calla was talking excitedly to a nice- looking man Lyle didn't recognize. Julia made her way to where Calla was while Ray and Lyle watched her. "Who is that she's talking to?" Ray asked.

Lyle's brow furrowed in annoyance. He had no idea, but she sure looked like she was having a good time. He shrugged. "I don't know. I've never seen him before."

"Me either," Ray said. "I didn't even notice he was here today. That was pretty sloppy of me. I should have welcomed him. I know I really appreciated it when I first came and people took the time to say Hello to me."

"Yeah," Lyle agreed absently. He wasn't thinking so much of welcoming the handsome man as he was in prying Calla away from him. "Would you excuse me, Ray?" he asked, wheeling his chair toward Calla and the man.

"Sure, I'll be seeing you, Lyle. Write to me," Ray called after him.

Lyle turned around long enough to assure Ray that he would keep in touch, before homing in on his goal again. As he wheeled up, Calla turned to him laughing heartily about something the man was saying.

"Lyle!" she exclaimed. "I want you to meet someone. This is Jesse Redcloud. He was walking by the church today, and he heard the music and decided to join us. Isn't that wonderful?"

Jesse turned to Lyle, an amused look on his face. He wore nice street clothes and his black hair was rather long, pulled back in a neat ponytail. He was dark-complected, clean-shaven, and smelled like the men's section of a department store. His slim fingers were idly toying with a crystal that hung from his neck by a leather cord. Tall and lean, he stood about a head higher than Calla, forcing her to look up at him. Lyle felt an immediate rush of jealousy.

"Wonderful," he agreed, his tone suggesting that he thought it was a little less than wonderful.

"Jesse has been telling me a little about himself and where he grew up. Lyle, he lived in the same town I did when I grew up . . ."

"We've got to leave," Lyle interrupted, grabbing her hand possessively.

"We can't leave yet, Lyle. That would be rude. Why, Jesse wasn't through talking. Were you?"

"That's OK," Jesse replied smoothly. "I need to get going anyway. I really only wanted to see what was going on. Do you have any books or pamphlets or any other information about your church that I could take with me?"

"Oh yes, I'm sure we do," Calla said quickly. "Let me find you something." She turned to the literature rack beside the front door while Lyle waited impatiently. Nothing she looked at seemed to be what she wanted. Finally with an exclamation of triumph, she pulled a small book from the rack and handed it to Jesse. "This should answer any questions you might have. All the verses it mentions can be found in your Bible."

"I don't have a Bible," Jesse said quietly. Lyle groaned.

"Don't have a Bible?" Calla said. "Then take mine. I have several." As she held it out, Lyle saw her wince a little. That was when he noticed that it was the Bible he'd given her for her birthday the year before.

"You . . . can't . . ." he sputtered, face flushed. "But . . . that's . . ."

"Nonsense," Calla said firmly, the line of her jaw telling him that if he knew what was good for him, he wouldn't make a fuss. "As I said, I have several at home. You take this one. If you ever get one of your own, you can return it to me."

"I couldn't," Jesse began, but he seemed to read the same message in her face, and he let the matter drop. "OK. Thank you very much." He looked warmly at Calla and then dropped his gaze to Lyle. His eyes were as black as midnight and completely unreadable. Lyle refused to look at him directly.

"It was nice meeting you both," Jesse said. "I hope I see you again sometime soon."

"Yes, you must come back and visit us again," Calla said warmly.

Lyle forced himself to look at the man. Was that pity he saw? He felt all his muscles stiffen up. "Yes, you really should come back soon," he managed.

Jesse dipped his head in a nod and turned to make his way out the door. He got three or four paces before another one of the church ladies stopped him. Calla grabbed the handles of Lyle's wheelchair and wheeled him, protesting every step, toward the back door. "How could you be so rude?" she hissed.

"At least I didn't kill him with kindness," Lyle replied angrily. "What was that all about anyway? I'll bet you didn't even tell him that we were engaged."

"Engaged? Why should I? The subject never came up," Calla whipped his chair around and stood before him, hands planted on her slender hips. Wisps of her blond hair had pulled free of the fancy braid she'd done, and they fell around her face in be-witching strands. Her eyes flashed with fury, and Lyle began to feel just the least bit uncomfortable for making an issue out of nothing.

"You should have told him," Lyle grumbled, studying his lap.

A loose thread on his pants drew his attention, and he began to pick at it. Calla grabbed his hand and pulled it away.

"You keep that up and I'll have to mend those. Leave it be. I'll take care of it later. Now, what is the matter with you? You've been acting funny all morning and then this. Lyle Ryan, I've never been so embarrassed in all my life!"

"I'm sorry," Lyle chewed the words and spat them out distastefully. She should be the one apologizing, he told himself. He wasn't the one who had made a fool of himself over a perfect stranger. "Perfect" being a more operative word even than "stranger." He wondered if he would have been so upset if Jesse Redcloud had been old and ugly.

"What did I tell you?" Warg asked. "The world you live in judges by outward appearances. You just proved that. What makes you think you can judge by appearances and expect her to judge by what's inside you?" He leaned over and flexed his long crooked fingers. They snapped, making Shelan jump. She edged away from him to Lyle's other side. She didn't like the way this was going. Not one bit. Lyle and Calla, embroiled in a stand-off, were glaring at each other. Had they not been so preoccupied, they might have noticed the object of their discussion studying, not them, but the exterior door of the church before yet another church member accosted him.

CHAPTER 5

Toby was sitting on the steps of the mission admiring the moon as it rose full and heavy from the horizon and swung up laboriously into the sky. It wasn't dark yet, and she could clearly see across the compound. One of the native nurses, it looked like Djema, was getting water from the well while she talked to Flory. Marcus, freed for the time being from his father, was playing with several of the children who lived on the mission compound.

Every now and then, he would pause in his play and glance across the baked earth toward Niamey where Shay had gone with Madina to take care of her father's legal affairs over the telephone at Wahabi's. She expected to be back in a couple days, but she hadn't returned yet. Marcus was clearly worried, but whenever Toby brought it up, Don just shrugged her off, surmising that Shay probably had trouble getting through to the States and it was taking longer than she planned to settle everything. Chances were, he was right, but that didn't help Marcus any.

Toby let her eyes wander across the mission compound looking for the long form of Nwibe resting somewhere while Marcus played, but she didn't see him. It was unlike him not to be close by, but for the past few days he had complained of a headache and had been staying in his room. He could get around the compound pretty well by himself, but it was still easier for him when Marcus assisted him.

"Marcus," Toby called when the boy missed the ball his companion threw to him. The boy gave him a disgusted look, and Marcus shrugged apologetically before he trotted over to where Toby sat.

"Yes, Madame Toby?" he asked politely.

"Where's your dad?" Toby asked, handing him the other half of a banana she had just peeled.

He accepted it gratefully and stuffed the whole thing into his mouth, mumbling around it. "He didn't feel well. He's lying down inside. He looked pretty bad to me, but he said not to worry. His face looked funny, though, and his eyes were bright red."

"Red?" Toby asked, her concern growing. Not malaria, she prayed silently. Please don't let him have malaria. "I think I ought to go see how he's doing."

Marcus tried to protest. "He says he'll be fine. He doesn't want to trouble anyone."

Toby took Marcus's arm. "I know that, but I think we're past that now. You come with me. I can't just go barging in on him."

Marcus went along grudgingly. "Okey dokey, but he isn't going to like it," he warned her.

"You just let me worry about that," Toby said grimly. There was such a thing as too much pride, she decided as she followed the boy toward the family's quarters near the back of the mission compound. As they neared the room, they began to hear the sound of violent vomiting. Marcus wrinkled his nose.

"He's been doing that all day," he reported. "Akueke sent some food in to my father, but he could not eat it." He opened the door slowly and pointed solemnly to the tray of food untouched on the table by the window. "See?"

Nwibe sat on the bed, stripped down to his undergarments, cradling a bowl into which he was vomiting. It was half full of a slippery red liquid mixed with black specks that looked like coffee grounds. The smell made Toby struggle to keep her own supper down.

"Nwibe?" she said gently, approaching the bed. When he looked toward her, she could see that the entire white area of his eyes was a brilliant red. His face was an expressionless mask, his eyes fixed and staring. The eyelids were slightly droopy, which made it seem as if his eyeballs were popping out of his head and half-closed at the same time. There were bright red starlike speckles covering his face. Toby laid her hand on his forehead and found that he was burning up.

"Nwibe? Do you know who I am?" Toby asked as she reached for his wrist and counted out his pulse. It was sluggish. Nwibe nodded.

"Madame Toby," he replied dully. "Where is my wife?"

"Shay is in Niamey with Madina, remember? They went to take care of her father's affairs."

Nwibe didn't say anything, and Toby motioned Marcus back out of the room as she followed him out. "Marcus, this is very important. You run and get Dr. Germaine immediately. Do you understand? Don't stop to talk to anyone. Just go get Dr. Germaine. Now!" Toby gave him a little shove and tried to ignore the frightened look in his eyes.

She leaned back against the cool cement wall and sank down, her head in her hands. Nwibe was very sick, that much was certain. But it looked like nothing she had ever seen before. Don came at a fast trot, Marcus right on his heels.

"What's up?" he asked.

Toby took his arm, her fingers digging in as she squeezed unconsciously. "Nwibe is really sick." She lowered her voice and turned slightly away from Marcus so he wouldn't hear her. "I mean *really* sick. I've never seen anything like it before."

Don turned to Marcus. "Marcus, you stay out here in the hall while we examine your father, OK? Stay right here."

He pushed open the door, and Toby followed him back into the room. She gagged immediately at the smell. It seemed, if anything, to have gotten worse. It was like a slaughterhouse. Don took the bowl of horrible liquid from Nwibe and handed it to Toby. She fought the bile that backed up in her throat.

"*Vomito Negro*," he said. "Black vomit. Empty that, would you? Dig a hole out back and pour it in. Then bring the container back. He's going to need it again." Don grabbed her arm. "Don't touch it, and don't spill it. And on your way back bring that box of supplies we stored in the back of the clinic. The ones marked 'Ebola.' "

Toby's eyes widened. "Ebola?" she gasped. "He's got Ebola?"

Don's normally golden complexion was ashen. "I've only seen this one other time. In a small village just outside of Nairobi. It was Ebola. Almost everyone died." Don reached up and took her face in his hands, forcing her to concentrate on him. "Let's just take care of Nwibe first and then we'll deal with the rest."

"Rest?" Toby echoed blankly. "What rest?"

"Listen, Toby, I need you with me. There are going to be a lot of people getting sick soon. There are probably a lot of people sick already. A lot of them are going to die, maybe all of them. We've got to be careful we don't catch it, and we're going to have to watch the people who have been exposed to this to see if they come down with it. It's going to take both of us and more. Now, pull yourself together. OK? OK?!"

Toby shook her head. "I can't believe this. After all I've been through. Now this." Then her head snapped up. "What about Shay? And Madina? They were exposed before they left, weren't they?"

Don sighed helplessly. "I don't know. Probably. But, there's nothing we can do about that right now. They either have it or they don't. Maybe that's why she's not back yet. I don't know. If they don't have it by now, they're probably safe. What we do know is that Nwibe has it, and Marcus could very well get it. And we're going to have to take precautions that we don't get it."

Toby shivered in spite of the fact that it was still very hot. To her, the temperature had suddenly plummeted. She walked carefully with the bowl. As she passed Marcus, he turned away but not before she saw the reality in his eyes. He knew. She found a shovel and dug a large hole in the back of the compound. After she poured the bowl of blood into the hole, she rinsed the bowl out with disinfectant, and for good measure she poured half the bottle into the hole as well. Then she covered the hole back up and made her way to the clinic to get the Ebola supplies.

The boxes were stacked in the back of the clinic like an afterthought. She remembered the day they'd piled them there, complaining about supplies they didn't need. Dorsey's ears must have been ringing that day. They wanted more bandages, more needles, more medicine.

They didn't want a bunch of isolation supplies: paper surgical masks and slippers and gowns and gloves. They didn't want blood tubes and syringes. They especially didn't want the orange Racal spacesuits, a positive-pressure spacesuit with a battery-powered air supply, the ones Dorsey had chuckled with glee at having been able to obtain, in slightly used condition from the CDC.

She hefted two of the boxes into her arms. They were light, and she had no trouble carrying them, but she wished with all her might that they contained something less ominous than those supplies. With every mental fiber she tried to deny what was happening. It just couldn't happen. It wasn't possible.

When she reached the room, she was just in time to pass Don the cleaned out bowl as he helped Nwibe lean over and vomit copious amounts of hemorrhagic blood into it. She began ripping open the boxes and pulling out the supplies. She laid one of the spacesuits down on the bed beside Don.

"I'm not putting that thing on," he growled.

She stared at him blankly. "Why on earth not?"

"He's sick enough. He doesn't need to be treated by some

compassionless alien. I'll take basic precautions, but I refuse to dehumanize myself by wearing that contraption. Besides, I've already been exposed. If I get it, I get it," he said simply.

"Well, I'm going to wear one," Toby said stubbornly, pulling the lightweight suit on. "I'm going to live in it." It felt weird, and everything outside the mask seemed surreal. But it was when she saw the terrified look on Marcus's face that she realized that like it or not, she wasn't going to wear the suit either. She peeled it off and helped Marcus get settled into another room just down the hall from Nwibe.

"But, why can't I stay with my father?" he asked in a piteous whine. "I want to stay with him. He needs me."

"Look, Marcus," Toby said gently. "You've taken good care of your father all of your life. You really have. Now it's our turn to take care of him. What I want you to do is to stay in this room and rest. I'm going to take care of you and make sure that you don't get sick like your dad. OK? I'll try to bring you some things you can do, but I'll probably be too busy to keep you company much." She squeezed his arm compassionately. "There is something you can do for your dad," she told him. "You can pray."

Marcus swallowed hard and looked directly into her eyes. "Isn't it too late for that?" he asked.

"No," Toby replied firmly. "It's never too late to pray, Marcus."

"Okey dokey," the boy said bravely. "I'll pray that God will make my father well again."

"You do that," Toby said. "I'll be back in a little while to check on you. Try to rest some."

She closed the door behind her and leaned heavily against it. "Dear God," she breathed out loud. "Please be with him. Protect him. Be with all of us and protect us too. We're scared, God. We don't want to die. But if we're going to die, be with us and comfort us and help us to comfort each other."

"I did it!" Lucien crowed with satisfaction. Merck looked at the puny human, doubled up on the flimsy cot.

"Did what? So, one person is sick. What kind of victory is that? I hardly think it's anything to get worked up over."

"Oh, you don't, do you? Well, I'll have you know that this is just the beginning. They'll all be sick soon. And once they get sick, that's it. They'll die. They have no chance." Merck looked skeptical, and Lucien blustered defensively. "OK, so they have a fifty/fifty chance. Take my word for it, enough of them will die that they'll leave this place, no not leave, flee from this place. And that will be the end. Do you understand what I'm saying? This is the end of this miserable mission. I, Lucien, have brought about the demise of the mission."

He couldn't control himself any longer. Whirling excitedly, he danced around the room. Breathlessly he collided with a massive, dark, menacing figure that blocked the doorway. "Sparn," he gasped, clamping his mouth shut before anything unfortunate could escape.

"What's going on here?" Sparn asked, his curiosity aroused. "What are you talking about? You've brought about the end of the mission? How? Is the prayer warrior dead? Why have I not been informed?" He pinned Lucien down with a disapproving stare. "Have you been going about behind my back?"

Lucien gulped. "No, sir. I've just been doing my job, as you would have wanted me to . . . had you been doing your job." The last bit slipped out before he could catch it, and Sparn jumped on it. Lucien never even had a chance.

"Are you accusing me of neglecting my duties?" he shrieked. "I'll have you know that I've done nothing each day but dream up ways to shut this place down. It's been impossible, just impossible. And now that I've come up with a way, here you are dancing around taking credit for it."

"Me?" Lucien croaked. "But it was my idea!"

"Silence!" Sparn shouted, the power of his voice sending Lucien crashing into a wall where he lay panting and bruised. "You will observe silence in my presence. Speak only when you *are spoken to. And never, NEVER, forget your place here. I am in charge. Don't forget that. Now, my plan is to wipe out this mission outpost with a deadly virus. You will take orders from me. Do you understand that?"*

Merck had trouble hiding his smile as Sparn seemed to expand with his newly assumed role of authority. It was as if Lucien had breathed new life into him. Lucien, on the other hand, had shrunken in size to make as small a target as possible. Even then, Sparn had no trouble back-handing him as a reminder before he left to rally the forces.

"It was my plan," Lucien whimpered. "I thought of it myself. I worked hard to bring it to pass. And now he's going to take all the credit for it. He who did nothing but sit in defeat day after day. Well, I won't let this happen. I will get what's coming to me. I will." His voice rose to a shriek before he thought better of it and quieted down. There was no telling who might be listening and willing to relay his rebellion to Sparn. Merck certainly wasn't above it.

Merck was inclined to agree with Lucien, despite the friction in their relationship. He believed wholeheartedly that Lucien would get what was coming to him. He just wasn't at all sure that Lucien knew what that was. And he was pretty certain that if Lucien did know, he wouldn't like it much.

Three days later, it was all over for Nwibe. He was the first one to die. In a way, Toby was glad that there was no time to think about that, to mourn for him, because there were so many others sick as well. Infected villagers straggled in from surrounding areas with tales of entire villages sick and dying. Most of the natives were coping in their own way, setting up shelters as places of quarantine. Toby could only hope they were managing OK without any medical assistance. They were able to do so little it hardly seemed to matter. Still, she felt sorry for them, fighting this unknown and deadly assailant.

Between Don, Toby, Flory, and a couple of native nurses, they were able to continue to run the clinic, but they accepted only those with the disease. Everyone else was sent home. Some of the patients fled, taking their bed linens with them and disappearing into the night.

In the beginning, when Nwibe had first become sick, Don had taken a blood sample and shipped it off to a lab. The report came back quickly. Too quickly. Nwibe did not have Ebola. He had Marburg, Ebola's sister. It was called the "gentle" sister because its kill rate was not as high as either of the two strains of Ebola that were lethal to humans. That had been the first good news they had received.

Toby watched Marcus like a hawk, but other than ceaseless crying, the boy appeared fine. He had convinced himself that his mother and sister had contracted the disease as well and perished in Niamey. When his father died, he was inconsolable. Toby did the best she could, but she was so busy taking care of the rest of her patients that the boy spent most of his time alone and uncomforted.

Seven days after the outbreak, Don began complaining of a headache. His eyes were red, his face covered with starlike splotches. Toby reeled away from him but not before he saw the truth in her eyes.

"I've got it, haven't I?" he asked dully.

"Yes," Toby sobbed violently. "Oh, Don! You can't die. You can't die!"

"Are you going to be able to manage? I really shouldn't see patients like this, though you know I'd work until I keeled over." He stood up and paced the floor. "My back's killing me," he complained and then chuckled wryly. "I guess that's the least of my problems, huh?"

Toby's hands flew to cover her face. "Don't joke about this! How can you joke? You're going to die! What am I going to do?"

"You're going to go on, that's what you're going to do," he replied harshly. "Don't make me shake you!" he warned. "I knew the risks. You did too. I don't want to alarm you, but for all we know, you might catch it too."

"This never would have happened if you hadn't been so stubborn and worn the Racal suit," Toby hollered. She shook her finger at him accusingly. "If you had worn one, I would have. Now your pride is going to cost you your life!"

"I only hope it doesn't cost you yours as well. But, this would have happened anyway," Don said quietly. "I didn't tell you because I didn't want to worry you, but while you were gone, Nwibe vomited again . . . in my face. Some of it got in my eyes. That's how I was infected. I kept hoping that I wouldn't get it, but . . ."

Toby sobbed into her hands. "Why didn't you tell me?" she moaned. "All that stuff about wanting to be humane . . . why?"

Don shrugged in a tired sort of way. His shoulders sagged in defeat. "I didn't want to worry you. And I wasn't sure." He lifted his head, and there was a little of the old flash in his eyes. "I don't regret it though. I'll never regret it. I did the right thing. It was more humane. I think Nwibe appreciated it. I'm glad I could do that one thing for him."

Toby rocked from side to side, her arms clutched fiercely around her torso. "How can you say that? I'm going to lose you when we've just found each other."

"I'm sorry for that," Don admitted. "I love you, Toby. I think I've loved you from the beginning, even when I hated you."

Toby looked up through her tears. He'd never said that before. A thousand times she'd dreamed of the moment when he might. Never, never had she thought it would be like this. The end was not supposed to come before the beginning. "Why didn't you ever say anything before this?" she sniffed, wiping her nose on the sleeve of her shirt like a little kid.

"I thought there would be time," he replied, sitting down heavily on his cot and leaning back against the cold cement wall. "I never expected, that is, I didn't see this coming. Who could? I guess I shouldn't have waited. I'm sorry. And I'm sorry to leave you like this, with all these sick people. You should wire Dorsey as soon as you can to let him know what's going on, although I expect the press has leaked enough that he's got some idea already. He'll send you some replacements. You'll also want to find out what happened to Shay and those two nurses we were expecting from the States. They were supposed to be here a week ago."

Toby listened to his voice as he rattled on about practical matters. She wasn't so much paying attention to what he was saying as she was memorizing his voice, his face, his expressions. She refused to think about "after." It was unthinkable that he would die . . . like Nwibe . . . such a horrible death. It had taken them two days to work up the courage to clean Nwibe's room after he had died.

There was blood everywhere, the walls, the floor, the ceiling. Two nurses had scrubbed for hours, but you could still see the stains. There was talk about painting them after this was all over. But first, Toby thought, it had to end.

In the next few days they lost a total of eight more patients, each of whom died the same way Nwibe had, crashing and bleeding from every orifice. Don continued to get worse. His fever skyrocketed. Toby made sure that someone was beside him at all times. He lay passive and distant. "I love you" was the last thing he'd said to her.

Julian approached the heavenly courts with a sense of relief and a feeling of homesickness. For too long now he'd been commissioned to earth. He had seen things, horrible things, that had broken his heart, bit by bit. Breathing deeply of the fresh air of heaven reminded him that there was a place in the universe where sin had no quarter, a place where its ugliness did not stain everything in sight. He wanted to tarry beside the Sea of Glass and commune with old friends he saw infrequently, but his mission urged him onward. There was not much time. He had to find Gabriel.

The archangel wore a preoccupied look when Julian found him. Noble was by his side and the two were in deep discussion. They made an impressive sight striding down the golden street. Julian halted and waited for them to reach him. He wasn't sure he wanted to interrupt them.

Noble glanced up and caught sight of him first. Julian lifted one hand in greeting but didn't speak, as he saw the grim set of Noble's jaw. It could have been carved in marble; it was so smooth and so solid. The angel's brow was furrowed into deep ripples, and he looked tired. He took hold of Gabriel's arm as they reached the spot where Julian stood studying them. Gabriel looked up, pain in his eyes.

"Hello, Julian. It's been a long time, brother," he said softly. His voice gave the impression of a gentle wind caressing chimes of crystal. It echoed pleasantly but didn't seem to fit the somberness that lay upon him like a shroud.

"Greetings, Gabriel. Do you have word from the Master about my charge, Don Germaine?" Julian asked anxiously.

"The Master's heart is broken by the suffering at the mission and over all of the earth," Gabriel said. "I have just come from His side. The faithful prayer warrior, though weak, has been praying night and day for relief at the mission and for Don Germaine's life to be spared. It has taken the last of her great strength, and her request will be honored. But," Gabriel warned, "you must be prepared, because all will not go well for your charge. He will soon enter into a very trying time, and he will need your help more than ever."

Julian nodded his understanding. "I will be there. I will guide him and point him to the Master.

"The devil and his accomplices would like very much to see the end of the mission. Even under their constant attacks, it has grown and flourished. As long as the people there keep their hearts close to the Master and their priorities heavenward, they will be safe in the Master's hand." Gabriel gazed across the deep azure water of the Sea of Glass toward the purple mountain peaks beyond. Snow glistened on their crests in a rainbow of colors, and yet the air surrounding them was fresh and clean but not cold. Every breath was refreshing. "Soon," he murmured, "soon they will be coming home."

Noble reached over and squeezed Julian's arm gently. "Courage, brother. Return now to your charge. There is much work for you to do."

In an instant, Julian was by Don's side. Scores of demons hovered about the room. Don thrashed restlessly on the bed. Every now and then, he screamed or yelled incoherent half sentences. Once he threatened the nurse who was sponging off his forehead. "Get away from me, do you hear? Leave me alone!" he bellowed. Flory, the nurse, ignored him and continued to apply the wet, cold cloth to his feverish brow.

Julian laid a cool hand on Don's forehead. His clear, vibrant voice rang out in songs of praise and deliverance. The bright aura around him burned brightly, enveloping Don and making the demons who strove to push in next to him scramble to avoid touching it. They hissed and spat at him, but he paid no attention to them. "Don," he called. "You will get well. The Master has sent me to you."

A legion of angels converged around the bed and began to join his song, lifting high praises to the Master. Don relaxed visibly, and the flush abated. His breathing became easier. Julian knew that he could hear them singing, and he appeared to be listening. A slight smile tugged at his colorless lips, and for the first time since he'd become ill he drifted off into a peaceful sleep.

Toby was stretched out on a cot in one of the abandoned rooms when Flory gave her the news. "What do you mean he's better?" she asked cautiously.

"He is better," Flory replied simply. She shrugged her shoulders and absently brushed at a lock of black hair that had strayed from her neat chignon. "He has no more fever, and he sleeps like a baby. I have been watching him. There's something," she hesitated then studied the floor sheepishly, unable to look directly at Toby. "You will think I am only a foolish girl, but there is something very peaceful in the room. It feels warm and comforting. I . . . I should have come to find you sooner, but I could not tear myself away from it." She lowered her voice to a whisper. "I think there are angels in his room."

If she expected Toby to laugh, she was disappointed. "Angels?" Toby asked. After the words "He is better," nothing could surprise her. "I'm going to go see him," she announced determinedly.

Flory shrugged her slim shoulders. "I will go with you. You will see that I am not lying."

"I don't believe you're lying, Flory," Toby assured the young nurse. "I just want to see it with my own eyes." Even after she saw the wonder of Don sleeping peacefully with no fever, she refused to get her hopes up.

"What if it's just some sort of remission?" she asked. "I won't believe that it could be for good. No one else has gotten better yet. Why should he? I can't, I just can't hope that he will get well. If I did, and he did die, it would kill me."

Instead, she spent every free moment reading the material that Dorsey had sent them through Wahabi. The bartender had come within shouting distance of the mission and left a large canvas bag containing literature on filoviruses, what there was of it, and also a letter from Shay. Apparently word of the outbreak had reached Niamey, and Shay was worried. She wanted to know what she was supposed to do while she was stranded there, and she was worried about Nwibe and Marcus.

Reading that line had made Toby wince. How on earth could she tell Shay that her husband had died? She was carrying his child, which meant that at twenty-six she was a widow with three children to care for. The prospect was daunting to Toby, and she refused to dwell on it. There would be plenty of time for that later. She was getting good at shoving emotional dilemmas under the carpet to deal with later. So good that she was beginning to feel more than a little bit like Scarlet O'Hara. "I'll think about it tomorrow. Tomorrow is another day."

And then the impossible happened. Two of the other patients began to get well, and Toby stumbled across some information about cases of others who had recovered. Maybe all was not lost. Later that day she found herself by Don's side relieving Flory, who had been up for forty-eight hours straight. She laid one hand on his now cool forehead and marveled that he slept so peacefully. Inside his body a war still raged as his immune system fought the remnants of the hot agent that had tried to destroy him.

Tears trickled down Toby's face as the realization swept over her. "You're going to live, Don," she whispered gratefully. "You're going to live." It crossed her mind that she might still break with Marburg, but they had not had a new case in five days and were nearing the end of the incubation period. As long as their luck held. . .

She smiled ruefully at the thought of luck. "I know it's not luck that got us here," she murmured, casting a quick glance upward. She sank to her knees beside Don's cot. "Lord," she prayed, "thank You so much for watching over us all. I know there have been times during this whole ordeal when I've questioned Your presence. But we're still here and by Your grace, we'll still be here tomorrow and the next day and the next."

Lileah joined Julian and the other angels beside Don's bed. She spread her wings out and let them settle with a flutter around Toby. "Surely he will save you from the fowler's snare," she quoted from Psalm 91, "and from the deadly pestilence. He will cover you with his feathers, and under his wings you will find refuge; his faithfulness will be your shield and rampart. You will not fear the terror of night, nor the arrow that flies by day, nor the pestilence that stalks in the darkness, nor the plague that destroys at midday."

A portion of one of the psalms flitted through Toby's mind, and she felt peace enter her being with the power of the words. Her thoughts turned to those they had lost, and for the first time, she allowed herself to feel the agony of her grief. A sob caught in her throat as it squeezed shut against the onslaught of emotion.

"I know in every battle that there are casualties. Nwibe was a good soldier, and I'm sure I'll see his smiling face in heaven some day." It occurred to her then that he would also be able to see her face. The thought softened the loss she felt. For Nwibe, the fight was over. All that was left for him was to enter into the joy of his Lord. She made a mental note to relay her thoughts to Shay when the time came.

"Please, Lord, be with all the families who have lost someone from this disease. It's going to be hard on a lot of us for quite a while. Comfort us and strengthen us. Amen." When Toby finished her prayer, she looked up and found Don's gray eyes focused on her.

"I'm still here," he whispered in awe.

"Yes," Toby said, taking his hand. "You're going to come out of this. You're going to make it."

"I am?" Don asked, disbelief in his voice. "How is that possible?"

Toby chuckled. "With God all things are possible, remember?" she kidded him.

The muscles in Don's face tightened, but he couldn't manage a smile. "I love you," he whispered, before closing his eyes and drifting back to sleep.

"And I love you," Toby replied softly. She stayed by his side for the rest of the evening, but he didn't wake up again.

CHAPTER 6

It had been a long day at work. The first inkling Davy had that he should have stayed in bed was when his teller drawer came up short by a thousand dollars. Five o'clock came, and he still hadn't found it. Carole Grayson, the bank manager—also known as the Dragon Lady—made him fill out a report, and he wondered if this meant he was going to be fired. The way she studied him—her narrow eyes squinted into suspicious little slits and her lips scrunched up on one side of her face and then the other as she chewed nervously on the insides of her cheeks—made him think that she suspected he had pocketed the money.

Laurie cast him surreptitious looks of sympathy behind the Dragon Lady's back and appeared as if she would like the opportunity to commit mutiny. Davy tried to ignore her, expecting some kind of offer to get together and discuss his problems. He wasn't far off.

"What a witch," Laurie hissed, coming up behind him in-between customers. She made like she was getting some coin rolls, but she only grabbed one of each. "Tell you what, I'll take you out tonight, my treat, to get your mind off this," she offered.

Davy groaned inwardly. Why couldn't she let it go? "I really can't," he apologized. "I'm not feeling that great."

Laurie snorted. "I can understand that. She's been on your case all day. I think she actually believes you stole it!" She glanced around before going on. "You didn't steal it, did you?"

"Of course I didn't steal it," Davy snapped. "Haven't you ever come up short before?"

"No, not once," Laurie replied honestly. "That is, nothing that we didn't find later." She patted his shoulder comfortingly. "Don't worry; it'll turn up. I'll go over your batch list after work, and we'll find it. I'm sure it's just some transposed numbers or something. You sure about dinner?"

Davy nodded sullenly. The last thing on his mind was going out to dinner. "I'm sure," he grunted.

"Your loss," Laurie shrugged unhappily.

Long after the bank officially closed, Davy pored over his teller batch trying to find the error that had left him out of balance by a thousand dollars. "Why couldn't it have been the other way?" he complained. "No one would really mind if I was a thousand dollars over."

"We'd still have to find it," Laurie replied, scooting her chair closer to his. From her glass-walled office everyone referred to as the "fishbowl," the Dragon Lady had a clear view of them as they worked. She had stayed late to finish some mortgage applications. Laurie was apparently ignoring her. She put one hand on Davy's, flinching as he pulled his away.

"I'm sorry," he said, as he watched her eyes fill with hurt. "It's just that . . . I'm really upset about this, Laurie. I can't think of anything else until I find this money."

She pulled away. "I understand," she replied coldly. "Don't worry, we'll find it." She studied a run of numbers. "What's this?" she asked, pointing with the tip of her pen.

"What's what?" Davy asked, his attention drawn to the row of numbers. Something did look funny about them.

"This," Laurie circled the numbers triumphantly. "That's not supposed to be an eleven hundred dollar cash out, it's only supposed to be a hundred dollar cash out. There's your problem."

"Really?" Davy exclaimed. "It's really that simple?"

Laurie sniffed. "We've been looking for it all day, Davy. I wouldn't exactly call it simple."

Impulsively, Davy grabbed Laurie by the shoulders and kissed her. Her mouth dropped open in shock.

"What was that for?" she stammered.

"For staying late to help me," Davy replied, suddenly just a bit sorry he'd been so spontaneous. "You have no idea how worried about this I've been." He grabbed the tape. "I'm going to go show this to the Dragon Lady, and then we can get out of here. How about some supper?"

Laurie's mood did an about-face. "Sure!"

From the moment they stepped foot in the pub, Davy regretted inviting Laurie to dinner. The choice of the pub had been hers, and she was obviously at ease there. But that wasn't what bothered Davy. It was how she clung to him that he couldn't take. Maybe, he told himself, the lines of friendship couldn't be blurred this way.

In the end he'd shortened the evening, saying that he had a headache, which was entirely true. Laurie didn't seem to believe him, and he could hardly blame her. He'd been lousy company. By the time he turned the key in his door and staggered inside, he could barely see straight.

"A nice shot of whiskey would just about do the trick," Belial suggested. "You can almost feel it going down, can't you? Can you feel the fingers of fire ease the ache right out of your body? Put on a little soft music, pour yourself a glass, and relax. You earned it. You deserve it. You've been through an awful lot today. Do this for yourself."

"Drinking will not solve anything," Jes warned as Davy gave thoughtful contemplation to Belial's suggestion. "Drinking will only dull your senses and poison your body."

Davy didn't give her advice a second thought. He headed, as if magnetized, toward the cupboard where he kept a few bottles of liquor. He pulled out some whiskey and poured a stout glass. Then he made his way into the living room, popped a Kenny G CD into the stereo, and collapsed into his favorite chair, the blue velour one that was so worn out it looked hideous but so comfortable he couldn't bear to part with it.

He sat sipping the whiskey, letting his head fall back now and then and closing his eyes. Soon the whiskey did exactly what Belial had promised. Thin fingers of warmth spread out over his body, massaging his aching muscles. A pleasant feeling of detachment pushed aside the tension he'd bottled up from the day's events.

Unknown to Davy, the whiskey was also doing its vicious work, cutting off the oxygen supply to his brain and killing brain cells. The Still Small Voice was quieted as his senses became dull. When his head became so heavy that it seemed like an effort to hold it up, he let it drop onto the back of the chair and closed his eyes.

The now familiar nightmare began again.

"Remember the plane crash?" Belial prompted him. "Remember how scared you were? Terrified. I know, I was there with you. Do you remember sending Toby out of the plane in her chute, not even sure you were high enough for it to work? You could have been signing her death warrant. Real nice guy, you are."

Belial settled back to toy with Davy's mind. It was totally in his control. "Those trees, didn't they come racing up fast? Whew! I've never seen anything move that fast. They were in your face before you even realized it. The wing cracked up against that one tree, and that's when you realized the mistake you had made."

Davy's breath began to come in little pants as his heart raced at the memory.

"That scream you heard? It wasn't the metal. It was your own voice screaming as the inside of the plane erupted into flames. Pow!" Belial slapped his hand into his fist, making Davy jump and moan in his sleep. "The force of the crash slammed you up against the cockpit windshield. And you passed out, but not before you felt the heat. Remember the heat? It was so hot! Your face felt like it was melting."

"Yes, Davy, remember the flames?" Jes prompted, interrupting Belial's guided tour of the plane crash. "And then suddenly you were cool. Hands, my hands, lifted you out of the wreckage and placed you up against the tree. I tended your wounds until help arrived. Do you remember? I held back the flow of blood from the cut above your eye, and I prevented you from going into shock. Remember, Davy!" It was no longer a question. Jes commanded him.

"Yes, Davy," Belial continued smoothly with a threatening gesture toward the angel. "Remember the accident. Remember how horrible it was. Twisted steel and flames and cold. Horrible, just horrible."

Davy woke in a sweat, his heart racing. He looked wildly around before realizing that he was in his own apartment, safe and sound. "Arghhh!" he howled, clutching his head in his hands. "I've got to get past this! I've got to get beyond this!" He struck his head repeatedly with the flat of his hand. "Come on, Davy. Remember something besides that stupid accident."

Jes, sensing an opportunity, approached from a different tack. "Davy, do you remember the auction you and Toby went to? Remember how you bought her that old, ugly farmhouse desk? The one you paid too much money for, just because you liked it? Remember how she used it even though she hated it and how you both laughed because of it?"

Belial made a threatening gesture. "I don't know what you're playing at, but if you don't stop now, you'll regret it."

His words caused a hush to descend on the group of demons

that were clustered in the living room near enough to jump into the fray at a moment's notice.

His words appeared to bounce off Jes. "Do you remember how you would walk down to the Charles and throw stones in the water and make wishes? And how you talked about join-ing the Peace Corps and flying a bush plane in Africa? And how she used to have a fit whenever you used her toothbrush? Do you remember, Davy?"

Davy clutched his head. It pounded out a rhythm that rivaled any rock band's drummer. He had a nagging feeling that there was something he was supposed to remember. He glanced over at the chipboard desk he'd acquired when he moved in. It was so horrible that the previous owner had left it in the apartment when he'd moved out. Davy kept all his bank statements on it and balanced them there.

In a quick rush, he remembered the one he'd bought for Toby. He'd loved it, but she called it a dinosaur and teased him for buying it. He'd paid more money than it was worth, he remem-bered that. He wondered what had happened to the desk and then recalled that Toby had sold everything in the house, so it was probably the proud possession of someone else by now. He smiled a little at the memory. It was one of his first.

He'd had a few isolated memories, usually related to some-thing he was doing, but this was the first one he'd had out of the blue. In a sudden rush, he remembered a few more. Trembling, he stood up and rotated in a confused circle. What was happen-ing to him? Was his memory coming back?

The CD ended, and Davy reached over automatically and flipped on the radio. Jes reached out, her fingers wrapping around the antenna. The signal of the oldies station that Davy usually tuned in to traded places with the signal for the local Christian radio station. A deep, sonorous voice drifted into the room. "And if we confess our sins He is faithful and just to forgive us our sins and cleanse us from all unrighteousness."

Guardians

Davy halted and stared in confusion at the radio. What on earth was that station? It certainly wasn't the soft rock station his radio was usually tuned to. He bent down to change the station, but the voice halted him.

"When we accept Christ as our Saviour, we become new people in Christ," the beautiful voice was saying. "Our old selves die, and we are reborn, so to speak. We begin our new lives with a clean slate. And we keep that slate clean by . . ."

But Davy didn't get past his first sentence. "A new life!" he exclaimed. "That's what I need. I need to be a new person. I need to start over. But, first I have to understand who I am." He dropped to his knees and clasped his hands together. "Oh, God!" he cried. "If you're up there, can you help me? I want to know who I am."

Jes couldn't refrain from expressing her joy. "Hallelujah!" she exclaimed. "Davy, in the Master's hands you will be safe and whole."

"Bah!" spat Belial. "Your past will bring you nothing but moral dilemmas and trouble. Leave it alone, I tell you!" He flew at Davy, an evil-looking dagger clutched in one fist, an intense look of hatred on his face. Alarmed, Jes intercepted him, driving him back with powerful blows.

Snarling, Belial came at Jes, his arms wind-milling wildly, the knife in his hand posing a real threat. One flailing arm caught Jes, and she tumbled sideways, narrowly correcting her trajectory before the idle gang of demons converged on her.

Beside her, Davy clutched his head and moaned in agony. "God, please, get rid of these awful voices in my head. Give me peace, please! Jesus, help me!"

When Jes looked up next, the room was bathed in a warm light. The demons attacking her ceased immediately, falling back with shrieks and howls. In the next moment, they were gone. Only Belial remained, warily watching the strong group of angel guards who had arrived as he panted and oozed ha-

tred from every pore.

Davy jumped up and began pacing up and down the living-room floor, racking his brain, willing it to release more information. Finally he collapsed back onto his chair in exhaustion. Nothing else occurred to him. Maybe it was one of those things you couldn't force, he reasoned. Maybe if he just cleared his mind, another memory would present itself. He drew a few deep breaths and tried to be open. He shook his head, fighting the fogginess caused by the alcohol.

Nothing.

"Please, God," he whispered. And then . . .

"Chicken," Toby's voice taunted him. She sounded faraway, like an echo, and he could almost feel a cold snowball slap him upside the head.

"You're in for it now," his own faraway voice hollered in reply. Her giggles accompanied his frenzied attempts to scoop up snow and turn it furiously into snowballs. Their shrieks of pleasure mingled, and he had a vague impression of the familiar Boston skyline. Maybe they had been in a park somewhere.

He grabbed her, and the two of them had tumbled onto the snow, furiously making snow angels. He heard her breathless laugh, saw her sparkling eyes, and felt her kiss as though it had happened yesterday.

"Toby!" he exclaimed, starting up from the chair in excitement. He remembered . . . he remembered Toby. At least he remembered Toby a little bit. He was so excited that he didn't think he could possibly go to sleep, but fifteen minutes later he collapsed onto his bed and fell into the deep sleep of mental exhaustion.

"Sleep, Davy," Jes said soothingly. She touched the top of the radio, and the comforting voice talking about salvation was replaced by the soft sounds of yesterday's favorites. "You're going to need your rest. You have a long road ahead of you, and you've only just begun."

GUARDIANS

"He's going to need his sleep, all right," Belial agreed, lips curling back to reveal dirty, yellow teeth. "But not for the journey you have planned for him."

Jewel knew that something important was going to happen as soon as he saw Noble. The archangel only visited to relay special messages. His first words confirmed Jewel's suspicions.

"We have vital things to discuss," he said, a twinkle in his sapphire blue eyes. "The Master has a job for you . . ."

Billie Jo wrinkled her nose at the musty smell of old books. She looked up and down the rows of ancient tomes and wondered how on earth she was ever going to find what she was looking for. She rubbed the slip of paper between her fingers and tried to make out the spidery writing scrawled on it. They were supposed to be directions, but they were not of much use.

"Where on earth do they keep the newspapers?" she asked herself, jumping at the sound of her own voice. She shivered. "It's like the catacombs down here."

She wished heartily that their little hick-town library would update and get with the program. She considered herself technologically illiterate, but even she could use a computer easier than she could find something in this literary tomb.

"Can I be of assistance?" a smooth, male voice asked from behind her.

Billie Jo jumped and whirled around, her breath automatically freezing in her throat. "Oh! You startled me!" she exclaimed.

The man in front of her was tall, even taller than Jimmy, and that was going some. His hair was a golden blond and on the long side. It was tied back in a neat ponytail. He wore an immaculate white T-shirt and faded blue jeans. His face was open and his smile wide. And, it seemed to Billie Jo, he acted as if he knew her from somewhere. It was uncanny, but she felt as though she knew him too.

"I, uh, I was just lookin', that is, I'm tryin' to find some old newspapers and such. Do you know where they keep them?" *Where do I know him from?* Billie Jo kept asking herself, mentally listing the places where she might have seen someone so striking, but she couldn't place him.

"As a matter of fact, I do know where the old newspapers are kept. Which date were you looking for?" he asked politely as he led the way through a maze of shelves that threatened to collapse on them.

"No special date," Billie Jo replied. "Just a few years. I thought I'd start with 1940 and go on from there."

"I see," the man replied as he pointed up to a long row of black cardboard folders, each neatly imprinted with the date in gold. "Are you searching for something specific or . . ."

Billie Jo swallowed hard, wondering just how much she ought to say. "Just lookin'," she replied finally, squirming a little uncomfortably. She was looking for something specific, but she wasn't sure she ought to tell him that. In fact, she hadn't told anyone what she was doing. She'd just asked her friend Leah if she'd watch the kids for a bit, and she'd driven straight over here.

She pulled down the folder marked "1940" and laid it on a nearby table to open it. The musty smell that wafted up from the old, yellowed newsprint made her cough. She opened it to the first page and sank down into a chair. This was going to take forever.

Not even Jimmy knew where she was. She'd been afraid to tell him. After that first night in the hospital, he'd been distant. She'd tried to question him about James's cryptic mention of Helen's past, but he just wrinkled his brow at her, frowned, and said he didn't know about no past. In fact, he didn't know too much about his Momma's family.

He looked puzzled for a while, but the thought was soon pushed aside in light of more pressing concerns. Helen was moved to the medical ward to recuperate. She'd regained consciousness two weeks after the accident, though she hadn't said much. Jimmy went to visit her every evening.

"Even from a hospital bed she can take him away from us," Billie Jo muttered. "Maybe that was part of her plan all along."

"Excuse me?" the man beside her asked.

Billie Jo jumped and then flushed with embarrassment. "I forgot you were here, mister," she said sheepishly.

"That's all right," he replied. His voice reminded her of an oboe she'd heard in an orchestra one time when Jimmy had taken her to one of those fancy-schmance symphony concerts. She'd felt a bit out of place—especially next to Jimmy who had been wearing jeans of all things—until the lights went out and the music started. Then everyone in the audience was equal, and nothing mattered except that beautiful music.

She didn't know much about the music except that it was wonderful, but one song she did remember, Pachelbel's "Canon." Even the name was pretty. It was the only time they'd ever gone to one of those shindigs. After that, Jimmy had his accident, and things had been pretty tight ever since. They were still paying back his hospital bill a little every month.

"Thank you for your help," she told the man.

"You're quite welcome," he said. "If you'd care to share with me what you're looking for, I'd be happy to help you find it."

Billie Jo was tempted, severely tempted, to tell him, but she bit her tongue. "Thanks, but I can manage on my own."

"Suit yourself," he replied pleasantly. "But if you need any help finding anything else, please ask. I'm well acquainted with the layout here."

"Thanks," Billie Jo said, almost wishing she had accepted his help. She sighed heavily and looked down at the first page. The ads on the pages looked funny and were for products she'd never heard of. Headlines talked about people she'd learned about in school. She scanned them carefully. She wasn't sure exactly what she was looking for, but she had decided that if there was something to be learned about Helen's family, it might be found here.

She was positive that James was hiding something, and she was determined to know what it was. Maybe it would help her understand Helen better. It wasn't long before she was engrossed in her task, and the flipping of pages settled into a steady rhythm. Two hours slipped easily by and when she happened to glance at her watch, she jumped up in consternation.

Leah would kill her! She only meant to be gone for an hour at the most. Hastily she replaced "1940" and "1941" on the shelf where they belonged. She snatched up her purse and nearly knocked over the chair as she scrambled for the steps that led up into the main library.

The man who had helped her find the newspaper archives was seated at a small desk reading. He looked up as she hurried past. "Have a good day," he called after her.

Billie Jo spared him a quick glance. "Thanks. You too."

CHAPTER 7

Cindi's alarm rang in strident tones, and she rolled over and slapped at it in groggy confusion. Marc groaned from his side of the bed and rolled away from her, pulling his pillow slightly over his head. Cindi forced herself to sit up and try to remember why she'd set the alarm to go off while it was still dark outside.

Reissa shook Cindi's shoulder urgently, "Wake up! You intended to spend time with the Master this morning," she reminded her.

Oh yeah, Cindi remembered, prying herself from the warm embrace of sleep with a long yawn. Today was the day she was going to start having her devotions early in the morning before Esther woke up. The only problem was that Esther had woken her up twice last night. The first time she'd had a nightmare and the second time, she wanted Cindi to sleep with her "just for a few minutes." The few minutes had turned into two hours in which Cindi had managed only a light sleep, constantly interrupted by Essie's tossings and turnings.

Cindi shuffled out to the living room, peeking into Esther's room on her way past. Her dark brown hair fanned out onto her pillowcase, exposing her face, sweet in its repose. Cindi felt her heart ache with love as she tiptoed past, hoping Esther would keep on sleeping. She made her way to the sofa and curled up on one end with her Bible in hand.

Her goal was to read one chapter every day. Sooner or later, she was bound to make it through the whole Bible. It would just take time and a little iron-willed determination. A morning person she definitely was not.

"In the beginning," she read, yawning again. "God created the heavens and the earth . . ."

Reissa watched Cindi's sleepy eyes droop as she read. Her intentions were good, Reissa knew, but her approach was all wrong. Sleep deprivation and Bible reading did not mix. In addition, failure of her new plan to become closer to the Master would discourage her. "Wake up, little sister," Reissa called softly. "Wake up!"

Before Cindi reached the end of the chapter, her head nodded heavily, and she caught herself falling asleep with no clear idea of what she'd just read. Doggedly she began again, picking up at the last thing she remembered reading. Marc's hand, shaking her shoulder, brought her fully awake with a kink in her neck from where she'd slumped over on the couch.

"What?" she asked thickly. "What happened? What did I do? Fall asleep?" She groaned. "I don't believe it."

"Believe it," Marc replied grumpily. "You also forgot to set the alarm again, and now I'm going to be late."

"Oh, Marc," Cindi said. "I'm sorry. But, I can't believe Esther didn't wake us up."

"Esther is still sleeping," Marc said. "I turned on her light on my way past, so she ought to get up soon."

"She's probably tired from being up so much last night," Cindi mused. "I know I am." She set her Bible aside and went to check on her daughter. Esther peeked at her from beneath a pile of blankets.

"It's time to get up, sweetie," Cindi said cheerfully. She hid another yawn behind her hand.

Rafe scowled as he watched Cindi enter the room. He had been hard at work all night long to take that sunshiny smile off her face. It was bad enough that he'd been demoted after his miserable failure with her employer, Ethel Bennington. Discouraging Cindi was a challenging and important thing—after all, she was in line to succeed Ethel. But working with her brat was another proposition altogether.

It was so easy it was beneath him.

All he had to do was fill her head with bad thoughts, and the child acted out on them. Between the power of the media and advertising in general, he hardly had to lift a finger. Most of his work was already done. As much as Cindi concentrated on prayer, for the most part she neglected her child in this area. Her spiritual concern for the child was sporadic at best, often forgotten altogether in light of more immediate concerns. Rafe found it deadly dull.

"You don't want to get up, kid," he told Esther. "You want to play with your toys, don't you? Then just tell her so."

"Esther, Jesus wants us to obey Mommy and Daddy. Remember your lesson from church last week?" Shania coached. She moved towards the little girl protectively, but the truth was that she had very little power to interfere because neither Cindi, Marc, nor Esther had asked for her protection.

"Don't want to get up," Esther grumped. "I want to stay in my room and play with my toys."

"I'm sorry, Essie, but we're going to see Grammy this morning, and we've got to get going. Today is Mommy's early day. The other visiting nurse has to leave early today."

"I don't want to go to Grammy's today," Esther howled, diving under her blankets. "I want to stay here and play with my toys!"

"Come on, Esther Julia," Cindi said, more firmly. "Let's go. We've got to go eat our breakfast, and then we have to get going."

"Noooooo!" shrieked Esther, pulling against Cindi as she

reached down and grabbed one of the little girl's hands. "Noooooo! I don't want to eat my breakfast! I hate my breakfast!"

"Esther, stop!" Cindi warned. She could feel her internal thermometer begin its daily climb. "Now, let's go. Daddy's late for work this morning, and I've got to help him get going. Be a good girl and come with Mommy."

Rafe moaned. "This is just too easy," he complained to no one in particular. "I'm overqualified for this job. Will no one see my talent? You there," he said gruffly, addressing Esther. "Remember that TV program you saw last night? Remember that that little boy hit his father because he didn't want to do something? Hit your mother."

Cindi fought with the child as Esther kicked at her. "That's not nice, Esther. If you don't stop that, you're going to have to go in time-out."

"Ah, the challenge," Rafe said sarcastically. "She doesn't mean it, kid. Go ahead. Test her. See if she does."

"Esther," Shania pleaded. "Obey your mommy."

Esther set her lips in a determined grimace and deliberately kicked at Cindi, striking her in the forearm. Cindi scooped up her belligerent daughter and strode purposefully toward the kitchen, where the "Time Out" chair was. She deposited Esther, a little rougher than was necessary, into the chair, where she proceeded to burst into wails of frustration and anger.

"Another day begins in the Trahan home," Marc intoned with a deadpan expression. "I think I'll just skip breakfast this morning and get to work." He dumped the remainder of his juice down the drain and set his glass in the sink. Cindi looked from his retreating back to Esther's unhappy, red face. What on earth was she doing wrong? Life wasn't supposed to be like this!

Days were supposed to start easily, with the family all gathered around a nutritious breakfast (that Cindi had risen early to prepare). After the meal was consumed and the chef complimented, they would adjourn to the living room where Marc would lead out in family devotions. They might sing a few cheerful songs, have a prayer, and then off into the day.

The fuzzy scene in Cindi's mind melted before the reality that was her life. Breakfast for her and Esther would consist of cold cereal and fruit. Not a bad breakfast, altogether, Cindi reasoned with herself, but far short of her ideal of homemade whole grain waffles and fruit topping or homemade granola. There would be no prayer as a family. Marc was rushing around looking for his briefcase. She would be lucky to get a quick peck on the cheek.

Where was all the power of God in her life? Where was the evidence of Him in her life? Somehow, she decided there was a short between her and God. Some vital link was missing. She decided to ask Ethel about it. If anyone knew, it would be Ethel. Not once had Cindi seen evidence of God's power lacking in Ethel's life.

By the time they reached Ethel's house, Esther still refused any breakfast and Cindi's nerves were jangled beyond repair. She was curt with Esther several times, and once she actually yelled at her. Then she immediately felt ashamed. She was the adult. She was supposed to be able to control herself.

Ethel sensed immediately that they had had a rough morning. "Hello, sweetheart," she said to Esther, holding out her hand in welcome. Esther slunk over and crowded in next to the wheelchair and under the old woman's protective arm. "How are you this glorious morning, Esther?"

"Bad," Esther growled. "Mommy was angry with me, and Daddy was angry with Mommy, and I am angry at both of them."

Ethel raised her eyebrows and gave Cindi a questioning look.

"There are no secrets at our house," Cindi shrugged in embarrassment. "We've had a bad morning. That's actually what I'd like to talk to you about. Esther, honey, would you go play with your toys for a little while? I'd like to talk to Grammy."

"I want to stay here," Esther pouted, shrinking closer to Ethel.

"Fine," Cindi sighed. "Stay then, but we're going to bore you to death."

Stubbornly Esther held her ground while Cindi waited to see if she might change her mind. "Suit yourself," she said finally.

"There's something wrong with me," she began and then stopped and gave a short laugh. "There's a lot wrong with me," she admitted, "but, what I'm worried about in particular is my relationship with God. He seems so . . . distant. I don't feel like He's really a part of my life. It's more like I know who He is and we get together once a week to talk for a few minutes, but the rest of the time I just barrel through life alone on my own strength."

"Honey," Ethel said, after contemplating for a few minutes, "I think you've summed up your own problem. You need to spend time with God in order to really know Him. Lots of times we Christians think we've got God all figured out. The stories we read in the Bible that were all fresh and alive when we started out are old and tasteless. So, we figure we're not babies anymore and strike out on our own.

"Problem is, we don't get very far without falling flat on our faces. We need God every moment of every day, and that's a fact. You know how in the Bible it says we're supposed to be the light of the earth?" Cindi nodded. "They probably had some sort of oil lamp in mind, but we'll bring the illustration into the modern world and say that we're like that floor lamp over there." She pointed one crooked finger at the art deco lamp standing in the corner of her bedroom.

"Unplug it for me, would you?" she asked. Cindi obligingly reached over and pulled the plug out of the wall. "Now turn it on."

"But it won't light," Cindi protested, turning the switch. Nothing happened.

"Exactly," Ethel cackled. "It won't turn on because it's not plugged in. And we can't be the light of the world unless we're plugged into God all the time, every moment. That's why He tells us to pray continually. Honey, you ever wonder what prayer is for?"

Cindi lifted her shoulders in confusion. "I don't know, I guess I've never really thought about it. I've just always prayed because I was supposed to and, you know, God says to."

"Now, mind you, I'm not saying that we shouldn't ask for things, because it might be in God's will to give them to us. And I'm not saying that prayer won't give God and His angels an opportunity to speak to others that He wouldn't have without it, because it will. But, the most important part of prayer, at least to my thinking, is for our benefit, not God's.

"Remember how Jesus prayed in the Garden? Father, not my will, but thine be done. What was He praying for?"

"That He wouldn't have to be crucified," Cindi answered promptly. "That God would take away the cup of suffering from Him if it was God's will."

"Was it?" Ethel prompted.

Cindi thought for a moment. "No, I guess it wasn't."

"I think Jesus knew what God's answer would be even before He started praying, don't you? If He did, it seems mighty silly for Him to bother praying for something He knew God wouldn't do, now doesn't it? But He wasn't praying to try to convince God to change the plan that He and God had created together. The reason He was praying was to acknowledge that God was the One in control and to submit Himself to God's will, no matter what it was."

Esther decided the conversation was boring after all and scooted away to find something interesting to do. Cindi sat thoughtfully for a moment before looking up at Ethel. The old woman smiled encouragingly at her. Cindi felt like one of the disciples being rebuked by Jesus. *"Have you been with me so long and yet you do not know . . ."*

She'd been taking care of Ethel for a long time. She thought she knew everything there was to know about prayer, and yet she hadn't ever considered this. Or had she? Had she once known this and forgotten in the face of the more immediate demands of taking care of Esther?

She reached over and patted Ethel's hand. "Thank you," she said simply.

"That's what I'm here for, child," Ethel assured her. "You know, honey, there are seasons in everyone's life. There's a time to be single and a time to be married, to have kids and not to have kids. There's a time to get old and a time to die. We have to make the most of the seasons of our lives. Right now, you're in a right hard season. You're raising Esther, and she's not an easy child. There are a lot of demands on you. Don't make God another demand."

Cindi's brow wrinkled in puzzlement. "I'm not sure I understand what you're saying," she said, groping for understanding.

Ethel chuckled. "What I'm saying is that you can't schedule God into your day at this season in your life. I'm not so old that I don't remember these days when your children take every blessed breath from your body and leave you limp as an old dish towel at the end of the day."

"You mean . . . you had . . . children?" Cindi asked, bewildered. In all the time she had worked for Ethel, she had never heard her mention any children nor had any children ever come to visit. As far as Cindi knew, Ethel had no living relatives.

The old woman's smile slipped from her face, and her eyes seemed to look right through Cindi. "Yes, I had children at one time," she said. "My son, Richard—oh, he was a bright one, that boy. He could take anything apart and put it back together again just like new. Now, mind you, he practiced a lot. I'll never forget the time he practiced on my husband's new pocket watch. It never did work again. He took sick with polio when he was ten and died in my arms."

"I'm so sorry," Cindi began, but Ethel didn't seem to be aware of her presence.

"My daughter Carol was a sweet child. She adored her brother. When he died, something inside her died too. She became cynical and stopped believing in God. My husband, Bert, bless his soul, tried to take the boy's place in her heart, but she didn't want any of it. He was so kind to her, Bert was. But she came back at him tooth and claw. I think she blamed us."

She shook her head as if to scatter the memories. "Anyway," she went on, her voice more in touch with the present and detached from the past, "she ran away when she was just sixteen, and we never saw her again. There's not a day goes by but I don't pray for her.

"Bert, of course, died about ten years later of lung cancer. Died physically, that is. His heart had died long before. I think it sickened when we lost Richard and passed on the morning we woke up to find Carol gone. He was a good husband and all, but he never opened up his heart again. It was as if he just closed that door and lived at the surface level for the rest of his life. When he got the cancer, he almost seemed to be relieved."

Ethel's watery blue eyes focused on Cindi's face as she listened intently. "Well, now, that's more than I've talked about myself in a good, long time." She took Cindi's hand and patted it gently. "I hope I didn't bore you, my dear."

Cindi leaned forward and gave the old woman an impulsive hug. "You could never bore me," she assured her. "I didn't realize what a hard life you'd had. How come it didn't shake your faith?"

"You know, I've never known anyone who had an easy life," Ethel said, "even Jesus. His life was harder than mine will ever be. I don't expect to do better than Him. As long as you're living, there are going to be trials to face. If we let them get the best of us, if we surrender, then we'll live the rest of our lives bitter people. But if we let God, He can help us to become better people because of those same trials. Everyone faces trials. It's how you get through them and Who you go through them with that makes the difference."

"I wish I could get through them better," Cindi sighed.

"Don't get discouraged," Ethel said firmly. "You won't always be in this season of your life. It lasts for a precious little while. Until you get through it, you might want to try practicing the presence of God."

"The presence of God?" Cindi asked. "What do you mean?"

"Just take God with you through the day. There's nothing in the Bible that says we have to talk to God only at set-apart times." She shook a crooked finger beneath Cindi's nose. "Now, I'm not saying it's not good to take breaks and get away to spend time alone with God. But God understands that you are having trouble making time to spend with Him the way you were accustomed to. He's with you twenty-four hours a day. Don't ever forget that. You can talk to Him every moment of every day if you have a mind to, even while you're doing other things. Your hands will still be here, but your thoughts will be in heaven. Try it and see if that doesn't help."

Cindi smiled with relief. "That sounds like a wonderful idea!" she exclaimed. "I can't wait to give it a try."

"Wait?" the old lady cackled. "Why wait?"

Jesse Redcloud studied the sheet of paper he'd laid out on the Formica table in his dinky little apartment. For the moment, he didn't notice the stench of the place or the fact that everything he owned was strewn all over the small living space as if it had been ransacked. The kitchen, which smelled of rancid oil and too many burnt meals, was only an extension of the main living space. It was a "studio" apartment, so there was no bedroom, only a tiny, filthy bathroom some ingenious designer located right next to the kitchen.

A small patio off the living room might have made up for it except that it faced the dirty brick side of the building next door. Garbage in the alley below created such a horrible smell that you couldn't even open the glass door for a little relief from the heat. Even plants wouldn't grow out there. When he'd moved in six months before, Jesse had tried to grow a cherry tomato plant there, thinking the tomatoes would be good in the chef salads he was so fond of. The poor plant had withered in less than three months, just as the baby tomatoes were the size of green peas.

That was one of his first disappointments, but it wasn't his last. Never having been one to keep a job long, he'd been laid off—again. If that wasn't bad enough, he had listened to a friend and placed a losing bet. Last night saw the end of his last ten bucks in exchange for a carton of cigarettes and some beer. That was when he decided that he had to do something.

He drew little doodads on the corner of the sheet of paper he was studying. On the paper was his best recollection of the lay-out of the church he'd visited. While talking to the pretty, friendly girl, he had been concentrating intensely on his surroundings. It had been simple, and he had actually felt a twinge of guilt that he'd deceived her so easily. Calculating the amount the church's sound equipment would bring him erased the guilt almost immediately.

He placed check marks on the paper at the places where he remembered seeing things worth stealing. They were bound to have things like a copier and maybe even a money box that was somewhere else in the building. He'd feigned having to use the restroom so that he could see more of the building. A helpful man gave him directions downstairs. Besides the restrooms, three rooms led off the main meeting and dining room downstairs. He'd opened one a crack and peeked inside before someone else had descended the stairs. There had been a television and VCR in that room on a metal stand, and he felt pretty confident that there were more things to steal behind those other two doors.

For a moment, he toyed with the idea of returning to the church again to complete his survey before he attempted to break into it. But a growl from his stomach reminded him that he had no money at all and couldn't wait that long. Besides, Sean, who was going to fence the stolen goods for him, had agreed to join him with his van to steal the stuff tonight. After that, Sean was busy with "more important matters," he'd said.

Jesse got up from the table and yanked open the fridge door for another beer. He popped the top and flopped into an old bean bag chair that he'd had to repair with packing tape. There was no other furniture in the room. He polished off three more beers before it got dark enough for him to carry out his plan.

He rummaged in the piles of clothes scattered around for black jeans and a long- sleeve black mock turtleneck. Stuffing a pair of gloves and a black ski mask in the waistband of his pants, he grabbed a long metal flashlight that could serve as protection as well as illumination. He also pocketed a switchblade and put on his black hightop sneakers. When he walked out of the apartment building he felt like Batman, almost invisible in the dark.

He met Sean in the parking lot of a grocery store a few blocks down. His van looked even worse than Jesse remembered. "Been in a little accident," Sean explained as they pulled out into traffic. Unfortunately, the "accident" had caved in the sliding door somewhat, making it stick until you nearly had to dislocate your shoulder to move the thing shut.

The insides of the van had been ripped out the day Sean stole it, to make room for the stuff he hauled. Jesse wondered why no one in authority had ever questioned Sean about that. Of course, he had been smart enough to make the usual changes as a precaution against anyone finding out the van had been stolen, but the gutted interior looked a little obvious to Jesse.

"Where is this place anyway?" Sean asked. He was slumped

over on the driver's side, steering with one hand while the other tapped a string of cigarette ash onto the floor of the van.

"Here, take a left," Jesse instructed. They pulled off onto a street that was a little less bright than the main street. Sean slowed the van and cruised past the dimly lighted fronts of houses lining the street. Finally, there was a break in the houses, and a sign, pinned to the darkness by two spotlights, announced the presence of a church.

Sean yanked the wheel sharply and pulled into the parking lot. "What's going on here?" he asked angrily. Jesse recognized the fear in Sean's voice, not because he'd heard it before, but because it was at that very instant coursing through his own veins.

Saiph was not alone. In fact, she was accompanied by a dozen other angels, each as large and powerful as she was. On this night, the veil that usually separated them from the human beings on earth would be lifted in order for them to protect the church from being vandalized. That was not their only purpose, of course. Saiph hoped that their presence might prompt her charge, Jesse Redcloud, to examine his life, to halt its downward spiral. She hoped that from the pit he had dug himself into he would look up and see Jesus.

As the van slipped noiselessly into the parking lot and prepared to park in a dark corner, obscured by a tree, the contingent of angels was suddenly revealed. Each held a flaming sword and towered over the van. Saiph clearly could see the startled, fearful looks of the occupants, and even if she hadn't known Jesse so well, she would have realized that he was questioning what he was seeing, hoping maybe it was some alcohol-induced hallucination.

His hands wiped his face, and he looked hastily back to the place where the angels were standing as if he hoped maybe he could erase them. A quick glance at his companion confirmed that if this was a hallucination, he was sharing it with Sean.

Tires squealing and smoking, the van's engine raced as Sean attempted to run over the angels. It was as if the van had hit a giant marshmallow. It rebounded gently, unable to cross the line of angel guards.

Steering wheel spinning frantically, Sean gunned the engine again and drove furiously out of the parking lot. Saiph left her companions with her thanks and followed Jesse as he shakily exited the van at the grocery store and made his way back to his apartment. He climbed the rickety stairs that smelled of cat urine and let himself into his apartment. Glancing skittishly around, he determined that there was no one else in the apartment with him, and he sat down at the Formica table.

With trembling hands he tried to open a can of beer, but it was too hard. Finally, he ran the water in the tap and filled a glass, downing it in one long swallow. He wiped at his mouth with the back of his hand. Never, ever, had he seen anything like what he had just witnessed.

"Jesse," Saiph said. "What you saw was the army of the Lord. It was not a hallucination, and it was not ghosts. It was angels, beings created by God just as man was."

Balor entered the room with a whoosh, and it immediately became darker, the air close and confining. Jesse ran his hands through his hair and jerked at the collar of his mock turtleneck. The color heightened on his face to a sickish shade of green. He looked as though he might throw up.

"Will you grow up?!" Balor raged. "What kind of sissy are you? If you think that was some impressive supernatural freak-show, just wait until I get through with you. You ain't seen nothing yet! You know those tarot cards you've got in the bottom of your backpack? How about that crystal around your neck? You've been wanting to see my master's power. Now I'll show you!"

He reached out one long hand and grabbed Jesse by the throat, lifting him up so that his feet dangled off the ground. Kicking and squirming, Jesse fought against the darkness that threatened to strangle the life out of him. His eyes bulged, and sweat beaded up on his forehead. Saiph knew that he felt the cold, oppressive presence of the demon. But because he had invited Satan by toying with the occult, even in such a seemingly harmless way, there was nothing she could do to help him unless he asked Jesus to save him.

Suddenly, in a blinding rush, a flash of light entered the room, catching Balor off-guard. The new angel, Atli, thrust a shoulder hard into Balor's midriff, staggering the demon who grew more furious at the interference than he had been at Jesse.

"GET AWAY FROM HIM, ANGEL!" he roared. "He is mine. I am here by his invitation, and I can do whatever I wish with him."

"Someone is praying for him," Atli responded, drawing his sword. "I have a right to be here."

"You think it's that easy?" panted the demon as he renewed his grip on Jesse's throat. "I will not give him up."

"You must give up," countered Atli. He swung his sword in a broad arc that would have ended at Balor's throat, but the demon, sensing that the angel would not relent, drew his own sword and the two parried, blow for blow, the force of their strength shaking the very walls. Jesse, suddenly released from the grip of the demon, slumped against the countertop, his hands groping for a knife or something with which to defend himself against this unseen attacker.

Instantly, Saiph recognized her opportunity. She thrust Calla's Bible beneath Jesse's searching fingers. He picked up the book and nearly threw it away in disgust, but Saiph halted his arm.

"You need a weapon with which to fight. This is the only weapon you need." She watched the look of understanding slowly penetrate his consciousness. She knew he was remembering something he hadn't thought about in years. Since he had been a child, he had been searching, always searching, for *something to fill the empty void in his life.*

At the age of three his father had left his mother, six sisters, four brothers, and himself. Being the youngest of eleven children, he was raised mostly by his oldest sister, Jennifer. She was a good girl and tried hard to help her mother with the children. At sixteen, she had left school to get a full-time job, working nights at a truck stop. During the day, she would look after the children while Jesse's mother worked full time at a diner. Between the two of them, they earned just enough to get by.

It wasn't until Jesse's oldest brother, Ed, also joined the work force two years later that they had enough money for extras like new clothes or food to fill the bellies of the whole family. When his mother died of exhaustion just after he turned seven, the family had been split up and sent to foster homes. He had never seen any of his brothers and sisters again.

The family he stayed with were nice people, but it seemed they delighted in telling him stories of hell and damnation. A confused and angry child, Jesse frequently acted out by lying, stealing, and beating up kids who picked on him. His new parents convinced him that his soul would be lost because of such behavior and tried to scare him out of it by telling him stories of torture in the afterlife. No matter what the infraction, he was told his soul was lost. After a while, he began to believe it.

Eventually, he ran away so many times that the people wouldn't take him back. It was not until he was passed along to the next family he stayed with did he hear of a loving God who forgave him for his sins. But by that time he was pretty much convinced that his was a hopeless case and that nothing would help him. Although it didn't mean much to him at the time, he often remembered this woman, whom he never could bring himself to think of as his "mother," cuddling with him and stroking his hair while she told him stories about Jesus.

She always told him that Jesus would help him no matter what his problems were. It didn't matter if they were big or small. Jesus would help. She died five years later and no matter how hard he asked Jesus to bring her back, He never did. So he ran away again one last time. He was seventeen and managed to stay "lost" until he was legally of age. He'd been on his own ever since.

"Your foster mother was right. Jesus will help you no matter what your problems are. And He is the only one who can help you right now. Ask Him to help you."

Saiph could see the turmoil wrenching him apart inside. The old doubts, the old fears, the old sense of distrust were as fresh today as they had ever been. Across the room, Balor had eluded Atli's defenses and charged toward Jesse. As the demon threw him to the floor, the Bible flew out of his hands, sliding across the linoleum and bouncing off a table leg.

"Jesus, help me!" Jesse shrieked in desperation before Balor's strong fingers once again circled his throat.

Atli plowed into Balor's back in the next instant and Saiph drew her sword to join the melee. Although Balor struggled valiantly, he was no match for the two angels. As soon as Balor released the hold on his throat, Jesse had crawled across the floor and picked up the Bible, clutching it to his chest like a shield.

"Jesus!" Jesse cried again. "Save me!"

Saiph blocked the swing of Balor's sword as the demon backed toward the open window. With one last venomous look, he fled, limping the remaining distance to the window. "I'll be back," he promised, with one last ragged breath before he threw himself out the window and disappeared into the night.

Jesse sat trembling and weeping on the cold floor, fingers clutched so tightly around the Bible that they were white. For two hours he didn't move. When finally he was able to peel his fingers from the cover of the Bible, he opened it, determined to find the Source of strength that had saved him.

Reverently, he opened the cover of the handsome, leather Bible.

"To my darling Calla," he read, "Happy Birthday! I'll love you forever. Let's spend eternity together. Love, Lyle." He smiled at the inscription and with Saiph's help, he opened to the book of John and began reading. Within moments he was so engrossed that he never noticed when his cramped legs lost all feeling or the sunshine began to filter in through the still open window.

Shay awoke with a dull ache behind her eyes and a sick feeling in the pit of her stomach. She had felt the same way for so long now she couldn't remember ever feeling "normal." Rolling over clumsily, she squinted her eyes against the glare of the sun streaming in the window and listened to Madina's squeals as the little girl played with Ray and Julia Vargas in the room adjacent to hers.

Downstairs in the bar, she could hear the clink of glasses as Wahabi cleaned up after what had sounded like an endless night of merrymaking. For nearly a month now, she had been staying with her brother-in-law. What had started out as a long weekend had turned into a living nightmare. First, there was the death of her father to deal with. She had barely gotten his affairs settled when she'd gotten word that there was an outbreak of Ebola at the mission.

"Now, now," Wahabi had comforted her. "Probably an exaggeration, Madame Shay. These villagers are cautious, maybe too cautious. A simple flu can turn overnight into the Ebola virus. You see how simple it is? Word travels fast in these parts. For all we know, it may not even be the same mission."

But it had been the same mission. No one was allowed in, and no one was allowed out, though many fled. It did them no good, because having told their fantastic tale of gruesome death, they were turned away and driven out of the town. Shay had heard that only the hospitals in the big cities would take them in, and she doubted that they made it so far. Many were believed to have perished in the desert trying to escape the death they carried inside them.

After she had been at Wahabi's for a week, the two new nurses bound for the mission arrived in town. Wahabi had generously agreed to let them stay also in his apartment above the bar. The quarters had been crowded before; now they were almost unbearable. The two nurses, Ray and Julia Vargas, were nice people, but Shay found herself avoiding them whenever she could. They were pleasant and outgoing, but they kept asking her questions about the mission that she didn't feel like answering at the moment.

As worried as she was, she couldn't concentrate on anything. By day she schemed ways to sneak back to the mission, but always her concern for Madina and the baby growing inside her kept her from carrying out her plans. When Wahabi received the shipment of literature for the mission, she offered to carry it in, knowing full well that he wouldn't let her. She had been right. In fact, he wouldn't even let her come along and talk to anyone from a distance.

"Too much shouting bad for the baby," he had said by way of explanation. Shay was sure he was worried about more than that. The second he had come back, she plied him with questions. How had the mission looked? Did he see Nwibe or Marcus? Who had he seen? Did he ask about Nwibe or Marcus? Why on earth not?!

Although he made excuses, she knew why he hadn't asked. The less he knew, the less he could worry her with. And worry or suspicion, in his mind, was better than knowing for sure. At least it was for now. As unstable as Shay was emotionally from the death of her father, she could hardly blame him for wanting to put off the possibility of any further bad news as long as possible.

So, she did the only thing she could do. She prayed. She prayed long and hard every day, mostly while lying in bed because she was so sick it was really all she could do. For that one reason alone, she was extremely thankful for Ray and Julia. They took over Madina's care as if she had been their own child. Madina loved them and had already taken to calling them "aunt" and "uncle."

Shay was just thinking about going in search of something her stomach could hold down for breakfast when she heard a light tap on the door. She struggled into a sitting position on the mattress that lay on the floor. She was wearing the same rumpled clothes she wore nearly every day. They were the only ones that fit her, and she didn't have money to buy anything else and was too proud to beg money from Wahabi.

The tall African's face peered into the room. Shay could tell immediately that something was wrong. His face was lined deeply and although he had brushed them hastily away, she could see moisture on his cheeks from recent tears. His eyes were bloodshot and blinked rapidly as if he hoped that movement would ward off any further rush of emotion.

"Madame Shay?" he began. "I have had a letter."

Shay felt her stomach tighten. "Yes?" she asked, suddenly feeling as though her mind floated somewhere outside her body, watching everything.

"There is bad news."

"Yes?"

"My brother, your husband . . ." Wahabi faltered and finally went on, his voice sounding very far away. Shay knew what he was going to say before he said it. "Nwibe is dead."

"Marcus?" she asked as the numbness began to penetrate her body.

"The boy lives," Wahabi said. Shay could hear the worry in his voice. Even now, he was more concerned for her than he was about his own grief. "He is missing you. The letter says that soon you will be able to return to the mission. The outbreak is almost over."

"I'll have to tell Ray and Julia," Shay said tonelessly. "They've been really anxious to get there. I'm sure they'll be relieved to finally be on their way. And you, I'm sure you'll be happy to have your apartment to yourself again. We've more than worn out our welcome."

"Madame Shay, you know well that you are welcome to stay as long as you like," Wahabi said, hurt in his voice. "Now that Nwibe is gone from us, you and I are both alone in the world. He was the only relation I had left. You, too, are without support, and you have the burden of his children. You are more than welcome to stay here with me for as long as you wish. It may be, in time, that you would consider allowing me to take my brother's place and care for you and the children as long as you live. As Nwibe's brother, this is my duty to care for you, but I would consider it a great honor."

This strange offer of marriage didn't really register with Shay. Suddenly, for the first time since her father had died, she knew what she was going to do. When she looked up at Wahabi, it was with eyes that were clear and purposeful. There was no hint of grief in them, and she could tell by the look on Wahabi's face that he feared she had taken leave of her senses. "Thank you, Wahabi, but I'm afraid that I will not be staying."

"In Niamey?" he asked, thinking she meant to return to the mission.

"In Africa," she clarified. "I am going to return to the mission for Marcus and to collect the rest of my things, and then I'm going to take the children back to America. My father left me half of a house in his will and a great deal of money. We can live quite comfortably there. I have some family and friends who can help me, if they haven't forgotten me."

"But, Madame Shay!" Wahabi exclaimed, aghast. "What about

the children? Africa is the only home they have ever known! What about the mission? Who will take your place?"

"They don't need me. There is no one to care for my children while I work. I would only be a burden to them."

"They would be happy to help you," Wahabi pointed out.

"They would pity me," Shay countered. "I do not want anyone's pity. I refuse to be pitied." In that one statement, she sealed off any way to reach her hurting soul, and she did it on purpose. At that moment, she began laying down the bricks that would wall her off emotionally from the rest of the world.

When she was allowed to go back to the mission, she barely recognized it. It seemed like a ghost town. Don and a few others, though recovering, were still quartered in the clinic, and Shay wasn't allowed in there "just in case." Toby had read that Marburg was especially devastating to unborn babies, and she was worried about Shay. She went so far as to suggest that Shay should leave all of Nwibe's effects to be burned.

As Shay looked around the room she had shared with her husband, she could feel the wall around her emotions tremble a little. Marcus tucked himself into her side, wrapping his arms around her and keeping silent as she surveyed the room. "We can't leave his things here, Marcus," she said quietly. "Can we?"

"No, Mama," he replied. "We can't."

"We can't take him to America with us, but we can take his things to remind us of him." Shay let out a long, slow sigh. "Besides, one day you and Madina and this little one inside of me will want something to remember him by. What could I tell you? That I was too afraid of a virus to take his things with us?" She looked down at Marcus. "You have been in this room, eating and sleeping, and you haven't caught anything from it. I think it's safe."

And so it was decided, and nothing could shake her. She took only the things that meant the most to them. The rest she left, knowing that Toby would burn them and she could never reclaim them after that. When she asked Marcus what he wanted to remember his father by, the boy took only one thing. The long, smooth pole that had tied the two of them together since Nwibe had become blind.

At the sight of this pole, Shay had felt warm tears slide down her cheeks. She brushed them away fiercely and asked Marcus if he was ready to go. They had left Madina with Wahabi and would pick her up on their way out of the country.

Shay never would have believed it would be so hard to say goodbye to everyone at the mission. Toby was crying, Akueke was silent and morose.

"Don says that he's sorry he can't see you off personally," Toby relayed through her tears. "He wanted me to tell you how much he appreciated all you've done here." Toby's voice cracked, and she couldn't go on. Shay nodded her understanding and wrapped her arms around Toby. She found it ironic that she was the one comforting Toby and not the other way around.

"I made you something for the trip," Akueke said, pressing a bundle wrapped in cloth into Shay's hands before she could protest. "You take it. The children will like. Someday you'll come back, so I won't say goodbye. Instead I will say, have a nice vacation."

Shay smiled in spite of herself, even though she knew it was wishful thinking on the part of the old woman. "I'll send you pictures of the baby," she promised, submitting herself to Akueke's embrace. The old woman hugged her tightly, and Shay was afraid for a moment she might change her mind. But then Akueke let go, and she took Marcus's hand, and they left.

Toby had asked Flory to drive them into Niamey and as they jostled along, the young nurse tried to make small talk, but Shay could only manage one or two syllable responses, and finally Flory fell silent. She wanted to tell Flory that she didn't hold her responsible for Nwibe's death, but she couldn't bring herself to talk about it.

Instead, she studied the landscape. She knew that she should feel excitement or nervousness or fear or *something* at the thought of returning home after so long, but instead, she felt nothing, absolutely nothing, inside. It was as if she, Shay Beauregard Okeke, had ceased to exist. She put her arm protectively around Marcus, and the two of them clung silently to each other all the way back to Niamey.

Lucien surveyed the spot of dust kicked up by the jeep. Two leaving, two coming. It seemed that he could never make any headway here. His lips twisted into a grimace of displeasure, and he looked around for someone to take his anger out on. Festus had the misfortune of being close by.

"You!" he shrieked.

Festus jumped and cowered away from Lucien like a dog who expects a beating. "Me?" he asked in a small voice.

"Yes, you," Lucien growled. "I have an assignment for you." He pointed to Ray and Julia, who stood a little uncertainly in the middle of the mission courtyard surveying their surroundings. "Those two are now your responsibility. I want you to make their lives miserable. I want you to make them want to go home more than they've ever wanted anything in this life. Understand?"

Festus studied the two hapless humans and then shrugged his shoulders. "Piece of cake," he replied.

"Don't be so sure," Lucien answered. "And don't fail. Because if you do . . ." He left the threat open and gloated at the look of fear on the little demon's face.

"I won't," Festus assured him, displaying a stubborn streak that Lucien hadn't known he possessed.

C H A P T E R

Calla propped open a copy of *Modern Bride* and idly flipped through the pages while she ate. She was in a foul mood. Lyle was still being a jerk about Jesse Redcloud, and Calla didn't much feel like planning her wedding to him at the moment.

"Ooh, I like that one," Aunt Bernie said, looking over her shoulder at a wedding dress on one of the glossy pages. "Do you like it?"

"If I get married one of these days I might," Calla conceded grimly.

Aunt Bernie chuckled. "Still fighting with Lyle, I see," she observed.

"He's such a jerk!" Calla said with so much force that she sprayed the magazine with little bits of egg. "What does he expect? That I'm never going to talk to another man as long as I live? Why doesn't he trust me? I've never done anything to betray his trust."

"Maybe it isn't you he mistrusts," Aunt Bernie said softly.

"Oh no!" Calla wailed. "Not you too! What is it about Jesse that you don't trust? How can you make such a snap judgment about him? You've never even talked to him. What's not to trust?"

"I wasn't talking about Jesse. I was talking about Lyle," Aunt Bernie corrected gently.

"Oh," Calla replied in a small, embarrassed voice.

"You must remember, Calla," Aunt Bernie admonished, "that Lyle has only just rediscovered his self-worth. You helped him to find it, so it's only natural that if you begin to doubt it, he will too."

"But I don't doubt his self-worth," Calla replied miserably. "All I was trying to do was be a good Christian. I treated Jesse no differently than I treated Lyle when I first met him."

"And what happened when you treated Lyle the way you treated Jesse?" Aunt Bernie prompted.

Calla refused to reply. He had fallen in love with her, that's what had happened. Aunt Bernie bent over and gave her a squeeze. "You're a very kindhearted girl, Calla. But you have to be careful, because that kindheartedness can be mistaken by many people whose motives aren't as pure as yours are. I don't believe you had any ulterior motives or any inclination that you might be inviting disaster when you spoke so kindly to Mr. Redcloud. But, no matter what your intentions were, you hurt someone.

"Your own sense of self-worth is strong. I know that because you are able to reach out to others so easily. Lyle's sense of self-worth is very weak. If something that you're doing is hurtful to him, even if it isn't necessarily wrong, it's probably the better part of wisdom to stop doing it."

Calla sat for a long time after her aunt had gone outside to tend to her garden. She stared unseeingly at the pages of the magazine open in front of her. It wasn't fair, it just wasn't fair. Why should Lyle's insecurities keep her boxed up like some kind of trophy? That's what she felt like. How was she to know what might set him off next? It was like walking around in a mine field.

The longer Calla sat feeling sorry for herself, the more de-

mons collected in the little room with her. Atli, her guardian angel, was pushed off in a far corner of the room where he watched helplessly as the demons taunted Calla.

"You are so right!" one agreed with her. "It isn't the least bit fair to you. I think you should dump him. He doesn't deserve you."

"He's limiting your Christianity," another piped up. "He's hedging you in. You can't do as much good with him around."

"Who does he think he is anyway? You're too good for him. Maybe he is only pretending to be a Christian so that you'll marry him. After all, his actions aren't very Christlike."

It wasn't often that Calla obliged the demons like this, and Atli hoped that she'd soon snap out of it. "Do not cause anyone to stumble," Atli quoted. "Whether Jews, Greeks, or the church of God even as I try to please everyone in every way. For I am not seeking my own good but the good of many. Do not seek your own good, Calla," Atli begged. "Seek the good of others. Seek Lyle's good. Put his needs before your own. You have agreed to marry him. He is your mission right now. Leave the rest in the hands of God, for His arm is not too short, nor His hands too small to hold them all."

Calla perked up as if she were listening to him. He saw a guilty look cross her face, and she looked at the pictures in the magazine as if she were really seeing them for the first time. Then she closed the magazine and pushed it to one side. Her Bible lay on the table beside the magazine, and she opened it up and began reading. One by one, the demons got bored and left in search of easier prey.

"Well, I may not be able to witness to him," Calla muttered under her breath, "but no one can stop me from praying for him." She bowed her head where she sat at the table and began to pray again for Jesse as she had often in the past few days. For some reason she felt compelled to, as if his very life depended on it.

When she finished praying, she jumped up from the table and headed out to her car. Aunt Bernie saw her before she could get in and close the door.

"Going somewhere, hon?" she asked, rubbing her dirt encrusted garden gloves together to remove some of the caked-on mud.

Calla didn't quite meet her aunt's gaze. "I thought I'd go down to the church. I've been meaning to fix up one of the bulletin boards, but I haven't gotten around to it. I don't have anything else to do, so I thought I'd run down this morning."

"Lyle going with you?" Aunt Bernie asked innocently.

Calla shrugged. "I don't know what he's doing today. I'll call him later."

"Have a good time, Calla," Aunt Bernie said.

Calla waved to her aunt and closed the door of the car, wondering why she suddenly felt as though she were committing some kind of sin. She didn't feel like telling Aunt Bernie that she hoped to find Pastor Hendricks at the church. She knew he often worked in the office there on the weekend. Maybe he would be there today.

She almost sighed with relief when she saw Pastor Hendricks's car parked in the parking lot. She pulled her beat-up Chevette in beside his and hopped out quickly. She found the pastor in his study working on a sermon.

"Hello, Pastor Hendricks," she said, forcing a cheerfulness she didn't feel. "How are you today?"

"Calla!" the pastor exclaimed. "I didn't expect to see you here this morning."

"I need to work on the bulletin board, and I thought today would be a good day," Calla explained. "But, also, I really need to talk to you about something. Do you have a minute?"

Pastor Hendricks pushed his keyboard across his desk and swiveled his chair around to face her. "Yes, Calla? What is it? What's troubling you?"

Calla drew a deep breath, but before she could push any words of explanation out between her lips, a tentative knock sounded on the door behind her. "Hello?" a strange voice said. "I hope I'm not interrupting anything."

Calla whirled to find Jesse Redcloud standing behind her. He looked awful, as if he had gotten no sleep. There were deep purple circles beneath his eyes. He was dressed all in black, and if it weren't for the openness and joy shining from his face, he would have appeared quite sinister.

"Jesse!" Calla exclaimed.

"Well, hello, young man," Pastor Hendricks greeted him. "What can we do for you today?"

Jesse looked from one to the other hesitantly. "I came because, ah, I have a confession to make, that is, well, it's a long story. Do you have time?"

Pastor Hendricks shot a quick look at Calla that she interpreted as an apology. She nodded her head quickly to let him know that she understood and turned to leave. "Certainly, certainly, come right on in."

Jesse put a restraining hand on Calla's arm as she went to pass him in the doorway of the study. "I'd like you to stay if you don't mind," he said.

Calla looked up, her eyes meeting his. She could feel her heart speed up, and she mentally castigated herself for it. For just a second, she wondered if she really ought to.

"Stay, stay," Warg encouraged her. He had been working overtime to split Calla and Lyle up, and finally he was beginning to see a glimmer of light at the end of the tunnel. "What harm could it possibly do? After all, Pastor Hendricks will be here. And Jesse did ask you to stay specifically. You wouldn't want to let him think that you didn't care for his eternal soul, now would you?"

"Yes, stay," Balor hissed agreeably. "Stay; maybe you can provide him with a distraction to all this religious hogwash he

thinks he's discovered."

"Shut up!" Warg snapped, lashing out at the demon. Balor twisted aside to avoid the demon's balled up fist. "You keep out of it. This is my project, and it will be my victory. I don't need your help."

"What's your problem?" Balor griped. "We both want the same thing."

"Maybe we do," Warg agreed. "But, I don't want you coming along on my ride to victory. I managed to get this far without your help, and I can finish the job myself. I'm not about to share the glory with you when you haven't done a thing to help me out until victory is in sight. You just keep to yourself, and you'll be all right."

Balor shrugged. "Fine. Have it your way." He pointed to Jesse. "But he's my responsibility, and you can't stop me from working with him."

"I wouldn't dream of it," Warg said sarcastically. "Just stay away from her."

"Of course I'll stay if you want me to," Calla agreed as pleasantly as she could. Even though she didn't feel as though there was anything wrong with staying, she couldn't shrug the uneasy feeling that clung to her as she turned back and took a seat beside Pastor Hendricks.

"Mind if I close this?" Jesse asked, indicating the open door.

"Feel free," Pastor Hendricks acquiesced, waving his hand toward the door. "Now," he asked as Jesse sat down on the remaining chair and fidgeted nervously. "What's on your mind?"

Calla looked at the floor, the ceiling, and Pastor Hendricks as Jesse related his fantastic tale. She looked everywhere except at Jesse. The uncomfortable feeling in her chest was growing, and it was hard to concentrate on anything else, even this incredible story.

"I'm really sorry that I was planning on ripping you guys off," Jesse was saying when Calla managed to concentrate on his voice again. "It's nothing personal, believe me. I've been stealing stuff for, oh, years and years. My mom never had any leftover money for us kids to spend on stuff, you know, and my foster parents would never let me have an allowance. And I wanted things like my friends had." He paused and shrugged. "What choice did I have?"

Without waiting for Pastor Hendricks to answer the question, he went on. "I know it was wrong. At least, I do now. I never thought much about it before. But, man, when I saw those guys guarding your building, it really made me think twice, you know? Who were they? I mean, were they . . . real?"

Pastor Hendricks drew a long contemplative breath before he said anything. Jesse played with the ends of his long hair, which hung loosely from his shoulder. He stuck the end of one strand in his mouth and chewed on it nervously as he waited for an answer.

"Young man, we do not, nor have we ever, employed guards to safeguard the church property. In my opinion—that is, what I believe—you saw heavenly angels guarding the church."

"Wow," Jesse breathed, his hands ceasing their purposeless activity. "Angels? Really? I mean, wow."

"It is also my opinion that you struggled with the forces of darkness." At the puzzled look on Jesse's face, he elaborated quickly in layman's terms. "That is, Satan—the devil. There are many stories in the Bible of demon possession. From what you've told me, I think that you were fighting with demons. Tell me, are you involved with the occult or anything of that nature?"

"Occult?" Jesse asked.

"Ouija boards, seances, tarot cards, runes, witchcraft, magic, that kind of thing," Calla supplied. Without realizing it, she'd become so absorbed in his story that she had forgotten why anyone, like Lyle or Aunt Berniece, might have objections to her being there.

Jesse's face lighted up with understanding. "Shoot, yes!" he said enthusiastically. "I've got a couple of friends who are into that sort of thing. I've been playing with it myself the last few years. Mostly just for fun," he assured them.

"I'm afraid Satan doesn't play for fun," Pastor Hendricks replied. "What you are doing when you participate in those sorts of activities is inviting Satan into your heart."

"I don't want to do that!" Jesse cried. He looked anxiously from one to the other. "After the room stopped shaking, I read through half of that Bible you loaned me. I haven't left my apartment or even eaten since that night. I was never so scared in all my life. I don't want anything to do with the dark side, or whatever you called it. I had a foster mother once who told me about Jesus. She said He would help me with any problem. Well, He didn't make her come back after she died, so I never did believe in Him anymore after that. But last night He made whatever it was that attacked me go away.

"I'm not saying that I understand everything I read in that Bible, but it got me to thinking. Maybe Jesus had a good reason for not bringing my foster mother back. If He did, I'd like to know what it was. I guess what I'm saying is that I owe Him one and I'd like to give Him another chance."

Pastor Hendricks swallowed a smile, but not before Calla saw it. She, too, was slightly amused by this unorthodox theology. She had grown up a Christian and wouldn't, in her wildest dreams, think about giving Jesus another "chance" if she felt He let her down. She'd just swallow her bitterness and her questions and go on. In faith. That's what she'd been taught to do. It made her wonder, just a little, if this—for all practical purposes—heathen, who admitted to dabbling in the occult, had a healthier relationship with God than she did.

"Jesse, I would be happy, and honored, to study the Bible with you if that's what you want," Pastor Hendricks said.

"Yeah, I guess, well, that sounds great! You'd do that? How

much does something like that cost? Because I don't have any money, like I said. In fact, I'm going to have to go on down to the mission today for lunch because I . . ." Jesse stopped suddenly and looked sheepish. "Well, I told you already. I didn't steal anything, so I don't have any money. Not that I'm sorry about that," he added quickly. "Anyway, I couldn't pay you right off, but I mean to get a job just as soon as I can."

Pastor Hendricks took out his wallet and pulled out several crisp twenty dollar bills. He handed them to Jesse, who tried to resist taking them. "For food," he insisted. "And whatever else you need."

Jesse reluctantly took the bills and folded them neatly. An embarrassed flush had crept up his neck and stained his cheeks. "I didn't come here for money," he said defensively. "But, thank you just the same." He choked on the emotion that backed up on him, making him blink rapidly to check tears of gratitude.

"I know," Pastor Hendricks said simply. "And you're welcome. Now, when would you like to start studying?" He glanced at the calendar that lay open on his desk. "Are Monday nights OK with you?"

Jesse nodded. "Unless I get a job," he replied, half joking.

Pastor Hendricks penciled the appointment in. "And you, Calla? Are Mondays all right with you?"

"Me?" Calla squeaked. "I, that is, I wouldn't want to intrude . . ."

"I'd really like you to come," Jesse said quietly. "If you hadn't given me your Bible, I might be dead now. And I know it's pretty special to you. That is, unless you don't want to come. If you're busy or something, I'll understand."

"No, no, no," Calla gushed. "Of course I want to come. It's just that, well, Mondays are fine with me," she finished weakly. *What have I done?* her mind shrieked. If she ever thought she had a problem saying No, she was sure of it now.

Lyle was never going to understand this.

"And there's no reason for him to find out," Warg said

smoothly. "After all, it would just upset him. And it isn't as if you're doing something wrong. You act as if helping with a Bible study were illegal, for pity's sake. You're simply doing your Christian duty. There's nothing to feel guilty about."

"Calla, tell them you appreciate being asked, but you're sorry you can't make it," Atli warned. "You are setting yourself up. You are doing this for all the wrong reasons. You have helped as much as you should. Leave the rest to Pastor Hendricks. He is more than capable of conducting the Bible study alone. Jesse may be disappointed for a moment if you don't agree, but he will be more disappointed, and hurt, if you lead him on in this way. It's plain that he is looking to you for moral support. Offer to fill this need by finding a male friend who would go with him to Bible study."

"Oh please!" Warg scoffed. "You'd think he were asking to marry you! All he wants is someone to show they care. And you do care, don't you, Calla? I think you care more than you're willing to admit."

Calla squirmed uncomfortably in her seat as Pastor Hendricks said goodbye to Jesse. She had the impression that there was a small window of opportunity in which to back out. She had to do it now before she lost her nerve. But, then, why should she? She was making a big deal out of nothing. Precisely what she had accused Lyle of doing. Lyle and Aunt Berniece were making her jumpy about the issue, that was all. She was being silly.

She looked up at Jesse and caught his eye. His smile deepened, and she knew she was blushing without even putting her hand on her cheeks and feeling the heat. Now if she could only keep her emotions in check when she was around him, maybe she could actually believe there was nothing wrong with being his friend.

"Bye," Jesse said, peering around Pastor Hendricks. "See you Monday."

"Yeah," Calla replied, ignoring the flip-flopping of her stomach. "See you Monday."

Pastor Hendricks escorted Jesse to the door and then returned to his study. "Now, Calla, I'm sorry about the interruption. What's on your mind?"

Calla looked up at Pastor Hendricks and swallowed. Hard. "Uh, nothing, nothing at all." She shot up from her chair and backed out the still-open study door. "It's not important. It can wait. Really."

"If you're sure," Pastor Hendricks replied cheerfully. "But you know I'm always here to talk. Always. If you ever need anything, you feel free to come and talk to me about it. All right?"

Calla nodded vigorously. "All right. I'll see you later."

Pastor Hendricks began to turn back to his desk and then paused with a puzzled look on his face. "Weren't you going to work on the bulletin board?" he asked.

"Not today," Calla gulped. "Some other time. Later. This week some time. Bye, Pastor Hendricks." Calla pulled the door shut just in time to hear his muffled, if perplexed, "goodbye." She leaned against the door for a minute. Logically, she couldn't see anything truly wrong with what she'd done, but if there wasn't anything wrong with what she'd done, why did she feel so bad?

She took a deep breath and headed out to her car. The entire morning had given her a terrible headache. All she wanted to do was go home and rest.

Billie Jo shuffled out into the kitchen, squinting at the sunshine as it streamed in the big picture windows of the living room. She covered a yawn with the back of her hand and ran her fingers through her tousled hair as she took in the messy

one I have. I only get it out for special occasions. Don't know why I bothered. Might just as well have used it every day. Then at least I'd have gotten some use out of it."

"Don't see what you're getting all worked up about," Jimmy complained. "I can fix it easy enough. A little glue and it will be good as new."

"It will not!" Billie Jo cried. "I won't be able to cook in it. The glue fumes would get into the food. I'll never be able to use it again!"

"Well, you could look at it then," Jimmy exclaimed in frustration.

"I don't want to look at it! I want to use it!" Billie Jo gunned the engine and began to pull away.

"Billie Jo! Stay and settle this issue with Jimmy before you go off," Jewel pleaded. "If you don't resolve it, it will go with you and build into something much worse. Don't give your anger a chance to fester. Stay. Talk to Jimmy. With love you two can straighten this out right now and put it behind you."

"What are you waiting for already?" Nog complained. "You're wasting my time. Get out of here. You can fix this mess when you get back. He'll have had time to cool off and become remorseful, and you can cherish your vengeful, angry feelings for a little while longer. They feel good, don't they? You spend so much time being a goody-goody; doesn't it feel good to get some anger out of your system?"

"Where you going?" Jimmy demanded.

"To the library," Billie Jo replied.

Jimmy grabbed ahold of the window and stubbornly refused to take his hand off. "Why you been spending so much time at the library?" he wanted to know.

"Research," Billie Jo shot back.

"What research? What do you need to do research for? You ain't writing a paper or going to school," Jimmy said.

"Jimmy, let go. I'll be back in an hour," Billie Jo said.

Jimmy reluctantly loosened his grasp on the window. "Fine. Be sure you are, 'cause I got work to do."

Yeah, right, Billie Jo thought as she backed the car up and turned around to head down their long, unpaved driveway. Likely as not when she returned, Jimmy would go down to his workshop and putter around with his tools and chunks of wood. Maybe he'd work on an old piece of furniture he'd salvaged from some dumpster or clean some chisels. One thing would be certain. It wouldn't bring any money in.

And they were hurting.

Billie Jo couldn't count the number of times James had offered to help them out of their financial "slump." She couldn't count them because she had begun to tune him out. It was embarrassing to see him try to slip Jimmy some money. Jimmy never took it, but still, it hurt.

When he'd recovered from the accident, Jimmy hadn't returned to his old job. He'd tried, but the first day on the job he'd returned looking ashen and said he couldn't do it, he just couldn't do it. From then on, he'd taken odd carpentry jobs, remodeling and such. Most of the time he had work, some of it even paid well, but then there'd be a dry spell with no money coming in.

Billie Jo had suggested that she go to work. It was something she hadn't done since before they'd been married. At that, she hadn't worked long and only at the local grocery store bagging groceries and stocking shelves. She wasn't sure she even possessed a marketable skill, but it was better than going hungry.

Little by little their winter stores, those seemingly endless shelves filled with her sparkling jars of canned fruits and vegetables, had disappeared. Now there were a precious few jars holding down those shelves, and soon they would be gone too. And it was another month before the harvesting season got into full swing. Until then, they had to live on the early crops and hope for the best.

"I know hoping ain't what's keeping us going, Lord," Billie Jo muttered as she concentrated on the road and paused for a moment in her thoughts. "It's only by Your grace that we have enough to eat. Why, if You hadn't given us so much out of our garden last year, we'd be starving by now. As it is, we'll just barely make it."

Billie Jo applied the brakes and put on her blinker as she turned slowly into the library parking lot. There weren't too many cars there that time of day. The ones that were there were probably young mothers bringing their children to story hour. Billie Jo kicked herself for not suggesting that Cassidy and Dallas accompany her to the library.

She sighed, knowing that if they had, she could have kissed her research time goodbye. Dallas was at an age when everything that came out of his mouth was prefixed by "why."

"Why did the dinosaurs die?"

"Why do fish live in water?"

"Why did Grandma Raynard shoot her head?"

Billie Jo had the hardest time explaining the last one. Even Jimmy hadn't shed much light on the subject yet. At first, she thought maybe he was protecting his mother by not telling her why she might have done something so positively outrageous, but now she was beginning to suspect that he genuinely did not know why his mother might have wanted to kill herself.

She'd tried talking to James about it one more time, but he had feigned innocence, claiming he didn't know what she was talking about. She could see in his eyes, however, that he knew quite well what she was talking about. She was half-tempted to tell him what she was doing at the library a few days every week in the hopes that maybe it would scare him into telling her, but then she'd never be sure it was the truth.

Billie Jo parked her car and followed her now well-worn route through the building and down the rickety stairs to the library archives. She knew what she would find even before she arrived. Jay, the man who had helped her the first day, would be there.

He was usually sitting at a small desk reading something. The folder for the year she had left off on would be waiting for her at the same table she always occupied. Sometimes, there would even be a glass of water next to it.

Billie Jo had felt uncomfortable at first, accepting kindness from this strange man, until she'd figured out why he was doing it. He worked for the library, she decided. That had to be it. Otherwise, why would a complete stranger be so accommodating and go out of his way to help someone. Besides, if he didn't work for the library, why was he in that basement all the time?

The place gave her the creeps. It was gloomy and stuffy. The air down there tickled her nose and made her want to sneeze. Billie Jo hiked her purse up further onto her shoulder and stepped off the last stair. Her eyes adjusted slowly to the light.

Jay looked up from his book. "Well, hello Mrs. Raynard. How are you today?"

Billie Jo started to reply that she was fine, but something in his expression made her uncomfortable about telling the acceptable white lie. "Hi, Jay," she replied. "Not well, I'm afraid. I've had one humdinger of a morning, let me tell you. I feel just awful."

"I'm sorry to hear that," Jay replied. "Is there anything I can do to help?"

"No." Billie Jo smiled a tight-lipped little smile. "There's nothing anyone can do to help." She wasn't going to say anything further, but as she sank into her usual chair at the table and noticed the glass of water beside the 1944 folder, something inside her broke, and she began weeping.

Jay shot up from the desk and walked over to her. "Mrs. Raynard? Are you OK?"

Billie Jo waved him away, half-laughing, half-crying. "It's so silly, so *stupid*! I shouldn't be crying about this. I'm such a basket case. Why is this bothering me so much?"

Jay pulled a chair over and sat down next to her. "Why don't you tell me what happened. Maybe I can help."

Billie Jo drew a ragged breath. "Oh, it's nothing really. Just something stupid, like I guess all fights are in the beginning. My husband, Jimmy, broke my best pot this morning." She laughed recklessly. "See? Something mighty upsettin', ain't it?"

"Obviously it is," Jay observed.

"It's just that it was my best one, see? It cost a fortune. Not to us," she hastened to add. "If you bought it at a store, that is. Jimmy found it at a lawn sale last year. I only used it for special things. I . . . I took it down to make our favorite dish for our anniversary last night, and before I could get it put back, Jimmy broke it."

"You can always replace the pot," Jay assured her.

"No I can't," Billie Jo said. "That's just it. I maybe could if I found one of those fancy kitchen stores, but we could never afford that."

"God provided the first one, maybe He'll provide another one to take its place," Jay suggested.

Billie Jo glanced sideways at him to see if he were making fun of her. "I'd like to believe that," she agreed, "but that pot was a one-of-a-kind find. Jimmy will never find another one like it. I ain't never even seen another one like it. I ain't saying it *can't* happen," she said. "Just that it ain't likely in my lifetime. And Jimmy wasn't even sorry. That's what hurt even more than losing the pot."

"You know," Jay said slowly, "men are not famous for being overly sentimental. God made men and women to complement each other. I'm sure that if your husband knew how much that pot meant to you, he would have shown you more compassion."

Billie Jo squinted at Jay. "You sure know an awful lot about God. Are you a Christian?" Suddenly she was overcome with embarrassment. "I'm sorry. I don't mean to pry or nothing, it's just that you don't talk like anybody I know."

Jay smiled gently. "How's that?"

"Well, the way you talk about God, natural, like you knew Him personally or something. I mean, I pray and all, but when you talk, I feel like He might just wander on down here and ask where they keep the Dead Sea Scrolls or something!" Billie Jo laughed at her own joke.

"God is here," Jay insisted. "Don't you think so? Oh, He's not looking for scrolls or anything like that, but He's here just the same."

"Yeah, I guess so," Billie Jo replied. "I know for sure He's helped me out of some real tough spots, and I trust Him more than anything, but I can't say as I cozy up to Him all the time. Seems most like I talk to Him when something's going bad. Not that I don't believe He's there other times; I just don't seem to talk to Him as much when I don't need Him."

"I'm sure that makes Him sad, Mrs. Raynard," Jay replied, and for an instant Billie Jo thought the man might actually cry. She could feel his sadness penetrate her own heart, and she wondered if he was right. Did God miss her when she ignored Him? It wasn't like she meant to, but it was awful hard finding time to spend with God and get everything else accomplished that she needed to do too.

Besides, Jimmy had been real religious after the accident, but within a year he'd gone back to his old ways. Oh, he went with them to church, usually, but slowly family worship had slipped away, and he almost never prayed with her before he left the house anymore. Mostly his religion consisted of "Bless this food we are about to eat. May it nourish and strengthen our bodies. Amen."

Right after the accident, Jimmy had taken to reading his Bible. He said it comforted him. Lately, Billie Jo couldn't remember the last time he'd picked it up. It sat on his bedside stand collecting dust. She'd asked him about it once and received some vague reply. She hadn't asked again.

It wasn't as if Jimmy stopped her from practicing her religion or even gave her a hard time about it, but it was like fighting an uphill battle without him walking by her side. If she wanted to have family worship, *she* had to instigate it. If she wanted to read a couples devotional with him, *she* had to bring it up. And on the mornings when they went to church, she was the one prodding them all to get out of the door so they wouldn't be more than a half hour late.

It was tiring, and now Billie Jo wondered if maybe it hadn't worn the edge off her own faith. It seemed as if she'd gotten too tired to push anymore, and so she'd just let everything slide. She still considered herself a Christian, and she still prayed and relied on God, but as far as seeing any practical evidence of Him in her life, she couldn't point to one thing.

"That's right," Nog agreed. *"It's too hard to try to please God. Isn't it much easier this way? What a relief, huh? Not to carry that burden with you? Forget about it. Who needs it."*

Afterward, Billie Jo couldn't have said what made her think of it, but suddenly she remembered the mother's group she used to belong to with her friend Leah. They had begun meeting at the home of an elderly woman. She'd had an absolutely massive house. It was wonderful going there. She'd always felt like royalty going in that house. And the other women were really nice.

At that moment, she couldn't remember why she'd stopped going. Maybe one of the kids had gotten sick and she'd missed a meeting. Maybe she'd stopped when she had to drive Jimmy to physical therapy. It had been hectic for a while. She just couldn't remember. She wondered if they were still meeting and decided to find out.

"I really enjoy getting together with my friends and praising the Master," Jay was saying.

Billie Jo glanced at him. His face was positively glowing. "Yeah," she murmured absently. "I used to enjoy that too."

Jay pushed his chair back and stood up. "You should have stopped me. I've been keeping you from your research."

"No, no," Billie Jo protested. "Thank you for talking to me. I feel much better now."

Jay smiled. "I'm glad. You let me know if you need anything else."

"I will," Billie Jo promised.

When she finally looked up from the last page of the last newspaper of 1944 a little bleary-eyed, Jay was gone. She couldn't remember hearing him leave, but then she'd been pretty absorbed. Every time she turned a page, she felt as though she was getting closer and closer to finding out the deep, dark secret of Helen's past.

Billie Jo replaced the folder, collected her purse, and headed up the stairs. She glanced at her watch. She'd been gone for a little over an hour. She quickened her steps. Jimmy would be having a fit soon.

On the way home, she noticed a "Garage Sale" sign. Impulsively, she pulled into the driveway. Jimmy was going to be upset anyway, she decided; why not have some fun before she got back? She hopped out and began to peruse the tables full mostly of junk. Just as she was about to turn back to her car, she noticed a familiar looking handle.

With a glad shout, she flung some clothes off the table and uncovered a pot very similar to the one Jimmy had broken. The only difference was that this one was slightly larger than the one she had. And that was the only thing she had wished she could change about the other one. With a family of four, it had been hard to find a recipe small enough to fit into the pot.

Billie Jo didn't realize she was crying until the old lady who was running the garage sale spoke to her. "Honey? What's wrong? Why are you crying? Did you hurt yourself?"

"God loves me," Billie Jo bawled. "He really loves me."

"Of course He does, honey. Didn't you know that?"

Billie Jo smiled through her tears. "I reckon I'd forgotten. How much for this pot?"

"Fifty cents," the old woman replied with a steel glint in her eye. "And I won't take a penny less."

Billie Jo fished two quarters out of her purse and handed them to the old woman. "Thank you," she said before returning to her car.

When she returned home, she found that Jimmy had pulled out the plastic pool from underneath the back porch and filled it with water. Cassidy and Dallas were chasing each other around in it, splashing water in all directions. Jimmy lounged at a safe distance in a dilapidated lawn chair that threatened to collapse beneath his weight.

When he heard the car, he got up, placing the newspaper he'd been looking at on the seat of the chair. Walking over to the car, his arms wrapped around her as soon as she stepped out of the car. "I'm sorry, darlin'," he said. "I didn't know that old pot meant so much to you. And you didn't even ask after my foot. It really hurt."

"I'm sorry, too," Billie Jo breathed into the fabric of his shirt. "Look what I found on the way home." She produced the pot from behind her back, and Jimmy stared at it dumbfounded.

"Where?" he asked.

"God found it," she said simply. "At a garage sale. For fifty cents."

Laughing, they hugged each other again.

CHAPTER

Davy was working in the garden when he heard the truck pull up to the front of the duplex—a big truck, by the sound of it. Brushing dirt off his knees, he walked around to the front of the house and stared in amazement at the huge moving truck emblazoned with the slogan "College Guys Moving Service—We Move U." Two burly guys in T-shirts and cutoffs threw open the large back doors and began hauling boxes out and carrying them into the apartment adjacent to his.

"Party's over," Davy muttered to himself. While he watched a long, white New Yorker pulled up and parked in front of the moving truck. A tall, thin black boy jumped out of the front passenger side and ran back to the moving truck. A tiny little black girl Davy judged to be no more than four or five climbed out of the back seat and stood sucking her thumb while she watched the commotion.

A woman who looked neither black nor white struggled to get out of the driver's side. She rocked from side to side as she made her way around the car and as soon as she came clearly into view, Davy could see why. She was pregnant. Very pregnant.

Masses of long, black hair were done up in tiny little braids and held out of her face by one of those bright red clips that always reminded Davy of a clam shell with teeth. Even though her hair was pulled back, a thin layer of sweat glistened on her face. She was not overly tall. In fact, compared to most of the women he knew she would be short. And her protruding belly only emphasized her lack of height. She had to be really uncomfortable carrying that burden in this heat, Davy reflected.

Before Davy worked up the nerve to walk over and introduce himself, a bright red sports car zipped into the space just ahead of the New Yorker. Deniece practically flew out of the car, squealing like a bad brake job. As soon as the woman saw her, she began an identical squeal and they flew at each other. Before he knew it, they were laughing and crying at the same time and then both of them tried to talk at once.

"Girlfriend!" Deniece said, "I've missed you so much. We've got so much to talk about. Where are your beautiful babies? Show me, show me!"

The woman put her arm around the tiny girl and drew her close. "This is Madina. Marcus? Come here a minute." The boy ambled over, but hung back shyly. "This is Marcus. Marcus, say hello to my friend Deniece."

"Hello," Marcus said obligingly, but he didn't approach her and he didn't smile.

"Hello kids," Deniece said with a big grin. "I'm your Aunty Deniece. We're going to have lots of fun."

Marcus wandered back over to watch the movers, but Madina sidled up to Deniece, grabbed one of her hands and popped her thumb out of her mouth long enough to give Deniece a fetching smile. The girl's mother turned to retrieve something out of the trunk and at that moment Deniece caught sight of Davy.

"Davy, man, what are you doing over there?"

"I live here, remember?" Davy pointed out.

"Here?" Deniece looked puzzled for a moment. "Get out! Do you really? I guess I had forgotten. Hey, you two will be neighbors. Come on over here and meet your new neighbor, Davy. This here is my best friend in the whole world. Shay Beauregard. Whoops! I mean Shay Okeke."

The woman winced when Deniece said her last name. She stuck out her hand. "Guess I'm your new landlord," she said. "It's nice to meet you."

"Likewise," Davy replied, shaking her hand. "Did you buy this place?"

"Inherited it," Shay replied quietly. "My dad left it to me in his will."

Deniece put her arm around Shay's shoulder and gave Davy a threatening look. "Girlfriend, you could have stayed at his house, you know. It's much bigger."

Shay shook her head. "Too many memories. Besides, Dad always thought of me living here. Now I will."

"I'm sorry about your father," Davy said. "I didn't realize he had passed away. Is there any way I can help?"

"Yeah, you can carry that for her. Where are your manners, boy?" Deniece chided him. "The woman's with child. She shouldn't be carrying heavy objects."

Davy took the suitcase from Shay's hands. She let it go without protesting and meekly followed her vibrant friend up the walkway to the apartment. Madina skipped alongside Deniece, looking up at her every once in awhile, her eyes crinkling when she smiled.

Davy offered Shay his free arm, but she declined. "I'm not that pregnant," she protested. "Not yet. I've got a long ways to go."

"Girl, you look like you could pop any second," Deniece observed candidly.

"Yeah, well, I only wish. I'm afraid it's going to be a long uncomfortable summer. I thought I was over the worst part when I stopped throwing up. Little did I know that the fun was only beginning."

Davy shifted uncomfortably at all the unpleasant girl talk. He looked around for a likely place to set the suitcase, but there were boxes piled up everywhere. "Uh, where would you like this, uh, Shay was it?"

Shay smiled. "You can call me Shay. You can call me Mrs. Okeke. You can even call me Mrs. Landlord. Anything. Just as long as you don't call me Madame Shay. Because if you do, I will burst into tears."

"I, uh, I'll try to remember that," Davy promised.

"You can just set it down anywhere. It's going to take me forever to get this place in order and until then I won't be able to find anything anyhow." She surveyed the room with a look bordering on desperation. "I don't know what possessed me, but I took a bunch of the stuff out of storage that my father left for me. I'll probably regret it. I'm not sure what's in half of these boxes."

"Well, we'll find out," Deniece promised. "I'm not leaving here tonight until everything is just the way you want it."

"Oh yes, you are," Shay argued. "It will take at least a week just to unpack all these boxes, forget about putting everything where it's supposed to go."

"Want to bet?" Deniece challenged. "I say it's done before eleven o'clock. Davy, start with that one."

In the end, Deniece was right. Although Davy seriously doubted that she would have won her bet if she hadn't pressed him, Marcus, and eventually the two moving guys into service. Before he'd left that night for his own apartment where he fell into the sleep of the terminally exhausted, they had unpacked every box, hung the shower curtain, and fixed a pick-up, albeit surprisingly delicious, supper.

He expected Deniece to stop by and see him the next day at work and he hadn't been disappointed. She showed up talking on her cell phone as she walked up to his teller window. She snapped it shut with one quick flick of her wrist.

"Davy! Thanks so much for all your help last night. Shay just got back in the country, you know? I couldn't let her do all that unpacking alone, especially in her condition."

"No problem," Davy replied. "I was happy to help. That's too bad about her father."

Deniece rolled her eyes. "That's not the half of it. First it was her father and then her husband. They hadn't even been married that long. Some sort of virus hit that mission she was at. Wiped out practically everyone. If it hadn't been for her father dying she might have caught it too."

"Wait a minute," Davy said, his eyes lighting up. "Is this the friend you were telling me about that night we went to the football game?"

"The very same one," Deniece agreed. "I'm so happy to have her home. I wish it could be under better circumstances though." Deniece leaned across the counter and put her face close to his. Davy was distinctly aware of the fragrance of her perfume.

"Davy, would you do me a favor?"

He shrugged. "Sure."

"Would you watch out for her? I mean, she's all alone with those hree kids. Well, two and one on the way. I'm worried about her. She's gone through so much lately. I don't know how she's going to cope. Just keep any eye out for her. Be helpful." She smiled coyly at him. "I know you're good at that."

"It just so happens that they gave me an A for helpfulness in school and I play well with others too," Davy replied sarcastically.

Deniece straightened up. "Oh, don't get snotty on me. Will you do it?"

"Yes," Davy agreed. "I'll do it.

"Thanks Davy, you're a real pal," Deniece said. She turned to leave and had dialed another number before she even made it to the door.

"Yeah, Davy, you're a real pal," a voice behind him mimicked.

Davy jumped in surprise and turned to face Laurie. "Does she ever stop using you?" Laurie whined.

"What do you mean? She's not using me," Davy protested.

"Like a cheap towel," Laurie retorted. "She sure is. Davy, help my friend unpack. Davy, watch out for my friend. What's she going to want next? Davy, deliver my friend's baby."

Davy laughed at the mental picture that evoked and he was suddenly struck by a memory. In his mind's eye, he could see Toby sitting on the side of his bed after the accident saying something about how he always fainted at the sight of blood and how she wished he'd get better quick so they could go home. "I hardly think so," he replied absently. "I'm no good around blood."

"How do you know?" Laurie snapped.

"I remember," Davy said simply, a smile of wonderment on his face.

Laurie stared at him in amazement. "You remember? You mean, like, everything?"

"Not yet," Davy replied with an edge of conviction in his voice that he hadn't used in years, "but it's coming back. It *will* come back."

That evening, as he walked out to his car, he noticed a white paper held onto his windshield by one of the wipers. He groaned at the all too familiar site. He could have sworn he had put enough money in the meter, but there it was. Another parking ticket.

Leaning over the car he pulled out the paper and was about to put it in his pocket when he noticed that it wasn't a parking ticket at all. It was a piece of paper folded in half. He opened it expecting to see some crackpot joke about his parking skills, but instead he read, "The Power of Prayer - 10 Reasons To Pray" in big bold letters. Underneath that was a lot of small writing.

"Ha!" Belial yelped. "Someone is out to get you. First the radio station, now this. Looks like a conspiracy to me. Throw it away. Stupid religious fanatics only want to get you hooked into their church so they can get all your money. It's spiritual

propaganda. They don't really care about you. And God doesn't love you. If He did, would you need a little piece of paper to tell you? No, He'd show you, that's what He'd do. Pitch it."

"Davy," Jes interjected calmly. *"You've started searching for answers. Here is one way to start. At least read what it has to say and then make up your own mind. Don't dismiss this, Davy. You asked for God's help and He's trying to help you. Don't turn away from Him."*

Davy crumpled the paper up and stuffed it into his pocket. Who would have put something like that on his car? Glancing around the parking lot he noticed little white papers fluttering from many of the windshields. He let out a relieved breath, glad to see that it wasn't personal.

"What's this?" he heard Laurie exclaim as she ripped a paper off her own car.

He hopped into his car, not bothering to answer her. As he drove along Route 66 toward home, he couldn't get his mind off the wadded up paper in his pocket or overcome the urge to read it. What harm could it do?

"What harm?" shrieked Belial. *"It could mess up lots of things for me. You don't need to read it. Religious propaganda. It's worthless."*

"Davy, it's been a long time since you have spoken with the Master," Jes said. *"I probably remember it more clearly than you do. But, Davy, He misses you. He's given you this opportunity to come closer to Him. Don't reject it. You thought your life was full before the accident, but what you couldn't see, what you were too busy to see, was that it was full of worldly things that were dragging you down to death like cement boots. Look ahead, Davy! The Master is waiting for you. He's been waiting patiently ever since you left Him."*

"Waiting patiently, ha!" Belial snorted. *"Like a vulture. Like a trap. Like a slave driver. He doesn't want you to have any fun, Davy. You'd be stupid to talk to Him. He doesn't approve of all your wicked ways. He'd turn you into a self-righteous hypo-crite like all those church going folks. Don't do it," he warned ominously.*

"When you were trying to remember, Davy, and you called out to Him; He answered you. Let Him give you more answers," Jes implored.

Davy swerved his car over to the side of the road making the guy behind him honk in annoyance. Panting, he sat there while the engine idled. He wiped one hand across the back of his fore-head. It felt as if he were burning up. His heart was racing and he wondered if this was what people called a panic attack. The knuckles on the fingers that gripped the steering wheel were pure white and his hands felt clammy.

"Calm down, Davy boy," he muttered to himself. "It's prob-ably stress." But, he knew it wasn't stress. Something was hap-pening to him, but he didn't know what it was. It was like a war inside. He wanted to beat on his chest and make his heart stop skidding around. He wanted to bang his head against the steer-ing wheel and make his thoughts stop.

He wanted peace.

Before he even realized it, his hand crept into his pocket and he pulled out the piece of paper and began reading. As he read, he remembered.

He remembered things about his childhood that hadn't come back to him since the accident. He remembered things about Toby that he hadn't been able to recall before. But, most of all he remembered, how involved he used to be with his church, par-ticularly with the youth group. When he got his pilot's li-cense, he'd had a dream to go to Africa and become a bush pilot for some mission.

Later, after he'd married Toby and his attention had shifted to the business of making money, his church attendance had slacked off. Then the dream had mutated. He still wanted to go to Africa and be a bush pilot, but in this dream they would just be philanthropic do-gooders, wealthy enough to champion lost causes out of the goodness of their hearts.

It was odd, really, how they had stopped going to church. They'd both been brought up by godly parents and had gone to church as long as either of them could remember. But, there had been something perfunctory about their experience, at least, that was all Davy could attribute it to. He knew he'd never felt particularly close to God, though he did have fun with his church friends. He didn't remember Toby ever spending any quality time with God either. If she had missed going to church, she had never mentioned it to him.

Looking back, he could see how easy it was for them to slip out, unnoticed. Not one person from the church had ever called or stopped by to see them and invite them back and so they hadn't returned. Oh, they went to church for the customary occasions, like Christmas and Easter, but it hadn't been to find God there. It had been more out of a sense of duty or because it was expected of them.

Davy leaned his head back against the headrest as the car shuddered with the drag produced as a car whizzed past him. He wondered about God. What was He like? What did He get out of helping people? Why did He care? The words on the piece of paper caught his eye: The Power of Prayer.

What power?

He decided to find out. Hesitantly, he closed his eyes. "God," he prayed awkwardly, "I really don't know that much about prayer, but it says here that there's power in it. If that's true then I'd like to see some, please. I don't know how, but I need to find out where my wife is. That is, I mean, my ex-wife. I think I still love her, at least I love what I remember of her and I want to see if she'll give me a second chance. So, if you can do something about that, God, I'd really appreciate it. Uh, thank you."

Davy opened his eyes, half expecting to see a large road sign appear saying "Toby: 420 Miles," but nothing happened. Sighing with disappointment, he wadded the piece of paper up and tossed it onto the floor of his car. Flicking on his blinker, he pulled back onto the main road his mind already on what he would fix for supper.

Jes didn't wait for Davy to finish praying. She went immediately to Shay's. She found her sitting morosely on the living room couch. Madina had curled up on a beanbag and was sound asleep. Marcus was off with some new friends. Shay stared into space, her eyes blank.

"Shay! Wake up!" Jes urged. "The Master needs you. There is work to be done."

"I hate it when you do that," Don grumbled.

Toby put an extra fluff into his pillow before plunking it down behind him and giving him a little push to settle him back onto them. "What? You hate it that I want to make sure you're comfortable?"

"I don't like people fussing over me all the time," he griped. "They make me feel like an invalid."

"You just ought to be thankful you're around to not appreciate any of it," Toby said sternly. "If you had any idea how close we came to losing you . . ." She stopped, unable to speak past the lump in her throat.

"I don't remember any of it," Don said. "It actually seems like some kind of really bad dream." He patted the cot beside him. "Come. Sit. Tell me about the mission. What's going on? How are you all managing without me?"

Toby sank down to the side of his bed and took his large hand in her own. She traced patterns on the top of his hand as she talked. Although she tried to sound cheerful, she knew she would never fool him. "Fine, fine, just fine. Even with Shay gone, we've got plenty of manpower. Yesterday, Julia and I flew out to the clinic to see how things were going." Toby squirmed under Don's intense stare.

"How were things?" he asked.

She hesitated. "You know," she said, hopping up. "You're really not strong enough to be worrying about all of this stuff. Why don't we talk about it some other time, when you're feeling better."

"I am feeling better," Don growled. "Just what is it that you don't want to tell me? I know you're hiding something. Now out with it. What's wrong?"

Toby sighed and sat down on the bed again. "Well, you've been sick a long time, Don, and things just kind of fell apart. People are afraid to come here because of the outbreak and some villagers destroyed the outpost clinic."

"THEY WHAT?!" Don roared. "How could they? The ingrates!"

Toby threw up her hands to silence him. "Now, just hold on. You don't understand. They're afraid of us now. They're afraid maybe we caused the outbreak."

"Us?" Don said incredulously, but his voice lost much of its fight. "Preposterous."

"Not really," Toby countered. "We didn't start it maybe, but we are responsible for spreading it to a certain extent."

"We don't even know how it started," Don protested.

"I think we do," Toby replied quietly.

"What do you mean?"

"I spent a lot of time thinking about it when you were sick. Do you remember those men who stopped at the clinic just before the outbreak? They were English? The one we spoke with said he was a doctor and one of his friends needed a shot of penicillin?"

"So? He was sick. That doesn't prove that he had Marburg."

"No," Toby agreed. "But, do you remember when one of the

kids got too close to their Rover and upset the monkeys? That guy said the monkeys were for lunch."

"Oh, for Pete's sake! He was kidding you!"

"Was he?" Toby quipped. "You know as well as I do that it isn't uncommon for people to eat monkey in this country."

"Yeah, but . . ." Don's voice was deflated.

"But, nothing. I think they caught an infected monkey and they ate the meat. They got infected by the blood of the monkey. I also remember Shay telling Nwibe to get a vaccine that day and then later you said she found Flory using the same needle for every patient. She must have given the Englishman with Marburg a shot and injected Nwibe and countless others with the same needle." She shrugged her shoulders. "It makes perfect sense to me. I only wish I knew what happened to those guys."

"So, where does that leave us?" Don asked.

"I don't honestly know," Toby replied. "We have a clinic, but no patients. I guess we could sit around and wait to see what happens. Or . . ."

Don finished the sentence for her. "Or we could quit."

"I don't like that prospect, but what can we do? Sit around here waiting for people to lose their fear of us? We have no idea how long that will take. C.A.R.E. isn't going to finance us to be on vacation here."

"No," Don mused. "No, they're not." He fixed his gray eyes on her and she squirmed beneath his stare. "I wish I could help you, but I can't."

"Don't worry about that," she replied, laying her hand on top of his. "You just concentrate on getting better. Hopefully you'll have a clinic to work in once you do."

"I guess we don't have to worry about getting replacements just yet," Don stated.

"No, and it's a good thing, because Dorsey said we can't have any."

Guardians

Don shook his head. "I should have known that. So, tell me something. When I get better, are you going to marry me?"

Toby gasped. "My, aren't we tactful." She cuffed him playfully on the shoulder. "Haven't you ever heard of a little thing called romance?"

"If I learned one thing from nearly dying it's that I don't have time to waste. I need to get on with the business of living. Romance takes time."

"Well," Toby huffed. "There are a few things a girl likes and romance happens to be one of them. So what if it takes . . ."

But, she never finished her sentence. Don's grip on her hand tightened and he pulled her down against his chest, kissing her fiercely. She felt herself go limp and when he released her, she pulled away and grinned at him, dazed. "I'll settle for that," she laughed breathlessly.

"Just look at them," Lucien complained. "Love makes my skin crawl." He ran his gnarled fingers up and down the flaccid skin on his forearms as if to prove his point. His eyes narrowed as he studied Toby and Don talking in soft tones about their rosy future together.

"You!" he shouted, slapping Festus who happened to be standing nearby. "What are you doing? Or, more to the point, what are you not doing? Are you slacking off again? I gave you explicit orders. Why aren't you with your charges?"

"I was, I was," Festus whimpered, cradling his head in his hands. "I've been with them all day. I manufactured a dust storm this morning when they drove back from Niamey with supplies. I hoped they might get lost, but they didn't. And then I provoked them into fighting over something trivial and they haven't spoken a word to each other since. I've been telling them each how worthless and miserable they are all day. The girl is in her room crying. She wants very much to leave. She misses her little girl and her father and her friends. The man is banging around the clinic scrubbing things that have already

been scrubbed." Festus rubbed his hands together gleefully. "He is very angry."

"Hrmphh," Lucien grunted. He had greatly hoped to find fault with Festus so that he could slap him around some more. He backed off and took another tack. "You have done well. So well, in fact that I have another job for you."

"Really?" Festus simpered, scrambling onto his feet. "What? What?"

Merck watched the exchange from a distance with an amused look on his face and Lucien wished mightily to smack him around as well. With great difficulty, he ignored Merck and wrapped one long, bony arm around Festus' shoulder. "There is one outpost clinic left. They haven't checked it yet, but I expect them to do so in another day or two. When they do I don't want it to be standing. Arrange for it to be robbed and burned to the ground. I want it gone. Take care of it."

"I'll be happy to," Festus exclaimed eagerly.

"Then do it," Lucien replied. "NOW!"

Festus scampered away, limp black wings flapping lifelessly behind him. Lucien turned his complete attention on Merck. "What is so almighty funny?" he demanded.

Merck raised one cool eyebrow. "Nothing. Nothing at all."

Lucien sauntered up to the other demon. "You find me amusing, yes?"

Merck backed away slightly, not enough to make Lucien believe that Merck was afraid of him, but enough to acknowledge Lucien's superiority in the demonic pecking order. "I find you amusing," he repeated, casting his eyes down.

"And you find me intimidating," Lucien gloated.

"Well, yes, you are so masterful, so proud, so brilliant," Merck responded, unable to keep the chuckle out of his voice.

"YOU MOCK ME!" Lucien screamed, leaping towards Merck, his outstretched hands ready to strangle the other's throat.

"What is going on here?" a voice demanded.

Lucien stopped before he had taken more than two steps. That voice. That was the voice that came to him in lonely hours when he wished with all his might to get out of this wretched dustbowl. That voice was the only one that could offer him a promotion, toast his success, and send him on his way. Lucien turned slowly to face Sparn.

Since his defeat some years previous by the old prayer warrior, he was only a shadow of what he once had been. His rule at the mission was a mere charade. Lucien, however, felt it necessary to patronize his leader. Even since Sparn's shameful loss, Lucien had been scheming up ways to get promoted away from the mission. It would not further that cause to rile Sparn now.

"A matter of a disagreement," he said smoothly. "Nothing important." Merck lifted his head in acquiesce as Lucien glared in his direction, daring him to disagree.

Sparn seemed distracted. "I think there has been an improvement in our status," he said, taking Lucien's arm and steering him a short distance from Merck. "Are there fewer angels? Or is it my old mind playing tricks on me?"

Lucien swallowed his disgust. "Yes, sir. I engineered an epidemic that thinned out the defenses of the humans. There are few left and the people are scared to return for medical care because the stink of the plague surrounds this place." He strove valiantly to hide his pride. "I believe, sir, that it is only a matter of time, a short time, before they close this mission down."

"Amazing," Sparn breathed. A new light began to flicker behind his eyes. "I can't imagine what I did to cause this. I thought all was lost."

Lucien felt a panic begin to well up in his chest threatening to explode from him. "Well, sir," he said politely. "As I said, I engineered a plague. It killed many people. It drove scores away from this place."

"Yes, yes, I see," Sparn said absently. Lucien could tell that his role in the impending victory had still not become clear to Sparn.

"I was very happy to help," he elaborated, emphasizing his instigation of the events. "You have no idea how hard I worked, how long I schemed to come up with such a perfect plan. But, I really think I outdid myself with this one. Why, it borders on sheer genius."

He cleared his throat, convinced that he had gotten his point across. "Do you have any plans? For when we move on from here, I mean?

Sparn blinked at him for a full minute before he spoke. "Leave?" he asked in bewilderment. "Why on earth would we leave? We've done such a great job."

Lucien gaped at him. "Why, well, that is, no one will be left. It's only a matter of time. They will all be gone. There will be no one here to bother any more."

Sparn clenched one fist and held it over his head. "Then we will move with them. We will hound them to the very ends of the earth. We will never rest until they have been crushed into the very dust."

Lucien cringed at the word dust. He'd seen enough dust to last him until eternity. "But, sir, I was hoping that maybe I could be sent to High Command? This strategy was such a success and I would very much like to plan others as well. I could be of much more use to you and to our leader's cause if I were relieved of my duties here and free to plot their demise without any distractions."

"Nonsense," Sparn bellowed as he slapped Lucien on the back. A cloud of dust lifted off Lucien's cloak and he coughed with the force of Sparn's attention. "You will go wherever I go. We make a magnificent team. Now, I must make a trip to the States. I think I may be instrumental in ridding us of the last vestiges of that irksome prayer warrior. I sense that her time is very near. I leave you in charge until I return."

"But," simpered Lucien. He never had the opportunity to finish his protest. In the next instant, Sparn was gone, leaving Lucien to curse the space where he had so recently stood. He turned back to Don and Toby only to find them studying a couples devotional book. "Great," he muttered to himself. "Just great."

Cindi pulled open the kitchen door at Ethel's house with an oven mitt on one hand and Esther wrapped around her leg. She greeted her visitor, one of the women from the women's prayer group, and attempted to make her way into the kitchen to check on some banana bread she'd put in the oven as refreshments for the group which was meeting that morning.

"Hello, Leah. Esther, let go. You're too old for that," she said in the same breath. She tried to give Leah an apologetic smile and Esther a warning look, but she just ended up looking frustrated.

"Hi, Cindi, how are y'all doing? Busy, I see," Leah said, side-stepping around Esther's prostrate form as Cindi tried to drag her limp body towards the kitchen.

"Esther, I'm not going to tell you again," Cindi warned. "Now, let go. I have to get the bread out of the oven before it burns. Esther! Now, or you're going to get a spanking."

"Don't let go," Rafe commanded the child. He grinned with satisfaction as Esther dug her tiny hands into the fabric of Cindi's jeans and hung on with determination.

"Noooooo," she squealed.

Cindi bent down and lifted her bodily into the air, grunting at Esther's weight. She turned the child swiftly over her knee and smacked her bottom a few times with the wooden spoon she grabbed off the counter, glancing a little guiltily at Leah. Leah's children gaped at her open-mouthed and looked pityingly at Esther.

Esther began immediately to wail and thrash around. "Ow, ow, you hurted me!" she shrieked. "Not so hard!"

Cindi grabbed Esther's hand and yanked her over to a kitchen chair propelling her up onto it. "You sit right here in time-out until you're sorry for disobeying," she said sternly.

Esther glared up at her.

"Uh, Cindi?" Leah ventured, watching the ongoing scene with discomfort.

Cindi looked up, ready to defend her parenting techniques. "What?" she asked.

"I do believe whatever is in that there oven is likely to start a fire soon," Leah pointed to a thin column of smoke rising up from the front of the oven.

With a cry of anger, Cindi leapt across the room and ripped the door open. A black crust covered the entire top of the banana bread. She reached in to pull it out with the hand not gloved in the oven mitt before she realized what she was doing and yanked her hand back with a yelp of pain. Finally, she managed to extricate what was left of the banana bread from the oven before collapsing to the floor and bursting into tears.

Leah shooed her children into the adjoining room and sat down next to Cindi, putting her arm around the latter's shoulders and uttering soothing sounds like you might offer a child who had been hurt. Cindi rocked back and forth cradling her burnt hand and crying like a baby.

"Go get your mama a bowl of cold water," Leah instructed Esther. Wide-eyed with fear, the girl immediately hopped off the chair and did as she'd been asked.

"Here, Cindi, put your hand in here. It'll stop the burning." She guided Cindi's hand into the bowl of water and patted it gently. "Now, now, it's just a bad day, that's all. We all have them now and again." She looked up at Esther. "Thank you, child. Now, go in the other room and play with my kids. Go on."

"What is wrong with me?" Cindi moaned. "I can't do anything right."

"That's for sure," Rafe agreed wholeheartedly. "I don't know why you even try. It's too much trouble to keep having this group over and you never get so much as a thank-you for doing it. Forget them! Let them meet at someone else's house for a change. See how they like it then."

"Cindi, listen," Shania begged. "Don't let Satan discourage you. He wouldn't be after you if you weren't doing something important. If what you were doing made no difference he'd leave you alone. Don't give up."

Cindi took a shuddering breath. "I don't know why I put myself through this," she said slowly. "I want to think I'm doing some good, but then sometimes I wonder." She glanced darkly at the closed door. "It's probably just you and me today. It doesn't look like anyone else will show up. I . . . I think we ought to just cancel the meetings."

Leah sat back and scrutinized Cindi until she began to feel uncomfortable. "Are you certain that's what you want?" she asked. "Seems to me that you're getting mighty discouraged by one little incident."

"It's not one little incident," Cindi protested. "Last time, Mary Lou brought Jonathon with her and he gave Esther his cold. She was sick for two weeks and miserable too. The time before that, Meg's kids knocked over Ethel's vase, the one that cost $2,000. I felt like it was my fault. And the time before *that*, Mary Lou and Meg disagreed so strongly about a point of doctrine that I thought they'd never make up. And as you can see, neither one of them is here today. Is it really worth it?"

"That all depends," Leah replied, "on what you're trying to do here."

Cindi sniffed. "What do you mean? What I'm trying to do? All

I've ever wanted was to provide a place where mothers could get together and support each other and share Christ while their children played."

Leah laughed. "No place where mothers and children get together is going to be quiet. And truth is that children get sick. A lot. And they pass it on to other kids. That's just the way it is. And sometimes they break stuff. It just happens."

Cindi buried her face in her hands. "It's not just that. It's everything."

"What everything?" Leah coaxed. Before Cindi could answer there was a tentative knock on the door.

"Would you get that?" Cindi pleaded.

Leah nodded and stood up to answer the door. "Hi, Billie Jo!" Cindi heard her exclaim. "Come on in. We missed y'all lately. Where you been keeping yourself?"

Cindi scrambled up, clutching the bowl of water and hastily wiping her tears away. "Hi, Billie Jo," she murmured. She managed a faint smile. "I'm having a bit of a rough day."

Billie Jo bit her lip. "Me too. Guess we're all in kind of the same boat."

"Let's go into the living room," Cindi suggested. The three of them, with Billie Jo's kids following along behind, moved into the small living space attached to the spacious kitchen area. Considered more the servant's eating quarters, it had served as the main living space since most of the house had been closed off after Ethel's husband's death.

"Made it easier on me," Ethel had told Cindi. "I was getting too old to have to clean this big old house. I hope someday, when I've passed on, someone will be able to do wonderful things with it. I rather hope they'll make it into an orphanage or some such thing. It's really too big for one family."

As Cindi seated herself on the couch she looked up hesitantly at Leah and Billie Jo. Of the two, Leah's face wore the most serene expression. She laughed a little as she glanced from one to the other.

"Now, if you two don't beat all with those hang-dog expressions. I know things are tough on you both. I can't see anything else on your faces except that. But you know what? My God's bigger than y'all's problems. Come on."

She took one of Cindi's hands and one of Billie Jo's hands and sank down to her knees on the floor, tugging them along with her. Even the children grew quiet while she closed her eyes and began to pray. "Oh, Lord," she sighed deeply, as if in that breath of air passing through her lips she could expel all the negative things inside and blow all their problems right out the room. "We got a lot of burdens, Lord. We're bringing them all to You, 'cause we know that You are big enough to carry them for us. Take our burdens, Lord, and lift us up. Comfort us and give us Your wisdom to do things right."

Shania joined the other angels as they made a circle around the women and their children. Each angel supported one of the women and eased the burden she was carrying off her shoulders and laid it down. Shania's wings fluttered with excitement as she watched peace steal into the features of the women.

From outside the circle, Rafe scowled at the proceedings. "Hey, Esther," he called softly. "Now would be a good time to scream. Aren't you sick of sitting still like that? Don't you want to jump around the room? Go ahead, do it."

Esther squirmed in her place and darted quick glances at the other children. Her lips twitched and she snuck a peek at her mother, wondering what would happen if she let loose with a blood-curdling scream. It might be fun, she reasoned, to watch what the grown-ups would do.

"Pray for protection for the children," Shania urged Leah just before "amen" slipped from her lips. A frown of concentration wrinkled Leah's brow and her face lit up as if she'd just remembered something very important.

"And also, Lord, please be with our children. Send Your holy angels to watch over and protect them. Keep them safe from all harm and send the bad angels from this room. Amen."

Shania turned as the prayer ended and drew her sword. "Leave!" she commanded.

"I will not," Rafe responded hotly.

"You will," Shania contradicted him. "Now." Each of the angels beside her drew a gleaming sword and prepared to drive the demon from the room if necessary.

"Don't think you've won," Rafe informed them as he wrapped his wings around his body and made ready to depart. "When I return, I'll bring others with me. You have gained nothing. You've only goaded me into trying harder the next time. Until then . . ."

With a whoosh, he left the room. It appeared to the angels as if the humans could actually feel his presence depart. As they sat back down in their chairs, Billie Jo and Cindi had small smiles of relief on their faces.

"Now, that did wonders, didn't it?" Leah asked cheerfully.

A chuckle escaped Billie Jo's lips. "Sure enough did," she agreed. "Seems to me my problems ain't nearly as heavy and burdensome as they were when I stepped through that door just a few minutes ago. I don't know why I don't come more often."

"Seems like we all have trouble getting together for one reason or another," Cindi said. "It makes it hard to plan. Some weeks, no one even shows up. It makes me wonder if maybe I ought to cancel the meetings altogether. But, then, something will happen like today and I think it's just Satan trying to discourage me."

"Please," Billie Jo begged. "Please, don't cancel the meetings. I know I haven't got much right to speak up since I been gone so long now, but I really need this place. And I need to know you all are praying for me when I ain't here." She dropped her eyes onto her lap. "Least, I hope you all are praying for me when I ain't here. I count on it. Sometimes it's all that keeps me going. You really don't know, you can't understand what a blessing you are. I know it puts you through a lot to have to be responsible for setting them all up and I wish I could help, but, right now I just can't. So, like I said, maybe I don't have much right asking you not to stop them."

Cindi reached forward and laid her hand on one of Billie Jo's that was fidgeting in her lap. "No, it's me that doesn't have much right to stop the meetings. I'm just the servant here. The meetings are for God to minister to us. Sometimes I forget that."

She leaned back in her seat. "It's just that it gets so overwhelming. I can't handle it. I have my job. Not that I don't love taking care of Ethel. I do. But besides that, I take care of Esther and she's a real handful." She shot a quick warning glance at Esther who was trying to rip a toy out of Dallas' hands. "I never have any time for devotions. Lately, I've been trying to squeeze in a minute here and there. I listen to the Christian radio station. That's been helping some, but I really long for that close relationship I had before Esther was born. Seems like nothing I do really gives me that."

"We've all been there, honey," Leah assured her. "And maybe some of us aren't out of it yet. I know my kids seem to take up all my energy too and they're mostly older than yours, except for my little Lilly." The girl turned and gave Leah a gummy grin at the sound of her name, holding out her arms for Leah to take her.

"I had my first child when I was but sixteen. Next year, she'll turn sixteen herself," she blushed and averted her eyes. "Tommy says she looks just as pretty as I did at that age. 'Course now, after the battles of child raising I'm sure a sight to look at. And me so young still. But I'm totally worn out. Kids do that to you."

Billie Jo threw her arms impulsively around Leah's neck. "You don't look a sight. Why there are days, sometimes three or four in a row, when I can't even get a shower much less wash my hair. It's better now than it was, but when Cass and Dallas were littler and Jimmy was laid up, why a body'd a'thought I was a vagrant judging from the way I looked. We've got to face it. With little ones like ours, we don't always have time for ourselves. Lots of times we don't have time for our families, much less God."

"But, we can't just leave it at that," Cindi protested. "You can't tell me that I'm going to have to wait until Esther is older to have my times with God again. I can't wait that long."

Leah shook her head. "Not wait, honey. Just be creative, that's all."

Cindi nodded. "Ethel told me about practicing the presence of God, so I could bring Him with me through the day. And I've been doing that. But I still miss reading my Bible and having a quiet time set apart for God."

"There are a lot of ways we can keep ourselves fed spiritually, even with the little ones around," Leah agreed. "I like to pin prayer requests to a ribbon that I hang on the window by the sink. I pray for those people while I do my dishes."

"And I write out Bible verses and put them on the frig and mirrors," Billie Jo suggested. "And I keep a stack in my purse to look at if'n I have to wait when I go to pick up the kids or Jimmy."

"I think that's a good place for us to start, don't you?" Leah asked cheerfully. "What do y'all say about giving these ideas a try and then we'll meet again in two weeks and let each other know how we've done?"

As Cindi saw her friends out the door later, she couldn't help but be thankful that she hadn't canceled the meeting. For the first time since Esther had come to live with them, she thought she'd caught a glimpse of God. At least now she was pretty sure she knew where to find Him. And she was excited about meeting Him again.

CHAPTER 10

Jes's excitement rose as she waited for Davy to finish proving his teller drawer so that he could lock it in the vault and go home for the evening. Davy himself had been on edge all day, but it was only half Jes's doing. Belial had been trying all day to convince him that he needed to go to a bar after work for a drink.

So far, Davy had resisted the temptation, but Jes knew he was wearing down. It didn't help that Belial had provoked Laura into a fight with Davy. He was feeling just a little put-upon and sorry for himself. Right about now, Jes knew, that drink was starting to look very inviting.

"Davy, go straight home," she urged. "There is something important waiting for you there. It is the answer to your prayer."

Belial watched her impassively. He seemed quite sure that things would work out his way. "Laura, you know, maybe if you invited Davy to go for a drink with you, the two of you could make up. You know, down the hatch and that sort of thing. Let bygones be bygones. He probably didn't mean to be a jerk. Men are just like that sometimes. They don't think about a woman's feelings."

Laura shot Davy a sideways glance, and Jes intercepted it, crowding in protectively close to Davy. "Davy, go straight home," she insisted. "Go see Shay."

Davy shook his head and took a deep breath. He'd lost count again. He put the bundle of twenties back into a single stack and began over. He'd been fidgety and anxious all day long, and he couldn't figure out why. It was as if he were expecting some sort of news, only he wasn't.

Laura walked over to stand beside him. She pretended to be busy refilling the deposit slip blanks next to her station, but Davy knew for a fact they didn't need refilling. Her closeness irritated him, and he shifted away from her. It was a slight shift, but to him it defined his space. That was Laura's problem; she was always crowding his personal space.

"Um, Davy," she began. "Look, I'm sorry we got into a fight today." She conveniently skipped over the fact that she'd started it, Davy noticed. "I was wondering. Would you like to go out for a drink after work? My treat," she added hastily.

Davy made no attempt to hide the annoyance in his voice. As much as he wanted a drink right now, he had no intention of going anywhere with Laura. "No, thanks. I really can't tonight," he said coolly.

His tone was not lost on Laura. "Fine," she spat. "If you want to be that way, I didn't really want to go out with you either. I don't know what possessed me. Jerk!" she said, hurling the last word at him.

Davy flinched, but he forced a smile. "Thanks. See you to-morrow . . . loser," he added under his breath.

"Jerk," Laura repeated as he walked away from her toward the door.

Outside, the air was heavy, and clouds hung low and ominous in the sky. Raindrops that had broken free of the clouds earlier in the day had hit the sidewalks and pavement, drying up immediately. If Davy hadn't been told by customers all day that it was sprinkling outside, he would never have known. The streets were bone dry.

He made his way quickly to his car, almost wishing he'd brought his umbrella. Just before he reached his vehicle, the sky opened up, and a deluge dropped all at once. Davy gasped from the force of the water and ran the last few steps to his car, yanking open the door and jumping inside. He watched the water stream down the windshield as he tried to shake out his clothing without success.

"Man," he muttered. "What a storm!"

Lightning split the sky a moment later, lighting up everything. It seemed as if it were directly above him. Thunder cracked, and the mighty sound of it rolled down the street. Davy eyed the confines of his car nervously. The light and the noise transported him back to the accident.

"You're never going to be free of it," Belial laughed. *"It's going to go with you for the rest of your life. It doesn't really matter that you have more memories. You're never going to lose this one, and that's what counts. For the rest of your life you're going to live in fear of this memory. I'll see to it that you do."*

"That's not true, Davy," Jes said sternly. *"If you'll just yield your life to the Master, He will protect you from the power this memory has over you."*

Davy's breathing became labored and shallow. He pulled at his tie. It was too tight. How come he hadn't noticed it before? Man, and this car. It was too small. A dull roaring filled his ears, and panic burst over him in a cold sweat.

Screaming incoherently, he jammed his shoulder against the car door. For a second it held, then the latch opened all the way. Thrashing wildly, Davy fell out onto the pavement of the parking lot. Passersby gawked openly at him as he sat there, disheveled and wild-eyed like a man gone mad. No one offered to help him.

Davy sat next to his car for a full fifteen minutes, his Armani trousers soaking up the muddy rainwater, his leather loafers becoming dark and soggy. When he finally stood up, he felt a little dizzy and his mouth, in contrast to the rest of him, was dry as cotton. He slid back into the driver's seat, shaking slightly, and began to drive home.

When he arrived, his only thought was to go straight to his apartment and have a tall glass of whatever alcoholic beverage happened to be in his cupboard. But as he pulled up in front of the duplex, he saw a strange sight. Outside her apartment, in bare feet and a baggy dress that was almost large enough to be a pup tent, was Shay. One slim hand shielded her eyes as she scanned the street up and down, looking for something.

The rain beat down on her, and even her braids seemed to droop forlornly. Davy hopped out of his car and made his way up the sidewalk. "Something wrong?" he hollered.

Worry lined her eyes, but when she saw Davy, she seemed suddenly to become conscious of the picture she presented. The wet dress accentuated her girth and with cumbersome movements, she tried to turn aside. Davy sprinted up the last few steps of the walk.

"What's the matter? What's wrong?" he demanded, catching her arm.

A sob caught in Shay's throat. "It's Marcus," she said. "He . . . he . . . said hateful things to me, and then he ran out. I don't know where he is. I'm afraid he'll get lost and not know how to find his way back."

"You stay right here," Davy said, his voice full of an authority he did not feel. "I'll go look for him."

Davy jumped back into his car and peeled away from the curb. As he drove slowly up and down nearby developments, he kept a sharp eye peeled for Marcus's tall, lanky figure. He found him unexpectedly as he turned a corner. A group of boys had congregated around a construction site. One of the boys was Marcus.

GUARDIANS

As Davy pulled his car up and slowly got out, all of the boys except for Marcus took off running. Davy walked deliberately up to him. Marcus glared at him belligerently but didn't say anything.

"I can give you a ride home, son," he said.

Marcus's glare deepened, and a flush of anger spread over his face. "No, you cannot. And I am not your son," he said, enunciating each word so there could be no mistake. "I am not her son either. My parents are dead."

"Look, Marcus, I don't know what happened. All I know is that when I got home from work, your mother was outside in the rain looking for you. I would think that you'd know better than to upset someone in her condition."

"She does not understand me. She refuses to let me meet with my friends," Marcus cried. "I have lost everything . . . mother, father, country. I do not like America. I did not want to come here. She made me. I want to go back home!"

Davy tried to embrace Marcus, but the boy pulled away angrily, wiping away his tears as if he could erase them. "I'm sorry, Marcus. Look, what happened to you was horrible. I can't even imagine what you must have gone through. But your mother is trying to do what is best for you and your sister and for her. Can you understand that?"

"I understand that she is doing what is best for her," Marcus agreed sullenly. "What is best for me is to go back to my country. My uncle, Wahabi, he would let me live with him. It was not so bad there, I think. Not like America. I am not welcome here."

"Look, I know things look bad, but it's that way no matter where you are. We all have trouble figuring out how to fit in to new places and experiences. I had a hard time when I first moved here too."

Marcus looked skeptical. "You did?"

"Sure, I did," Davy said. "I didn't know anyone, and I didn't

CELESTE PERRINO WALKER

have a job. Then I found a job and met some people, and now I feel as though this is my home."

"I made some friends," Marcus said. "But my mother does not approve of them."

Davy glanced in the direction the group of boys had fled in. "Were those your friends you were with when I showed up?"

Marcus nodded. "Yes."

"Well, Marcus, I don't know them, so it's kind of hard to tell, but why did they run?"

"Perhaps they did not wish to speak with you," Marcus suggested defensively.

"Or maybe they had something to hide," Davy countered.

"They have nothing to hide," Marcus spat. "I know them."

"How well can you know them, Marcus? You haven't been here that long."

"I know them very well," Marcus insisted. "When I went to the big school on the yellow truck, these boys said they would be my friends. They have a new word for friend here. It is "homey." I am their homey, and they are mine. We "hang." When I am with them, I do not miss my father so much and all my friends at the mission."

Davy put one hand on Marcus's elbow. "I believe you, Marcus. It's just that in America you have to be careful who your friends are. They aren't always how they appear."

"I am not stupid," Marcus said. "I know who my friends are."

"Come on, I'll give you a lift home," Davy said.

Marcus did not resist as Davy led him to his car and they drove back to the duplex. Shay met them at the door with towels. She had wrapped herself in a thick robe and put a towel, turbanstyle around her head. She pointed Davy to a seat at the kitchen table and served him a mug of hot chocolate before taking Marcus to his room.

Davy enjoyed the warmth as the chocolate seared its way through his innards. He hadn't realized just how cold he was until he began to warm up. The emotional and physical stress he'd just been put through paired up with the heat radiating from the hot chocolate, making him feel very sleepy.

"Davy," Jes said. "Get up. Walk around."

Afraid he might nod off right there at Shay's table, Davy got up and began to walk around. He wandered over to the fireplace mantle to look at some photographs that had been put up since he'd been in the house last. As if drawn by a magnet, his eyes were pulled to the first one. It was a picture of a man and a woman standing next to an ultralight. The man didn't look familiar at all, but the woman he'd seen before.

"Think hard, Davy," Jes pleaded after she had tugged him over to the pictures. She was having a hard time controlling her excitement. "When was the last time you saw that face?"

Davy leaned forward trying to see the woman's features better in the dim lighting. Suddenly, in his mind, that face became animated. It was Toby's face. A chill shot through him, making him feel cold all over again. He sank weakly onto a chair by the fireplace just as Shay emerged from Marcus's bedroom.

"Where did you get that picture?" Davy croaked.

Shay wrinkled her brow with a frown. "He's fine, thank you. We made up. What picture?"

He pointed. "That's Toby, Toby O'Connell."

Shay squinted the picture as if she were afraid that the subject might have changed in her absence. "Yes, of course it is. So what?"

"Where was it taken?"

Shay rolled her eyes at him. "In Africa, where else?"

"Africa," Davy whispered, his face getting soft. So she'd gone to Africa, just as they had planned.

"What's the big deal?" Shay demanded. "Do you know her or something? An old girlfriend?"

"No, not a girlfriend," Davy corrected. "Wife. She's an old wife."

"Wife?" Shay squeaked. "Toby was your wife?"

"The illustrious Mrs. O'Connell," Davy replied. "One and the same. Didn't she ever talk about me?"

Shay's eyes got round. "Oh, yeah. But nothing I can repeat. She always referred to you as `my ex-husband' in a voice that could slice brick. I'm not sure I ever did know what your name was. If I did, I had forgotten."

Davy chuckled. "That doesn't surprise me. Tell me about her," he begged. "Tell me everything you know."

Shay groaned. "But that will take all night," she complained. "I didn't get a nap today, and I'm tired."

She'd caved in finally when he offered to make her dinner and massage her feet in exchange for learning everything she knew about Toby. Shay talked and talked as they ate. Davy even suspected her of lengthening the story just to draw out her foot massage, but finally she'd rubbed her eyes and said she couldn't think of another thing to tell him about Toby.

"You drive a hard bargain, Shay," Davy grinned as he made his way out the front door.

"No," Shay disagreed. "A hard bargain would have included dessert."

Davy reached into the pocket of his suit coat and pulled out a chocolate bar he'd bought after lunch but hadn't had time to eat. He handed it to her with a grin. "That's the best I can do."

Shay laughed. "Go home, you nut case!" she said, pushing him out the door and closing it behind him. He heard her muffled "Goodbye" as he stood on the doorstep looking up in amazement at the clear black sky studded with glittering stars.

He drew in a deep breath. "You found her, God," he admitted. "I didn't think You could do it. I really didn't. But You did. Thank You."

"Oh, Davy!" Jes exclaimed. "He has so much more to offer you, so much more to show you. Won't you let Him?"

"IT WAS A COINCIDENCE!" Belial roared. "Can't you see

that? Are you such a sap that you think God took time out of His busy day and helped you find the wife you spurned? Get real! Why would He bother? What good will it do anyway? So you know where she is. Big deal. Like that's some real important information there."

"Davy, you blew it with Toby once," Jes said. "But Shay says that she hasn't remarried. Maybe she still has feelings for you. Go to her. Ask her for a second chance."

Davy stared at the stars. He could hardly believe the thoughts racing through his head. A profound gratefulness welled up in his heart, and it was quickly being matched by an excitement he hadn't felt in recent memory as an idea so remote, so incredible, so inconceivable began to take shape in his mind that his heart began to beat faster.

"I couldn't," he whispered to himself. "I just couldn't."

"Davy, with God all things are possible," Jes quoted. "You have nothing to lose and everything to gain. You were thinking about quitting the bank soon anyway. Now that your memory is coming back, it will soon be obvious to you as well as everyone else that you should rightfully be a vice president, not a teller."

"Don't even think it," Belial warned. "She wouldn't take you back if you paid her a million dollars. Why on earth would you want to traipse all the way out there and make a complete idiot of yourself? She'll humiliate you. She'll grind you into the dust. She'll chew you up and spit you out. Do yourself a favor. Don't go. Don't even think about it."

Davy felt as though he was floating a foot off the stoop. His breath came in smoky puffs, and his eyes sparkled in the moonlight. "Oh, God," he whispered. "If I go to Africa, You've got to come with me. I'm not going there alone."

"YOU'RE NOT GOING THERE AT ALL, I TELL YOU!" Belial shrieked. "Aren't you listening to me?"

"No," Jes replied peacefully. "He's not. He's listening to me."

Lyle sat at the kitchen table drumming his fingers absently. Outside a steady rain poured down. Occasionally a gust of wind beat the drops into sheets that slapped against the window. It had been raining for five days straight. That wouldn't have been bad in itself. Lyle didn't mind the rain. But Calla had been mighty scarce.

Every time he'd called asking if she was coming over or if she wanted to go out and do something, she had a good excuse. He was glad that she had some girlfriends who liked to do things with her, but they were engaged. They ought to be spending time together. He stared at the phone and contemplated whether or not he ought to give her a call tonight.

He wasn't exactly sure what he would say if she had another excuse. Busy was one thing; evasive was quite another. He pushed his chair back from the table with one quick motion and wheeled over to the phone. Picking up the receiver, he dialed the number without even thinking of each digit consciously. It was burned into his memory.

Berniece answered. "Hello?" she asked cheerfully.

"Hi, Aunt Bernie, it's Lyle. Can I talk to Calla?"

There was a hesitation that made Lyle's stomach drop. "I'm afraid Calla isn't here," Berniece replied.

"Oh?" Lyle said wryly. "Where is she this time? Candle party? Tupperware party? Library? Movie?"

"No," Berniece said slowly. "She's at a Bible study."

Lyle was puzzled. Calla hadn't said anything about a Bible study. "Oh? With whom?"

"Pastor Hendricks," Berniece said. "And Jesse Redcloud."

"Jesse Redcloud?" Lyle's voice was steely, and he was so calm he surprised himself. But Berniece seemed to sense it was a calm as frightening as the eye of a storm.

"Lyle, now I know Calla should have told you about this, but frankly, I think she was afraid of what you might say. Not that that excuses her," Berniece said rapidly, trying to fill in the silence.

"Afraid?" Lyle spat with disgust. "What did she have to be afraid of? Was she afraid to hurt the cripple when she broke up with him? Is that it? Well, she doesn't have to worry. Maybe I'll break up with her first and save her the trouble."

"Lyle," Berniece pleaded with desperation. "It's not like that at all. You know Calla loves you."

"I thought she did," Lyle agreed. "But now I'm not so sure. Is it love, Aunt Bernie, to go sneaking around behind someone's back? Perfect love has no fear, remember?"

"But nobody is perfect," Berniece countered.

"No," Lyle agreed. "No, they're not, are they? Goodnight, Aunt Bernie."

"Lyle, wait . . ."

But Lyle didn't wait to hear what Aunt Berniece had to say. He put the phone down gently onto the cradle and sat staring at the wall as emotions crashed over him. Hate, jealousy, anger . . . he thought he'd mastered these monsters years before. Now here they were again, just as fierce as they had ever been.

"Lyle!" Shelan called, trying to reach him over the clamor of the demons whirling with a sudden frenzy around his chair. "Lyle, God will help you! Ask the Master to help you. Emotions are normal, but don't let them dictate your life. Don't let them consume you. Use your reasoning. Do not rely solely on your emotions."

Warg let out a blood-curdling yell that would have scared the stuffing out of the toughest warrior alive as he homed in on his prey. Victory was in his grasp, and he lost no time in pressing his advantage. He barreled through the fray, collaring Lyle and pressing up tight against him.

"You're right, boy!" he exclaimed jubilantly. "Isn't this what I've been telling you all along? She doesn't love you! Why, she's afraid of you. Yeah, right! She's afraid that you'll find out what she's doing; that's what she's afraid of."

Lyle clutched his head as thousands of accusations and questions bombarded him. Humiliation and anger threatened to explode from his chest and leave a huge gaping hole where his heart had once resided. "God, where are You?" he cried.

God seemed farthest away of all.

He felt himself reaching toward God, but it was as if he were a blind man groping around in a warehouse. If God was there, Lyle couldn't feel His presence and the space was just too big to search one inch at a time. He didn't have the patience or the time.

"She's going to break up with you. You know that, don't you? She's lost interest in you. You're yesterday's cause. She's on to bigger and better things." The demons packed in closer, egging Warg on. He drew strength and daring from their support.

"Life isn't worth living!" they clamored.

"What have you got to live for? Nothing! Are you such a coward that you can't do away with your miserable existence?" Warg challenged. "End it all right now, if you're man enough." He drew Lyle's attention to the row of kitchen knives all sticking out of the proper slots in their holder on the counter.

"Lyle, the Master will help you. Call on the Master," Shelan repeated. Sensing that she wasn't getting through, she gave Lyle one last pitying look and fled to find help.

Lyle looked frantically at the kitchen knives. He wondered if he could do it. He wondered if he should. And he wondered what was stopping him. Roughly, he yanked one wheel of his chair to turn it in the direction of the counter.

Back from her errand, Shelan pushed the kitchen chair out just enough so that it caught on the wheel and stopped the chair dead. Frustrated, Lyle jerked it back, but when he tried to go forward again, it stuck repeatedly on the leg of the chair. Jamming the chair back and forth, his rage spewed out of his mouth in a roar. The chair, free now of the table leg, drunkenly rammed up against the wall. Lyle didn't seem to notice that he was free.

Crying and screaming, he rammed the chair over and over against the wall. When he got close enough, he slammed it with his fists. He didn't even stop when Berniece knocked tentatively on the door.

"Lyle?" she called tentatively. Not waiting for a response, she pushed the door open and burst into the kitchen. "Lyle!"

She crossed the floor in one giant leap and grabbed his chair. He thrashed against her blindly. "Lyle! Lyle!" she cried, shaking him until he came to his senses.

"Aunt Bernie?" he asked dumbly, staring at her as though she might be an apparition. "She doesn't love me anymore, Aunt Bernie," he sobbed.

"Lyle, that's not true," Berniece's voice held accusation and sympathy but very little conviction. "You haven't even talked to her, given her a chance to explain. Now, I don't approve of what she's doing, but I know for a fact that you're jumping the gun. Why, Lyle, you don't know anything for sure. What you're supposing is just that, supposing. It's not facts."

"It's a fact that she's with him right now, isn't it?" Lyle demanded bitterly. "And it's also a fact that she didn't tell me about it. And it's a fact that she's been ignoring me for the last week. What does all that add up to? She doesn't love me anymore," he spat.

Shelan responded immediately to Berniece's prayer for wisdom. There was a bit of desperation in it. She knew that Berniece, from her position as outside observer, was seeing the horrific flaw in the cornerstone of Lyle and Calla's relationship.

Berniece had been wary of Lyle at first. He seemed so odd, so warped. She had been hesitant to give Calla her blessing when they became engaged. In fact, their engagement shocked and terrified her. She was afraid that Calla was responding to the romantic element in rescuing Lyle rather than really loving him. Calla had dealt well with his disability, and her tact in that area had really helped Lyle to stop feeling sorry for himself, but they were like two emotional children. He ate up her vivacity, and she wallowed in his adoration.

Now Lyle was "fixed" on the outside, and Jesse presented her with a whole new challenge. It was a challenge that Berniece recognized all too well. Calla's father had been an alcoholic before he died, and Calla had thrown herself into "fixing" things in their lives when her mother left them and started her life over with another man. Calla presented such a normal front to the world that few people had realized the extent of her father's problems.

Lyle had really blossomed under her care, and the past year or so Berniece had come to think that perhaps they had a chance despite the odds. Now she wasn't so sure. Here, at the very first sign of a problem, Lyle was melting down. It only proved to Berniece that he wasn't nearly as stable as he appeared and that maybe Calla was overlooking his emotional instability and "covering" for him the way she had with her father.

"What you have been considering in your heart is the truth," Shelan said to Berniece. "These two young people have a lot of growing and sharing before they are ready to enter into such a union as marriage. Their relationship is a shallow one. It stopped at one level and never progressed to the next. They would both benefit from counseling."

Berniece took a deep breath. "Lyle, I think it would be a good idea for you and Calla to go see Pastor Hendricks for counseling."

Lyle gaped at her as her words penetrated the cloud of rage that filled his mind. "Counseling? For what? To find out whether or not Calla loves me?"

"No," Berniece replied steadily. "To find out if you're ready for marriage. I'm actually surprised that no one mentioned it before."

"Aunt Bernie, that's preposterous," Lyle argued. "Whether we're ready for marriage or not isn't the question. The question is whether Calla loves me and wants to marry me. Why, we've hardly ever fought in the entire time we've known each other."

Berniece nodded. "I know, and that's one of the things that troubles me. Neither of you have any conflict/resolution skills. What you're going through right now proves what I'm trying to tell you." Berniece took a deep breath. "Lyle, I'm fond of you, you know I am. I've grown to think of you as a son. And that's why I'm telling you this. Right now, what's important isn't whether or not Calla loves you or doesn't. What's important is whether you're ready to enter into marriage with Calla or with anyone else. Do you honestly believe that you are?"

"Don't take this lightly," Shelan warned. "Think about what she is asking you. Are you prepared to trust Calla, really trust Calla, with yourself forever? Are you prepared to love her through difficult circumstances as well as pleasant ones? Do you really think the best of her, believe the best in her, and want the best for her more even than you want it for yourself?"

"What a line!" Warg howled. "It's not a big deal. Don't sweat it. If the relationship doesn't work out, you can always get a divorce and start over. Lots of people do it. You're lucky. You live in a disposable age. There was a time when you would have been shackled by your morals to a bad relationship for the rest of your life. Now you can just throw it away."

Lyle stared into Berniece's frank eyes. He searched his heart fearfully and found it hard to reply with anything less than total honesty. "I'm not sure, Aunt Bernie," he admitted finally.

He didn't know which hurt worse, thinking that Calla didn't love him or admitting that he might not be ready to get married.

The years he'd spent alone before he'd met Calla had been so overwhelmingly lonely and Calla had filled his life so completely that he couldn't bear the thought of going back to life without her.

Berniece patted his hand reassuringly. "That's OK, Lyle. What's important is that you're willing to find out now and not later. Believe me, there are many people who are not big enough or forward thinking enough to bother until it's too late."

Lyle hid his face in his hands. "What am I going to do, Aunt Bernie?"

"You're going to take it one step at a time. When Calla comes home tonight, I'll send her over."

"I don't think that's a good idea," Lyle said. "I would rather talk with her at your house in case things get out of hand. If you don't mind, I'll come over in a bit and wait for her to get back."

"That would be fine, Lyle," Berniece agreed. "The important thing is that the two of you talk honestly about your future, and if you are still interested in having one together, you need to make plans to get some counseling."

Lyle nodded. "You're right," he said. "I don't like it, but you're right."

Berniece squeezed his hand. "Are you going to be all right?"

"Yeah. Thanks, Aunt Bernie. I'll be fine. I'm just going to collect my thoughts for a minute, and then I'll come over." After Berniece left, Lyle sat for a long time in the darkened room listening to the old mantle clock ticking and feeling a cool breeze sweep through the house from the general direction of the dogwood trees.

Finally he drew a choppy breath and bowed his head in prayer. "Lord," he prayed out loud, "I can't see You, and I feel very alone right now. I'm alone, and I'm scared. I don't need to know all the answers right now, but could You just comfort me and be with me right now? That's all I'm asking for. Just give me strength to face this and wisdom to know what to do.

"I love Calla, Lord. I really do. Not just because she's pretty and she loves me but because she's a good person and she's funny and thoughtful and for a million other reasons. But, I'm not sure I trust her with my heart.

"I'm sorry that I thought about taking my life, Lord. Please forgive me for my weakness. Give me strength to face my problems. Thank You for hearing me and for answering. Amen." As the last word died on his lips, Lyle felt the presence of God settle around him and infuse him with peace.

"Thank You," he murmured again.

"Praise God!" Shelan shouted. She linked arms with other angels who had responded to Lyle's prayer. They formed a ring around him and comforted him as he sat communing with God in the soft darkness.

"It ain't over," Warg snarled as he headed out to find some place not glowing with the radiance of heaven.

CHAPTER 11

Billie Jo heard the crash at the same time a knock sounded on the front door. She wasn't sure which to investigate first. A howl followed closely behind the crash and galvanized her into action. "What happened?" she screamed, racing down the hallway.

"I bumped my head," Dallas wailed, clutching his forehead, his features twisted up in a grimace of pain, tears spilling out of his eyes and liberally splashing his cheeks.

"I told him not to jump on his bed, Momma," Cassidy said sagely. She was coloring on the floor and looked up with such an adult expression of superiority that Billie Jo had to stifle a smile.

"Oh, honey," she crooned, scooping Dallas up and rubbing his forehead vigorously.

"Owww, that hurts," he complained.

"It'll make it all better," Billie Jo promised him. "Let me see." She pried his hands away from his forehead and brushed back his hair to expose a red welt the size of a Ping-Pong ball.

"Doesn't anyone answer the door anymore?" a shrill voice complained from the hallway.

Billie Jo felt her stomach drop at the sound of that voice. For months, Helen had been blissfully absent as she recovered from her suicide attempt. Once a week, Jimmy hustled the entire family into the car and drove over to visit her, but that didn't seem nearly as ominous as hearing her voice echo down the hallway of her own house.

"We're in here," she called weakly. "Lord," she prayed under her breath as she helped Dallas to his feet. "Please, give me strength. You know I want to love her. OK, I'm willing to love her. All right, I'm willing to like her. But, I'll never do it on my own, Lord. I need help. And I know You can do it. Thanks. Amen."

As the last word slipped out of her mouth, Helen came into sight in the doorway. Her face looked different, but not bad, really, considering what she'd been through. The plastic surgeon said that for the most part no one would ever know anything had happened to her. Her family was more likely to see it, mostly because they'd had to remove quite a few of her teeth on the side of her face the bullet exited, and the replacements didn't look exactly the same. Billie Jo was amazed that something so slight could make such a difference.

There was also something in her eyes that said things weren't right. Despite her narrow brush with death, she projected herself no differently. She'd been thrilled with all the attention during her recovery, of course. Although Jimmy brought them all over there only once a week, he stopped by on his way from work every day he worked. But the thought of nearly dying didn't soften her in any way. If anything, it made her rougher and more impatient than ever. Especially with Billie Jo. For reasons she never talked about directly, she blamed Billie Jo for what happened, as if Billie Jo had shot her.

An emerald green silk scarf was wrapped around her neck despite the high temperature, probably to hide a scar, Billie Jo reasoned. The color brought out the paleness of her cheeks and the unnatural brightness of her eyes. Her lips were pursed together as if she'd just bitten into something that had set her teeth on edge.

"What happened in here?" she asked curtly, eyeing Dallas's head. "At it again, I see."

Billie Jo bristled immediately. Would Helen never believe that she was capable of caring for her own children? "Strength, Lord," she murmured. "Boys will be boys," she said lightly.

"Ha," Helen laughed shortly. "That one will be lucky to grow into a teenager in this house."

"That's telling her," Nog laughed, slapping his knee with vigor. "The old gal's back, and there's no stopping her now." He gave Jewel a triumphant look that was short-lived.

Rather than succumb to Helen's taunts, Billie Jo kept up a steady, silent petition to heaven for strength and wisdom. Jewel was gathering such a solid force around Billie Jo that Nog feared the entire visit would be in vain. He wasn't about to let this prime opportunity for fireworks go by with a fizzle and a pop.

"Are you going to take that? She belittles you all the time. Isn't it about time you stuck up for yourself?" he hissed in derision. "You're more affected by her attempted suicide than she is. It's made her stronger, and you've only gotten weaker. If you won't stick up for yourself, at least defend your children."

"Billie Jo, remember there is more to Helen than you are seeing at this moment. There are reasons she was led to try to take her own life. Offer her your pity, compassion, and God's love. With those you will not go wrong," Jewel urged. "Freely take the love God offers you for this woman. Will you accept?"

Billie Jo swallowed hard. She felt an overwhelming sense of pity for Helen. James's words at the time of the accident came back to her. *"I knew it would happen someday,"* James had said. *"Ever since her mother . . ."* Ever since her mother what? Billie Jo had an odd feeling that Helen's mother had done something terrible and it had tainted the rest of her life.

She knew from the Bible that the sins of one generation affected the next, sometimes for four generations. In some ways, she wished that Helen's mother had lived long enough for her to see if she was as vindictive as Helen herself was. Maybe that would explain Helen's disposition. Maybe her mother had treated her the same way Helen treated Billie Jo.

"Can I get you anything?" she asked humbly, forcing her thoughts away from Helen's past and into the present.

Helen sniffed. "Have you really got anything worth eating? I suppose I could take a glass of cold water, if it isn't too much trouble and if it is very cold. If it isn't cold, I'd rather not have it."

"I think I can find cold water," Billie Jo replied, trying desperately to keep the sarcasm out of her voice. She headed out the bedroom door for the kitchen. Her fingernails were dug into her palms so hard to keep her focused on her responses that she was afraid she might draw blood. Before she got out of earshot, she heard Dallas exclaim, "Grandma, I'm so happy to see you!"

She cringed at the words. Every fiber of her being wanted to yank the children away and shield them from Helen's insidious influence. They were too young to understand that she used them only to fill her own pathetic need for affection and dependence.

By bringing them gifts every time she came, she was assured of their enthusiastic love. Even Cassidy, who remembered more than her brother about the terrible time when Helen had tried to take them away from their parents, was inclined to be forgetful of the past in order to gain the favors of her grandmother.

Billie Jo let the water in the tap run extra long before she filled a glass for Helen. Her fingers drummed on the glass as it filled, wondering if Helen would run true to form and have gifts for the children. She didn't have long to wait. As she returned to the room, she could hear them exclaiming over something.

Cassidy was ripping a Barbie doll out of its box, and Dallas was zooming a toy airplane around the room. "Look, Momma," he said gleefully. "Look at the new airplane Grandma gave me."

Helen looked at her with an expression that was half-smug, half-proud. Billie Jo felt her temperature rising, but at that instant she heard the front door open and Jimmy stomped inside.

"Ma?" he called. "That you? Can't believe you got outta the house finally. Where are y'all? Billie?"

Billie Jo handed Helen the glass of water and went out to meet Jimmy in the hallway. "We're all in Dallas's room," she said out loud. Under her breath she added. "She's done it again, Jimmy. Are you going to say something to her this time?"

Jimmy brushed by her in irritation. "Done what?" he muttered, but Billie Jo knew that he was well aware of what his mother had done. Again. He just wasn't going to do anything about it this time either.

He always had one excuse or another. In the beginning, Billie Jo had wondered if he was just uncomfortable bringing up an issue of conflict with his mother. Since the accident, she'd begun to suspect that Jimmy was afraid of his mother. He was afraid that he might drive her to attempt suicide again. Helen had become even more powerful.

Billie Jo followed on Jimmy's heels as he made his way down the hall to Dallas's room. "Hi, Ma, good to see you out again." Helen accepted a hug from Jimmy, and Billie Jo could have sworn that she wilted physically in the presence of her son to make herself seem more pitiful.

"Hello, Jimmy," she said softly. "Your father offered to drive me over, but I said it was about time I started doing things for myself again. It's practically done me in as you can see. Too much excitement for my first time out, I suppose. Maybe I should have let your father bring me. He likes to feel useful."

Billie Jo stifled a groan. There was absolutely no chance Jimmy would bring up the issue of her giving the kids gifts all the time now. She'd wielded her most powerful weapon. Check and mate.

She eyeballed the kids playing with their new toys, and Jimmy made small talk with his mother. Helen was holding the glass of water limply in one hand as if it might drop out at any moment.

"Let me take that for ya, Ma," Jimmy said. "Here, we'll set it down right here on the bureau."

Helen sighed morosely. "I was so parched, but I simply can't drink that water. Tepid water makes me nauseous."

Jimmy handed the glass to Billie Jo. "Would you freshen that, darlin'?" he asked.

Billie Jo accepted the glass and trotted back out to the kitchen to empty and refill it with water of exactly the same temperature. Cassidy followed her out into the kitchen with her Barbie.

"Momma, ain't she beautiful? Like a princess," Cassidy breathed. She didn't own a single Barbie. Billie Jo didn't approve of them.

"Don't get too attached to her," she warned. "After Grandma leaves, we'll be puttin' her up. You know I don't think they're fittin' for girls to play with. Those dolls are hard images for little girls to live up to. Nobody looks that perfect. Ain't right. It ain't normal," she hissed.

"That's not fair!" Cassidy wailed. "Grandma gave her to me. She thinks they're fine for girls like me. I'm growed up, you know, Momma," she added as if perhaps Billie Jo, though she shared the same living quarters, might have become blind in that area. She clutched the Barbie to her chest. "She's mine. I'm keeping her."

"Are not," Billie Jo said firmly. "We'll talk about this later. After Grandma leaves."

"I'm gonna tell Daddy," Cassidy said firmly, playing her trump card.

Billie Jo grimaced. Jimmy was as likely to say the doll could stay as he was that it had to go. The last thing she wanted that evening was a fight with Jimmy. "We'll talk about it after Grandma leaves," Billie Jo repeated.

Cassidy followed her back into the bedroom where Helen accepted the fresh glass with a tired sigh as if it took all her effort.

With incredible intuition, she divined that Billie Jo had spoken to Cassidy about the doll. "What's wrong with my princess?" Helen crooned.

Cassidy's sullen look became hopeful. Before Cass even opened her mouth, Billie Jo could see the thoughts whizzing through her brain. She latched onto the hope that Helen would be sympathetic to her and somehow force her mother's hand.

"Momma says I can't keep the doll," she said, with a challenging sideways glance at Billie Jo.

"Whyever not?" Helen exclaimed, as if she hadn't heard Billie Jo's reasons a million times before. "It's just because I gave it to her, isn't it?" The accusation in her tone was unmistakable.

"No, it's not because you gave it to her," Billie Jo replied with as much patience as she could manage. "I don't approve of Barbie dolls. They focus little girls' attention on the way they look, and all Barbie does is go off on dates and such. There are lots more constructive things for Cassidy to be playing with."

"Ah, I see," Helen said. "So I'm luring her away from constructive play, is that it?"

"No," Billie Jo said. "I mean, yes. The doll is," she tried to explain, but Helen wasn't paying attention any more. She'd heard what she wanted to hear.

She drew herself up haughtily. "I don't know why you disapprove of me so. I've tried everything I know to please you, and nothing ever seems to get through to you." A cold tear slid down one pale cheek. "I'm sorry I can't live up to your high standards. Cassidy, sweetheart, give Grandma the doll."

Cassidy handed the Barbie over with disbelief and then burst into tears. "I want my doll," she sobbed.

"I know, sweetie. I'm sorry," Helen replied with patronizing sweetness. "But your mommy won't let you have it."

Dallas stopped flying his new airplane around the room in dismay. "Do I have to give my plane back too?" he wailed.

"I'm afraid so," Helen said. "I can't let you keep your nice toy if your mommy won't let Cassidy keep hers. It wouldn't be fair. Now, I'd better be getting home. I tire easily these days."

Jimmy glared at Billie Jo and then took his mother's arm. "I can drive you home if you want, Ma," he offered.

"No, Jimmy, I couldn't let you do that," Helen protested weakly. "That would be too much trouble. How would you get back?"

"Billie Jo could follow along with the kids and give me a ride home," Jimmy said quickly. "Billie Jo, get the car keys. Come on, kids, we're going to bring Grandma home."

Cassidy and Dallas followed them out the front door, both wiping back sniffles and hiccuping soft sobs. Giving Billie Jo dirty looks, they opted to ride with Daddy and Grandma, leaving Billie Jo to follow along in a silent car that was heavy with disappointment and anger.

"What did I do wrong, God?" she hollered, beating the steering wheel in frustration. "She wins at every turn, and it ain't fair. I love my kids, and I end up being the one who looks like the devil himself. All she ever does is use them, and she looks like some kind of saint spreading toys around like chicken feed. What am I doing wrong?"

As she drove, anger and frustration mounted until they were ready to explode from her. She dreaded the ride home with Jimmy and the kids. She knew it was not going to be pleasant. She didn't have long to wait.

As she pulled up in the driveway, Jimmy and the kids were trouping back out of the house. They hopped quickly into the car. Billie Jo backed out onto the road and headed in the direction she'd just come from.

"I want to know why you did that," Jimmy said, his voice stone cold and void of any emotion.

"Did what?" Billie Jo swallowed. The tension in the car was palpable.

"I want to know why you treated my Ma that way. It was her first time visitin' us since the accident, Billie. Why'd ya have to go an spoil it?" he elaborated.

"Me?" Billie Jo choked. "We've spoken to her countless times about not givin' the kids presents when she comes over, and does it do any good? No. Not only does she give them gifts when she ain't supposed to but seems like she goes outta her way to pick ones we disapprove of."

"But, why couldn't you let it go this time, woman?" Jimmy bellowed. "It's as if you set out to upset her on purpose. Can't you at least wait until she's well?"

Billie Jo felt an emotional steel door slam shut over her soul. Her mouth closed with a pop, and she stared straight ahead at the road, her knuckles white as she gripped the steering wheel. They passed elegantly groomed lawns surrounding the homes of rich people and rolling farmland before coming into more mountainous terrain where she turned onto their long, dirt drive-way.

"Ain't you got nothin' to say?" Jimmy demanded.

Billie Jo shook her head stubbornly. There was no use talking to him if he was going to be like this. Nothing she said was going to make any kind of difference, and he would invariably stick up for his mother anyway.

"Well, I'll be," Jimmy huffed, jerking open the car door when they had rolled to a stop. "If you don't want to make an issue of something, then why bring it up? You got Ma all worked up, the kids all worked up, and I ain't in that good a mood either now, thanks to you. Really, Billie, you ought to be thinkin' more clear before you stir up the waters like that."

He slammed the door behind him, and Billie Jo sat biting her lip and blinking back tears as the kids extricated themselves from their seatbelts and clambered out of the car after their father. Billie Jo didn't make any movement for a long time. She simply sat there, feeling sorry for herself.

"That's right," Nog encouraged her. *"You're so misunderstood. I don't know how you handle it. You know it would be much*

easier if you divorced Jimmy, took the children and moved far, far away from here. He doesn't understand you, and he loves his mother more than he loves you. Probably wouldn't even bother him. Unless he started missing the kids. Think of it. No more Helen. Isn't that appealing?"

Billie Jo shook her head, but the thought persisted. Divorce. She'd never even thought about it before. Even during the dark times when she thought Jimmy would never wake up. For one instant, she let herself think of what life would be like without Helen.

Bliss.

Heaven on earth, she decided. "No more meddling in my affairs," she muttered. "It'd be such a relief just knowin' the kids would be safe from her influence. Oh, Lord," her spoken thoughts slid easily into prayer. "It would be wonderful to be rid of that burden. You didn't see fit to take her when she tried to kill herself, but Lord, would it be a real big sin to move away from here?"

Even as the words left her mouth, she knew she would never consider divorce as an option. Leaving was just wishful thinking on her part. As angry as she was at Jimmy and as hurt as she felt from his words, she knew that he would regret them all when he cooled off. He'd always been real good about apologizing when things had time to sit a spell.

"Lord, forgive me for my discouraging thoughts. Please send your angels to protect me from the old devil. He's trying real hard to get to me today, Lord."

The clash of swords was so unexpected that Nog tumbled over backwards away from his prey. Never had he expected so much backbone from Billie Jo. He'd thrown every weapon at her, and she'd parried stubbornly with her blasted prayers. As Jewel bore down upon him, his gleaming sword slicing the air in front of him, Nog turned and fled. This was only one battle. He may have lost this time, but soon he would prevail.

Jewel and the other angels turned to group around Billie Jo

after they successfully drove Nog away. Jewel smiled with pride at his charge. Since she'd decided to practice the presence of God, as her prayer group called it, she'd become more aware of the power of heaven at her disposal.

Little by little, day by day, she'd begun to pray more often. When she was confronted by problems in life, she sought direction from heaven quicker than she used to. Jewel was happy to be able to give it. He followed her as she pushed open the car door after one final prayer for guidance and made her way into the house.

Shay curled up as best she could on the sofa and stared moodily into thin air. She'd had another fight with Marcus that night when he'd come home late with no explanation. Finally in desperation, she'd sent him to his room. He hadn't come out.

Also, between Shay's troubles with Marcus and the fact that it was all she could do to get through each day because the pregnancy took so much out of her, Madina was suffering. The child alternated between being weepy and cross. Shay felt guilty about finding ways to distract her so that she could get some rest, but she didn't know what else to do. There was only so much of her to go around.

Exhaustion throbbed through her body. The baby growing inside her pelted her from all angles. Just as she was finally able to get some rest from the other two, this one started to warm up for the Olympics. Even when she was able to ignore the thumping from within her, sleep was light and restless. She would wake up over and over with no clear idea of what woke her.

Just as her eyelids drooped heavily, a knock sounded at the door. She was half-tempted to ignore it, but it persisted. Heaving herself up from the couch, she shuffled her way to the door and opened it, knowing full well who it was.

Deniece smiled at her.

"Are the kids asleep?" she asked in an exaggerated whisper.

Shay nodded. She had been really glad to renew her friendship with Deniece when she moved back to the States. They were so close they might have been sisters. But lately she was finding it hard to talk, to really open herself up to Deniece. She wasn't sure if it was because they had been apart for so long. She didn't think that was it, because in some ways it felt like she'd hardly been gone at all.

She was disappointed that Deniece wasn't more help with the kids, but she told herself that Deniece could hardly be blamed for that. After all, she was a busy professional woman with commitments of her own. The children of her best friend weren't her responsibility. Still, the disappointment persisted, and sometimes Shay felt it change into resentment.

For fleeting moments, she found herself wishing she were single and free to do as she wished. When Marcus answered her with a smart mouth or tried to make her feel guilty for bringing them all to the States and Madina was clingy beyond all reason, she would catch herself thinking wistfully of Deniece's unfettered, carefree life.

She eyed Deniece's tiny waist enviously as the latter pounced on the sofa and hugged a pillow to her middle. She looked up at Shay with a bright, infectious smile and patted the sofa next to her. "Come on," she urged. "Sit right down here and tell me about your day, girl."

Shay suppressed a smile. If Deniece really knew what her days were like lately, she'd know better than to ask. Shay waddled over to the couch and sank down gratefully beside her friend. "You don't want to hear about that," she assured her. "Why don't you tell me what you did today?" She tried to hide a yawn behind her hand, but Deniece saw it.

"Are you tired?" she asked sympathetically. "I shouldn't stay. It's just that I had meetings after I got out of work and, well, you know, one thing and another. Before I knew it, the whole day was gone. But I feel like I haven't seen you in ages, so I just had to stop by." She twirled the tassel of one of the pillows. "By the way, what do you hear from Davy? Anything?"

Shay's eyes compressed into little slits as she glared suspiciously at Deniece. "Is that why you really came? To get the scoop on Davy?" she exclaimed.

Deniece threw up her hands in defense. "Now, don't go getting all uppity on me. Of course that's not why I'm here. But, as long as I am . . ."

"You're incorrigible," Shay admonished with a laugh. "To tell you the truth, I'm not sure whether to be happy about your interest in that man or to feel sorry for you. Toby, his ex-wife, and I were never what I would call close, but she talked about him often. Mostly when she was upset. And I personally think he's on a wild goose chase."

"Really?" Deniece perked up.

"Of course, she might be really impressed that he thought enough of her to sell practically everything he owned, leave a respectable job, and go halfway around the world to make up with her." Shay shrugged. "I know that would sweep me right off my feet."

"Oh," Deniece said darkly. "I hadn't thought of that." Then she brightened. "Oh well, it's actually kind of romantic, don't you think? I mean them getting back together after all this time and that tragic accident?"

"I guess so," Shay said doubtfully. "But, I'm not sure I want them to get back together. It would break Don's heart, and he's been through enough already. The two of them really changed. They used to be so angry all the time. It kind of started to happen after Madina was born. And then he . . . he almost died in the outbreak. I thought it was plenty romantic that they managed to find love after all both of them went through. What will happen to them if they lose that?"

Shay's thoughts flew to her own loss, and she was immediately saddened. Deniece noticed it and reached out to shake her arm gently. "Hey," she said. "Don't go there. Not tonight. I'm sorry. I didn't mean to bring back painful memories. Let's talk about something else. How are the kids?"

Shay sniffed and wiped away a stray tear. "I thought you didn't want to depress me," she asked with a brief smile.

"It can't be that bad," Deniece said. "They're such sweethearts. I can't wait until I have babies."

Shay rubbed her belly absently. "Oh, babies, I thought you said the kids. The baby is fine, thanks. Very active. I think she's going to be an Olympian. A gymnast, maybe."

"Is Marcus doing any better?"

"Not good," Shay admitted. "He was late getting home again tonight. I'm really worried about him. Whenever I try to talk to him about it, he gets so angry. I don't know what to do. I can't handle him like this. He's always loved me so much. Now it seems like he hates me."

"That's not true," Deniece contradicted her quickly. "He's just growing up, that's all. Every kid goes through it."

"Maybe, but that doesn't help much. I wish . . ." Shay caught herself before she finished the thought out loud. What she wished was that Nwibe were there. That she weren't a single parent. That she could get answers from God. But, right now He wasn't speaking to her.

"That's not true," Gaius said. "You have blocked yourself off from His help. You have hardened your heart toward Him. Express your grief. Open your heart. Give your pain to Him. His shoulders are wide enough to carry all of it. Let Him share your burden."

"Oh, puh-leese," Jezeel spat. "Where was God when your husband lay dying? Where was God when he stood in line and got

that shot? He could have gotten his vaccine any day; why did God let him do it that day? He could have stopped him. He could have sent those sick guys somewhere else. God's mad at you, that's what's going on. He did this to you on purpose because He's vindictive. Who needs Him? Forget about God."

Gaius's lovely wings drooped by his side as he concentrated completely on his charge. Ever since Nwibe's death, she had struggled, in vain, to reach God. There was a chasm as wide as the earth's Grand Canyon between the two of them. If only Shay would let Him, God would fill it in and rush to her side.

She harbored hatred toward many people for Nwibe's death. But she hated God most of all. She did blame Him, but she wouldn't admit it. Good Christians didn't hate God, and so she hid it, even from herself. And it was this hatred that separated them. Shay had kept her emotions buried so deeply since her husband's death. Gaius knew that if she was ever to move from this place and grow in her trust in God, she would have to uncover them, release them, and deal with them.

Deniece studied Shay until she squirmed uncomfortably. "What?" she asked irritably.

"You think He's responsible, don't you?"

"What do you mean?" Shay said, refusing to look directly at Deniece. Instead, she studied the carpet, the pattern on the sofa and the wallpaper.

"You think that God is testing you or something. First, He took your father and then your husband. You're worried you or me or one of the kids might be next, aren't you?"

Shay's head snapped up, fire in her eyes. "What do you know about it? So what if I do. What am I supposed to think? People are dropping out of my life like flies lately. People I love." A sob caught in her throat. "People who are closest to me. Why shouldn't I take this personally? How am I supposed to know? Maybe He's not done yet." She dropped her voice to a whisper, afraid that maybe if God heard her He'd zap someone immediately.

"Girl, I've known you forever. I mean forever. You're the one who brought me to church the first time. We were baptized together. I know you. You wouldn't be thinking like this if it were happening to me or someone else you knew. Your grief is clouding your mind."

"Butt out!" Jezeel said, crowding in close to Deniece. "What do you know about it anyway? You're not attached to anyone. You have virtually no responsibilities. How do you know what it feels like to lose the people who are closest to you? She has a right to feel any way she chooses."

"That's the point," Gaius said. "She chooses how she feels. She can choose to hate or to forgive, to love or to harbor anger, to let go or to hold on. She can choose freedom or slavery." He turned to Shay. "Let go. Seek truth. Be free."

Tears streamed down Shay's cheeks. "My grief is clouding my mind?" she cried. "You have no right to lecture me on grief. You aren't the one who is raising two children, about to have a third, with no husband. You aren't the one who feels as though every breath is an effort, every day a burden. God isn't out to get you. You have everything."

Inside somewhere there was a huge, angry ball of emotion that threatened to explode and shatter her to pieces. She struggled to settle it down, but she could feel it fragmenting around the edges. Deniece had hit too close to home.

She trembled like a leaf battered by storm winds. Pieces of the wall she had hastily built at the news of Nwibe's death began to fracture and crumble. Emotions leaked out and the moment she felt them, the dam burst, flooding her with grief, anger, and frustration.

"Oh, Deniece," she sobbed. "I'm sorry."

Deniece gathered her into her arms as Shay sobbed wildly. "No, Shay, I'm sorry. I'm sorry all this has happened to you." Shay shook as her emotions spent themselves and washed away in her tears. Deniece patted her shoulder and whispered the same comforting words over and over. "Everything is going to be OK. It'll all work out. You'll see."

Gaius sighed with relief, and Jezeel cursed under her breath as the little scene in Shay's living room played out. Gaius knew that Shay had taken the first step toward healing the breach between herself and God. Now if she'd only make the next step, He would meet her more than halfway.

"Lies, all lies," Jezeel hissed fitfully, pacing back and forth, helplessly watching while months of work were destroyed. "Everything will not be OK. Nothing will bring back your father. Nothing will bring back your husband. Marcus still hates you, and you deserve it. Madina still has problems adjusting to America. You are still pregnant and have no means of supporting yourself. Your father's money won't last forever, you know. You're going to have to find a job sometime."

Jezeel threw up her hands in disgust. "Just look at you. Nothing has changed."

"Yes, it has," Gaius contradicted her. "Her heart has changed."

Shay gripped Deniece as her heart melted like snow kissed by chinook winds. The violent emotions that shook her so fiercely ebbed away and were replaced by relief at their passing. Slowly, she was aware of a great love filling her heart. It wasn't her love. It was God's.

"Oh, God, I'm so sorry," she whispered. "Please forgive me. Please help me."

Gaius watched happily as the Master's face reflected joy and He reached out to meet her.

CHAPTER

12

Don pushed himself up gingerly and hung his legs over the side of the bed. The slight exertion made him pant. His large, now rather bony hands, wrapped around his torso. He marveled at how gaunt he had become. His ribs stood out in sharp relief like ridges carved into a sand dune by the wind. His flimsy T-shirt felt heavy as it draped over his frame.

Shaking, he leaned forward, peering out as far as he could into the courtyard, looking for Toby or Julia or Ray or anyone who might launch into a tirade of protests that he shouldn't be up and around yet. Seeing no one, he slid himself tentatively off the bed, praying that his legs would hold him up. They buckled immediately, and he crumpled onto the floor with a yelp of surprise. Other than the bruise to his ego, he didn't feel any injuries.

"Arghh," he growled, searching the area around him for some way out of his predicament. Nothing presented itself. "Great," he muttered. "Now what am I going to do?"

"You could try staying in your bed until you have sufficient strength to leave it," Flory suggested sternly as she darkened the doorway and stepped inside the clinic.

Don grinned sheepishly up at her. "You won't tell Toby, will you?"

Flory planted her hands on her hips and gave him a stony glare that just barely hid her amusement. "You will not do this again?"

Don shrugged. "Not for a while, I suppose."

Flory wedged herself in behind him and locked her arms around his torso, pulling him into a semistanding position. Don reached out and gripped the edge of the cot and helped her as she pivoted him around and eased him back onto the bed. With one slim hand, she easily pushed him backward onto his pillows.

"Now rest," she commanded. "There will be time for adventures later."

"Adventures?" Don protested. "All I want to do is take a little walk. I haven't been out of here since . . . well, I can't even remember when. I want to feel the sunshine on my face. I want to see people doing things. I even want to feel the dust blow against my face. Is that a lot to ask?"

Flory raised one long black eyebrow at him. "That depends on whether or not one has just cheated death. Now, were it me, I would be concentrating on praising God for saving my life and regaining my strength so that I could use it in His service once again. You have nothing to rush for. The mission will still be here when you are finally able to get around it and make us miserable once more."

Her words rang in his ears as she left him to ponder them. Something about them made him uneasy, and soon he realized what it was. He was worried. He was worried that the mission wouldn't be there when he was able to get around. He was worried that in his absence it would fall apart. Already, Toby admitted that villagers prompted by fear had destroyed the outpost clinics. They had no patients.

All around him, empty cots mocked their efforts and reminded him of just how much the mission was suffering. What if they were forced to close it down? He knew that Toby didn't want him to worry—like that was possible—and he wondered just how much she was glossing things over. Were they even worse than what she had related to him?

Angry villagers were capable of many things, not the least of which was harming innocent medical personnel. The memories of Rwanda that had once plagued him continually began to push themselves into the fringes of his consciousness. Average, ordinary citizens, full of anger and fear, had clubbed or stabbed to death thousands of their neighbors, friends, and other ordinary citizens. Only the rich had been able to pay for the privilege of being shot.

"Is that what you want to happen to these friends too?" Merck asked. He knew full well what Don had been through, although for the past few years he hadn't been able to make use of Don's experiences in Rwanda to such a great advantage as he once had. He sensed this would be a prime opportunity to revisit painful memories and use them to get what he wanted . . . namely for Don to leave the mission. "How would you like your beautiful Toby to be clubbed to death by angry villagers who blame her and this mission for the deaths of their loved ones? Would you really like that on your conscience?"

"Don't let fear guide you," Julian warned. "Satan would very much like you to believe that if you only avoid things that you fear, they will never happen. The truth is that you cannot control what happens here or anywhere. That is in God's hands. And His hands are plenty big enough to carry them all. Leave the ones you love in His hands where they are safe."

"Yeah," Merck jeered. "Leave them there where they're as safe as the children at the orphanage were. You remember how safe they were? Not one of them was left alive."

Don could feel a bead of sweat break out on his forehead as painful old memories washed over him. As if it were yesterday,

Don could see the faces of the children he loved so well as he had seen them the day he returned, a bag of beans and rice slung over his back. It was meager rations maybe, enough only for them to have a cup apiece, but to the children who hadn't eaten anything for three days, it would have made a feast. Except that the children were all dead. Later, he found out that members of the vicious *interahamwe*, the secret police, had discovered their hiding place.

Maybe it *would* be better to close down the mission for a while. The locals could stay if they wanted to. Don figured they would want to, since they really had no alternative. He and Toby could take a vacation, maybe even get married. Ray and Julia, well, they hadn't been married that long, they could go on a honeymoon trip somewhere or let Dorsey assign them to another mission. If this one was ever reopened, they could always come back. That only left Flory, and she would be leaving soon anyway.

"Hey, I hear you were trying to get out of bed," Toby's accusing voice brought him back to the present. "What did I tell you about pulling stunts like that? You doctors make lousy patients."

"Flory wasn't supposed to say anything," Don complained.

Toby leaned over and gave him a peck on the cheek. Her lips felt soft and warm against his cheek. Don reached up and took her hand. His own felt so weak. "Hey, I want to talk to you about something."

"Oh yeah?" Her eyes sparkled. "What?"

Don licked his lips uneasily. He wasn't really sure how she would react to his suggestion, but he had an idea. "What would you think about blowing this popsicle stand for a little while?"

Toby grinned wickedly. "What did you have in mind?"

"A vacation, first and foremost," Don elaborated. "I haven't taken one in years. It's about time. Maybe a honeymoon."

"Don Germaine, are you proposing to me?" Toby asked, doing a lousy job of acting shocked.

"No. Not yet," Don replied. "But I've been thinking about it."

"Oh," Toby sniffed haughtily. "In that case . . ."

"Come on, you could use a vacation too," Don said.

"I don't want to shoot your idea down, good as it is," Toby countered. "But we can hardly leave a couple of new nurses here to look after everything while we take long-overdue vacations."

"Careful," Merck warned. "Don't spring it on her. She's not going to like it much as it is. Try to break it to her gently. Talk her into it."

Don cleared his throat. "I wasn't thinking of leaving them here."

"You want them to come with us on our honeymoon?" Toby asked, sarcasm and laughter mingling in her voice. "That I'd like to see. That is, I wouldn't like to see it, but that will be the day."

"I wasn't thinking of them coming with us either," Don replied quietly. He felt Toby's attitude quickly change from levity to unbelief. "I was thinking of closing down the mission for a while."

"What?"

Merck leaned back, disgust written on his face. "Oh, great. Now you've done it. You call that talking her into it? Now you've got her on the defensive. Way to go, Romeo."

"It would only be temporary," Don protested. "Just until I'm feeling better and the situation isn't quite so volatile."

"What situation?" Toby immediately began to pace the length of his cot. Her face worked stormily, a flush creeping up her neck. "What situation?"

"You know perfectly well what situation," Don retorted. "You know even better than I do, but you don't know what happens when things get like this. This isn't Boston. It isn't even New York. If people beat you to death, no one much will care about it. They certainly won't try to help you."

"That's good," Merck observed. "Play on her fear. Work it from that angle. If that doesn't do it, then try playing on her sympa-

thy. *Tell her you were worried about her. Tell her that you didn't want to see her get hurt. And then if she still won't go along with it, put your foot down and tell her the way it's going to be."*

Toby whirled around and stood facing him, her hands clenching and unclenching at her sides. The veins in her neck bulged. "Beat? To death? Are you having a hallucination? Just what is this about?"

Don pushed himself up in bed, but it was an effort. "Did you or did you not tell me that the villagers tore down one of the outpost clinics?"

"Well, yes, I did," Toby sputtered.

Don didn't let her continue. "Let me tell you something. They didn't do it because there was nothing else going on in the village that night."

"No, of course . . ."

"They did it because they are afraid of us. People who are afraid, especially ones who are as superstitious as some of these people are, are dangerous people. What do you think might happen when you start going back out to the clinic?" Don tried to interject some patience in his voice. "I know you haven't been here as long as I have, so take some advice from me. Be careful. Move cautiously."

"I have been."

Toby's words felt like a slap across the face. "You don't mean to tell me that you've gone back out there?" he gasped.

"Yes, that's exactly what I mean." The icy waters of the Atlantic couldn't have been cooler. "Jean-Robert and I have been going out a couple days a week and rebuilding. He talked to the villagers. He made them understand, in a crude way to be sure, about the virus and how it got here. They aren't afraid of us anymore."

Don fell back weakly against his pillows. His face whitened nearly to the same color as the pillowcase. "You could have been killed."

Toby stepped closer to the bed and took one of his hands in hers.

GUARDIANS

"And I could have been killed in Boston by a bus while stepping off a curb. And I could have been killed in the plane crash that night. And I could be killed any time I take off in that ultralight. If I never did anything again because I was afraid of being killed, I'd have to live out the rest of my life in one of those Biospheres."

"Why did you do it?"

Toby appeared to ponder this over for a minute before answering. "Partly, I guess, because I want to help them. And partly because I didn't want to let you down. I was afraid that the clinic would go under while you were recuperating and by the time you got well, there wouldn't be anything to come back to. I was afraid I'd mess up and cost you everything you've been working for."

She grew thoughtful. "You know, though, I was never afraid going back. I felt very calm and peaceful. Jean-Robert and I always prayed first, and I believe God protected us. Not once did a villager threaten us, and when we explained what had happened, they actually understood it. Jean-Robert thought that was a miracle in itself. They were so open to us. Some of the men even helped us to rebuild."

Lileah's face shone. "You felt God's presence because there were faithful people praying for you, and you asked for strength, wisdom, and protection. God will always give you His best. He longs to give you His best. All you need to do is ask for it."

"You're just lucky," Merck grunted. "That's all it was. Sheer luck. Maybe the next time you won't be so lucky. Do you really want to take that chance? You say you're relying on God, trusting in Him, but this is your life you're talking about. You only get one of them. Are you really sure you want to repeat a gamble like that? What if the villagers were just playing along with you to give you a false sense of security? Maybe that's part of their plan. You still aren't safe."

"This life is unimportant in the scope of eternity," Lileah countered. "If you lose it working for the Master, you have done nothing but gain."

Don stared at Toby's face. It shone with confidence. "I don't know . . ."

"What? Don't you believe me?"

"Of course I believe you, it's just that, what if next time . . ."

"Look," Toby said firmly. "God will protect us next time and the time after that and the time after that. This is His work. I'm just glad to be able to help in it. And your part of helping is to get well. We need you! Now, enough talking. You rest. I'll stop in and see you later."

Toby bent over to kiss him. Don could smell the faint aroma of engine grease on her hands as she brushed the hair back off his forehead, stared searchingly into his eyes, and then smiled faintly before turning to leave. After she was gone, he lay on his cot staring up at the ceiling, seeing spots of the blue sky beyond where there was a hole in the roof. That would have to be taken care of once he was up to it.

"I'm sorry I doubted you, Lord," he prayed. "Will You forgive me? Show me how to be strong in Your will, how to be confident, and how to step out in faith. It's hard for me. Especially right now. I feel so helpless. I know that there's a lot I can do right here from this bed. I can be a prayer warrior just like Ethel. My body may be weak, but my prayers can be strong. Will You help me?"

Julian smiled broadly before leaving Don's side to carry his request to the Master. This was his very favorite kind of request to bring. He had a feeling he would be very busy shortly, and he lifted his arms over his head in a victory salute as he shot toward heaven as quick as thought.

Calla turned off the ignition in her car and sat there for a few minutes. She knew her face was flushed, and she could feel her eyes sparkle. One palm felt warm and tingly. It was on the hand that Jesse had shaken after Bible study, just before he left. She knew without a doubt that if Aunt Bernie saw her at this moment, she would guess the truth, that she was attracted to Jesse.

Her heart raced in her chest, and every few minutes a feeling of panic would overwhelm her. She wished the churning of her stomach was just the result of eating something disagreeable. The real cause was too hard to face and much too complicated to want to think about.

What was she doing? She was practically married. She loved Lyle. At least she thought she did. But, if she loved Lyle, how on earth could she be attracted to someone else? It just didn't happen. Maybe she only thought she loved Lyle but really she didn't.

Calla moaned and clutched her head in her hands. "What am I going to do?" she groaned. "I can't be in love with two people. This has to be just some stupid crush. I'm sure I'll get over it once I get a grip on myself. What'll I do if Lyle finds out? He'll hate me. I hate me already. God, what should I do?" she wailed.

Atli watched Calla with compassion. He knew her past and had been able to watch it slowly shape her into the person she was. Her intentions were good. She always went out of her way to help others. The proverbial good Samaritan, she would give a complete stranger her last buck without thinking twice.

But she did this partly to fill a desperate need she had for acceptance. By doing nice things for others, she felt better herself. Her good deeds were a little like a drug. The high she got out of helping others and building them up made her forget her own childhood and the fact that her mother had abandoned her and her father. It dulled the pain she felt when her father leaned on alcohol after her mother left and completely forgot he had a daughter who needed him.

"Be honest with yourself. Be honest with Lyle. Be honest with God," Atli advised. *"Without honesty there can be no love."*

Calla wiped a stray tear out of her eye. She searched her heart and tried to decide exactly how she felt about Lyle. Did she really love him? Or was her love based on pity and the good feeling it gave her to do nice things for him?

"I don't know how I feel," she finally admitted to herself. The admission brought little relief. She sighed and shoved open the creaking car door. Wrapped up in her thoughts, she made her way into the house.

"It's about time you came in," a voice said crossly as she quietly let herself in the side door so she wouldn't wake Aunt Bernie if she had gone to bed early. Calla gasped and spun around.

Lyle leaned forward, his arms propped on the armrests of his chair. His eyes were bloodshot, as if he'd been crying and his face was pale. He looked like a man called to the coroner's office about to view the body of a loved one to confirm identity.

"Lyle," Calla whispered as dread filled her. "Wh-what are you doing here?"

"What were you doing that you weren't here?" Lyle countered.

"I was at a Bible study," Calla said defensively. Suddenly she knew that Lyle knew where she'd been and who she'd been with. He just wanted to hear it from her.

"I didn't know you were giving Bible studies," he said, his voice so cold Calla took a step back. "Who was at this Bible study?"

"Pastor Hendricks," Calla replied with resignation. Better to just get it over with. "And Jesse."

She half-expected Lyle to explode, but he sat calmly, studying her with cold, calculating eyes, waiting for an explanation or an apology or something. Calla realized that whatever it was he wanted, she wasn't able to give.

She was tired of hiding from him. She was tired of feeling guilty. She was tired, just plain tired. "Look, Lyle," she said, her voice deadpan. "I don't know what you want from me. He asked that I be at the Bible study. I wouldn't have gone otherwise. Not that I think I've done anything wrong," she added defensively.

"No?" Lyle questioned.

GUARDIANS

"The truth," Atli insisted. "The truth will set you free."

In that one word, Calla recognized her opportunity to be honest with herself and with Lyle. She opened her mouth to tell him everything, to say she wasn't sure about how she felt anymore, to say that maybe they needed some time apart to grow and to learn about themselves before they were joined before God as one person. But something in the look in his eyes, half-begging to hear that everything was all right, half-challenging her to admit the truth, clammed her up. "No," she said simply.

"Calla," Aunt Bernie said. Calla whirled to face her aunt. She had been so absorbed with Lyle that she didn't even realize Aunt Bernie had been there the whole time, seated in a chair by the fireplace, her Bible open on her lap. There was accusation in her voice, and Calla fought to maintain her composure. "Open your eyes. Don't you see what you're doing is wrong?"

"No," Calla replied icily. "All I see is that the two of you are making a big deal out of nothing. It isn't like I've been on a date! I've been at a Bible study. I wasn't even alone with him. Pastor Hendricks was there. He knows Lyle and I are engaged. He doesn't see anything wrong with it. Why," she gasped, throwing her arms into the air, "he has more trust and faith in me than you two do. And you should know me better."

"We do know you better," Aunt Bernie said softly. "That's why we're concerned about you. We know how tenderhearted you are. We know how easy it is for you to be taken in."

"So that's what you think has happened here? That I've been duped?" Her voice took on a hard, mocking edge. "Poor Calla, tricked into a Bible study by the wily Mr. Redcloud, who hopes to lure her away from her betrothed. What a joke! Get real. You're seeing demons where there are none."

"Calla listen," Atli pleaded. "You know Aunt Bernie and Lyle love you. They have your best interests at heart. He who ignores discipline comes to poverty and shame, but whoever heeds correction is honored. Listen, Calla."

"Oh, what do they know?" Warg taunted. *He edged close to Calla. "They aren't privy to your intentions. They can't see that you only have Jesse's best interests at heart. They can't see that your only concern is helping him, making sure that he becomes a Christian. That's a noble cause. Who are they to try to stop you? It's your Christian duty, after all."*

"That's not what I meant," Aunt Bernie said. "Calla, it's easy for you to give your heart away. It can happen so quickly. I think you can see that it's already happened." At those words Lyle flushed darkly, his fists clenching and unclenching until his knuckles whitened with the force.

"I know you didn't mean for it to happen, and I think it's confusing you. You are engaged to Lyle, and you feel guilty that you're attracted to someone else." Calla felt the blood drain out of her face and hands as Aunt Bernie clarified all of the things she felt, as if she had been eavesdropping in her mind or something. "What you may not realize is how your past has set you up for this. I've watched you and Lyle over the past four years, and I've really worried about you both.

"Lyle, you were starved for affection and attention for so long you just soaked it up when Calla came along. And Calla, honey, I know that what happened with your mom and dad was painful for you. Because of it, you crave attention just as much as Lyle does. What you both need to realize is that two needy people shouldn't be getting married. You each need to stand on your own two feet. You need to learn to dance alone before you dance together."

"Aunt Bernie, you don't know what you're talking about," Calla said hoarsely. "Tell her, Lyle. Tell her she's wrong."

Lyle looked from one to the other. His eyes were full of anguish. "Calla," he said, swallowing hard. "This is probably the hardest thing I've ever done in my life, but I'm breaking our engagement."

Calla felt the air whoosh out of her lungs as if someone had belted her in the midriff. "What are you saying?"

"I'm saying that I think Aunt Bernie is right. I think we need to be on our own before we can be together. I sincerely hope that at some time down the road we can get married, but that time is not right now."

Calla blinked at Lyle, sure that this whole conversation had been a horrible nightmare that she would awaken screaming from at any moment. "I can't believe you'd say that. Don't you love me?" she asked.

"Yes," Lyle replied. "I love you very much. I've never loved anyone else. But I don't trust you. I don't trust you now, and that wouldn't change if we got married. I'd always wonder if I was good enough for you. I'd always feel like you settled for being with me because you felt obligated and that eventually you'd feel trapped in our marriage. I'd always be suspicious of every Jesse Redcloud who happened along."

"If you don't trust me, then you don't love me," Calla whispered. She felt as though she was free-falling through space. It was a sickening feeling.

"I'm willing to go to counseling if you are," Lyle suggested.

"Counseling?" Calla exclaimed in horror. That was not the kind of thing normal people did, was it? Just the thought made her inside writhe in shame. To have to bare her soul to a counselor she didn't know, or even to Pastor Hendricks, was more than she could bear. "No. So where does that leave us?" she asked, bitterness filling her voice.

Lyle shrugged tiredly. "Friends?" he asked. "If you want to be friends."

Calla shook her head stubbornly. "You have to trust your friends too," she said. "I wouldn't want a friend who didn't trust me."

"Maybe you should both sleep on it," Aunt Bernie suggested. "When you've both had time to cool down, you'll be able to discuss it better. Until then, you can think about the direction in which you want your relationship to go."

"I think you've done quite enough for one evening, Aunt Bernie," Calla snapped. "I have a perfect right to choose my friends. If I don't want a friend who doesn't trust me, then that's my decision. I'm the one who has to live with it."

"Calla, I think we can be friends," Lyle began, but Calla cut him off.

"Your kind of friendship I can do without," she said haughtily. "Now if you don't mind, I want to get to bed. It's been a long day, and I'm tired. I'm sure Aunt Bernie will see you to the door."

Without waiting for a reply, Calla spun around and walked quickly down the hallway to her room. It was an effort not to slam the door behind her, but she closed it softly. Not quite knowing what to do first, she stood in the middle of the floor and stared around at the walls of the room she had occupied for such a long time now.

Just days before, she had begun packing up some things that she didn't use in preparation for her wedding. The boxes were stacked neatly against one wall. She was going to take them over to Lyle's and store them there. There would be no need for that now.

"You've already got them packed," Warg suggested. "Why don't you just pack the rest of your things and move out?"

"Don't do anything rash," Atli begged. "Wait, pray, ask God for direction."

"God's made a mess of your direction already," Warg said. "I don't see any benefit in asking Him for any more."

She walked slowly to her bed and sat down, her mind churning slowly with a new idea. Since she was already packed, what was there to prevent her from moving out? She was sick of living with Aunt Bernie. It was time to get out on her own. It was time to leave "home."

She wondered for an instant if she could move in with her mom and stepfather but immediately dismissed the idea. No, if she moved out, she was going to move out on her own. She wasn't going to trade one bad situation for another.

Excitement mingled with fear as she began to consider her options. She'd been an advertising executive with Rowe Collins for just over a year now, and she'd been sacking nearly all of her paycheck away in anticipation of wedding expenses that she was going to have to foot herself. If she wanted, she could afford to get her own apartment.

It was a tempting thought.

For the first time, she'd be her own boss. She'd be on her own. Not responsible *to* anyone else, not responsible *for* anyone else. A chill shivered down her back, not caused by cold, but by the thought of stepping into uncharted territory. In many ways, the thought scared her.

Living alone sounded great compared to the thought of living with Aunt Bernie right now, but what if she were so lonely she couldn't stand it? She'd never been alone. She definitely didn't want to go busting out into the big, wide world and then have to come crawling back to Aunt Bernie because it was too much for her. If she was going to do this, there would be no turning back.

"Pray about it," Atli suggested. "The Master will lead you if you will only ask. Do not make a decision of this magnitude in your own wisdom."

"Hah! Yeah, right," Warg said. "God's not listening to you. If He was, He would have spared you from having to go through this in the first place."

Calla sucked in a sharp breath. It occurred to her that she ought to pray about her decision and ask God to guide her. Stubbornly, she decided not to ask Him. "Just do it," she muttered to herself.

Not wanting to waste a single moment now that her mind was made up, she began to pull things out of her drawers and stuff them into the empty boxes that lined the opposite wall. It was going to take her a couple hours to get it all packed, so she'd get little sleep that night. Which was fine, she told herself. She'd call the office tomorrow and take a personal day. No one would mind.

Facing Aunt Bernie and telling her that she was leaving was not going to be pleasant. She pushed it from her mind. That was later. This was now. Concentrate on now. One thing at a time. The words kept buzzing through her head like radio static, and soon she forgot everything else but the packing. Keeping her hands busy kept her mind off unpleasant thoughts of Lyle and Aunt Bernie.

When she finally finished three hours later, she sat on the edge of the bed and contemplated the mountains of brown cardboard boxes leaning precariously around the room. It occurred to her that she was no longer engaged. As a free agent, she wondered what she would do now about Jesse.

She fell back onto the bed with an exhausted groan. There would be plenty of time to think about that tomorrow. In seconds, she fell asleep with the lights on. At first, she slept with the abandon of a child.

Warg wasn't through with Calla. He wanted to be sure, certain, absolutely positive, that she would leave in the morning. As she slept, he invaded her dreams, making her relive the fight with Aunt Berniece and Lyle. He provoked her into anger again and again as she was subjected to their accusations. In her dreams, he gave her no opportunity to defend herself.

When he thought she'd been through that dream enough, he gave her dreams about Jesse. In those dreams, Jesse was always one step away and Calla was chasing him. Although she got close, she never caught up to him. The dream ended with a start when she bolted up in bed reaching out to touch him.

She blinked in confusion a few times and then lay back feeling sick inside. Before she went back to sleep, she staggered over to turn off the light. The rest of the night, Warg took her through the same dreams again and again. He knew that all the next day she would carry a feeling of uneasiness and despair from the dreams. That was what he wanted.

GUARDIANS

Flory squinted and held her hand up as a shield as she looked out toward the slowly sinking sun. Distracted, she moved away from Toby's side where they had been bent over packing some medical supplies to restock the outpost clinic. Toby tugged her sleeve in irritation.

"Come on, Flory, we're almost finished, and I want to get this ready for tomorrow. My back's killing me." When Flory didn't respond, Toby glanced up at her. She stood slowly, easing her back into an upright position with a groan. She'd been bent over half the day. "What is it?" she asked, following Flory's finger as she pointed.

A jeep bounced across the desert in their direction. "What? It's just Wahabi," Toby said. "He's made at least fifteen excuses in the last month to get out here and show off that new jeep of his. I think he likes to rub it in."

"But someone is with him," Flory said. "Mr. Okeke always comes alone."

Toby looked again. "You're right," she said. "There is someone with him."

She felt her stomach tighten in fear as the jeep grew close enough for them to see the occupants. There was something familiar about that figure in the passenger side. There was something very . . .

Toby sucked in a hasty breath and choked on the dusty air. It couldn't be! That wasn't . . . there was no way . . . it couldn't be.

The jeep pulled up with a belch of dust and a tiny flourish yards from where Toby and Flory stood. Wahabi unfolded his tall body from the driver's side, and a dark-haired man stepped gingerly out of the passenger side.

"Hi, Toby," Davy grinned sheepishly.

"Davy," Toby gasped, feeling faint. "What are you doing here?"

"Am I here?" Davy asked softly. He shot an accusing glance at Wahabi. "If I hadn't just been bounced all the way from Niamey, I would think it was just a very vivid dream. How are you?"

"How *am* I?" Toby repeated. "I'm, I'm . . ."

Lucien, who had gloated over the arrival of Davy, stood watching the exchange nearly as speechless as Toby. Finally he found his voice. "What are you blathering about, woman?" he demanded. "Tell him where to get off. What is he doing here in the first place? Just who does he think he is?"

"Easy, Toby," Lileah cautioned. "Give him some time to explain. After all, he came all the way out here."

"Who cares?" Lucien squealed angrily. "He dumped you. Remember? Whatever he does doesn't interest you anymore."

Toby felt anger well up inside her, replacing the dumbfoundedness that had tied her tongue. "Davy, what are you doing here?" she asked icily, ignoring his question.

Davy flashed her a charming smile that had never failed to melt her insides, but Toby stood firm. Davy glanced uncertainly from Wahabi to Toby. "Uh, thanks for the lift," he told Wahabi. "I'll get my stuff out, and you can go. I don't want to keep you."

"Not in the slightest," Wahabi assured him. "Take your time. I would not miss this for the world. Why do you think I would not take your money? Free ride, free entertainment. It is an even trade." Toby scowled at him, but Wahabi only continued to grin gleefully.

"Oh, uh, well," Davy turned toward Toby and took a hesitant step in her direction. "It's like this, uh, you see, my memory came back. Yeah, isn't that great? And you know, mostly it's back. There are some things that are a little fuzzy still, but I'm working on them. And I'm different, Toby. Really, I'm a changed man. I've been talking to God, praying, you know, and God's been talking to me; at least I think it's Him, and well, I've been thinking about you."

"That's nice, Davy," Toby said, her voice flat. It was anything but nice. "And I suppose God told you to come out here and find me."

"Actually, you'd probably be surprised, but He did. At least, I think He led me out here. How else can you explain my meeting Shay and her telling me all about you? I didn't know where you were. I hadn't the slightest idea."

"You saw Shay?" Toby asked in disbelief. She curbed the urge to ask how Shay was doing.

"I was her neighbor. I was renting the other half of her father's duplex. Weird, huh? I had been asking God where you were. I wanted to apologize. I wanted a second chance. I wanted to make things right with you. And He answered me. He told me where you were. Isn't that awesome?"

Toby winced. "*You* want, Davy? What about what I want? You left me. I didn't leave you. What makes you think I want to *give* you a second chance?"

"Aw, come on, Toby. I lost my memory. I didn't know what I was doing. Can't you forgive me?" Davy pleaded, walking toward her.

Toby took a panicked step back and nearly stumbled into Flory. "I don't know, Davy. I don't know if I can forgive you."

Davy sighed, and his shoulders drooped. "I understand. I know it's a lot to spring on you all at once. Can I at least stay here while you think about it? I'm serious, Toby. I want a second chance. I left everything behind to come and find you. I can't leave now."

Toby studied Davy. If there was one word that described Davy O'Connell, it was "transparent." He was incapable of deception. She believed what he said. Even if she hadn't, she could hardly send him back without the benefit of consideration. "If you stay, you're going to have to work," she warned.

Davy brightened immediately. "Great! I can't wait. What'll I do?"

"Clean bedpans," Toby said dryly. She wasn't even aware of Don's approach until he was right beside her.

"Hey, Toby, aren't you guys done yet? Wahabi, nice to see you. And who's this?" Don's forehead crinkled as he took in the little group, his eyes resting on Davy. He leaned heavily on the cane he relied on to help him get around. Every day he was getting stronger and soon he wouldn't need it.

Toby grimaced. "Don Germaine, meet Davy O'Connell."

"Not funny, Toby," Don quipped, giving her a shove that staggered her a few paces. The look on Davy's face darkened. "Dorsey sent you, right? You're here to check out the outpost clinics? I think you'll be pleased. We've made some real improvements. Of course, we had to totally rebuild, but the clinics are better than ever. Our clientele has really dwindled since the outbreak, but we're hoping to implement new programs that will build it up again."

Davy stuck out his hand. "Actually, no, I'm Davy O'Connell, and I'm here to make peace with my ex-wife. Not that I have anything against your outpost clinics, you understand. I'm sure they're in fine shape. Really."

Don's jaw went slack, and he simply stared from Davy to Toby. She shrugged her shoulders sympathetically and squirmed uncomfortably from the tension.

"So . . ." Davy finally said. "Where do you want me to stay?"

"STAY?" Don roared. "Surely you're not staying?"

"Well, the ticket was a bit pricey for a ten-minute visit. I thought I'd stay, oh, I don't know, my plans aren't firm, indefinitely, I guess."

Don turned to Toby, who was beginning to look miserable. "What is he talking about?" he demanded. "What gave him the idea that he could stay here, and what does he want?" he asked as though Davy didn't exist.

Toby glanced sideways at Davy before replying. "He says that he wants me to give him another chance, that his memory has come back. And I kind of told him that he could stay for a while, until we get things sorted out."

"I thought you had things 'sorted out,' " Don said, his voice low and murderous.

"Guess you thought wrong," Davy said cheerfully. "So, now will you tell me where I can stay?"

Don felt the expletives practically explode from his mouth. Part of him was shocked at his own behavior, but part of him was unbelievably satisfied. "He's staying over my dead body," Don said.

Toby felt her anger flare up in the face of his. "Look, there is no need to get all worked up over this. We're all adults here. This is all happening too fast for me. I want some time to sort things out. I can't send him back tonight anyway, and we could use the help."

"Not his help," Don snarled. "I don't know why you're doing this, Toby, but I don't like it."

"There's nothing to like or not like," Toby said simply. "He's staying. We'll talk. And then he'll move on."

"Not likely," Davy muttered under his breath, but neither Toby nor Don responded. They were so intent on the anger they were directing toward each other that they barely noticed him.

Merck, sensing an unprecedented opportunity that would earn him a promotion rivaling Lucien's status, dove into the fray. "Leave," he offered solicitously. "Just leave. Quit. Go home. You need a vacation anyway. What have you got to lose? Just tell her that if he's not gone in 48 hours, you will be."

"What do you think you're doing?" Lucien asked menacingly.

"I'm going to cut the heart out of the mission," Merck responded calmly.

"I've already weakened it," Lucien countered. "Anything you do will only be an extension of what I have already done."

"I don't think our commander will agree with you," Merck said. So intent were they on their disagreement that neither

*noticed how silent Julian was. The magnificent angel simply
watched, not commenting, not cajoling, not advising. Had they
been paying attention, this would have given them both pause.*

Toby watched the anger work Don's facial muscles as he glared
at her. "One of us is not staying here," Don said menacingly. "If
he's not gone in two days, I will be."

"That is your decision, Don," Toby replied evenly. "I would
hate to see you go."

"Really? We'll see just how much you mean that," Don retorted as he turned and limped off. Toby slumped against the
ultralight, her body weak from the confrontation.

"He doesn't treat you very nice," Davy observed.

"Don't go there, Davy," Toby growled. "You don't have a leg to
stand on. Flory, would you show Davy where he can stay? Put
him in the east wing. I'll finish up here."

Long after Flory had led Davy away and Wahabi had driven
off, his throaty chuckle carrying back to her on the wind, Toby
stood with her back against the ultralight, not moving. Around
her, shadows formed as the sun dipped below the horizon. "Oh,
God," she whispered between trembling lips. "What am I going
to do? What do You want me to do? I prayed for this very thing
for so long, and now that it's here I don't want it."

She blinked away tears as she thought about Don and how
much he had come to mean to her. She'd had every intention of
marrying him someday. And now, in one instant, her whole future was uncertain.

Her mind was flooded with memories of her life with Davy.
He'd meant everything to her, too much almost. Being with him
was so exciting that she'd let go of God. They had been everything to each other. People jokingly said they were joined at the
hip.

For a long time after her world shattered and she'd come to
Africa, she had asked God, begged Him, really, to restore Davy's
memory, to send Davy looking for her, to make him into the

godly husband she knew he could be. And nothing happened. At least, nothing that she could see. It stunned her to realize that somewhere along the line she had given up hope.

She'd fallen in love with Don. And, she reminded herself, biblically there was nothing wrong with that. Davy divorced *her*, not the other way around. Why shouldn't she move on and be happy? She had every right.

Except that here was Davy, messing things up.

The cocky grin, the flashing eyes, the easy way he had about him all brought such strong feelings flooding back to her that she could hardly think of anything else. What if they could get back together? Would she want that?

Toby sank weakly into a sitting position beside the ultralight. "Oh, God, I don't know what I want. Can You help me?"

"Delight yourself in the Lord," Lileah advised, *"and He will give you the desires of your heart. Commit your way to the Lord; trust in Him and He will do this: He will make your righteousness shine like the dawn, the justice of your cause like the noonday sun. Be still before the Lord and wait patiently for him; do not fret."*

Lucien brooded a short distance away. He was unsure of how to proceed. He had not foreseen Merck's surprise move to oust Don, and now he felt one swing behind the game. He debated what to say to Toby. Would it be in his best interest to advise her to stay? To go? To give Davy a second chance? To send Davy packing? While he was mulling over his options, Toby made up her mind.

"Thank You, Lord. I will wait on You. I won't make any decisions until I know which direction You want me to take." Toby pushed herself onto her feet and went back to packing. Even though her life hadn't changed, her outlook had, and that made all the difference.

CHAPTER

13

The print in front of Billie Jo's eyes was beginning to blur. She hadn't gotten much sleep the night before and almost hadn't bothered coming to the library. But Leah had called her out of the blue and offered to watch the kids. Billie Jo was almost at the end of the 1945 folder, and she wanted to finish it.

She stifled a yawn and took a few deep breaths to clear her head. Lately, she was beginning to think she was on a wild goose chase. Even so, she felt compelled to return time after time when she could have been doing something else. She turned each page with a sense of urgency, as if what she sought might be on the very next page.

She flipped the yellowed page over, her eyes scanning the columns. She missed the headline, but a picture of a forlorn-looking little girl caught her eye. The caption read: "Mother takes own life and lives of seven children ages 5 months to 12 years. Lone daughter survives."

Billie Jo gasped. "How awful," she murmured. She didn't usually bother reading the articles because it would take up too much time, but this time she couldn't help herself. Before she knew it, she was reading:

"Authorities were called to the home of Randall Kennedy early Wednesday morning. Mr. Kennedy, who had gone to the market for groceries, returned to find his wife, Annabel Kennedy, had shot and killed six of their seven children, the youngest a five-month-old baby. The seventh, ten year old Helen Kennedy, had been presumed dead, though only wounded superficially. After taking the lives of her children, Mrs. Kennedy turned the gun on herself. She left a single round in the chamber and a note to her husband that the remaining bullet was for him. Mrs. Kennedy had been known to have a family history of depression and suicide. Her doctor believes she may have been suffering from post-partum depression. Services will be held . . ."

The article went on, but Billie Jo was too stunned to read further. Kennedy was Helen's maiden name. Little ten year-old Helen Kennedy had grown up and married James Raynard and become her mother-in-law.

"No wonder she don't want to let Jimmy go," Billie Jo muttered. "She lost almost all of her family in one fell swoop. Somethin' that awful probably made her want to hang on for dear life to everybody."

"What's that?" Jay asked kindly. "Were you speaking to me?"

Billie Jo looked up with a start. "Huh? Uh, no, just talkin' to myself." She stared up at him with a blank expression on her face. "I'm sorry, I've had a bit of a nasty shock. I don't mean to be rude."

Jay brushed her apology off. "Think nothing of it. Is there anything I can do?"

Billie Jo shrugged helplessly. "No, I don't think so. I just can't seem to take it all in is all." She sighed. It would feel so nice to talk to someone about Helen. Before she knew it, she was telling Jay everything. "And now," she concluded, "I think I know why she's done it all."

"And how does that make you feel?" Jay prompted.

"Sorry for her," Billie Jo said. "I feel plumb sorry for her. I mean, how awful! No one should have to go through what she went through. I can just imagine her as a little kid. She probably figured she'd lose her father next. Then she married James and wondered if she'd lose him, then Jimmy. No wonder she clings to them so hard. Her past has been haunting her something fierce all these years.

"Seems like she got worse when Jimmy had the accident, probably 'cause we came so close to losing him. Then when he got better, he kinda drew back from her 'cause she tried so hard to take our kids away from us. I think now that it scared her. She felt like she was losing all of us. That's why she did it."

"Did what?" Jay asked, watching her intensely.

"She tried to kill herself," Billie Jo said, more to herself than to him. "That's why she tried to kill herself. And that's why she hates me so much. In her eyes, I'm the one who took her only son away. I'm the one who's standing between her and her grandkids."

As she began to understand Helen, Billie Jo became more and more excited. "She's jealous of me. I have all the attention of her son and grandkids, and she's got nothing. Most times James barely knows she's alive. That's why she's always invitin' herself over and giving the kids presents. She figgers she needs to buy their love to be sure she'll get it. She's not taking any chances with love."

Jay nodded. "Sounds logical," he agreed.

Billie Jo temporarily forgot he was there. Her mind raced ahead to what she could do with this new knowledge. A scene played out in her mind. She saw herself approach Helen with what she knew. She saw Helen, stricken, but relieved to have someone to share her burden with. The dream-Helen broke down, sobbing on her shoulder, realizing that Billie Jo understood her. They had a heart-to-heart in which they straightened out all the misunderstandings of the past.

With the clean slate of their relationship in front of them, they wrote terms they would live by. Helen became the model grand-mother, a godly woman that Billie Jo was thrilled to leave her children in the care of. The time she spent with them, she used to instill Bible truths and reenforce Billie Jo and Jimmy's instruction. In every way, she supported their efforts to raise their children to be good Christians.

Billie Jo's bubble burst just before the dream-Helen grew old and died, a revered family patriarch. As if someone had splashed cold water over her, she realized with a start that just because she knew what had shaped Helen into the person she was didn't mean that Helen would change at all. The fact that she had remained the same despite all the attempts Billie Jo had made in the past to be nice to her were precedent enough.

Her shoulders slumped, and she sat staring dejectedly at the photo in the newspaper. "All this has been for nothing," she muttered. "It don't matter if I know why she's like she is. That don't change her none."

"You know," Jay said, startling her. "God's love, when it touches a heart, is so powerful it can melt it even if it is as cold as the ice on the North Pole."

"You don't know this woman," Billie Jo said angrily. "A blow-torch wouldn't melt her heart."

"I wasn't talking about her heart," Jay replied softly. Billie Jo looked up with a start.

"You think I got a cold heart?" she asked in dismay.

"No," Jay replied. "I think your heart is tender, but it takes more than a tender heart to deal with hard people. There are some people who are difficult to love in our humanity. But God can give us His love to pour out to them. It may never change them, but we're not called to change them. Only to love them. And we don't even have to do that out of the love in our own hearts."

Billie Jo had to think about that. "Guess I never looked at it that way. I wanted her to change. I just figgered it'd be easier and that would be what God wanted. Suppose I can't expect everyone that's hard to get along with to change just 'cause I'd like 'em to." She knew the skepticism she felt showed up on her face. "I'm not real sure I know how to do that," she admitted. "I been hating her for a long time. I'm afraid of her, see? And you know how we hate the things we fear. I'm afraid she'll corrupt my kids."

"Prayer," Jay supplied. "Prayer is our hotline to heaven. It's how God delivers His power to us. Try it and see if it doesn't work."

"Prayer?" Billie Jo asked doubtfully.

"Prayer," Jay repeated.

Billie Jo glanced at her watch with a gasp. "I gotta go," she said suddenly. She looked at the open book on the table, but Jay waved her out.

"Go on. I'll pick up," he assured her.

"Thanks, Jay," she said, scurrying up the stairs breathlessly. Leah would be wondering where she was.

"Hello, Billie Jo," Robin, the librarian greeted her. "Find everything you were looking for?"

"Sure did this time," Billie Jo said. "You know, you ought to give Jay a raise. He's so helpful."

"Jay?" Robin asked, a puzzled look on her face.

"Yeah, Jay. The guy that works in the basement."

"But Billie Jo," Robin began.

"I'm sorry, Robin," Billie Jo cut her off apologetically. "I can't stay to talk today. I've got to get home before Leah kills me. My kids are probably driving her nuts by now. I'll stop in again soon. I promise."

Billie Jo shrugged off the weird look Robin was giving her and raced out to where she'd parked her car. She had a lot to think about on the way home, but first she had to pray. "Dear Lord," she started.

Guardians

Ethel Bennington had a lot of dreams these days. She realized it was because she was asleep much more than she could ever remember. As a young mother, she'd craved sleep when she couldn't have it. As a middle-aged widow, she had begun to suffer from insomnia. Her latest struggle with sleep was not to find it but to evade its clutches.

No sooner would she begin to pray than her eyelids would feel heavy and her chin would sink onto her chest, only to snap up in panic. She lived with a constant feeling of frustration, because there was work to be done for her Master, and her weak body prevented her from doing it. She didn't need the soulful look on her doctor's face to know that her time was short.

Rather than dread what was coming, she looked forward to it with great anticipation. Death held no fear for her. She had spent a lifetime with God on this side of eternity, and she was anxious to see Him face to face. They had so much to talk about!

She did have some reservations about leaving Cindi. Although they never talked about her impending death, she had the feeling that Cindi didn't really expect it. Esther kept her so distracted that Ethel feared the event would be a terrible shock to her. And she wasn't sure how to break it to her gently.

How did one go about saying, "I'm going to be dying soon. Prepare yourself"?

Ethel did have one regret. From the moment she had discovered her daughter Carol's absence, she had prayed fervently to see her one last time. She often wondered what had happened to Carol. There were times when she was sure the reason she had never returned was because she had met with an accident. Still, that didn't prevent her from praying for Carol's safety throughout every day.

Now that she had come to the end of her life, she wished she could know for sure what had happened to her vivacious daughter. "But it's OK, Lord," she murmured. "I know that wherever Carol is, You're keeping Your hand on her. I'll see her here or there one way or the other. And I'd appreciate it, if she still walks this earth, if You'd walk with her. After I pass on, there'll be no one to remember her and uplift her in their prayers."

Ethel sighed deeply. She was tired again. With a slight yawn, she closed her eyes. It was time to pray. She made a mental note to mention Carol to Cindi again and ask her to remember her in prayer after she was gone.

A gentle breeze whistled in through the window, brushing the strings of the wind harp Cindi had placed there at Ethel's request in the hopes that the sound would help her stay awake. The sound of the strings varied in strength, and the soft sound, rather than wake her up, made her sleepy. Within minutes, Ethel's eyes closed, and her chin sank one last time onto her chest.

"Rest now, dear saint," Reissa murmured. A crystal tear slid down her golden cheek. She backed out of the room as it filled with rejoicing demons. Sparn triumphantly led the charge. "You have fought the good fight and run a good race. The Master will be so happy to welcome you home."

Sparn spun happy circles around the room, whirling in joyful abandon. "She is gone, and they are cut off!" he shouted jubilantly. The very air in the room suddenly seemed stale. Demons began to crowd in, elbowing each other for space. Their happy countenances sent a shiver down Reissa's back. She gave one last pitiful look over her shoulder before vanishing in a flash of light. It was time for a new assignment.

Calla woke up more tired, if possible, than when she'd fallen asleep. The last vestiges of sleep clung to her with clammy tenacity. She sat up and tried to shake off the feeling of dread that persisted in spite of the sunshine streaming cheerfully in the window.

She could hear Aunt Bernie rattling pots and pans in the kitchen. Before she dared to face her aunt, she needed to call in to work.

"Linny?" she asked, when a female voice picked up with a sickeningly happy 'Hello.' "It's Cal. I'm going to take a personal day today. I've got some stuff to do that won't wait. Is that all right? Great. I'll be in tomorrow. See you."

She replaced the phone in its cradle and pushed herself out of bed. No time like the present. Running her hands through her hair and flipping it over to one side, she padded down the hall and stood in the kitchen doorway waiting for Aunt Bernie to notice her. Finally, she cleared her throat.

Aunt Bernie looked up. "Good morning, Calla. Aren't you going to be late for work?"

"I'm not going to work today, Aunt Bernie. I'm going to be moving out."

"I see," Aunt Bernie said slowly. "Are you sure that's wise?"

"Wise?" Calla bristled. "Why wouldn't it be wise? I'm an adult. I have a job. I can't live here for the rest of my life. I was going to be moving out in six months when I got married anyway. Now it looks like I won't be getting married, but I still think it's time for me to move on."

Aunt Bernie's eyes filled with tears, and she brushed at them with the back of her sleeve. "Oh, Calla, I'll miss you so!"

"Give me a break," Warg growled. "The old broad won't miss you at all. She's secretly rejoicing that she'll have her house all to herself again. Don't let that sob trick you into thinking that she cares about you, because she doesn't. Brace yourself. Weepy females have a way of making people melt. Don't fall for that old trick. She may be crying on the outside, but inside she's jumping for joy."

"Calla," Atli said, moving protectively closer to her. "Your Aunt Berniece has taken care of you all these years. In many ways, she's been more of a parent to you then your biological parents. She deserves your love and your respect. Think of these things before you answer."

Calla felt a lump in her own throat. "I'll miss you too," she said quietly. "I've enjoyed living here. I just . . . I just think . . ." She fought them, but tears of fear and loss burst out with a fury that startled her. "Aunt Bernie, I'm so scared!" she wailed.

She wasn't sure how she got there, but she became aware of Aunt Bernie's arms around her as she sobbed her heart out. Her aunt's comforting hands patted her head as reassuring "shhh-shhh's" penetrated the cries of her heart. When her emotions had spent themselves, she pulled away from her aunt's embrace and stumbled over to the counter for tissues.

"I-I'm scared to live by myself, Aunt Bernie," she confessed as ragged breaths hiccuped between sobs. "But, it's something I have to do. I have to prove to myself that I'm responsible, that I'm independent. I don't want to rely on other people anymore. I need to learn how to rely on me."

"Can't you do that here?" Aunt Bernie asked.

Calla shook her head and blew her nose loudly. "No. This place has been like home. It's time to leave home." She shrugged her shoulders helplessly. "You were right. I need to learn how to dance alone. I've got to prove to myself that I'm enough. That I don't need to depend on someone else for my happiness. I've got to lean on God and let Him support me. If I don't learn that now,

GUARDIANS

I'll just have to learn it later, and the lesson might be more painful then."

Aunt Bernie wiped her eyes in the sleeve of her bathrobe. There was a hint of a resigned smile on her face. "Well, it sounds like you're growing up already," she sighed. "How can I help?"

Calla looked around the small, cheerful kitchen and spied the newspaper open on the table. A short embarrassed laugh cleared her throat. "Actually, I need an apartment. Did you happen to notice anything in the paper?"

Aunt Bernie sat down and flipped the paper open to the classified section. "Nothing caught my eye," she smiled. "But I'll take a look for you."

Calla prepared herself a quick breakfast of toast and grabbed a banana. As she moved around the kitchen, Aunt Bernie read her interesting selections from the paper. She sat down opposite her aunt and tried to eat, but everything tasted like sawdust. What was she doing? Things were OK here with Aunt Bernie. Did she really have to leave now? Maybe she could just stay a while longer.

But, you've got to prove yourself, Calla, she reminded herself firmly. *It was probably normal to be nervous about leaving "home." Besides, it was time to stretch and take some risks. It was time to grow.*

The remainder of the day passed in a blur. Aunt Bernie managed to locate an acceptable apartment and with some savvy negotiating, she arranged for Calla to move her things out that very day. She even volunteered to rent a moving van. Calla began transferring the boxes from her bedroom to the living room while she waited for her aunt to return.

Just as she was about to break down thinking about all the good times she'd had living there, Aunt Bernie drove up and tooted the horn. Calla laughed out loud watching Aunt Bernie put her fingers to her lips, whistle like a truck driver, and yell "Come on. We're burning daylight."

"If I get this truck back by five, they'll give me a refund," she panted, as she helped Calla lug boxes out to the truck.

"Aunt Bernie, I'm going to miss you," Calla laughed, shoving her knee under a box for leverage and hoisting it up onto the bed of the truck.

"I'm going to miss you," a quiet voice said.

Calla whirled around to see Lyle watching her. His eyes were bloodshot, and he looked as though he hadn't changed clothes from the night before. In fact, he looked as though he hadn't slept all night. "Lyle," she stammered. "Hi. What are you doing?"

"I saw the van. I couldn't believe that you were moving out, so I had to come see for myself. But it's true, isn't it?"

Calla hung her head. "Yes, it's true. It's something I have to do."

Lyle nodded tiredly. "I understand."

"I'm sorry about the way things worked out," Calla offered.

"Yeah, I am too," Lyle agreed sullenly. "Is it over then?"

"I honestly don't know, Lyle. I wish I did. I agree with you though. We need to be on our own before we know if we're ever going to be together. You have to be able to trust me, and I have to be able to trust myself."

"It's all Jesse's fault," Lyle said bitterly. "If he hadn't showed up, none of this would have happened."

Calla approached his chair hesitantly. "Don't blame Jesse, Lyle. It's not his fault. It's my fault. You were right. There would have been a Jesse sooner or later." She swallowed carefully. "I know this has been hard, but I'm glad that it happened before we got married. It might have been much harder to fix afterward."

"So you don't care if I start dating?" Lyle challenged.

Calla tried to keep the hurt out of her eyes. "Of course I care," she replied. "But I think you should. You need to realize that people love and accept you for who you are, not because they feel sorry for you. I hope they improve on my example. I know it hasn't been great. That doesn't have anything to do with you though. I have some stuff of my own to work out. Aunt Bernie talked to me about seeing a counselor, and I'm beginning to think she's right."

"You're going to see a shrink?" Lyle asked incredulously. Then he added slyly, "You're not that messed up."

Calla felt a smile warm her face. "Thanks, coming from you that really means a lot. I wish you all the best, Lyle. I really do."

"Are you going to let me take you out sometimes?"

Calla thought about the question for quite a while before she answered. She could tell that Lyle was getting uncomfortable about the pause. "Not right now," she finally said. "But later, I would like that very much."

Lyle nodded. "I understand," he said glumly. He pushed his chair in a tight circle. "Have a good one, Calla," he said.

Although his back was to her, Calla was quite sure she heard tears in his voice. Her whole heart wanted to cry out to him to come back. She ached to tell him that they could just work this out, maybe go to counseling together, postpone the wedding rather than cancel it. She twisted her lips together to keep from blurting her feelings out.

It was better this way. If things worked out later, then their relationship would be much stronger for this time that they were going through. And if they never got together, it was easier to break things off cleanly right now than to hack the relationship to pieces trying to work things out in their personal lives.

Toby glared across the compound. Davy's laugh carried the entire distance with no trouble. He was joking with some of the locals as he tried to teach them baseball. The trouble was that they were actually enjoying it. The children who were on recess from school flocked around him like pigeons to a statue in the park.

In the two weeks he'd been there, Davy had managed to ingratiate himself into the hearts of not only the patients but the locals and the mission staff. Even Wahabi, who took at least a year to begin to warm up to her, had made several trips out to the mission to talk to Davy. Wahabi had delivered a letter to him that had it been addressed to her would have languished at the bar until she made her way into town the next time.

Toby stuffed supplies into her flight bag with much more force than was necessary. It irritated her to no end that Davy was so well liked. It would have been so much easier to send him packing if everyone had hated him. So far, the only person who truly hated Davy was gone.

True to his word, Don had packed his bags and departed for the States exactly two days after Davy's arrival. At first, Toby had been sure that he was bluffing. He'd maintained a bristling silence after Davy showed up, waiting to see what she'd do.

Toby knew what she *wanted* to do. She wanted to toss Davy out on his ear. It would have been so *satisfying*. But something stopped her. Even she wasn't sure exactly what it was. There was a small voice inside that just kept saying, "Wait." So she waited.

The morning Don left was burned into her memory. Jean-Robert packed the jeep while Don approached her in the clinic. "Is he going?" he'd asked shortly.

She'd studied him, wanting to say Yes, but she couldn't bring herself to do it. "No," she'd replied. "Not yet."

"I'm going home," he had said without preamble.

"Well, you need a vacation. Dorsey's always telling you to take one," she'd replied lightly.

"I'm not taking a vacation," he'd replied. "I'm going home for good."

"You can't," she'd said, trying to keep her voice steady.

"Watch me," he'd said. His gray eyes were cold and hard. "It's been real . . ."

No "goodbye." No "I love you." No instructions. Nothing. Not even a wave as Jean-Robert drove him into Niamey.

For a few days she hoped, insanely, that he would come back, hoping to have scared her into sending Davy away. But he never came back. When she realized that he was gone for real, she'd called Dorsey in a panic.

He assured her that Don had a volatile personality and was no doubt just taking a long-overdue vacation. It was about time, really, and Dorsey was pleased, even if it did leave them in a tight spot. No doubt Don would be back once he thought he'd taught her a lesson. Toby wasn't so sure. In the meantime, Dorsey was confident that she could manage the outpost in Don's absence. He had every confidence in her. Toby wished she had confidence in herself.

Not only was she saddled with the most perplexing personal problem she had ever faced but she'd driven away the man she had planned to marry because of her own stubbornness. On top of that, she had a temporary nurse and two greenhorns besides a meager staff of local nurses. Davy had managed to fill her role as pilot, ferrying Flory to the clinics while she looked after things at the mission. Now she wondered if the clinic should just be closed down for a while, maybe permanently.

She was quite concerned that there was no doctor. Her own nursing skills had expanded to cover nearly every area she was likely to encounter, but there were still things she had no ability to cope with. Dorsey had blown off her request for a replacement doctor. Doctors were in short supply, and there was no one who could be shipped out there for the short time Don would probably be gone. He assured her that he would make every attempt to locate Don, and he was positive that within four weeks at the outside he would return, contrite and refreshed with an improved outlook.

"Deep thoughts?" Davy's voice jerked her out of her reverie.

She scowled at him. "Why would I have deep thoughts? I'm only responsible for an entire mission post, thanks to you."

Davy threw up his hands in a gesture of surrender. "Hey, I didn't make him leave. If you ask me, he was overly touchy about the whole situation."

"I didn't ask," Toby responded dryly. "And what do you know about it anyway? You just barged in here into the middle of my life. I didn't invite you," she pointed out.

"No, but I'm an answer to your prayers," Davy said. "Aren't I? Isn't this exactly what you prayed for?"

Toby clamped her mouth shut tight to prevent a gasp of surprise. "What makes you think that?" she demanded.

"Pompous, arrogant, egomaniac," Belial supplied her with adjectives to apply to his charge. "But, intuitive. Deny it. Go ahead."

"Toby, what he's saying is the truth," Lileah reminded her. "I, myself, heard your pleas to the Master on his behalf. You asked for his heart to change. You asked for him to find you against incredible odds. Because of these requests, the Master was able to approach Davy and invite him to accept His love. The Master ceaselessly pursued Davy's heart, and it was changed. Look at the evidence before you. This is precisely what you asked for."

"Shay told me how much you wanted me to change and come looking for you."

"She had no right," Toby muttered darkly.

"She had every right," Davy countered. "Toby, look at me." He reached over and gently cupped her chin in his hand, forcing her to meet his eyes. His face was soft, open. His expression was loving. Toby felt her heart melting in spite of herself.

"I'm sorry about what happened after the accident. I was confused. I didn't know who I was. I didn't know anything. All I wanted to do was fill up the emptiness inside me with stuff so I wouldn't have to think about how I didn't even know who I was. I wasn't fit to be a husband.

"What I did was wrong. I know that now, but that won't change the things I did. I realize I hurt you, and I'm very sorry. I wish I had it to do all over again. Do you think you can forgive me? Or is it too late?"

Toby hesitated, biting her lip. Davy's face was lined with sorrow. She could hardly question his repentance; it was written all over his face.

"The Master calls you to forgive each other as He forgives you," Lileah supplied. *"He will help you to forgive. And He will help you to love again. Love is a choice, not a feeling. If you choose to love this man again, the Master will help you."*

"Bah!" Belial snorted. *"Do you really want to go through the rest of your life with no loving feelings for this guy? I think not! He's the one who dumped you, after all. Why even give him a second chance? Forgive him, sure. Why not? But then tell him to take a hike. You don't need him. Forget him. You were doing fine without him."*

"I'll understand if it's too late," he said huskily, misinterpreting her silence. "I'll just pack my bags and go. I'll leave you alone. You don't have to worry about it. I won't hang around here and be a nuisance."

"I don't know if it's too late, Davy," Toby said quickly. "I'm angry with you for what you put me through. The accident was traumatic for me, too, and then I lost you. But in the time I've been here I've really changed. I've gotten a lot closer to God. I have a relationship with Him now, and that's very important to me. Even if I were willing to give you a second chance, I could never go back to the way we were living.

"That part of my life is over. I don't know where I want to go from here. I don't know if I want to stay here forever. But whatever I do, I will feel led by God to do it. I can forgive you, but I'm just not sure if I can . . ." Toby paused with irritation. Davy looked like he was bursting to say something. "What is it?"

"I agree with you," Davy said excitedly. "God's been talking to me too. I'm different now. God's helped me a lot. In fact, some really weird things happened to me. But I think He's been trying to talk to me. He's the one who showed me where to find you. I don't think that running into Shay was a coincidence."

Festus had been bored lately. There just wasn't much to do. Patients had been few and far between. The staff for the most part had been bored slightly, but relaxed. It was hard to start any fights. The new nurses from the States were so in love they could barely keep their eyes off each other. Newlyweds. They made him sick to his stomach.

Until Davy arrived, Festus had been at his wits' end for pranks to pull. Now opportunities were ripe. One bright idea popped into his head and without even bothering to evaluate it, he acted, sweeping a ragged wing over the surface of the baked landscape, sending a spray of fine sand blowing directly toward Toby and Davy as they stood talking. His purpose was merely to annoy them.

"What are you doing?" Belial shrieked, flying toward him, trying to block the spray of sand. "Stop!"

Festus danced with surprising agility out of his path and laughed a taunt as he blew more sand into the thick cloud. "I thought of it first," he called to Belial, who was pursuing him with evil intentions. "I get all the credit."

"You're going to be sorry when I catch up to you, you little pip-squeak," Belial promised.

"Is that any way to talk to your betters?" Festus jeered. "You're just sore because you didn't think of it first."

"You're ruining everything," Belial screeched. With an extra lunge, he caught the hapless little demon around the neck and nearly choked him senseless, but it was too late. The damage was done.

Toby turned her face away from a scorching breeze that kicked up, sending dust scuttling across the courtyard. It pelted the body of the ultralight in such a fine spray it hissed. The sand felt like needles pricking her exposed skin. Davy grabbed her hand and shielded his face with his hand.

"The clinic," Jes suggested, using the demon's mistake to her advantage. "Run for it." She followed along closely as Davy and Toby ducked their heads against the onslaught and ran toward the open door of the clinic.

"Come in here," he said, pulling her into the darkened clinic. Since the outbreak, there had been no overnight patients. In fact, if it hadn't been for the outpost clinics, they wouldn't have had much of anything to do. Toby guessed that if Don had to be gone for a while, now was a good time. She allowed Davy to guide her into the refuge of the clinic.

Stray grains of sand fell onto the corrugated tin roof like hail, but most of the noise was muted as the sand beat against the cement walls. Toby tried to catch her breath and shake sand out of her hair and gradually became aware of the fact that Davy's arm was around her waist. It seemed so natural that she hadn't even noticed. She looked up with alarm and found him watching her with a tender expression on his face.

"What's that sappy look for?" she asked, feeling panic fill her chest. All of a sudden, the clinic felt like a small closet.

Her hostility didn't seem to dampen Davy's attitude at all. "You're beautiful, do you know that?"

"Ha! You pick a fine time to tell me something like that," she growled defensively. "I've been working on that engine all morning. I'm covered with grease, and now my hair has so much sand in it I almost qualify as a terrarium."

Davy tipped her chin up and before she fully realized what he was doing, he bent down and placed his lips on hers. His kiss was warm and familiar. Toby felt her knees wobble, and she leaned against him heavily.

"You don't play fair," she said weakly, trying without success to collect her thoughts. Everything was too much like she remembered. Even the faint smell of bay rum aftershave on his sun-warmed skin was the same. She felt her hands creep up and her fingers tangle in his thick black hair.

"I've missed you so much, Toby," Davy breathed.

"Yeah," she croaked. "Ever since you remembered me, right?" She half hoped he'd lie to her and say he'd always missed her, even when he hadn't remembered her. She wanted to hear that the ghost of her memory had made every other relationship seem empty and meaningless. She wanted to believe that, even if she knew it wasn't true.

"Every memory I had made me miss you more," he said. "When I began to realize what I had let go when I walked out of your life, I thought I would die. We had the greatest relationship. Remember?"

Toby laughed. "Yes, I've always remembered. The question is, do you remember? Do you really remember?"

"I remember everything," Davy assured her. "Once my memory started to come back, it was like cracks of sunlight coming through a brick wall. As the wall crumbled, more and more light got through until the wall was gone."

"This isn't going to be easy," Toby warned him. "Just because I give you a second chance doesn't mean that it will work out. We are divorced, after all. And a lot of things have happened since we saw each other last. And just because I'm still attracted to you doesn't mean I'll ever feel love, real love, for you. But . . . I believe that if you don't do anything to destroy my growing trust in you that it will happen."

"Then you'll give me a second chance?" Davy asked excitedly.

Toby nodded and grinned at him. "Yes, I'll give you a second chance. I loved you more than anything at one time. If there's even a chance to reclaim that love, I want to know."

"Whoopee!" Davy yelped, jerking her off her feet and swinging her in dizzying circles around the room until they crashed into a cot and tumbled headlong across it. Laughing breathlessly, Davy cupped her face in his hands and peppered her face with kisses.

"Whoa," Toby protested. "A little of that goes a long way. Cool it, will ya?"

Davy grabbed her hand and pulled her unsteadily to her feet where she swayed slightly, overcome with emotion. "You OK?" he asked.

"I'll be fine," Toby said. "I think."

Belial groaned at the dizzy look on her face. Any idiot could see she was falling in love with Davy. Any idiot, except . . . He tightened his grip on Festus's neck, and the demon kicked and squirmed against his grasp. "Come," he said. "You and I are going to take a trip. I hope your insurance policy is paid up." Belial cackled at his own joke.

Festus's eyes widened with fear, and he struggled to free himself, but he was no match for the stronger Belial. As he was dragged to see Captain Lucien, he felt the cold hand of fear grip him. This was not going to be pleasant.

CHAPTER 14

It was drizzling lightly when Don heaved himself wearily out of the cab and handed a wad of bills to the driver.

"Keep the change," he said thickly. He hadn't slept for more than a few hours in the past few days. The lack of sleep dulled his emotions. He hadn't seen his sister, Cindi, in probably seven years. He thought he ought to at least feel some excitement, but there was nothing besides a dull ache in his chest that blocked out everything else.

He left his bags on the sidewalk and staggered up the walkway to the front door. The house hadn't changed much since he'd been gone. There were a few more flowers in the flower beds, but there were more weeds too. He knocked hesitantly on the jade-colored door and thought that perhaps it had been a different color last time.

The door opened a crack, but Don saw no one look out to discover who had landed on the doorstep. He blinked owlishly, trying to see inside the house from the crack in the door.

"Who are you?" a small voice asked from somewhere down by his knees.

Don refocused, searching for the source of the voice. An elfin face looked up at him, full of curiosity.

"You can't be Esther," Don said trying to comprehend four years worth of growth in the flesh.

"Yes, I can too," the elf insisted. "I am, too, Esther. How come you know me? I don't know you."

Don squatted onto his heels and looked directly into the elf's face. "Sure you do. I'm your Uncle Don."

"Uncle Donny," the elf squealed, throwing the door open wide and launching herself into his arms, staggering him.

"Esther," a woman's voice scolded. "I told you never to open the door to strangers."

Don picked Esther up and swung her easily onto one hip. "She didn't," he said, unable to keep the catch out of his voice. "How are you doing, Sis?"

Cindi came around the corner, her mouth open in surprise. She gaped at him like a stranded goldfish. "Donny? Is that really you? Donny! Marc," she screamed over her shoulder, "it's Donny!"

"No joke?" he heard his brother-in-law reply as Cindi flung herself into his arms, tears of joy streaming down her face.

"Hey, Cindi," Don murmured, struggling to hang onto Esther and hug his sister at the same time.

"Why didn't you tell us you were coming?" Cindi asked. "Don't stand out there in the rain. Come in, come in. Marc, would you get his bags? Oh, Donny, I can't believe you're home."

Don allowed Cindi to lead him into the house. He gratefully set Esther down on the floor where she proceeded to study him intently. "Did you know Grammy died?" she asked suddenly.

Don felt fear clutch his heart. "What?"

Cindi made a grab for Esther but was too late to hush her up. "Essie, shhhh," she hissed. When she looked up, Don guessed the truth from the pain in her eyes.

"Ethel is dead?" he asked, numb with shock.

"I'm sorry, Donny. I wrote you. I had no idea you were coming home. I'm sorry you had to find out so abruptly."

"No, it's OK," Don said. "I think I need to sit down."

He found a chair just before his legs gave out from under him. His mind still reeled with the news. "I can't believe the old war horse is gone," he choked out, his throat painfully tight. "I never even had a chance to say goodbye."

Weeping softly, Cindi pulled up a chair opposite Don and reached out to hold his hands in her own. "Neither did I," she said. "I never even saw it coming. I realize now she'd been trying to prepare me in her own way, but I was blind to it. I never saw the changes; they came so gradually. Her health had really been going downhill for the last few years. I'm just amazed I didn't see it. I should have called you. I should have let you know that she was failing. She hadn't been the same since that illness a few years ago, and she just gradually got worse. I never saw it. I was too preoccupied with Esther."

"It's not your fault," Don said gruffly. "Even if you had told me, chances are good that I wouldn't have come home. You know me. Dorsey's been trying to get me to take a vacation for years now."

Cindi attempted a smile, but it was weak. "Well, I'm glad he finally succeeded."

"He didn't," Don said. "There were some issues at the mission that I couldn't handle. I needed a break. I have no idea how long I'll be staying. I don't even know where I'm going."

"You mean after this?" Cindi asked, confused. "You aren't going back to the mission?"

"I don't know," Don said. "I haven't decided yet."

"What happened?" Cindi asked, concern etched on her face.

"I'm really tired, Sis. I don't much feel like talking about it," Don apologized. "Maybe later. OK? What I could really use is some sleep. Do you have some place you could put me up, or should I get a hotel room?"

"Hotel room?" Cindi exclaimed. "You aren't serious? Of course you'll stay with us. You just sit here for a minute. I'll have the guest room fixed up for you in a jiffy."

Don sat and cradled his head in his hands as Marc moved uncomfortably around the room. He cleared his voice a few times before filling the silence.

"How was your flight?" he asked.

Don heard the question, but it took him awhile to focus his brain on an answer. He sat up and tried to look sociable. He didn't know Marc well enough to be comfortable around him. "Not bad," he said. "Uh, there were some rough spots. Thought we hit a moose at one point. That turbulence can be bad."

Esther giggled at him. "Your airplane ran into a moose?" she giggled. "That can't happen. Moose don't fly!"

Don smiled in spite of himself. "You don't think so? Maybe it was just a real big seagull."

"I saw seagulls last year," Esther confided, drawing closer and closer to him until she finally climbed up into his lap. "It was when Mommy and Daddy took me to the ocean."

"Oh, yeah? That sounds nice. Maybe I'll get to see the ocean while I'm here," Don said absently. "It might be nice to see lots of water for a change. I'm pretty sick of sand." Despite his words, he felt a sharp pang of homesickness.

"Room's ready," Cindi said cheerfully. "Esther, come on down. Let's let your Uncle Donny get situated here before we over-whelm him." She smiled sympathetically at him before leading him to the guest room. "Let me know if you need anything. Do you want me to wake you or let you sleep as long as you want?"

"No," Don said. "Don't trouble yourself. Let me sleep. I need it. Thanks, Sis. I'll see you when I get up." He kissed Cindi's cheek in a perfunctory sort of way and then turned to survey the room as she closed the door quietly behind him.

The bright yellow and blues of the room were irritatingly sunny. Don tried to block them out as he shucked his wet clothes down to his boxers, letting them drop onto the lemon yellow carpet.

Looking at them lying there in a heap, he reconsidered and placed them neatly folded on the wicker chair by the door instead.

Shivering, he rubbed his arms briskly and crawled gratefully between the crisp sheets. Staring up at the ceiling, he was amused to see that Cindi had sponge-painted pale golden stars onto the dusky blue ceiling so that they resembled an old-fashioned night sky. He pictured another night sky far from where he was and wondered what Toby was doing at that moment.

He'd thought of nothing else since he'd left.

"What are You trying to tell me, God?" he asked out loud. "I thought this was it. But it's not, is it? What is it You have planned for me? Do You want me to spend the rest of my life alone? I'm lonely. I want a companion. Toby and I . . . we were made for each other. Who else am I going to find who likes the same kind of life that I do?

"It feels like You fixed me up and then set me up. You know? What is it You want me to learn from all this? I'm no quitter, You know that. But, how can I go back? What if she gives him a second chance? How can we work together? It would be like a constant reminder of what I'd lost. How can things work out?"

Julian shook his head sorrowfully. "The Master has no need to test you, Don," he said. "You reached out and took His hand when Satan had beaten you down, and He helped you up. Your relationship with Toby was part of your own plan, not God's."

"Lies, lies, all lies!" Merck shrieked. Not only had he been forced to leave the mission before he could witness Lucien's comeuppance but Don had been particularly resistant to any of his suggestions. He was wounded, dazed, and confused, but he wasn't alone. With both hands he was clinging to God with the tenacity of a barnacle. Merck was weary of bloodying his hands trying to remove him.

"She was up for grabs. He had every right to enter into a relationship with her." Merck turned to Don. "God was teasing you. Don't you think He knows how lonely you are? Don't you

think He knew her ex-husband would show up sooner or later? Of course He did. But, He let you get involved with her anyway. He let you give away part of your heart. Why do you even want to listen to Him? Listen to me! I won't steer you wrong."

"Don, the Master can fill your heart up with love," Julian said, edging closer to where Don thrashed on the bed as the struggle for his soul battered his consciousness. "He can erase your loneliness if you'll only let Him. You've trusted Him this far; give Him the opportunity to show you the full power of His love. Let Him fill your heart until it overflows."

"Will you shut up?" Merck snapped. "Love, love, love, is that all you can talk about? Look around you. Do you see much evidence of love? His world is falling apart, and you prattle on about love as if it were the antidote to all human suffering."

"It is," Don blurted out, sitting up suddenly and startling himself by answering the nagging voice in his head out loud. "It is the antidote, because God is love, and He is the answer to all human suffering." He flopped back onto his pillow, marveling at the clarity of this revelation to his sleep-deprived mind.

"But how, God?" he whispered as he fought the heavy blanket of sleep that began to settle on him. "How can I live love? Will you show me?"

"Yes, Don," Julian whispered comfortingly. "He will show you how to live love. But first sleep. We'll talk about it more when you wake up."

"That we will," Merck growled unpleasantly. "That we will."

As Don's eyes closed gratefully in sleep, a bright light flashed into the room. Merck screeched as though he'd been scorched and dove to one side to avoid it. Julian turned to welcome Noble as the archangel watched Don carefully.

"He has come a long way," Noble observed. "He learned much after Rwanda."

"Yes," Julian agreed. "He learned to trust God. I was unsure whether this lesson would carry through, but after his initial

hasty reaction to the situation, he has handled himself well. He has been awake for nearly two days now flying back here, and that entire time he has been reading the Bible."

"I know," Noble responded. "The Master has been weeping for the hurt in his heart. They have spent much of that time together. His questions have revealed a level of honesty about his feelings that would not have been possible if not for his strong relationship with the Master. I am pleased that he had time to build that relationship before this time."

"How will it all work out?" Julian asked.

"Yeah, how's it going to go down?" Merck taunted from the other side of the room. "I'd like to know too."

Noble ignored the demon. "The Master has a commission for Don. He will learn to live love and as he does, he will draw closer to the Master himself."

"Fat chance," Merck argued. "Don't underestimate me. I haven't finished with him yet."

As the trio looked on, Don's features softened perceptibly. Arms flung over his head, he slept with the abandon of a child, a light flush on his face. When Cindi peeked in on him hours later, he hadn't moved an inch in either direction. She smiled gently at him and closed the door softly behind her.

Ayala shuddered at the thick cloud of evil that hung in the air at "Home Base," the condemned building where Marcus's gang liked to hang out. The stench was overpowering, and the shrieks of demons unnerving. Ayala waited anxiously with the rest of the angels just outside the building. It was the closest they could get to their charges who had given themselves up to the evil influences smothering them.

GUARDIANS

Marcus had been coming here more and more often. Although Shay had gone looking for him on occasion, she had never found this place. Ayala wished that someone with the power to break up the gang of kids would find it. The convenient, out of the way location was ideal for the perpetuation of evil.

When several of the boys emerged from the darkened building surrounded by a thick cloud of demons, Ayala and the other angels moved back to make room for them. She caught sight of Marcus's recently shaved head in the midst of the boys. Fearfully, she followed along behind.

"Marcus," she called, but he hadn't listened to her since coming to America. He felt alienated by Shay's pregnancy, the death of his father, and the relocation to a country he knew nothing about. Her words bounced off him as though he were made of cement. "Marcus, please stop! Return home. Your mother is worried about you."

Several of the boys were smoking marijuana, but Marcus refused when the joint was passed to him. Their sway had not yet extended to using drugs or drinking alcohol, for which Ayala was grateful, but she knew that unless someone helped Marcus, it was only a matter of time before he would cave in under peer pressure.

A thick fog reduced visibility to near total oblivion in some spots. A hard rain had soaked the pavement, but the heat that followed was evaporating it rapidly. The smell of wet pavement was new to Marcus's nostrils, and he wrinkled his nose in disgust. He missed the familiar smells of home.

"Hey, I gotta idea," JoJo said, tossing his cigarette butt onto the road where it continued to burn. "How would you boys like to see some action? Come on."

Alberto grabbed Marcus's elbow and urged him to keep up with the others as they sprinted after JoJo. All the excitement was intoxicating to Marcus, and he tried to keep up, stumbling over the unfamiliar territory. By the time the group of boys reached the overpass, they were all panting.

"What we gonna do?" Dogpound asked, bending over and bracing his elbows on his knees as he gasped for air. Dogpound was everything Marcus was not. White, blonde, and fat enough to be two boys in one. He was immensely popular, and Marcus wished with all his might that one day he would be just like Dogpound.

He had asked Shay if he might get his head shaved and a nickname written on his scalp like some of the other boys had, but she refused. He'd done it anyway. Marcus attributed it to her negative attitude about everything to do with him since his father died. He was beginning to wonder if she wasn't angry with him because she had to take care of him, and he was not her true son. Sometimes he thought she wished that she could leave him and Madina and start life over with only her new baby to worry about.

JoJo was searching the wet grass on the other side of the guardrails for something, and Marcus hesitantly joined the other boys as they crowded around, shouting instructions. JoJo had descended part of a rock strewn hill that ended down on the highway on the side of the overpass. He clung to the slippery side of the slope and tried to pry something loose.

"What is he doing?" Marcus asked Alberto curiously.

"Dunno," Alberto shrugged. He took another drag of the joint clamped between his fingers. "But it should be fun."

Finally JoJo made his way back up the slope, slipping several times as he attempted to negotiate the distance with something large and heavy tucked against his stomach, like a football player clutching the ball on his way to a touchdown. Helping hands reached over the rail and eased him over it with his burden.

JoJo stood up revealing a rock about the size of a person's head, cradled in his arms. "Here it is," he said triumphantly.

"What we gonna do with some old rock?" Dogpound whined.

"This," JoJo said smugly as he led the rest to the side of the overpass.

Marcus peered over the side. Beneath, cars whizzed past on the highway. Their shapes were nearly obscured by the fog. He wondered what was going to happen. It felt as though an excited, fearful hand was clutching his stomach. His breath came in little puffs out his open mouth as he watched, wide-eyed.

The oncoming roar of a car filled their ears and as the boys watched, JoJo cocked his head, timing his release. Whoosh! He dropped the rock from the bridge, narrowly missing the car because his timing had been off due to the fog. It bounced harmlessly to the side of the road where it came to rest. Grinning, he turned to the others.

"Whoever climbs down and gets that rock, gets to drop it next," he announced.

There followed a mad scramble down the hill to retrieve the rock. Dogpound got smart and while the others raced for the fallen rock, he went over the other side to get his own. Marcus, being the least intoxicated and the quickest, won the race for the rock, and he lugged it proudly up the hill to receive the congratulations of others who had watched from the top.

"I get to go first," Dogpound insisted. Everyone looked over the side as Dogpound sized up an oncoming vehicle. A truck by the sound of it. Whoosh! He, too, miscalculated, and his rock dropped to the pavement, shattering into a thousand pieces. "Have to get a new one," Dogpound muttered.

The others made room for Marcus as he breathlessly took his place by the railing of the bridge. He could hear a car coming. The fog lifted slightly, allowing him to see a long white car approaching. He was so intent on releasing the boulder the precise instant that would allow him to hit his target that he never even considered the consequences of his actions.

"No!" Ayala screamed a split second before Marcus let the boulder go. Demonic shrieks of joy punctuated her cry.

The instant the boulder left his hands, everything seemed to move in slow motion. Marcus saw the horrified face of the driver look up. The face was Shay's. She threw up her arms in self-defense, and the rock hit the windshield as if it had a bullseye painted on it. With a screech of tires, the car zigzagged off the highway, blew through a guard rail which slowed its progress, and came to rest in the sunken median between the north and southbound lanes.

Smoke rose lazily from the engine, and one blinker flickered on and off. Marcus took a single, agonized look at the car before following the other boys in a headlong retreat back to "Home Base."

Ayala paused with a sad look toward the stricken car and its occupants. A cloud of demons, thick around the car as it had careened off the highway, were withdrawing with blood-curdling shouts of victory. Angels were ministering to Shay and Madina as they waited for the accident to be reported to the police. Ayala stayed until she heard the shrill shriek of sirens before she turned and made her way after Marcus. He was going to need a great deal of comforting when he reached the hideaway.

Billie Jo was working in the garden when the idea occurred to her. At first, she blew it off as too preposterous to possibly work. Instead, she tried to concentrate on the damp earth beneath her hands; the nicely shaped bell peppers hanging on the vine, almost ready to pick; the glistening tomatoes—anything but the thought that had just popped unbidden into her mind. In the background, she could hear the shrieks of her children as they raced through the sprinkler that Jimmy had set up before he left for work that morning.

He'd been working pretty steadily lately and for Billie Jo, life had slowed down, advancing with a comforting cadence, except for the times Helen blew in like a whirlwind to disrupt it. Billie Jo clutched her stomach as a sick feeling washed over her at the thought. Jabbing her trowel into the soft dirt, she peeled off her garden gloves and stood up slowly, arching her back with a groan.

Chasing a strand of hair back off her forehead, she wandered slowly over to the old chair she had placed beneath two stout trees that had grown up side by side in the yard. She sat down slowly, letting the peace of the place seep into her soul. The thought she'd had persisted.

"Billie Jo, why don't you make Helen your special love project?" Jewel suggested. "Make her your secret pen pal. Send her cheerful cards and thoughtful gifts. Pour the Master's love out onto her."

"You've got to be kidding!" Nog exclaimed. "Why? She certainly doesn't deserve any love, much less God's."

"Mankind would certainly be in a desperate condition if everyone received from God what they deserved. God's love falls like rain on the just and the unjust," Jewel told Billie Jo. "Everyone is a recipient of God's love whether they 'deserve' it or not."

Billie Jo chewed her bottom lip nervously. The idea was crazy, but it wouldn't leave her alone. She thought back to the time she had participated in a pen pal program at her church. It had been a nice feeling to receive unexpected surprises in the mail. At the end of the year, there had been a party during which Billie Jo found out who her pen pal had been. She remembered being surprised. It was a shy, young woman named Julia whom she didn't even know well. They had become casual friends until she moved away with her husband.

"Look, this is ludicrous!" Nog said impatiently. "She hates you! Why, you'd be sending her false messages. You'd be lying to her about how you felt. And it wouldn't make any difference in the end. She'd still hate you. It wouldn't change her at all.

Besides, this is Helen we're talking about. You hate her."

Billie Jo squirmed uncomfortably in her chair. She leaned down and plucked a dandelion, blowing the fuzz into the wind. She stared at the naked stem thoughtfully. It was true. She did hate Helen. Knowing why she acted the way she did didn't seem to help. Realizing that she hated her because she feared her didn't seem to make much difference either.

She wasn't at all sure she wanted to take heart in hand and place it in sicky sweet pen pal notes to be shipped off to the ogre's cave and ripped to cynical shreds. And she wasn't sure she wanted to make Helen happy. After all, Helen had never gone out of her way to make Billie Jo happy. Quite the opposite.

"That's right," Nog *agreed, sensing he might be gaining ground. He moved in closer. "What has she ever done to you but caused you grief? Give her the same back. Send her hate mail if that's what it takes, but don't send her anything nice."*

"Billie Jo, giving Helen love will free you," Jewel explained patiently. "Right now you're a slave to your hatred. It doesn't really matter how Helen takes your gesture. She won't even know it's from you. What matters is that you make the gesture. The object is not to change Helen. The object is to change Billie Jo into the likeness of the Creator."

Billie Jo straightened up in the chair, feeling as though things had just slidden into focus. "I'm going to do it," she stated firmly. Pushing herself up from the chair, she made her way into the house. If she remembered right, there were a few pen pal cards left over from before. She made a mental note to pick up some more at the store next time and chose a cheerful one. Rummaging around in her gift-giving stash, she found a bookmark with an inspirational saying on it.

A quick lick of a stamp and an address written on with her left hand was all that it needed. She slipped out the front door and waved to the children as she began walking to the mailbox to mail it. "Be right back," she hollered. In the pit of her stomach, replacing the sickening feeling, a tiny butterfly of excitement began to flutter.

Billie Jo reckoned that Helen was bound to mention the strange, inspiring notes sooner or later, and she wondered how she would handle it. She'd never been much good at hiding her feelings. Helen was bound to be able to read the truth all over her face. But time passed, and Helen never mentioned the weekly notes. Billie Jo was bursting with curiosity.

The whole ordeal continually surprised her. From the moment she'd placed the first note in the mailbox, an excitement had filled her. What had seemed like a tedious, odious chore in the beginning was turning into the most exciting secret she'd ever kept. Her entire outlook was shifting.

Wherever she was, she found herself watching for sweet, simple treasures to send Helen. Sometimes it was a perfect violet that she pressed between wax paper and sent along in a note card. One time, she found a set of hand-painted ceramic coasters with bright sunflowers that matched Helen's kitchen. Another time, she found an exquisite miniature quilt about the size of a credit card that some creative person had attached to a key chain ring.

Everything was sent in plain brown boxes with the address written out painstakingly with her left hand so that Helen wouldn't recognize the handwriting. She hadn't even told Jimmy or the kids what she'd been up to. Sometimes she thought they might guess, just because her attitude toward Helen was changing too. She couldn't really help it. It seemed to naturally follow her actions, since it was hard to do nice, special things for someone and hate them at the same time.

Billie Jo was cleaning the kitchen when a sudden knock on the front door interrupted her. When she turned to see who it was, she was surprised by Helen's face peering sourly in the glass of the door, trying to see if anyone was home. She dried her hands on a towel and went to answer the door.

"Helen," she said warmly. "How are you today?"

"I've been better," Helen responded darkly.

"Oh? Do you not feel well?" Billie Jo said solicitously.

"I feel just dandy," Helen said sarcastically. "Where are the children?"

"Jimmy took them to a church softball game. I was going to clean here for a while and then join them later." Billie Jo glanced at her watch. "You're more than welcome to join me if you'd like."

"A softball game?" Helen sniffed. "I think not. It's much too humid today to watch people running around a baseball diamond. I'm getting overheated just thinking about it. I'll just have to stop in again later when they've come home."

"I'm sure they'll be happy to see you," Billie Jo said, astonished to find that she genuinely meant it and that it didn't bother her.

Helen raised one hand to brush a stray austere gray curl from her forehead. Her keys jingled as she clutched them and pushed the curl back. The miniature quilt hung from the key chain. Billie Jo saw the bright patchwork and struggled to hide a pleased smile.

"I'll be back," Helen promised dryly as she turned to let herself back out the door. She stopped suddenly. "What's that look for?" she demanded. "Do you find something amusing?"

This is it, Billie Jo thought. *She's going to find me out.* Out loud she said, "What's that?" as innocently as she could.

"Tell her!" Nog yelled. "Go ahead. I dare you. Tell her. She'll be the one laughing, I assure you. Your pitiful attempts at friendship will only bring ridicule from her. Don't you know that? They'll never change her. She'll just despise you even more than she does right now."

Jewel was right there. "Billie Jo, if you concentrate on changing Helen, you will never get anywhere. You can't change another person. But with God's grace, you can change how you treat that other person. You can choose to love them and act on that choice. That is what you have been doing. The Master is pleased with you."

"Oh, He is not," Nog insisted. "He's playing you for a sap, that's what He's doing. He makes you do all these things you don't feel like doing. You're living a lie."

"Love is a choice," Jewel repeated. "Feelings are fickle."

"You have a smirk on your face," Helen informed her.

"Do I?" Billie Jo asked. "I sure don't mean to. Just happy, I reckon."

Helen eyed her suspiciously but turned and headed back out to her car.

Billie Jo nodded and closed it behind her, pausing to lean against it, her head resting on the cool frame of the doorjamb, her eyes closed. Joy filled her soul. "Thank You, Lord," she breathed. "Thank You for changing me. Thank You for making me free."

Jewel felt happiness surge in his breast as he watched Billie Jo. He had agonized for her and helped her as she had grown from being spiritually crippled, a victim of life and circumstance, to a strong individual, a healthy young eagle. Spreading her wings, she soared freely on the currents of God's love.

With His help, she was ready to gain even more height and grow stronger in His will. Jewel stationed himself solidly by her side. He wondered, with a smile, what Billie Jo would say on the day soon to come when he would walk up to her and introduce himself. Would she remember the nice, young man who had helped her in the library? He was anxious to find out.

CHAPTER 15

Lyle popped a wheelie and let his chair glide across the smooth surface of the track. He adjusted his gloves and pushed himself for one easy lap before he contemplated how far his next sprint would be. He was training for the Special Olympics, and he had precious little time left.

"Lazy," a female voice taunted him as Paula, a deaf paraplegic friend, raced past.

"I am not," Lyle laughed. He scrambled to catch up with her. Her long black hair was tied back with a simple rubber band and flopped rhythmically on her back as she bent over applying herself vigorously to the wheels.

Despite his best effort, she crossed the imaginary finish line before he did. She raised her arms in a victory salute and let her chair glide to a stop before turning to face him. "You're going to have to do better than that, my friend," she said, her hands flying in signs to accompany her words.

"It was just luck," Lyle signed back jokingly. She made a fist at him and shook it while she giggled.

"No it wasn't." The familiar voice made Lyle jump. He whirled his chair around to see Calla sitting on the grass, putting on her cleats. "You won fair and square," she told Paula.

"Calla!" Lyle glanced from Paula to Calla and back again.

Paula signed, Who is she?

"Uh, Calla, this is Paula. Paula, my, uh, friend, Calla." Lyle's hands faltered in their signs, and Paula gave him a quizzical look. He explained quickly in sign that Calla had been his fiancée until recently. Her eyebrows shot up in sudden understanding.

"What are you saying about me?" Calla teased. "Whatever it is, I hope it's nice."

"Yes," Paula explained hastily. "He said you were his very good friend."

"You read lips too," Calla said. "No fair. I feel like the odd man out here. I've got to get going anyway. Have fun but don't let her beat you all the time," she told Lyle before checking her watch and jogging off with a smile and a wave.

Lyle felt suddenly uncomfortable. Even though he and Calla had parted on relatively friendly terms, their breakup had been extremely traumatic for him. For weeks, he had questioned God continually. He waited for her to call, but she didn't. He thought about calling her, but he didn't.

Aunt Bernie had helped him through the worst of it. She gave him just enough information about what Calla was up to that he felt connected to her in a slight way, but enough that he was slowly able to let her go as well. He tried to believe that if it was God's will that they be together forever, then God would work things out.

Aunt Bernie had prayed with him when he felt his lowest. Hearing her prayers on his behalf had helped to heal his heart. Ever since the day he met Calla, he had believed that he could not live without her. Now he was finding out that being responsible for himself and meeting other people was an exciting learning experience.

Dating was another story. He'd had a rocky time in the beginning, but he was determined to see other women. The first few dates had been like living nightmares. He had prayed before, during, and after them. The one thing he had been unable to do was relax. Then he had become friends with Paula, and when he asked her out, it seemed like the most natural thing in the world.

Getting to know her had opened up a whole other world that he hadn't even realized existed, a whole deaf community that could be reached for Jesus. Paula was interested in the possibility of ministry to the deaf also, and together they had been meeting with Pastor Hendricks to see what opportunities could be made available. Lyle had even taken several courses in American Sign Language and sometimes talked so fast with his hands that Paula asked him to slow down.

"Deep thoughts?" Paula asked, signing her words. There was a sad expression on her face.

"Not too deep," Lyle signed. "Really. Let's go."

She matched him stride for stride as they attacked the track again. It was partly due to the fact that Lyle's thoughts weren't on his racing and partly because he enjoyed having her right beside him. They passed Calla so many times that Lyle lost count. By the time he and Paula were ready to head home, the track was nearly empty. Calla was gone.

As he and Paula pushed their racing wheelchairs toward the parking lot, Lyle glanced over at Paula. Her delicate features were flushed from exertion, giving her a healthy glow. No one would guess, looking at her, that she had nearly died as a baby. Lyle often forgot that she couldn't use her legs and expected her to get out of her chair and walk away.

Paula caught him looking at her and stopped her chair abruptly. "What?" she signed.

Lyle laughed. "Nothing! I was just thinking how beautiful you are."

Paula blushed lobster red and gave his chair a push. "Get out!" she commanded. "I am not."

"You are," Lyle insisted, signing vehemently. "You're beautiful inside and out." She truly was.

Vic Galle, a friend of Paula's who had been waiting in the van to drive them home, unfolded himself from the front seat and stashed the computer magazine he'd been reading beneath the driver's seat. He pushed black horn-rimmed glasses up on his nose. "I've told her that a thousand times," he signed, "but she's never turned that shade of red before."

"Will you hush up?" Paula signed. She buried her face in her hands in embarrassment.

"See that, you found a way to shut her up," Lyle said to Vic over Paula's head.

"I'm going to tell her you said that," Vic promised jokingly as he helped Lyle into the van from his chair.

"That's OK," Lyle quipped lightly. "She knows I love her."

"Do you really?" Vic asked seriously. "Because you know, if you hurt her, I'll hunt you down."

"Not yet," Lyle admitted, forcing himself to be completely honest. "But it could happen pretty easily."

"Ain't that the truth," Vic said before turning to help Paula. "I've been in love with her for years, but she won't have me. She's quite a woman."

"What are you two talking about?" Paula asked suspiciously. "Are you talking about me still? Stop that!"

Lyle threw up his hands in surrender. "OK, OK, we'll stop. Now let's talk pizza. Anybody want some besides me?"

"Pizza!" Vic cried. "My favorite food group! Now you're talking. Where do you want to go?"

"Somewhere with a juke box," Paula said innocently.

Vic rolled his eyes. "Very funny. The Pizza Joint it is. Charge!"

Lyle leaned his head back on the seat as Vic put the van in gear and drove, somewhat recklessly, out of the parking lot. He savored the feeling of living. As he looked back on his life since the accident, he could see God leading him in stages.

Always a tender Shepherd, He hadn't let Lyle experience too

much too soon, and He hadn't rushed him along. Every step in his life seemed to be leading him to the next one, and as he studied the tapestry God had woven in his life, he could see how every thread was necessary to make the weaving rich and complete. Even the dark threads had their place, though for so long he had tried to rip them out.

Slowly, being matched up with someone for life had stopped being an all-consuming passion. God had built his self-esteem up so much that he knew if he had to spend the rest of his life alone, that would be OK. He glanced over at Paula. But, he'd be just as happy to have a companion too.

Shelan rested one hand on Lyle's shoulder as his thoughts rambled on, sometimes converting into a prayer. She had been afraid, right after Calla left, that Lyle might let his faith slip and revert to how he was before he'd met her. The enemy had worked hard on him. She glanced over at Warg, who seemed to be snoozing on the far side of the car. In reality, she knew he was just waiting for the next opportunity to bring Lyle down. His languor was deceptive, like a lion basking in the sun.

"Just keep looking up," Shelan said softly to Lyle. "Keep your eyes firmly fixed on the Master, and He will lead you always. Soon, soon, you will be with Him forever, and this dark place will be but a dim memory."

Davy set the ultralight down as gentle as an autumn leaf floating to the forest floor. He grinned broadly as he hopped out and gave Julia a hand down. The young woman's face was ashen and tinged with green.

"Davy, where did you get your pilot's license? A bubble gum machine?" She waved her hands in front of her face. "Forget I said that word."

"License?" Davy asked, puzzled.

"No, bubble gum," Julia groaned. She clutched her stomach. "I think I'm going to be sick."

Ray rushed over, concern on his face. "Honey? Are you OK?"

"A little woozy, that's all," Davy said. "Caught some desert wind on the way back. It was a bit of a bumpy ride."

"Bit of a bumpy ride?" Julia gasped. "Ray, this man is certifiable. He asked me if I wanted to do a loopy-loo, and I think he would have actually done it except I screamed my head off."

Davy shrugged. "Seemed like a good idea at the time."

Ray struggled valiantly to swallow a smile. He put his arm around Julia's shoulders and led her away. "It's going to be OK, honey. Really. How did it go? Other than the flight, I mean?"

Davy didn't hear her answer. He chuckled his way into the clinic and found Toby setting a bone. "Whatcha doing?" he asked.

Toby looked up with an expression of tedium. "I'm setting a bone," she explained patiently.

"Yeah, I know that, I meant after. You know, what are you doing after? Want to go for a walk?"

"Where?" Toby asked incredulously. "In the desert?"

"I don't know," Davy replied, trying not to sound defensive. When Toby said she would give him a second chance, he didn't expect that it would take anywhere near this long to win her heart. Not only that, but every morning he was afraid that jealous doctor would return and talk her back to her senses. "Around the mission. Heck, I don't care if we walk at all. I just thought it would be nice to talk. I haven't seen much of you lately."

"Well, you know how busy we've been," Toby said evasively. "I haven't had much time."

"So, do you want to go or what?" Davy asked.

Toby shrugged. "Guess so," she replied.

Davy slunk out of the clinic and went to his room to change clothes and brood until she was ready to go. He pulled off his sweat-stained T-shirt and rummaged in the pile of clothes in the corner until he found a fresher one. He poured a pitcher of water over his head and let it collect in a basin. It might have been refreshing, except for the fact that the water was warm.

He dried his hair with a vigorous toweling. In spite of the warm water, he felt better. Spying his Bible on the crate beside his cot, he picked it up and sat down, flipping through it idly. He sighed heavily, realizing with a sudden rush that the closeness he'd felt with God just prior to moving to Africa had faded. With all his attention tied up in trying to make a good impression on Toby and win her back, he had neglected Bible study and prayer.

"Look to the Lord and His strength, seek His face always," Jes quoted. *"Davy, the Master misses you."*

"Yeah, like a toothache," Belial spat. *"What does God need you for? You're so attached to Him you can't even remember Him when things are going your way. Look at you. It's pitiful. You need something, so where do you go? You think God likes that? All you ever do is ask for His help and then ditch Him like yesterday's news after He helps you. Just forget it. You're unworthy to talk to Him now. He doesn't want anything to do with selfish ingrates like you."*

Davy sighed again and crawled onto his knees, Bible in hand. "God, I'm sorry," he said simply. "I don't know if that's enough to say or not. But I'm sorry. I've abused You in a way I never would have abused a friend down here. And You're God. I've got some kind of audacity, I know, to come now asking for Your help, but I need You. Not only to help me convince Toby to renew our marriage but to hang onto me in case she decides not to.

"I told You before I left, God, and I'm telling You again. I'm in this relationship with You for the long haul. I meant that. I'm sorry I got sidetracked. Please help me to put You first in everything. Thanks. Amen."

"That was a nice prayer," Toby said quietly. When Davy looked up in surprise, he found her framed in the doorway. She was dressed in a pale green sundress that he remembered from their life before the accident. She had worn the same dress the night he'd asked her to marry him. He fought back feelings of hope that swelled up at the sight of it. Was she trying to send him some sort of signal?

He clambered awkwardly to his feet. "Uh, thanks."

"Want to go for that walk now?" she asked sweetly.

Lucien couldn't understand it. Weeks ago, Sparn had returned with the glorious news that the cursed old prayer warrior had gone to her final rest. There had been celebrating. As the bearer of such wonderful news, Sparn would have been immortalized in song, had it been possible. It was as though he had instantaneously come alive, once again leading his troops with a vigor and purpose that was hideous to behold.

And still, they had made no progress. None. Rather than the mission staff slowly drifting off to all corners of the globe following the outbreak, Nwibe's death, and Shay and Don's departure, the remaining staff members had banded together with even more cohesion than they'd had previously. Merck's gamble in provoking Don into leaving had accomplished nothing besides removing him from the premises.

Lucien couldn't help but find a grim sort of satisfaction in that. In fact, when he was certain no one was looking, he allowed himself to gloat about it. His own battle strategy, "Project Outbreak," had earned him a commendation but little else. And now that Sparn was back in the picture, his dreams of earning himself a ticket out of there were growing dim.

As he watched Toby and Davy strolling arm in arm around the compound while natives gawked and surreptitiously pointed at them, chuckling in amusement to themselves, he couldn't help wondering where it was all going to end. When Festus sidled up to him, he was in no mood to hear the little demon's prattle.

"Cozy, aren't they?" he observed with a simper in his voice.

"You'll keep your mouth shut if you know what's good for you," Lucien said without even looking at him. Apparently Festus did not know what was good for him.

"What harm is it really? They're such a cute couple, don't you agree? So, they get remarried. That works to your advantage, doesn't it? If you caused the man to influence the woman to leave here, you could leave as well. After all, he is a new Christian. How hard could it be for a superior soldier such as yourself to wrap him around your little finger?"

Lucien turned to Festus with murder in his eyes, but as the demon cowered away from him, he thought over the implications of what had been said. It was true. The two of them were the last of the old guard. Soon Flory would return to Our Lady of Mercy. If he could persuade Davy and Toby to leave, to pursue their own pleasure, then the mission would be gone. Without them, Julia and Ray would be lost. Even if that cursed Dr. Germaine returned, he would return to an empty mission.

His bony hand, which had reached out to strangle Festus's neck, instead clapped him solidly on the shoulder, staggering him forward. "Festus, you little runt, I think you have a plan. How would you like to help me crush this mission once and for all?"

Festus recognized that Lucien's tone implied that the invitation was a command. "Certainly, my chief," he whined. "What would you have me do?"

"I will persuade them to take a flight in the ultralight, for old time's sake. I want you to find something that will break when they are in the air. We will only try to scare them away, but if they are killed, well, more's the pity. Do you think you can manage that without lousing it up?" Lucien scowled menacingly at Festus. He thought that perhaps he ought to involve Belial in the plan rather than the clumsy, worthless Festus.

Festus puffed out his rickety chest with pride. "Yes, sir. I can do that."

"OK," *Lucien agreed, with misgivings. "What are you wait-ing for? An invitation? Get lost already."*

No matter how many times he saw the sun sink slowly toward the horizon in this land, Davy knew he would never get over the breathless beauty of it. Its immense size took his breath away. His fingers unconsciously tightened around Toby's until she cried out.

"Hey, take it easy on my hands. I still use them," she said playfully.

"Sorry," Davy grinned. "I was just thinking how beautiful the sun is here."

"Yeah," Toby said dryly. "And hot."

"Oh, come on. You don't think that's beautiful?"

Toby squinted up at the blazing ball. "Yes, I think it's beauti-ful," she said finally.

"Why don't you take her up in the ultralight?" Lucien sug-gested, showing up with a puff beside Davy. Belial scowled at him.

"What are you doing here? This is my territory," he said firmly.

"Work with me," Lucien said, steel in his voice. He turned to Davy with an oily smile. "For old time's sake. Maybe it will bring back some old feelings. Who knows?" He threw in an innocent shrug for effect.

Belial rolled his eyes. "You're trying too hard. It won't work. I've worked him over too much about the accident."

"I have an idea," Davy said suddenly, turning to Toby with a wicked grin. "Let's go flying."

"What?" Toby blinked at him in surprise. "Fly what?"

"The ultralight," Davy said. "We've never taken it up together."

"I don't know, Davy," Toby said warily. "I've got a bad feeling about this."

"Look, if there's one thing I learned from the accident, it's that you can't let your fears rule your life. You have to step out and take a risk now and then. I took a risk to get here and look where it's gotten me."

"*Watch and learn,*" *Lucien told Belial, arching his eyebrows with superiority.* "It'll be OK," *he told Toby.* "And it's such a romantic suggestion, don't you think? Haven't you missed Davy's romantic ways? Go on. Don't disappoint him.*"

"I guess it'll be all right," Toby conceded reluctantly.

Like two school kids, they raced for the ultralight. Davy reached it first and clambered into the pilot's seat. Toby pulled back. "Why don't you let me fly it, Davy?" she asked.

Davy reached down and grabbed her hand, pulling her toward the plane. "It will be OK. I promise," he said. "Come on. I need to do this. Besides, if we don't hurry, we won't get back in time."

Toby climbed hesitantly into the second seat and hung on tenaciously as the plane took off. Davy grinned back at her . "Beginning to empathize with your passengers?" he hollered. "It's a totally different feeling when you aren't the person flying, isn't it?"

Toby nodded.

"Relax!" Davy yelled. "You know what a great pilot I am."

"That's what I'm afraid of," Toby yelled back.

Festus clung with tenacity to the delicate framework of the ultralight. He was completely unwilling to admit that he had no idea what he was doing. But he was just as determined to complete his mission. Closing his eyes, he jammed his hand toward the nearest crucial-looking part of the plane.

Lileah thrust him aside with one mighty sweep of her wing. He never saw her coming. The next thing he knew, he was tumbling toward earth as the ultralight continued on, unharmed, above him. Desperately, he stuck out his ragged wings and attempted to regain his position.

Angel guards came at him from all sides. Shrieking protests, he allowed them to corral him back toward the mission. As he turned back, he saw Lucien and Belial streaking toward the plane. The host of heaven swarmed around it like bees on apple blossoms, but the two demons pressed on. Shoulder to shoulder, they slashed their way through the light, one goal in mind.

Festus watched them indecisively. Should he join in the fray? They were so desperately outnumbered they were sure to lose. As he watched, Lucien managed to get some leverage, and he grabbed onto one wing of the plane, causing it to tip precariously. Festus heard Toby scream and clutch for something to hold onto. Davy scrambled to right the plane, probably thinking that they'd hit a major gust of wind.

Filled with new determination, Festus propelled himself upward. He reached Belial's side just in time to ward off a side attack by an angel. Each time he lifted his sword to parry, he felt the shock of the blow through his whole body. He ached with weariness. Still, he pressed on. If they couldn't force the plane down, he would have failed, and his punishment was sure to be severe.

The fighting became fierce, and Festus was aware of an increase in angels. The light was overpowering. He was suffocating in it. With one last blind swing, he was forced to give up and flee before the powerful angels. He dropped to the ground and found himself next to Lucien and Belial, who regarded him morosely. Wounded and panting fiercely, Lucien turned on Festus.

"Mercy!" Festus cried hopelessly, while Belial looked on passively, and Lucien dove into him. He was no match to stand against Lucien's strength and anger. Holding his arms up to ward off the blows, he staggered out of reach and slunk off with furtive glances behind to be sure that Lucien and Belial didn't follow him.

"I should have known you'd foul things up," Lucien shrieked after him. "Get out! Get out and don't come back!"

Limping and whimpering, Festus half-flew, half-hopped as he made his way away from the mission. Fine, if that was the way they wanted it. He didn't need them. He would find some-

one who would appreciate him. With increasing resolution, he made his way to the nearest village.

As Davy lined the ultralight up with the makeshift airstrip, the little plane bounced through the air with the delicacy of a dragonfly. It seemed to Davy as though the sinking sun was about to swallow them up. He guided the ultralight to the spot where they usually parked it. It rolled to a jerky halt, and he jumped out to give Toby a hand. Clutching a handful of her skirt, she hopped lightly out onto the ground, and he put his arms around her.

She looked up at him with a smiling question on her face. "What?"

"Nothing," Davy said. "I was just thinking how beautiful you are. Do you remember you were wearing that dress when I asked you to marry me?"

Toby nodded. "I remember. I wondered if you would."

"Toby?" Davy felt his heart pounding like a bass drummer in his chest. "Would you marry me again?"

Toby studied his face for a long time before answering. "Yes, Davy," she said finally. "But I want a long engagement. I've changed since we were married, and you probably have too. I want to make sure that we're going to be happy together and that our goals are similar. And I want to be sure we're doing what God wants."

Davy wrapped his arms around her. "I love you, Toby," he whispered. "That hasn't changed. The rest we can work out."

As if interested in the proceedings at the mission, the sun hovered on the brink of the horizon, casting a ruby glow on the lovers like a benediction before sinking into the embrace of the landscape. Lileah and Jes stood shoulder to shoulder as they watched Toby and Davy begin to walk back to the mission.

"The path before them is rocky and steep," Lileah observed. "There will be much to overcome."

"Yes," Jes agreed. "But they are walking with the Master now.

How different they seem from the self-centered people they had become before the accident. He counts them both among His friends."

"I believe we will be here for a good, long time yet," Lileah observed. "Shall we go see what needs doing?"

Together, the angels followed behind their charges to fulfill their commission to guard, watch over, and minister to them. Joining hands with others as they went, they drove the forces of darkness away, forming a ring of light around the mission and its occupants. Every moment, more angels joined them at the request of the prayers of a few faithful warriors.

"What are you going to do this morning, sleepyhead?" Cindi kidded Don as he sat at the kitchen table forking down mounds of fluffy scrambled eggs and working on a stack of toast.

"I thought I'd give Shay a call and see how she's doing," Don replied, talking around a mouthful of food.

"Uncle Donny, don't talk with your mouth full," Esther instructed. "You'll choke."

Don swallowed hard and gave his niece a patronizing smile. "OK, Button," he agreed. "I don't know what I'll do after that," he said to Cindi.

After breakfast, his stomach pleasantly full and rumbling with contentment, he took the portable phone and sank with a groan into one of Cindi's newly upholstered chairs. It had an unbroken-in look to it, and he was determined that by the end of his visit it would be comfortably inviting. The phone rang and rang and just when he thought no one was home, a woman's voice answered.

"Shay?" he asked in confusion. This woman didn't sound like Shay.

"No," the voice said tiredly. "This is Deniece. Who's this?"

"Uh, this is Don Germaine. I'm sorry. I must have the wrong number."

"No, this isn't the wrong number," Deniece replied. "Don, you said? Don? Oh, yeah, the cute one! Um, I'm sorry, but you can't talk to Shay. She's at the hospital right now. There's been an accident."

Don felt a sinking feeling in the pit of his stomach. "Accident? Nothing serious, I hope."

"That depends on whether or not you think a five pound boulder hitting you through your windshield is serious," Deniece replied somewhat flippantly.

"A boulder through the windshield?" Don asked in bewilderment. "Whaæ"

"Yeah, that's right. Her son, Marcus, and his gang dropped it on her car from a bridge. 'Course they didn't know it was her at the time, but that's small consolation now."

Don shook his head, feeling as though he'd entered some strange, warped dimension. "Marcus did that? Gang? Never mind that now. What is Shay's condition?"

"Well, doctors say she'll make it OK, but that poor, little baby they got hooked up to every monitor in the hospital—they're not holding out much hope."

"Shay *had* the baby?" Don gasped.

"No, not exactly. The doctors took it by Cesarean because of the damage," Deniece elaborated. "It's a boy. Two pounds, five ounces, but there are a lot of problems." A wailing began in the background, which Don assumed was Madina. "Hold on, hold on," Deniece was saying.

"Give me directions," Don demanded. "I'm on my way."

In a blur, Don packed some stuff in a small bag and said goodbye to his sister, who clung to him and promised to pray until she heard from him again. He took a taxi to the airport and flew out on the next flight. Another interminably long taxi ride and he was deposited in front of the hospital.

He found Madina clinging to a beautiful, young black woman in the waiting room of the maternity ward. Marcus was seated on the stiff vinyl couch looking sullen until he saw Don, and then his eyes filled with fear.

"You're the guy in the picture," the young woman said, approaching him and shifting Madina to her other hip with no small effort. "I'm Shay's friend, Deniece Daignault."

Don reached out and took her outstretched hand. "Don Germaine. We worked together at the mission in Africa." He held his hands out to Madina, and the little girl went to him gratefully.

"Uncle Donny," she cried. "Mommy's sick."

"I know, princess," Donny cooed, stroking her braids. "But we're going to see that she gets better."

"How?" Madina demanded.

His thoughts went immediately to Ethel and what she would do at a time like this. "We're going to pray," Don said with conviction.

"Good idea," Deniece piped up. "Marcus? Are you going to join us?"

Marcus moved away from the couch as if it were exerting a gravitational pull that he was struggling against. His eyes were leery, his face set. His whole body trembled as he approached the group.

"You don't want to pray," Merck hissed at him. The boy took several steps backward. "You don't want her to get well. You want her to die, just like your father did. She deserves it for bringing you all out here. She quit. She ran. And she took you along for the ride."

"Marcus, ask God for forgiveness and forgive yourself," Ayala begged. "What you did was wrong, but nothing is outside of God's redeeming mercy. Ask Him to forgive you."

"Marcus?" Don asked, his voice carrying grown-up authority.

"Come over here, boy. We're going to pray for your mother."

"She's not my mother!" Marcus cried bitterly. Turning, he raced out into the hallway.

Encumbered as he was with Madina bouncing heavily on one hip, Don made remarkable time as he sprinted down the hallway after Marcus. He reached the boy just as he was about to press the elevator button. Grabbing him by the arm, he spun him around. Deniece panted to a halt behind him.

"What's going on here?" she asked. "Marcus, what's got into you, boy?"

Sobbing violently, Marcus struggled against Don. Letting Madina slide down to the floor, Don turned his full attention to Marcus. Pinning both wrists, he waited until Marcus tired and slumped heavily against him.

"The baby is going to die," Marcus sobbed. "I killed my brother, and I might have killed Madame Shay as well. My father would hate me, and Madame Shay will hate me, too, when she finds out what I have done."

Don wrapped his strong arms around Marcus and soothed the boy as his body shuddered with grief. "Marcus, son, it's going to be OK. You didn't realize what you were doing. Shay will understand that. She will forgive you. You'll see."

Marcus shook his head back and forth determinedly. "She will not. She will never forgive me. Where will I go? Where will I live?"

"You'll go home, and you'll live with your mother and your sister and, God willing, your baby brother," Don said firmly. "Everyone makes mistakes, Marcus. The point is that we learn from our mistakes, and we allow them to make us better people. This is a hard lesson for you to learn, and you will carry it with you always. But it's also a great lesson about God's grace. No matter how people treat you on earth, even if they can't forgive you, God will always forgive you if you ask Him to."

Marcus sniffed heavily and wiped his nose on his sleeve. "Are you sure?" he asked hopefully.

"I'm positive," Don assured him. "Now, what do you say? We're going to pray for your mom and the baby. Will you join us?"

Marcus nodded and allowed himself to be led back to the waiting room. They made a small but earnest group as they knelt there in a tight circle, pleading for the baby's life and Shay's recovery. Even Madina was curiously quiet as they prayed.

Ayala, Julian, and several other angels formed a protective hedge around the believers as they prayed. Ayala's face was shining as Marcus asked God to forgive him and heal his mother and baby brother. Like lightning, angels ascended and descended from heaven, ferrying the requests to the throne.

Several demons congregated around the little group, but for the most part, their barbs went unnoticed by the humans. Ayala wondered why there were so few attacking them, but a look at Julian's sorrowful face made her realize suddenly why. With a sinking heart, she followed as Don, Marcus, Deniece, and Madina rose from their feet and made their way to Shay's room.

Her face still bloated from the pregnancy and her head swathed in bandages, Shay barely looked recognizable to Don. She had an IV hooked up to the back of her hand and several bags hung from it, dripping dutifully. Dark circles ringed her eyes, but her skin was as pale as his own. He felt his heart melt at the sight of her. She'd been through so much.

As if she felt his presence, she opened her eyes slowly and focused on the visitors in her room. She attempted a wan smile and held out one hand for Don to take. He reached out and placed her small, cool hand in his and gently squeezed it.

"Hello, Shay. You've had quite a time, I hear."

"Some people will do anything to get some peace and quiet," Shay joked, her voice hoarse. "Hi, girlfriend. Have the kids been OK? Marcus, come here, honey. I need a hug."

Marcus began to approach the bed but before he could, a doctor rounded the corner and skidded to a stop when he caught sight of all the visitors. "What are all you people doing here?" he asked irritably. "Mrs. Okeke needs her rest. And I'm afraid I have some very bad news."

Shay gripped Don's hand with surprising strength. "Whatever you have to say, you can say in front of my friends and my children," she said with determination.

The doctor looked at them warily and then cleared his throat. "I'm sorry, very sorry, but we lost your baby. We did everything we could. It was simply not enough."

Don felt a shudder shake Shay's body, and tears flowed quickly down her cheeks. Silently, he prayed for strength for her as she bore this heavy burden.

"Oh, Shay, I'm so sorry," Deniece cried, her own cheeks wet.

"Where's my baby brother?" Madina demanded. "I want to see the baby."

Marcus's eyes lighted up with fear. Slowly he began to back out of the room.

"Marcus," Shay sobbed. "Come here."

Marcus made his way across the room as though he were moving through water. Terror was etched in every line of his young face. "Madame Shay, I am so sorry," he blurted out in anguish. "I did not mean to hurt you or the baby."

"Marcus," Shay said with a sharpness that Don didn't expect of her. But in the next breath her voice softened. "You haven't called me Madame Shay since I became your mother. I don't expect you to start now. I know you didn't mean to do this. I forgive you, Marcus."

The boy melted at those words and clung to Shay as though he were drowning and she were his life preserver. Together they sobbed until their tears were spent. Madina, who was confused by what was going on, was led out by Deniece with the promise that they would come back later, when Shay was feeling better. Don tried to sneak out, too, but Shay restrained him.

"I want to talk to you for a minute," she said, her voice low and scratchy. She patted Marcus on the head, being careful of the tubes coming out of her hand. "Marcus, we'll be OK. Do you believe that?" Satisfied with a nod from him, she continued. "Would you go out in the waiting room with Deniece and Madina? I'd like to talk to Dr. Germaine alone for a few minutes."

Marcus nodded and wiping the tears from his face, he straightened up and tried to look brave as he made his way out of the room. At the threshold, he looked back and gave Shay a weak smile, which she returned. Don waited as she seemed to gather courage before turning toward him.

"Why are you here?" she asked simply.

"Oh, now, you don't want to hear all my problems," he began, but stopped when the steely look she gave him didn't falter. "Davy showed up at the mission," he said. "You know me. I flew off the handle, and here I am. Guess I messed that up."

Shay nodded. "Probably," she admitted. "But maybe things are better the way they are."

"Maybe," Don conceded. "I thought I loved Toby, but now I don't know. I'm hurt, sure, but I can see myself getting married to someone else still, if I found the right person. But listen, enough of this. How are you feeling?"

Shay bit her lip and blinked back a fresh set of tears. "I've been better," she said wryly. "They told me the baby wouldn't live. They wouldn't let me hold him, but I could look at him through the glass. He looked just like Nwibe. I named him Nwibe. I think he would have been happy that I named the baby after him. He was a beautiful baby. Would you ask them to bring him to me?"

Don nodded and left the room. The nurse on duty didn't give him any trouble about it but swaddled baby Nwibe in a crocheted receiving blanket as if she had been expecting that very request. She blinked back tears as she handed him the perfect, tiny bundle. Don thanked her and returned to Shay's room.

She gingerly moved over and sat up, leaning back on the pillows propped against the headboard. She patted the empty spot she had made for him on the bed. "Sit with me," she requested as he laid the baby in her arms. He lowered himself onto the bed as the springs squeaked a protest and leaned toward her, looking down onto the tiny face that could be seen framed in the white blanket.

Shay pulled the blanket back enough so that she could extricate one perfect little hand. The lifeless fingers, which should have curled around hers, simply rested in the palm of her hand. "He's exquisite," she whispered, indescribable longing in her voice. "How I wanted him."

"He's a beautiful baby," Don agreed, putting his arm around her and letting her lean into his big shoulder, sobbing quietly. He didn't know what to say, so he remained silent and patted her soothingly while she cried. His own tears dripped onto her braids, and his mind formed prayers for strength and wisdom.

Finally, Shay brushed her hands across her face in an attempt to dry her eyes. She wrapped the baby up snugly and kissed his cold cheek. "Goodbye, little Nwibe," she murmured. "I'll see you in heaven."

She handed the baby to Don, and he returned him to the nurses' station. When he came back into Shay's room, she was staring forlornly out of the window. She looked older than she ought to, her face weighed down, not by years, but by sorrow. He felt his heart go out to her, and he sat back down on the bed next to her, hugging her to his chest as she cried some more.

"It feels like there is a gaping hole in my heart," she sobbed. "Will it ever feel any better?"

Don reached out to lay a hand on her head but realized at the last instant that her head was bandaged. Self-consciously, he withdrew it. "Yes, it will feel better," he replied. "I used to wonder the same thing. It won't ever go away completely, but it will feel better. There will be a time when you can remember them without sadness. The pain will fade. It won't always be this sharp.

But, it's important to feel it right now. Pain like this refuses to be buried. If you try, it will surface some other way and destroy you.

"That's a lesson I learned the hard way," he admitted ruefully. "Feel the pain, Shay, and then release it. Life is too short to dwell on the pain. Think about when there won't be any more pain. You'll be able to raise your beautiful baby in heaven, where he will never know what it's like to be cold or hungry or sad or afraid. Think about that."

Shay snuggled her face against his chest. "I'm glad you're here, Don. I know you understand. You've been there. God must have known I'd need you. I don't know what I would do without you."

Don chuckled. "Yes, you would. You've always known what to do. From the moment you looked up at me with those fiery eyes after I treated you for sunstroke. I know I was rough on you. I expected you to give up, but you never did. You've got grit. I've always admired that in you, even when I gave you a hard time for it."

Shay's smile was wan. "Don't be too impressed. I only worked myself to death because I was in love with you," she confessed.

Don was taken aback, but he tried not to show it. He had never considered anything between them but a working relationship. The thought of romance had simply never entered his mind. He found himself wishing it had. The silence grew awkward.

"Don't worry," Shay said hastily. "I got over it."

"Maybe you shouldn't have," Don suggested, then immediately felt ashamed. "I'm sorry. I've got a lot of nerve. With Nwibe and now . . . oh, man, I can't stop myself." He jumped off the bed. "Look, Shay, if you need anything, anything at all, you let me know. OK?" He scrawled the phone number of the hotel he had booked on the back of a napkin lying on her bedside table. "I'll be waiting for you to call. I'll come see you again. I'm not leaving until you're well. Understand? You call me if you need anything."

"Stop already," Merck said, rolling his eyes. "Can't you see what a fool you're making of yourself? I didn't bring you all the way back here to find a lifelong companion. Get a grip!" Then he turned on Julian, who was watching the entire performance with a bemused expression. "You planned this, didn't you?" he hissed. "I should have known. You're a lot more sneaky than I give you credit for. I'll be more wary the next time. Don't think you've gotten away with anything. They are not together yet, and they never will be."

Don backed out of the room, practically fleeing from the bewildered look on her face. What a fool! What an idiot! What was he thinking? Exactly what? How selfish could he be? She'd recently lost her husband and now her baby, and he was practically asking her out. He slammed an open palm against his forehead in the age-old sign for stupidity.

"What is wrong with you?" Deniece asked as he burst into the waiting room as though pursued by demons.

"Don't ask," Don groaned, sinking onto the lounge.

"Fine, don't tell me," Deniece said, sounding miffed. "But we need to talk. I've taken a short leave of absence from work to help Shay out, but it's over today, and I have nowhere to leave these children. They have no relatives here. What do you suggest I do?"

Don glanced from Madina to Marcus and back again. "I'll take them," he offered, watching Marcus's face light up. "They know me. They can stay with me at the hotel."

"Hotel?" Deniece exclaimed. "Get out of town! You can stay with them at Shay's house until she gets out of the hospital. I don't know much about kids, but I think they'll do better in a place they know."

"All right," Don conceded. "But you tell her. I'm not going back in that room."

"She ain't going to bite," Deniece said haughtily.

"You tell her," Don repeated stubbornly. "Tell her if she needs anything, to call, and I'll get it."

Deniece narrowed her eyes suspiciously. "Is there something you're not telling me? What is it? You aren't," she gasped in disbelief. "You're in love with her!"

"That's preposterous," Don protested gruffly. "If I were in love with her, don't you think I would have asked her to marry me when I had the chance?"

"That all depends on whether or not you knew you were in love with her while you had the chance," Deniece replied evenly. "It doesn't matter what you say. I know it. I've seen that look a thousand times, although it's usually directed at me."

"Well, at least you're modest," Don huffed sarcastically, jumping up from the lounge and snatching Madina up. "Come on, Marcus, let's go get a taxi."

He hurried down the hall, but he couldn't walk fast enough to outdistance Deniece's smug laughter. It rang in his ears long after they were out of hearing range.

CHAPTER 16

"What you got, Dad?" Billie Jo heard Cassidy ask.

"Yeah, Dad, what's in the box?" Dallas's childish voice chimed in.

Billie Jo dried her hands on a kitchen towel and went to the door, looking above the heads of the children. Burdened down with a large box, Jimmy made his way through the garage, picking his way around the kids' toys. On his heels was Helen. She was dressed in designer jeans and a polo shirt and somehow still gave the impression that she had stepped, cool and clean, from the pages of an L.L. Bean catalog. Casual chic, Billie Jo believed they called it. She wiped a damp strand of hair back behind her ear and tried to mop up the sweat from her forehead. She hadn't been expecting company.

"Hi, darlin', what's in the box?" She asked, shooing the kids back and making room for him to get in the door.

Jimmy didn't reply but set the box down on her small desk in the living room. He turned around, grinning broadly and tapped the picture on the side of the box, which they could now clearly see. It was a computer. Billie Jo felt her jaw go slack.

"A computer?"

"A computer! A computer!" shrieked Cassidy and Dallas in

unison. "Cool!"

"I thought it was high time the children received the benefit of more sophisticated learning," Helen sniffed. "I know if it were up to the two of you, they would be lucky to know how to operate a toaster oven. At least this way, I know they will be prepared for high-paying jobs when they graduate from high school . . . and college."

"Get this one, Billie," Jimmy piped up excitedly. "Momma got us an account on the Internet. You know, that fancy computer highway. She says we can get onto a line and talk to other folk. Why, my cousin Farley, you remember him, why he's even doing it. They call it e-mail. Goes over computer wires lickety split. Ain't that something?"

"Yeah," Billie Jo agreed, too awestruck to say much. "That's really something."

"Of course I paid for everything," Helen added importantly. "And I got the best, the very best that money can buy."

Billie Jo waved her off. "Aw, you could've got them an old beater. They'd a never noticed."

"I didn't want the children using some kind of outdated piece of inferior equipment," Helen argued. "They might as well have the best as long as my money is paying for it. I can get what I want to get, right?" she asked lightly.

"Sure," Billie Jo agreed.

"She's got a lot of nerve, hasn't she?" Nog asked. "Rubbing it in your face that you could never afford something like that for your kids. You're a horrible mother. Why, everyone knows how important computers are these days. You should have been saving so you could buy them one. And you never even thought about it. Well, it's just a good thing you have the generosity of your mother-in-law to fall back on."

"It was a generous gift," Jewel agreed.

Nog eyed him suspiciously. "Quit agreeing with me," he snarled.

"It was generous," Jewel said. "Billie Jo, thank Helen."

"Thank her? What on earth for? She only did it to get your goat."

"It doesn't matter what her reason was. It was a nice thing to do. Respond to the gesture, not the motivation."

Billie Jo bit her lip as she watched Jimmy and the kids try to figure out how to get the computer running. Helen watched them as well and, surprisingly, didn't have much to say. Billie Jo glanced sideways at her. She knew she ought to thank Helen for the gift, but her self-righteous words still stung like salt in an open wound.

"I don't suppose you have any friends who are on the Internet," Helen observed.

"Actually, I do," Billie Jo replied, glad she knew something about the Information Superhighway. Just last week when the mothers' group met at Cindi's, she had shown them a new 3D Talking Globe program Marc had put on their computer. "My friend Cindi got it. I guess she can't be the only one. Seems like everybody's on that Internet these days. You been on?" The question was innocent enough, but Helen took affront at it.

"I've been surfing the Net at a cybercafe in town," she replied scornfully. "I don't have any need to own a computer. Besides, I could hardly afford to get two, and the children need it so much more desperately than I do. I'll just have to make do, I suppose."

"Suppose so," Billie Jo agreed amiably.

"Of course," Helen added slyly. "If I wanted to spend some time surfing, I could always come over here and use this computer." She shrugged her shoulders nonchalantly. "After all, I *did* pay for it. There's no reason I shouldn't be able to use it if I feel like it."

"Yeah, you can show us," Cassidy piped up.

Inside, Billie Jo felt steel bars clamp down on her soul. A scream welled up inside her.

"Yeah, now you're talking," Nog chuckled. "Bet you didn't see that one coming. The old gal isn't one to be held back long.

She's a sly old dog, isn't she? I couldn't have planned that one better if I had thought it up myself. Take that, Billie Jo."

"Billie Jo, there is no reason you must feel Helen can walk all over you," Jewel said. *"Remember why she is doing this. Now set limits before it's too late."*

Billie Jo took a deep breath. "Helen," she said. "This is a wonderful present; it's really too much, even." Helen inclined her head modestly. "And we'd be happy an all if you come over and help the kids with it. Me and Jimmy, we got no clue about these technical things, really. An we'd be happy to set up some times, prearranged like, to do that."

Helen looked to Jimmy for support, but he had his head in the computer box and missed her look of uncertainty. "Yeah, Ma," his voice was muffled. "It'd be neat to have you tutoring the kids, like in computer. It'd save Billie a lot of time, I'm sure. Maybe she could even get out of the house and do something, with you baby-sitting and all."

"Baby-sitting?" Helen sniffed. "I don't baby-sit."

Billie Jo stifled a laugh. It was true. Helen never offered to baby-sit. She felt a rush of love for Jimmy as he supported her attempt at boundaries. "You just let us know when you want to start. I'm sure I can find stuff to do that's awful hard to do while hauling kids around. Maybe I could take a class in pottery. I've always wanted to do that."

"Certainly not!" Helen sputtered. "I mean, well, I'm not that available. Probably it would be better for you to teach the children yourself. I'm sure it can't be that hard. You'll figure it out."

"You're not goin' already?" Billie Jo protested.

"Yes, I forgot that I left a load of laundry in the dryer, and it doesn't always stop when it's supposed to. I didn't tell James. I'd better get back before the house burns to the ground." Without another word, she bolted out the door.

"Just because you won this time doesn't mean you will always win," Nog informed Jewel as he passed through the door

on Helen's heels. "And wipe that self-righteous look off your face."

Jewel smiled joyfully as he watched Billie Jo join her family. Together, they managed to set up the computer and get it up and running. Jimmy was like a kid in a candy store. He continued to marvel over new features long after the kids became disinterested. Each time he found something new, he called Billie Jo over to show it to her. And each time, she patiently dropped what she was doing and came to see the new discovery.

When he insisted that she send Cindi an e-mail, she squeezed onto the chair next to him and obligingly began to type a message. "Hey Cindi! You ain't never gonna believe this . . ."

Calla slipped out from between her warm flannel sheets, grabbed her Bible off the stand near her bed, and headed out to the kitchenette of her new apartment. It was small, and most days she had only the overheard quarrels of her neighbors for company, but she was learning to be comfortable being alone. Right now, as much as she wanted companionship, it was better this way.

Sliding up the low window beside the kitchen table, she ducked through it and stepped out onto the fire escape. "An adjacent porch," the ad had read. Hardly. But Calla did find herself out there often, sitting cross-legged on the narrow metal slits praying or thinking or reading. The sounds of the neighborhood, which had been so foreign to her when she had first moved, were familiar now.

Directly below her lived an elderly blue-haired lady. While wrapped in a tacky polyester bathrobe, hair twisted in a jumble of curlers, she was out on the sidewalk calling her cat. "Here, Mousetrap!" she called. "Here kitty, kitty, kitty!"

GUARDIANS

From her vantage point on the fire escape, Calla could see the fat and sassy Mousetrap's hind end sticking out of a garbage can on the other side of the street. "He's over there," she called, pointing.

The old lady looked up, startled for a moment, then smiled gratefully and waved before crossing the street to retrieve her pet. Calla wondered, with a pang of loneliness, how Hershey was doing at Aunt Berniece's. When she moved, she'd had to leave him behind. Aunt Bernie said she was grateful, because she couldn't imagine parting with the dog, but Calla missed him.

For a second, she considered getting a cat. Then she sighed and opened her Bible to where she'd left off the day before. At a small-group study she'd been attending, one of the members had mentioned that there were thirty-one chapters of Proverbs, which worked out nicely when you read the one that corresponded to the days of the month. First she read the Proverbs chapter of the day, and then she flipped over to the New Testament and continued reading in Philippians.

Lately, she had found comfort in Paul's writings. His utmost priority and foremost relationship had been with Jesus. More and more, she was learning to rely on Jesus for her strength and purpose. It surprised her to realize what a shallow relationship she'd had with Him before.

Too soon, her watch told her it was time to get ready to go to church. Reluctantly, she closed her Bible and reentered her apartment. Church had been a hard place for her to be lately. Lyle and Paula usually attended together. Paula's friend Vic was usually hanging around with them, helping out. Although Calla was happy Lyle had found someone, she experienced a pang of regret and sadness every time she saw them together.

Aunt Bernie usually overcompensated, trying to distract Calla, but her intentions were good. Most weeks Jesse was there, but their relationship had never progressed past friendship, and Calla was happy to leave it there. Right now, she needed this time to be alone and lay down her priorities in life.

Just as she was getting out of her car at the church parking lot, Vic Galle's van pulled up beside her. She hesitated, not knowing what to do. Should she offer to help Lyle and Paula out? Should she simply wave and walk on?

"Whatever you do for one of the least of my brothers you do for me," Atli quoted. "Offer them your help, Calla. That is what the Master would do."

"Forget about them," Warg blustered, zipping over to where she stood indecisively. "They wouldn't help you out of a pothole. They obviously don't care about you, or they wouldn't flaunt their relationship in front of you. Keep moving, sister."

"Calla, I know you will do the right thing," Atli said firmly.

"Poppycock!" Warg snarled. "Isn't it enough that he humiliates you in front of everyone you know? The gimp's got a girlfriend already, and you're still alone? What does that tell you? Anything? Hello?"

Convicted that she should offer her assistance, Calla tried to walk toward the van, but her legs wouldn't move. "Lord," she muttered. "I'm going to need some help here."

The light surrounding Atli blazed so brightly and so unexpectedly that it enveloped Warg, and he cried out in terror. Shaken, he retreated to a safe distance and railed her with curses. Atli appeared not to notice him as she escorted Calla to the van.

"Can I help?" Calla found herself asking cheerfully. She took a wheelchair from Vic, who relinquished it with astonishment. Without giving it a second thought, she unfolded it, locked it, and reached up to help Paula out of the van and into the chair. She stopped abruptly when she realized all three of them were staring at her.

"What?" Calla asked. Lyle was the first to break the silence.

"It's nothing. Thanks a lot, Calla." He gave Paula a nudge, and she smiled shyly at Calla as Calla helped Vic to lower Paula into

291

the chair and position her legs and cath bag.

"Thank you," Paula said, signing as she spoke.

Calla patted her on her shoulder. "No problem," she replied. "Glad to help."

With Vic's help, Lyle swung down and settled into his chair. He looked up at Calla with a sincere smile on his face. "Thanks," he repeated, and Calla knew he was thanking her for much more than her help.

"Sure," she said. "See you guys later."

As she made her way into the church, she felt a tingly, warm feeling all over her body. "Thank You, Lord," she said under her breath. "I couldn't have done that without You."

She was so absorbed in relief and wonder over the incident that the sight at first made no impression on her. As her mind began to take in the details, she didn't know whether to laugh or be scandalized. She drew to a halt and took everything in, her mouth hanging open.

In front of her, right in the vestibule of the church, sat the biggest dog she had ever seen. He sat calmly, as though he had every right to be there. A frayed rope on his collar attached him to his mistress, a woman Calla recognized from town. Crazy Carol, they called her.

She'd never spent too much time thinking about Carol before. Oh, she'd wondered how she happened to come to be living on the streets, but then, that was none of her concern. Mostly, she just figured Carol was someone else's problem, the problem of some nameless, faceless, organization. Not that she had anything against the homeless, she'd just never given them very much thought before.

"I'm sorry, ma'am, but you can't bring that—that dog into the church," one of the church ladies was telling Carol.

Carol blinked at her. "Gotta stay here, Come Here," she sang, and the big dog flopped onto his belly right there in the vestibule.

"This won't do," the woman sputtered. "See here, you've got

to put him outside. This is a church, the house of the Lord. Dogs aren't allowed in here."

Tears sprang to Carol's eyes. "Can't leave him alone, all alone, can't do it. My dog comes with me, yessir, where I go. Gotta go see God, we gotta."

The flustered church member grabbed the arm of a passing elder. "Do something," she implored. "Make her understand she can't have that dog in here. It won't do."

Calla didn't notice him watching the scene, but when Jesse stepped forward, she almost sighed with relief. Jesse had a purposeful look on his face. "Carol, I'll watch your dog," he offered. "He can stay with me outside. He'll like it better out there anyway."

Carol sized him up like a robin choosing a twig to make a nest with. "You'll do, you'll do, you'll do just fine," she said, a low hum adding an undertone to her words. She handed Jesse the end of the rope, and the big dog heaved himself to his feet, patiently awaiting direction. "Good dog, Come Here," she told him. "Nice man, be safe. Gotta go see God. Be back soon."

Tottering unsteadily, she made her way past the group of curious onlookers who had gathered to watch the unusual scene and disappeared into the sanctuary. As she passed by, Calla nearly gagged on the body odor surrounding her. Filth clung to her clothes and hair. It appeared that she wore every item of clothing she possessed.

"Watch your purse," someone hissed from behind Calla.

Jesse turned and made his way out to sit with Come Here on the church steps. In the sanctuary, Calla could hear the organ music announce the start of the service, but she made her way instead out to sit beside Jesse for a few minutes. "Why did you do that?" she asked quietly.

Jesse squinted up at the sun before answering. "Carol is a good person," he replied. "She wouldn't hurt a fly, but they treat her as though she had some kind of disease." There was a long pause as he tried to collect his thoughts. "Do you remember how nice you were to me when I first came here? Everyone was nice to me. It wasn't because I was a sinner and they were the Christians and that's how they should have acted. It was because I looked respectable."

Calla squirmed uneasily at the truth of his statement.

"But I *wasn't* respectable," Jesse continued, as if unaware that he had insulted her by implication. "I was going to steal everything I could from this church. That's the only reason I came. Carol's never stole anything in her life, I'll bet, but they don't want her here. Can you tell me why that is?"

"I'm not going to argue with you, Jesse," Calla said slowly. "I think you're right. I'm not proud of that, but it's the truth. People were nice to you because you are nice looking. They treat Carol the way they do because she looks terrible and she smells terrible. She's a social misfit. Not that that's her fault."

"It's not," Jesse said. "Word on the street is that she was a runaway who took one hit too many and fried her brain. She got in with the wrong crowd. I know how that is." He shrugged. "Not that it matters how she got to be the way she did. That doesn't excuse them."

"No," Calla admitted. "No, it doesn't. And that's why it's so important for you—and for me—to treat her the way Jesus would. We need to teach people the same way Jesus did: by example."

"It makes me angry," Jesse confessed. "They should be teaching me, not the other way around."

Calla patted him on the back. "I know, but we can't look to people, remember? We talked about that the last time with Pastor Hendricks. We need to look to Jesus for our example. He was perfect; people are flawed. We want to look up, to follow Perfection. If you always ask what Jesus would do in your place, it will be hard to go wrong."

Calla took the end of the rope from his hands. "And now, if you'll allow me to do what Jesus would do, I insist that you go inside and sit with Carol. You know her, and I think it would help her to feel more comfortable. I'll stay here with Come Here."

At the mention of his name, the big dog lifted his head and cocked it at her quizzically as if wondering how she knew it. Calla reached out one hand and tentatively patted the broad forehead. "I had a doggie," she crooned as if she were talking to a baby. "His name was Hershey, yes it was. I miss my doggie."

Come Here seemed to understand this in some way and laid his big head down on the end of her shoe. "Aw, well," Calla sighed. "At least you don't drool like Hershey does, the old slobber hound." Cars raced past as Calla sat lost in thought, contemplating the ways she could help Carol and Come Here.

Atli positioned herself beside Calla and offered suggestions. A band of demons had congregated outside the church, and they heckled her, but she ignored them steadily. One, bolder than the others, ventured close and prodded the dog. A low rumble sounded from deep within his chest, and his lips fluttered as though in a breeze.

As if they were being lifted by puppeteer strings, Come Here's lips pulled back from his yellow teeth, and he snapped soundlessly at the demon. Calla became uneasy, pulling back to the very end of the rope. "Steady, Come Here," she said nervously. The dog laid back his ears and whined at her. The demon's gambit had been successful. She had diverted Calla's attention from helping Carol.

"Lord," Calla prayed silently. "Do something about this dog, would You?"

Cursing, the demon backed off just as Atli rushed toward her, sword drawn. "It was worth a try," she said smugly, retreating a safe distance from the gleaming blade and watching for another opportunity. Atli patted Come Here's head, and the dog wagged his fringed tail gently. Calla relaxed.

"Thanks, Lord," she murmured. "Now where was I? Oh, yeah, Carol. How can we help Carol, Lord?"

CHAPTER 17

Shay squinted against the bright sunshine and eyed the tall glass of iced lemonade Don had set beside her elbow. Off to the left, what remained of Davy's garden had grown into weed paradise. Only a few recognizable, edible plants struggled for survival amidst the jumbled heap of vegetation. Here and there, she could see a bright red tomato defying the odds. She thought casually about going over and picking them, but she knew Don would scold her, and although she had come a long way in her recuperation, she wasn't up to that yet.

Inside the duplex, she could hear Madina's squeals as Marcus and Don played hide-and-seek with her. Having Don around had really helped Marcus. The boy had stopped hanging around with his "gang," and he and Don did a lot of things together. Shay could see a connectedness between them, and she was glad Don was there to provide Marcus with male leadership. She realized keenly how much he missed his father.

As she contemplated the weeds in the garden, they suddenly disappeared from her view, and she saw instead an endless expanse of desert. A deep longing for Africa stole over her, and she began to wonder if she had done the right thing by moving them all back to America. She bit her lower lip thoughtfully.

"No!" Jezeel howled in frustration, panic gripping her. "Don't even consider going back there. This is where you belong now. And think about this, you can't be uprooting those kids every time you get a pang of homesickness. Make up your mind and stick to it. This is your home. Your father wanted you to live here."

Gaius sat down next to Shay and laid a compassionate arm around her shoulder. His voice caught in sorrow as he spoke, and tears slipped down his golden cheeks. "Little one," he said softly. "You have come through so much and clung so tightly to the Master. Let Him guide you. Go back to Africa. That is where you belong now. Nearly five years ago, you made the decision to make Africa your home. You planted your heart there. Return. Allow your children to fully taste their heritage. Continue your work there, and be of good cheer. The Master goes before you."

Shay wasn't even aware of the sudden quietness that had fallen in the house behind her. The slim, cool hand that touched her shoulder startled her. She looked up and saw Marcus smiling down at her. The sadness that had been behind his smiles since his father died had lessened a little, but there was a worried question in his eyes.

Ever since the accident, she'd had to remind him over and over that she forgave him for what he'd done. There were nights before she'd come home, Don told her, when Marcus had woken up in the middle of the night screaming in terror. No amount of comforting could calm him down enough that he could go to sleep again.

"How are you feeling, Mama?" he asked solicitously. "Do you want to come inside?"

Shay smiled. "No, honey, it's nice out here."

Don dragged a lawn chair over and sat down next to her, pulling Madina onto his lap. The little girl's sweet features showed delight in being cuddled. She reached up both hands and placed them on his cheeks, giggling at the roughness from his beard.

"You need a shave, don't you?" Shay laughed.

"No, no," Madina squealed. "It's more pickier this way. It tickles."

Don rolled his eyes at Marcus, who grinned. "Women," he said with playful sarcasm. "How are you doing?" he asked Shay, his voice growing serious.

"I'm fine," she insisted. "I'm sure you're only making me rest so much to keep me out of trouble. I feel like I could lick the world in a fair fight, and all you'll let me do is sit here like an old grandmother."

"Oh, I don't know," Don mused. "I know some old grandmothers who have pretty high adventure sitting in chairs." Shay knew he was thinking of Ethel, even though he hadn't spoken much of her since he'd arrived. She'd been afraid to bring up the topic herself. She didn't want to hurt him. There had been so much pain in all of their lives lately. They needed a break. Instead of acknowledging who he was referring to, she pointed to a hummingbird, zipping around a bright red geranium.

"Look at that," she exclaimed.

"Oh, my favorite!" Madina said, jumping off Don's lap to chase the hummingbird. The next instant, it was gone. "Where did he go?" Madina asked in confusion as the others laughed at her.

"You must have patience to watch the bumblebee birds," Marcus explained. "They frighten easily."

"Like me," Shay said softly. She looked up, wondering if they could see the tears shining in her eyes. "Marcus, Madina, I was wrong to move us here after your father died. I'm sorry for that. I want to move back to the mission, but I need to know how you two feel about it first."

Marcus looked as though he couldn't believe what he was hearing. "Go back to the mission?" There was wistfulness in the question.

"Could I see Felia again?" Madina asked excitedly. "And Akueke? And Uncle Wahabi? And Mrs. O'Connell? And Flory? And—"

Shay threw up her hands. "Hold on, hold on. Slow down. Now, most of those people are there still, but some have gone. Flory must have left by now." She gave Don a sideways look to gauge his reaction. "And I don't know about Toby. She might be gone now, too, for all we know."

To his credit, Don's face remained unchanged. It still registered the shock of her initial announcement. "You're serious about this?" he asked. "You really want to go back?"

Shay nodded. "I've never been more serious. I shouldn't have left in the first place. I was scared and angry and frustrated. I ran without really thinking or even praying about it. I think it's time to go back."

"What? Are you stupid?" Jezeel hissed. "There are horrible memories back there. If you return, you'll never go through a day without thinking about Nwibe and what happened to him and how you were helpless, holed up in that room at Wahabi's."

Changing tack in midstream, she fluttered over to Don's side. "Tell her," she insisted, digging long, black nails into his shoulder. Don flinched away from her. "Tell her what a mistake she's making. Don't let her go. You like her, don't you? Where she goes you go, isn't that it? You don't want to go back there. Toby's there. Davy's there. It would be awkward."

Merck backhanded Jezeel and she tumbled back hissing and spitting. "What's wrong with you, stupid?" she rasped angrily. "What do you think you're doing?"

"He's mine," Merck said. "I'll take care of him."

"We both want the same thing," Jezeel countered. "You don't want him to go back there, do you? I know what you did. You pressured him into leaving so that you could get away from Lucien. Don't think I won't tell him that if we get back. The old windbag thinks he got rid of you, no doubt. Imagine how sur-

prised he'll be to find out that you engineered a cushier assignment and managed to elude his clutches at the same time."

Merck's eyes narrowed dangerously. "Shut up," he warned. "Or I will personally see to it that you regret it."

"Your threats will not work with me," Jezeel taunted. "Your indignation will make a poor shelter if we end up back at that mission. And I will tell them that it's all your doing."

Merck appeared to ignore her, his eyes becoming unreadable slits as he turned his back on her and concentrated on Don. "As long as you continue to follow this path, I will hound you. I will torture you in any way I can, and in the end I will destroy you. Now listen to me and listen good. You will stay here. You will get a decent, well-paying job. You will start dating. Get married if you want, so long as the girl isn't a follower of the Master. But you will stay here. Make no mistake."

Julian, who had been observing the exchange, watched the expression on Don's face. He seemed to be contemplating the demon's words. Perhaps he was remembering Toby and wondering if he really was ready to face her again, especially in light of the fact that Davy might still be there and there was every chance that she had decided to give him a second chance. Julian sized him up, wondering himself if Don could stand that eventuality.

"Don, you cannot run from your problems. In order for you to experience any growth, you must face your problems and work through them. Don't let embarrassment and hurt feelings keep you from the work the Master has given you to do," Julian said. "I know your heart. I know that you miss your work and that no monetary considerations could ever make up for the joy you derive working for the Master. Go back, Don. Go back and face your fears. You will see that nothing is too big for you and the Master to handle together."

"Yeah," Don said finally. "I've been thinking I've been gone long enough for a vacation, myself."

Shay started. It hadn't occurred to her that he was on vacation. All this time he'd catered to her, taken care of her, watched her kids, cleaned her house. And he was supposed to be on vacation. She wiggled uncomfortably in her lawn chair; the quilt Don had laid on her lap slid off to one side and onto the grass.

"I'm sorry," she apologized. She could feel her face get red, and she hated herself for it. "I've been so selfish. Some vacation you've had, huh? I feel terrible."

"Don't," Don said quickly, reaching out and putting his hand on hers. "I've enjoyed every minute of it."

Shay was distracted by the pressure of his hand. She laughed off his response. "Yeah, I'll just bet. You're a doctor. The last thing you want to do on your vacation is take care of another sick person. And on top of that, you pulled baby-sitting duty and became a homemaker. I'm sure that's every man's dream of the ideal vacation."

"It's my dream of the ideal vacation," Don replied quietly. "I've really enjoyed it. I—I've come to see just how much I've missed not having a family." His voice took on a wistful quality. "Most people wouldn't have thought Nwibe had much of earthly value, but I believe he was the richest man on the face of the earth."

Merck groaned with disgust. "That is the sappiest thing I've ever heard. Liar! As if taking care of someone else's brats is such a wonderful time. She's not going to go for that line, trust me."

Gaius leaned toward Shay and tilted her face upward, causing her to see in Don's eyes the love he could not hide. He could feel wonder and fear course through her at the same time. "Do not be afraid," he said softly. "I know you believed that love was dead to you forever. You saw your path mapped out before you, alone with the children, and you accepted it without complaint. But the Master has plans for you that you cannot even begin to fathom. Leave yourself open to His leading. Don's feelings toward you have been changing. Open your eyes, little

GUARDIANS

sister. Trust him with your heart."

"Wh-what makes you think that?" Shay stammered, not daring to believe what she was seeing, trying to convince herself that she misinterpreted what she saw in his eyes.

Don looked at her for a long time before replying. Even the children had fallen silent as if they were waiting to see what he would say. "You know," he began, "when we first met, I thought you were young, naive, foolish. And you were so . . . happy. It was painful for me to even be near you." He paused a minute. Shay bit her lip and waited patiently for him to continue.

"When you married Nwibe, I was happy for you, of course. I was happy for him and for Marcus too. And you were able to give Madina a home. I really admired you for that. But I never expected it to last. I thought you'd end up getting tired of the mission and you'd pack your bags and head back to the States. But you never did.

"Oh, I saw you struggle with the culture. I saw you struggle to relate to Nwibe and his blindness and how limiting that was. I don't think the implications really occurred to you until it was too late. But I also saw you grow during that time. And my admiration for you grew."

"I didn't do anything someone else wouldn't have done in my place," Shay murmured. "I loved Nwibe. We had good times. We had bad times too. I wasn't really prepared for that, but I prayed a lot . . ."

"And you read those books your father sent you," Marcus pointed out.

Shay laughed. "Yeah, and there was that. My dad sent me every marriage help book ever published. I think he felt guilty he hadn't prepared me better. I learned a lot. Marriage wasn't what I had thought it would be. But once I made allowances, it was much better than I thought it could have been. Love is a decision, you know. Not a feeling. I didn't know that."

"In that case," Don said, "I have decided to love you."

Shay felt her jaw drop, and she hastily snapped her mouth shut. "You what?"

"I have decided," Don repeated, "to love you. I've felt it for a while, but I'm prepared to choose it too."

"You can't just tell me that you've decided to love me," Shay protested. "What about Toby? It wasn't so long ago you and she were serious about each other. And what about me? Nwibe hasn't been dead that long. I'm not sure if I'm ready . . ."

Don interrupted her, taking her hands in his own. "Stop already," he chided softly. "Anybody would think you didn't want me to love you, and I think you do."

"Well, you're . . . that's preposterous . . . I can't believe . . ." Shay sputtered. She stopped suddenly and eyed him quizzically. "And what if I did? That doesn't change anything. Are you still in love with Toby?"

"No," Don replied honestly. "I thought I was, but if I had been, I would never have left. I would have stayed and fought for her."

"What if we go back and she's sent Davy away?" Shay demanded. "What then?"

"I would choose you," he replied simply. "Don't you understand? I would have chosen you to begin with if you hadn't been in such a hurry to get married."

"I?" Shay bristled haughtily. "I? In a hurry? As if I—"

Don laughed. "Now, don't get your dander up. We were different people back then. I'm just saying that if you had given me time to work through things I was dealing with, I believe I would have come to love you then. I'm only just realizing it now."

Shay studied a grasshopper climbing up a grass stalk. "I don't know what to say," she said. "I had a crush on you once, I admit it. I think it probably would be pretty easy to love you." She looked up before going on. "I'm just not sure I'm ready."

Don nodded. "I understand, and I'm not asking you to walk down the aisle today. I just want you to know where I stand." He grinned. "I didn't want you to go falling in love with someone else and getting married again without knowing how I felt. All I'm asking is that you let me be your friend, your good friend; give me a chance. And when the time is right, if it ever is, we'll talk about getting married."

Shay glanced at Marcus, who was hanging on every word out of their mouths. Madina had tired of the conversation and was pulling grass shoots up. "How do you feel about this, Marcus?" she asked.

Marcus smiled shyly. "I would be happy to have Dr. Germaine to be a stair father."

Shay laughed. "Stepfather," she corrected him. Reaching out, she took his hand and pulled him close to her. "You know, Marcus," she said seriously. "No one will ever take your father's place. If Dr. Germaine and I were to get married someday, it wouldn't affect how you love your real father or how much you miss him. Do you understand that?"

Marcus nodded. "Yes, I do."

"How about you, Madina?" Shay asked.

The little girl looked up and smiled. "I like his whiskers. Can we have ice cream tonight?"

"You'd better stock up now, cricket," Don said, wiggling his fingers at her until she squealed with laughter in anticipation of being tickled. "Because we're going home, and you know how hard ice cream is to find there."

"Couldn't we bring some with us?" Madina pleaded, hitching herself up and preparing to flee.

"Sure," Don agreed, rising with exaggerated slowness. "We'll just pack it into a suitcase." The next instant, he launched himself toward her, but she was too swift for him and danced away with four-year-old agility. With a high-pitched squeal that was almost deafening, she raced across the lawn staying just ahead of Don. Shay and Marcus watched and laughed until Shay thought she might fall right off the lawn chair.

When they'd finally had enough, they returned, Madina tucked unceremoniously under Don's arm. He carried her like a sack of potatoes, arms and legs flailing. "Put me down!" she demanded, hiccuping loudly from laughing so hard. "Put me down!"

Don deposited her on the grass beside Shay and sank with relief back into the lawn chair beside her. "More, more," Madina begged.

"Honey, give him a break," Shay said. Then she glanced slyly at Don. "We wouldn't want you to wear him out before I decide whether or not to marry him."

Don groaned. "You're very funny, you are."

Later as she sat curled up on the sofa, listening to his deep voice coming from Madina's room reading "just one more bed-time story," she couldn't help the feeling of love that boiled up in her chest. She bowed her head, her heart racing. "Lord," she whispered, "I loved Nwibe, You know I did. I miss him. So much. Is it wrong to not want to be alone? To hope that I'll find some-one to love and share my life with again?"

Her stomach twisted in knots. "Is it wrong for me to want to find happiness again? Is it wrong to want my children to have a father? Help me, Lord; I can't go through this alone. I feel like I'm going crazy! This is ridiculous. I shouldn't even be thinking about this yet. What a traitor I am!"

Gaius smoothed the hair back off Shay's forehead. "You're never alone, little sister," he assured her. "The Master is inter-ested in every aspect of your life. Your choice of a life partner is a serious decision. A decision that has the potential to affect your relationship with Him. It is important that you choose someone who will encourage that relationship, not draw you away from it.

"Don Germaine walks with the Master. He has come through hard times, and he has learned how to rely on the Master for his strength. His relationship with the Master is strong, and he would be an encourager. He would make a good choice for a life partner. But now is not the time. That will come later.

"Be still. Grieve for your losses. Do not rush headlong toward the promise of love and bury what you must work through now. Feel your feelings. Feel them intensely. Offer them up to the Master. He will help you carry them. When you are ready to love again, Don will be there. And if he is not, then all the worrying you are capable of will not make any difference. Give it time, and give it to the Master. He will lead you in every area you allow Him to."

"He doesn't love you," Jezeel insisted, trying to sneak in by Shay's side. "He wants your money, that's it! No, he's on the rebound. He just thinks he's in love with you because he got jilted, and he wants to salve his ego.

"Forget him. Let him go back to that dusty, old place if he wants." Her voice took on a wheedling quality. "Stay here. Continue to enjoy the comforts of home. You'd miss all this if you went back. Besides, what about Deniece? She'd be heartbroken if you left again. You can't do that to her."

A knock on the door made Jezeel jump guiltily, and she glanced furtively over her shoulder, cursing the face that peeked in the door. "Go home!" she shrieked, flying at Deniece.

"Hey," Deniece called. "Can I come in? What's happening, girl? Why so serious?" Deniece looked as though she might bolt back out the way she'd come. "You OK? You want me to leave?"

Shay wiped tears that had slipped softly onto her cheeks. "No, no," she said. "Come in. Sit beside me. Would you like something to drink?" She pushed herself gingerly off the couch and headed for the kitchen.

"Where are you going?" Deniece said, her voice held suspicion. "Are you supposed to be up? I don't think Don would be happy."

"Oh, Don schmon," Shay pooh-poohed. "It's not as if he's my doctor or anything."

"I heard that," Don hollered from Madina's room.

Shay giggled. "OK, so he's my doctor. I'm a nurse. I know if I can get up or not."

"Yeah," Deniece agreed, "and I know stubbornness when I see it. Sit down, girlfriend. Let me get that."

"Oh, you guys," Shay complained. "I'll be an old lady before you let me do anything for myself."

"Not so old," Deniece contradicted her. "Enjoy it while you can. I'd love to have people waiting on me hand and foot. Now," she said, handing her a glass of seltzer water and studying her face as she got comfortable on the couch next to her. "What's up?"

Shay considered her words for a few minutes and then smiled sadly and took Deniece's hand in her own. "We're moving back."

"Of course you're moving back," Deniece said. "Tell me something I don't already know."

Shay was stunned. She had expected tears. She had expected arguments. She hadn't expected this. "What do you mean? How could you possibly know? I didn't even decide myself until this very afternoon."

Deniece shrugged. "ESP, I guess. Look, it wasn't that hard to figure out. You haven't been happy here. You've had a homesick look in your eye since you got here. I know you miss Africa. For the life of me, I'd like to know what they've got there that we don't have here."

"Dust," Shay laughed, relieved and sad at the same time. "Plenty of dust. The stuff is addictive, you know. Once you've gotten it under your skin, you're just not happy anywhere else."

"Yeah, well if you say so," Deniece replied skeptically. "I'm going to miss you, girl, that's for sure."

"I'm going to miss you, too," Shay wailed, throwing her arms around Deniece's neck.

"Uh-oh," she heard Don's voice say. "Women stuff. Well, it's time I get out of here anyway. I'll see you two tomorrow."

"You aren't getting out of here that fast," Deniece informed him, pulling away from Shay and wiping her eyes. "This is half your fault, isn't it?"

Don threw up his hands in innocent surrender. "Who, me? I didn't do anything. It was her idea."

"I'm sure it was," Deniece agreed. "I just wonder if it would have occurred to her so quickly if you hadn't been here."

"What? You think I coerced her?" Don asked incredulously. "I assure you. I didn't even bring the subject up. I couldn't believe it when she told us this afternoon about her plans."

"Yeah, whatever," Deniece replied, looking unconvinced.

"I'm outta here," Don said. "I'll see you tomorrow, Shay."

"Bye, Don. Thanks for all your help," Shay said.

Deniece waited until the door clicked shut behind him before she burst into peals of laughter. "Oh, girlfriend, I'm going to have so much fun with him!" she howled. "Did you see how red he got? It's almost criminal to have this much fun. I only wish you were going to live closer. It's a shame to waste all that fun."

Shay smiled. "We aren't getting married."

"You will," Deniece assured her. "Mark my words. Not that I blame you. He's cute in a rugged sort of way. He needs to get rid of that beard thing he's got going on. Doesn't work for him."

"Madina likes it," Shay said. "She says it tickles."

"Oh, well, then he should keep it, by all means," Deniece consented.

Jezeel stormed around, promising dire consequences as a result of this rash decision. She glowered darkly and hurled threats but otherwise took no action. Gaius kept guard until the wee hours of the morning while Shay and Deniece talked and prayed together. Finally, as they talked sleepily, Shay's head fell back on the pillow and Deniece yawned and checked her watch.

Seeming to realize she'd overstayed her welcome, she covered Shay with a quilt, checked on the children, and let herself out, locking the door behind her. Gaius never budged from his post. Shay moaned in her sleep and wriggled into a more com-

fortable position on the couch, but she never woke up.

"Sleep, little one," Gaius said. "There is so much before you. Rest now so you will be strong to take up the sword of light and enter the battle once again."

Cindi listened to Esther playing in the next room. She was singing quietly to herself, and every now and then she heard an odd thump, thump that didn't sound familiar. Making sure she was undetected, she made her way slowly into the next room to see what Esther was doing.

The sight that met her eyes made her clamp her hand over her mouth to prevent a shriek of laughter from escaping. Dressed only in a frilly white blouse, Esther had found a pair of Cindi's high heels and was clomping around the living room, singing to herself. Cindi dashed back to the kitchen and collapsed weakly against the wall.

"Oh, Lord," she giggled. "I know you created people for companionship, but I don't think you overlooked our entertainment potential either." She made a mental note to relay the story to Marc when he came home that evening.

There were only a few more chores to take care of before she planned to take Esther over to Ethel's house and finish cleaning and packing up Ethel's personal effects. She'd spent a lot of time there tying up all the loose ends after Ethel had passed away, and the house seemed so cold, so empty, so big. Cindi felt uncomfortable there.

In her will, Ethel had left her house to the church, with the stipulation that they use it as an orphanage, halfway house, or shelter of some sort. Just a week ago, the town council had approved plans to turn it into a homeless shelter. Cindi was glad. A house that big would be wasted on a single family when so many could find refuge there.

With a flourish of her towel, she wiped the last of the water from the countertop and spun to survey her kitchen. Neat, just the way she liked it. "Essie," she sang. "It's time to leave."

"Where are we going?" Esther asked, clomping into the kitchen.

"To Grammy's house. I have a few things to take care of."

Rafe slithered toward Esther like a cold, dark shadow obstructing the sun. "You don't want to go to that old place. It never fails that your mother starts bawling and makes you feel bad. Just tell her you want to stay here."

"I don't want to go to Grammy's," Esther said stubbornly.

"Essie," Cindi's voice was tired. Here they went again. It didn't seem to matter what she did; it met with resistance from Esther. "Remember what we talked about before? About how it makes Satan happy when you don't obey Mommy and Daddy? Remember what Mommy taught you to do?"

"Pray," Shania urged, putting her arm around the little girl. "Ask Jesus to help you."

Esther thought for a minute. "Oh, yeah," she said brightly and dropped to her knees on the floor. "Dear Jesus," she prayed. "Please help me to obey Mommy and send the good angels to make the bad angels go away. Amen."

As Rafe watched Esther drop to her knees, his complacency, his downright smugness, disappeared instantly. This was not supposed to be happening. He'd been hard at work to prevent it.

Before he could waste any time figuring out what was wrong, he was forced to defend himself. Gleaming angels, their robes of light so bright the entire house was lighted up, appeared by the legion. Rafe scuttled backward with a snarl. A few other demons who had been hanging around the house trying to discourage Cindi joined him, and together they presented a united front against the angelic host.

But they were hopelessly outnumbered. With little more than a brief scuffle, the demons were driven off, and an angel guard positioned around the house. Rafe and the others circled the house many times, but each time they attempted to penetrate the angelic barrier, they were driven back. Finally, they settled down outside the perimeter to wait patiently for their next opportunity.

Cindi gaped at her daughter. "Did I do it right, Mommy?" Esther asked.

"Oh, honey," Cindi cried, a sob catching in her throat. She fell to her knees beside Esther. "You did just beautifully."

Esther's face shone with pleasure. "Do you really think they're gone?" she asked.

"Oh yes," Cindi assured her, wiping the tears from her eyes. "The Bible tells us that the Lord will command His angels concerning us to guard us in all our ways. They will lift us up in their hands so that we won't stub our toes on stones."

Always literal, Esther contemplated that for a while. "What stones?"

Cindi laughed. "OK, maybe that wasn't the best illustration. Let's see, Jesus also tells us that if we call on Him He will answer us and help us out of trouble."

"And when we do what Satan says, we're in trouble?" Esther asked.

Cindi nodded. "Yes, sweetheart, that's right."

Esther seemed satisfied. "OK, let's go to Grammy's now."

She behaved like a jewel after that, and Cindi kept up a stream of cheerful chatter as she got Esther dressed and drove the short distance to Ethel's house. A couple of times, she caught herself glancing furtively around to see if she could see the angels herself. Their presence was almost palpable.

Shania cloaked Cindi and Esther with her wings, protecting them as they made the journey to Ethel's house. An angelic es-

cort accompanied them as well. To Cindi, Shania knew, this was just an ordinary trip to finish wrapping up Ethel's earthly affairs. What Cindi didn't realize was that there was one affair of Ethel's that needed particular attention.

When Cindi pushed open the door, she missed the cats brushing by her legs. They'd found good homes for all of them, fortunately. The house seemed close and dark. Cindi flipped the lights on and opened a few windows.

"Negative ions," she muttered under her breath, remembering what Ethel used to say about "foul air." A delicate breeze ruffled the curtains, and Cindi closed her eyes for a moment and inhaled deeply. Then she got Esther settled with some coloring books and made her way to Ethel's room.

No matter how many times she'd been in it since Ethel had died, she still always expected to see her there. In her mind's eye, she could see Ethel the way she'd found her that day. She had been sitting in her wheelchair, facing the window. The setting sun had colored her face with a rosy glow. Her mouth had been drawn up in a faint smile, and her hands had been clasped in prayer.

She could still feel the ache that had come over her when she realized that Ethel was gone. It was sharp and seemed to fill her whole chest. It was still there, though it had dulled with time. She sighed and turned to the stand beside the bed. She opened the drawer and pulled out the contents.

There were some copies of legal papers, some old love letters, and a few pictures. Cindi laid them all out on the bed and studied the photos. They were yellowed with age, and the people were dressed in outdated clothes. She recognized Bert from other pictures Ethel had around the house. In this photo, he was dressed in a striped short-sleeved shirt and trousers. Leaning on a rake, he stared into the camera with a carefree smile.

There were a few pictures Cindi deduced must be of Richard, Ethel's son who had died of polio when he was ten. A curly-headed tyke, he had Ethel's eyes and Richard's lean build. One photo, of a girl, caught Cindi's attention.

She sat on the hood of a large car, thin arms hugging her legs, an unhappy look on her face. Her long brown hair was pulled back and fastened on top of her head. She had a pretty face, marred slightly by what looked like a bruise beneath one eye. Cindi stared thoughtfully at that bruise. Somewhere, she'd seen something like that just recently.

"Don't you remember?" Shania prompted her. "At church this last week—the homeless woman? The one the others were ridiculing? I saw you look at her with compassion, wondering if perhaps this house might become a refuge for her if it was turned into a homeless shelter. Remember her face? Did it not look like Ethel's?"

Cindi's brow furrowed in concentration. Yes, she was quite sure she'd seen someone who looked like this girl recently. But where? She spent a few more minutes thinking about it as she shuffled through the rest of the documents. Most were simple Thank-you notes written by grateful people whom Ethel had prayed for. Cindi wondered if she should throw them away or put them in a box in storage. She finally decided to throw them away.

She placed the legal documents in one pile to give to the executor of Ethel's will in case they were of importance. The miscellaneous notes and letters she threw away. But the photos she kept. There was no one she could think of to give them to, but she couldn't bear to throw them away either. She decided to put them in her own photo album at home. Maybe some day she would place that face.

Cindi looked around the room with a melancholy smile. She'd spent many hours in this room, talking to Ethel, learning from her. She wandered over to the window and looked out one last time. Standing there, she couldn't help but think about the mansions Jesus was preparing for them. "I hope you live right next door to me, Ethel," she whispered before turning and leaving the room, closing the door one last time behind her.

Downstairs, she collected her things and was just about to call Esther when the phone rang. At first she simply stared at it. Who would be calling here? She considered just letting it ring, thinking it must be someone dialing the wrong number.

"Cindi, answer the phone!" Shania said. "There is one last affair of Ethel's that you must take care of."

Cindi lifted the receiver gingerly. "Hello?" she asked before remembering proper phone etiquette. "Bennington residence," she added hastily.

"Cindi, dear, is that you?" an elderly female voice asked.

"Yes," Cindi replied with hesitation, trying to place the voice.

"Oh, hon, this is Mrs. Webster. You remember me, don't you?" Cindi immediately pictured the friendly shut-in who had frequently called for prayer for her husband a few years back before he passed away. It had been a long time since she'd called.

"Yes, of course, Mrs. Webster."

"Sweetie, I need prayer something fierce. My lumbago has been flaring up, and it gits so I just can't stand it anymore. Would you ask Ethel to pray for me?"

Cindi struggled for something to say. "Mrs. Webster, I'm so sorry, I thought you knew. I'm afraid Mrs. Bennington passed away a couple of months ago."

There was a long pause. When Mrs. Webster spoke again, Cindi could tell she struggled to keep her voice even. "I'm sorry to hear that, dearie."

Cindi related the details as gently as she could.

"I guess you'll be doing the praying now," Mrs. Webster said finally. "Like Ethel did?"

"Me?" Cindi squeaked, picturing Ethel's determination, her sheer commitment to prayer. Ethel was a, well, a warrior when it came to prayer. Compared to her, Cindi felt like the bugle boy. "You want me to pray for you?"

"I sure do," Mrs. Webster replied. "Would you do that for me, honey?"

Cindi could hardly say No. Automatically, her hands found the notebook Ethel had called her prayer journal. She neatly penned in Mrs. Webster's request, assured her that she would be praying for her, and hung up the phone.

"Now what have I done?" she moaned. "I barely have time to pray for my own concerns, and now I've committed myself to praying for other people. I can't do this the same way Ethel did. I just don't have the same time resources."

"But you have other resources," Shania reminded her. "You are resourceful, creative, and your heart is tender. In time, you could become a wonderful prayer warrior. Give yourself per-mission to do things differently. Ethel's way might not be your way. The sword of light, after all, is not only used for battle but to point the way."

All the way home, Cindi mulled over her dilemma. By the time she had pulled in the driveway, she had come up with several ideas. While Esther ran squealing into Marc's arms and they began a game of hide-and-seek, Cindi went to the stand near the phone that held the phone books. She laid Ethel's notebook there. Now it would be right at hand whenever someone called with a request.

Then she wrote Mrs. Webster's request on a piece of paper and pinned that to the ribbon that hung by the curtain near her kitchen sink. She had been following Leah's suggestion with great success. She looked at it with satisfaction. She spent a lot of time in front of that window doing dishes. Before, she had just daydreamed. Now she prayed.

Her first prayer, she knew, would be one of thankfulness that Marc had never installed that dishwasher she'd wanted after all. The ribbon pinned right in front of her would help her remember each of the requests, and they could easily be taken off when they were answered, to make room for others.

Her next prayer would also be one of thankfulness that Marc *had* insisted that they join the cyber-age by getting a computer and teaching her how to navigate the Internet. Although she still felt very much like the "newbie" Marc jokingly called her, she'd at least managed to design a modest homepage and learned how to communicate with her friends. Even Billie Jo had gotten "on-line" recently, and they "talked" almost daily through e-mail.

She knew that alone she could never handle all the prayer requests she was bound to receive. But the Internet put the power of communication at the tip of her fingers. She could be the beginning, the source, of a national or possibly worldwide, prayer chain. By sending prayer requests to her friends, who sent them to *their* friends and so on, the burden for prayer would be shared among many and would not be so heavy for anyone in particular.

Their group would then affect so many more than just those who came to the meetings. They could even minister to those mothers who were isolated at home with no way to get to the meetings. When they did get together for their meetings, it would give them an opportunity to share how the requests had been answered. Cindi could see this strengthening their group, and the thought excited her.

Cindi began her e-mail to everyone in her address book. She had a hard time thinking coherently as her thoughts raced ahead to the endless possibilities this presented. "Hello everyone," she began. "Wait until you hear about my idea . . ."

Shania smiled broadly as she watched Cindi outline her plan. She knew that most of the people on Cindi's list would be happy to become part of the prayer chain. Like the ripple of a stone thrown into a pond, Ethel's influence had spread and grown. From her one intense light, other smaller lights would begin to burn brightly in the darkness, and it was only a matter of time before they would shine with a radiance that would light up the world, dispelling the darkness. Very soon the Master would return and banish the darkness forever.